Praise for Isabel Ashdown

'...ty, gripping, and utterly unpredictable.'

Will Dean, author of *Dark Pines*

'...aracter-driven mystery that's as enjoyable as it is satis-...'

Elle Croft, author of *The Guilty Wife*

'...el Ashdown's writing is as perfect as ever.'

Amanda Jennings, author of *In Her Wake*

'...ictive and brimming with dark surprises.'

Juliet West, author of *The Faithful*

'...iantly twisty and compelling.'

Sam Carrington, author of *Saving Sophie*

'... me up three nights in a row.'

Holly Seddon, author of *Don't Close Your Eyes*

'...ripping exploration of friendship and twisted family ...ts. Highly recommended.'

Cass Green, author of *In a Cottage in a Wood*

'...ngled web of secrets and lies.'

Louise Jenkins, author of *The Date*

'Fantastically written with intriguing, vivid characters.'

Karen Hamilton, author of *The Perfect Girlfriend*

Isabel Ashdown was born in London and grew up on the south coast of England. Her writing career was launched with her critically acclaimed debut *Glasshopper*, after an early extract won a national writing competition. Her 2017 thriller *Little Sister* (Trapeze) spent several weeks in the Amazon Bestsellers chart and went on to be shortlisted in the Dead Good Reader Awards. Alongside her work as a novelist, Isabel is a Royal Literary Fund Fellow at the University of Chichester, where she coaches students on all aspects of writing. She lives in West Sussex with her family.

For news, previews and book prizes, join Isabel's Book Club at www.isabelashdown.com

You can also find Isabel on:
🐦 @IsabelAshdown
📘 @isabelashdown_writer
📷 IsabelAshdownBooks

#LakeChild

By Isabel Ashdown

Glasshopper
Hurry Up and Wait
Summer of '76
Flight
Little Sister
Beautiful Liars

LAKE CHILD

How far would you go for your family?

ISABEL ASHDOWN

TRAPEZE

An Orion paperback
First published in Great Britain in 2019 by Orion Books,
an imprint of The Orion Publishing Group Ltd
Carmelite House, 50 Victoria Embankment,
London EC4Y 0DZ

An Hachette UK company

1 3 5 7 9 10 8 6 4 2

A CIP catalogue record for this book is
available from the British Library.

ISBN (Mass Market Paperback) 978 1 4091 7892 7
ISBN (eBook) 978 1 4091 7893 4

Typeset by Born Group

Printed and bound in Great Britain by Clays Ltd, Elcograf S.p.A.

www.orionbooks.co.uk

For my brother, Dom, with love

Falun Publishing International

PROPOSED MARKETING COPY:

A LIFE OF LOSS – A Grandmother's Story
An autobiography by Maxine Gregory

A Life of Loss tells the story of one woman's triumph over adversity, following the notorious disappearance of her baby granddaughter, Lorna Gregory.

The unsolved case of missing newborn Baby Lorna is one that both shocked and captivated the nation – and tore a family apart. In this frank and heartwarming memoir, Maxine Gregory tells her full story for the very first time, sharing insights into her own childhood growing up in London's poverty-stricken slums, and inviting the reader to hear the unflinching truth behind her daughter Tara's tragic life and death. Containing exclusive family photographs and first-hand testimonials, Maxine Gregory's autobiography delivers the most accurate and personal account of Baby Lorna's disappearance that the public have ever seen.

At once heartbreaking and uplifting – A Life of Loss is a story that will stay with you long after you turn the final page.

PART ONE

1

Eva, Valden Town, Norway

I'm in the passenger seat of a stranger's truck, on the snowy road between the forest and town, when the fox appears on the path ahead, her breath rising in the dark night, the white of her fur merging with the snow. Feet planted, eyes fixed; I know her. Beside me, the driver is a hazy figure, as indistinct as the fox is clear, a static fuzz, blurring into the snowstorm that sprays vicious slants of ice against the windscreen. There's a slow-motion quality about the way in which the vehicle moves along the road, and I'm wondering if I'm dreaming, when, with a distant shriek of tyres, we come to an abrupt halt and all but the fox disappears from the landscape. I lean in, pressing close to the windscreen, my gaze locked with that of the animal, some ancient communication connecting us in thought.

Just as I believe I might decode the creature's meaning, I turn to look at the driver. He opens his mouth to speak, but the piercing night-scream of the Arctic fox fills my head, and the scene disappears to a cool white blank. Blank, just like *the space inside my mind, the space where my memories are meant to live.*

I wake in the middle of the night, empty. In the space where waking dreams usually linger, there is nothing, and in the darkness I dwell on this thought for long minutes, wondering how it is that I've never experienced the sensation before. Fleetingly, it is liberating; I feel almost nothing, aware only that I am Eva, that I am sixteen, that I live with my parents in a forest by a lake. In my mind's eye I can picture the landscape beyond the shuttered windows of our red wooden lake house: the dense woodland to the front of us, a canopy of pine leading out to the water's edge, indigo-deep in winter, sparkling crystal in the spring. To the rear are snow-cloaked mountains, dazzling white peaks rising up to the heavens, a panorama of waterfall and heather and rock. Other than these clear images, anchoring me to my bed, my mind is a peaceful blank.

But this serenity is short-lived, because in a breathtaking rush my body catches up with my thoughts and pain rips through me, sharp as a knife, causing me to gasp into the darkness as my fingers clutch at the bedsheets in shock.

The room is silent and cold, black as the grave, and I am gripped by the sudden and irrational thought that perhaps I am dead. Yes, we are used to the quiet, we live remotely – and yet, *this* silence is disturbing. There is no creak of heating pipes, no murmuring snore of Pappa on the other side of the wall, no regular tap-tap of the willow branch as it brushes my bedroom window in the night breeze. Something is wrong; something is very, very wrong.

Summoning up every effort to lift my arm from my side, I reach out for my bedside table. Slices of pain scream through

4

me, from my ankles to the top of my head, slowing me down, confusing my movements. Where is my bedside lamp? My fingers fumble, not finding the switch where it should be, and I ease my legs from the bed. The surface beneath my feet is wooden. This is not my bedroom floor. I feel along the edges of the bedframe, not recognising the metal slats of its structure, the creak of its springs. Slowly, sluggish like my body, panic begins to creep through my mind; it connects with my heart rate and my blood begins to pump faster than I can stand. Fighting the swell of nausea, I rise, staggering across an empty space, my arms held out before me until my fingers make contact with the slatted surface of a wood-panelled wall. Where is this? Where are my parents?

Blindly, I feel my way along the contours of the wall, until at last I stumble down a single step and my palms connect with a door. Thank God! I breathe with relief, shards of agony punctuating my every movement. A way out! But when I curl my hand around the handle and turn it, the door remains shut. It's locked from the outside.

I have no control over what happens next, because fear overcomes me, and there is only one thing I can do. I scream. And the scream goes on and on, taking on a life of its own, until at last a crack of light appears beneath the door, and rapid footsteps make their way up the stairs on the other side.

'Eva?' a voice says, a low whisper as she draws back the bolt. It's Mamma. Oh, thank you, God, it's Mamma. 'Eva, darling, keep it down!'

2

Eva

When I open my eyes, I know it is morning, because the snow-reflected light makes its way through the shutters, casting white bars across the attic wall. Mamma is exactly where she was when I drifted back to sleep last night, curled around me, my head nestled into the crook of her neck. I can smell the scent of her favourite perfume, am comforted by the familiarity of her body, the soft brush of her hair against my cheek. It is warm beneath the covers, but the air of the room is cool, my breath a white mist.

'We'll have to get you an extra heater up here,' she says, alerting me that she's awake. 'I think the radiator must be on the blink. No wonder you woke up last night.'

I hold my breath as my mind leaps around, searching for explanations as to what's going on. Beyond the window a fox screeches, its cry childlike as the sound drifts and trails away. 'Why am I—' I start to say, but Mamma pulls me closer, her warm hands covering my ears as she kisses the top of my head.

'How are you feeling this morning?' she asks, releasing me and slipping out of bed, tucking the covers around my shoulders. She crosses the room, flipping on the desk lamp as she goes, and places her hand on the radiator, holding it there for a second or two. She's wearing a cream cable-knit sweater and flannel jogging pants, and her strawberry-blonde hair hangs down her back, fuzzy after a night's sleep. She bends to fiddle with the dial.

I blink, captivated by her casual movements, and try to find the right words.

'Why am I here, Mamma? Why am I in the attic?'

She turns to me and smiles, but I see sadness there and I know she's working hard to hold it together. 'We've talked about this, haven't we, darling? Remember?'

'Have we?' I reply as I stare at her, terrified by the fact I have no idea what she is talking about. 'I don't – I don't remember.' And then I recall that blank impression I'd woken with last night, the sense that I'd been wiped clean, that my mind had been returned to factory settings . . . that I was completely and utterly empty.

'Yes, we've been over it several times now – but you're still struggling to retain information. It's not uncommon after this kind of trauma, you know? You mustn't be afraid – it's temporary, we're sure.'

'Trauma?' I ask, and I try to sit up, but a stabbing sensation pierces my ribs and I swallow a yelp. 'What's wrong with me?' I push back the sheets, my hands shaking now.

Mamma comes to me and unfastens the last two buttons of my pyjama top, and that's when I see it for the first time. A criss-crossing of scars which starts at my sternum and runs down past my ribcage, to disappear into my pyjama bottoms. I glimpse the damage, and turn my head away, wide-eyed, horrified at the sight of my own mutilated skin.

'Oh, God – oh, no. Mamma? What is this? What happened to me?' I push her hands away, panicked, tugging at the sheets and wanting to cover myself up. Wanting to make it all go away.

'It looks fine,' she murmurs. 'The scars are tightening up a bit, that's all. We must keep using that special cream, to keep the skin soft – it'll help with the healing.'

I'm crying now, but I barely feel the tears, and when Mamma looks up my eyes seek out hers, silently pleading with her for some answers I can make sense of. This confusion feels like madness; I'm both inside and outside of myself, looking in and looking out.

Again, she sweeps me into her embrace, and, despite the physical pain it causes me, it's where I want to be. 'Please, Mamma,' I cry into her shoulder. 'Tell me.'

Before she is able to reply, we're interrupted by the tread of footsteps on the wooden staircase beyond the door, and Pappa's bearded face appears, smiling and bright. He's already dressed for work, in his thick plaid shirt and cargo trousers. I find I can replay a scene, like frames from a movie I've watched a hundred times. In it, we're in the kitchen, preparing supper, and it's dark beyond the window, and warm inside. Pappa comes in through the back, kicking off his snow-dusted work boots before padding across the flag-stones to kiss Mamma on the cheek. I look up from chopping onions and tell him he looks like a lumberjack; he says he only dresses like that to please Mamma; Mamma says she wouldn't change a thing. It's a love scene, I think now, and it makes me happy, except I have to leave it, because some-one's saying my name.

'Eva?' Mamma says, giving my shoulder a little shake, and I'm aware that she's said it a few times now. 'Pappa's here.'

Slowly, my mind returns from the past to the present, to me sitting in this strange bed with my mother at my side, and my father standing in the low doorway, the desk lamp casting his shadow huge across the ceiling. His expression is – what? Expectant? Hopeful? It's hard to tell.

'Hello, sweetheart!' he says, and for a moment I feel as though I'm looking at a stranger. 'How are you doing this morning? You gave us quite a fright last night.'

I open my mouth to speak, but Mamma answers for me. 'She's feeling much better now, aren't you, Eva? I think it must have been another bad dream – you know, you've been plagued by them since we got you home.'

'Where've I been?' I ask.

Pappa's smile remains, fixed, and I sense the change in Mamma instantly, the shift from soft and yielding to crisp and business-like. This is a thing I *do* remember: the way Mamma operates on two different levels. There's the gentle, funny, young-spirited Ingrid, the one who devotes her every spare moment to her husband and her only child, the one who dreams of off-grid living and world harmony, of a simple life. And then there's professional Ingrid, the neurosurgeon, the no-nonsense team leader and all-round grown-up. This is the one who's just materialised in the room, now brought into being, I suspect, by the expression on Pappa's face. It's only now that I recognise his smile is forced, tense.

'Is everything alright, Tobias?' Mamma asks.

Pappa looks over his shoulder, then back to Mamma. 'Oh, yes,' he replies, 'fine. Except the chief just phoned to say he and Bern are on their way over.'

'Now?' Mamma stands and crosses the room, to open up the windows and fold back the shutters, filling the room with

9

the bright reflection of a snow-covered landscape. 'Couldn't you put them off?'

Pappa picks up the empty water glass from my bedside table and leans in to kiss my hair. 'He asked if Eva was up and about, and I told him no, but still he insisted. He says it's been over a week now and he really needs to talk to her.'

'What's been over a week?' I ask.

'Since you came home from the hospital, sweetheart. Ingrid, he said he'll be here by nine-thirty – he wants to interview Eva properly.'

'She's not going to be able to help them. She's forgotten everything we told her,' Mamma says, her voice flat.

'Forgotten *what*?' I cry out, slamming my hands against my forehead. A crashing pain floods my temple.

'Whoa, careful!' Mamma soothes, lifting my fringe to inspect my forehead. 'This one's still quite sore, darling.' She sits again, takes my hands in hers, and in a matter-of-fact tone tells me, 'You were involved in a car crash, Eva. You broke several bones and sustained some internal injuries and a serious head trauma.'

Is this how she is with her own patients? Calm, controlled, factual.

'Have I got brain damage?' I ask. The answer must be yes, because that would explain the blank spaces of my waking mind, the confusion and weakness I now feel.

'Well – yes and no. Yes, in that your short-term memory is still affected, but no, in that we anticipate a full recovery. I see this sort of injury a lot in my line of work, darling – you're going to be fine.'

I shake my head, wanting to believe her; not believing her.

Pappa approaches, squatting down to my level. 'You've been home for a week, and we go over this with you most

10

mornings,' he says. 'But honestly, Eva, every day you seem a little clearer. You're definitely getting stronger.'

'What about my birthday?' I ask, knowing the answer before she even gives it. 'My seventeenth?'

'You missed it, I'm afraid, darling. You were still in intensive care at the end of February.' Mamma releases my hands, checks her watch and fetches me a hairbrush.

'What does Mac want?' I say, unable to articulate much more, only knowing that the prospect of seeing anyone right now fills me with fear. Why would Chief Mac want to interview me? Hearing I've been in hospital is shock enough, but how can I have been in this attic room for a week and not even know about it? What the hell is going on around here? My mouth is dry, my pulse racing again.

'We'd better get a move on,' she tells Pappa, shooting an irritable glance in his direction, and before I know it he's ushered out and it's just the two of us again.

'I don't want to see Mac and Bern—' I say, but she waves a hand through the air.

'Look, Eva, I'm no happier about this than you are. Let's get them out of the way. You'll have to give a statement sooner or later.'

I nod, my eyes falling to the hairbrush in my hand. 'I'm cold,' I mutter, though it's not what I mean to say. I mean to say, *No, Mamma! I won't see them! I won't answer their questions – not until you tell me more!* But I'm suddenly so tired, so worn out that right now I'll go along with anything.

For a moment Mamma gazes at me, as though I'm a puzzle to decipher, before she strips off her sweater in one fluid movement and drops it in a warm pile on my lap, indicating for me to put it on. She stands beside my bed, hands on hips, the skin of her slender arms pale against her dark vest. 'I would

11

have put him off if I'd taken the call. But Mac's got a job to do, I suppose. And he probably wants to see how you're doing – to wish you well. Everyone's been so worried, Eva.'

I'm looking at her as she says these things, and it strikes me that she's talking to herself as much as she's talking to me. 'Why?' I ask, though it's barely a whisper.

'Because you nearly died,' she replies plainly, and the truth of it is like a slap. She bends to scoop up a few pieces of clothing from the floor. 'I'll bring you up a bit of breakfast before Mac arrives,' she says, 'so you can take your painkillers. And I'll make sure he doesn't stay too long, OK? I promise.'

'Mamma?' I call after her as she retreats towards the door.

She pauses, turning back to me. 'Uh-huh?'

'What will I say to him?' I ask.

She looks at me blankly. 'Well, the truth, of course! That's all he wants to hear.'

The attic door shuts with a wooden rattle, followed by the hollow thud of the bolt sliding into place. The truth? God only knows I'd love to give it to him, but I have absolutely no idea what that is – or what I'm doing locked up here in my family's attic. I raise the hairbrush to my head, noticing only now that my previously thick dark hair is several inches shorter, and uneven, as though cut by an amateur. I run the brush through it, obediently, the lump in my throat growing as I feel myself waking fully to the horror of my situation.

Am I a prisoner in my own home?

3

Eva

Still reeling from the shock of my botched hair when Mamma returns, I try to refuse breakfast, pushing aside a bowl of oats, only agreeing to a few bites of pastry so that I can line my stomach for the cocktail of drugs she counts out into my palm. It's clear that I need painkillers, but there are six tablets here, and I'm not so groggy that I can't work out that some of them must do something else.

'Six?' I ask, swallowing them one after another, desperate to relieve this pain.

'You'll be off them in no time,' she says in reply.

'But what are they?'

The question goes unanswered. There's an impatient quality to Mamma's movements as she busies about the room, plumping up my pillows, straightening the sheets. When I realise I'll get no sense from her until the police have been and gone, I decide to drop the subject, and fall quiet too, silently listing questions to save till later, when I have her full attention.

Outside, the sound of tyres on gravel alerts us to Chief Mac's arrival in his jeep, and Mamma crosses to the window, wiping it clear of condensation with the sleeve of her shirt, turning back to me with a decisive nod.

'Ready?' she asks.

I don't reply.

'I'll tell Pappa to bring them up.' To my shock, she leans over my headboard, and I hear the soft click of static as she fiddles with something back there and speaks. 'Tobias? Eva's ready when you are. You can bring Mac and Bern up now.'

'What's that—?' I begin, but there's no time to object, because within seconds Pappa's here, with Chief Mac and his son Deputy Bern following close behind, sucking up the air in the room, making me feel like a freakish exhibit beneath their scrutiny.

Pappa places a stool beside my bed, and ushers the police officers in. I feel utterly exposed; ashamed. I detest this helpless feeling, and I can't stand to think of others looking on me as an invalid.

'Ah! Here's our little hero!' Mac says as he steps forward, stooping to avoid the sloping eaves. Bern follows behind.

Defensively, my hands fly to my head, pulling at what's left of my hair as I try to disguise the mess of it. I've known Mac since I was a baby, and over the years he's become a close friend of the family. He's Lars and Rosa's uncle, I remember that much. In fact, the everyday stuff, the larger elements of my life seem increasingly clear to me as the morning goes on. It's just the recent bits I have no concept of.

'*Hero?*' I reply. My voice is still hoarse with sleep. 'Hardly.'

Bern raises his hand to give me a small wave, and I notice how grown-up he seems in his uniform, how confident. In a small town like ours, everyone knows everyone else, and

Bern has always been there in the background, a few years older than me and his cousins, the sensible son who followed his pappa into the police force. I'd never taken much notice of him, but now I see how altered he is, his black hair a little longer around his ears, his sideburns fully formed. He looks like an advert for the perfect policeman: tall, strong, trustworthy.

'Hey, Eva,' he says, just as he would if he passed me in the street, and I feel grateful to him for treating me as though nothing has changed. 'How's the head?'

I widen my eyes, to let him know it's a stupid question, and he stifles a smile and looks for somewhere to sit. Mamma and Pappa stand awkwardly, unsure how to arrange all these people in so small a space.

'It's good to see you back home where you belong,' Mac says, glancing around the attic room with interest.

'Eva still sleeps a lot,' Pappa says, gesturing towards me in the bed. 'It's one of the symptoms of the head injury. It's quieter up here – more peaceful than downstairs.'

Mac nods, his expression saying, yes, that all makes sense, and I wonder whether he noticed the bolt on the outside of my door.

My mother settles on the edge of my mattress and Pappa moves to the foot of the bed to stand with his back to the window. The desk beneath the eaves faces me, and Bern perches on the corner of it, notebook in hand, as Chief Mac takes another sweeping glance of the room before pulling out the desk chair, sitting with his elbows on his knees, so that we're level. Four sets of eyes are on me, the girl in the bed.

'So, Eva . . .' Mac begins. His hair is as grey as Bern's is black. 'We were hoping to ask you a few questions, now you're awake.'

Downstairs, in the main house, I hear a woman's voice, singing 'This Little Love of Mine', and I look at my mother in surprise.

There's a brief, silent exchange between my parents, before she says, 'Oh, it's just Nettie.'

'Why is she here?' I ask, wondering what our old housekeeper is doing here at this time of day. Maybe she's come to pay me a visit? Part of me hopes so; I love old Nettie.

'She—' Chief Mac starts to say, but Mamma jumps in before he can continue, and he looks confused – and I'm completely perplexed by the weird atmosphere in the room, and by the strange expressions passing between them all.

'She popped in for a cup of tea, sweetheart, asking after you. I told her we'd only be a few minutes.'

Mac clears his throat; Mamma nods pleasantly; Nettie continues to sing downstairs. Without a word, Pappa crosses the room and pulls the door shut with a soft click. The singing fades to a faint murmur.

'So, Eva,' Mac says again. 'I expect your parents have filled in a few of the blanks for you?'

Mamma sits quite still at the end of my bed, her face impassive.

'A few,' I reply.

'You know you've been in a road traffic accident?'

I nod.

'And you know that the truck you were in was stolen?'

Now Mamma does react, and a pained expression crosses her features.

'Stolen?' I repeat. 'Who was driving? Was anyone else hurt?'

'We don't think so,' Mac replies, sitting upright, frowning. His focus shifts to Pappa, to Bern, then back to Mamma. 'We traced the truck back to a pest control company in Valden,

16

who'd reported it missing a week earlier, so whoever took it had probably been driving around in it since then. Forensics crawled all over it, and picked up a whole lot of fibres and prints, but nothing useful. With no firm suspects, and no print matches on our database, we're a bit stumped.'

I stare at Mac, unable to answer, watching as the crease between his eyebrows deepens.

'Ingrid, what exactly does Eva know?' he asks.

She sighs. 'We've told her *just about* everything we know, Mac, but she's not retaining it.'

Mac nods in a way that suggests he understands the code.

'We've had this every day for the past week,' Mamma continues. 'You're going to have to tell her from the start.'

The way they're talking over me is crushing. Am I so slow-witted, so damaged that I've really heard this all before? When Mac starts to talk, however, I somehow know that it's true: the information seeps into me like an echo of the past. He reaches inside his jacket pocket and brings out a newspaper cutting, which he unfolds and passes to me. The headline reads, 'Local girl escapes death: dangerous driver faces prosecution'. The photograph has been taken at night, and shows the image of a pickup truck, nose-deep in a snow bank, its front end entirely obscured. Surrounding the van are police cars, an ambulance and several people who appear to be emergency crew.

Mac reaches out and points at the front end of the truck.

'When this picture was taken, you were still inside,' he says. 'It took more than two hours to cut you free. In those sub-zero conditions, and with the injuries you sustained, you're lucky to be alive, you know?'

As I look up from the article, I have to fight the heat at the back of my eyes, and Bern meets my gaze. 'You're made of strong stuff,' he says, and I can't contain the tears any longer.

Pappa steps away from the window to sit between Mamma and me. 'Can we speed this along a bit, Chief?' he asks. 'Eva's exhausted.'

'Sure thing, Tobias,' Mac replies, and he opens his notebook and turns to a page of handwritten questions. 'I'm just going to fire away, Eva, OK? If you don't know or can't remember, just say, and we'll move on.'

I nod again, and Mamma rubs my foot through the fabric of my covers. *There, there*, she's saying, *let's just get this over with*.

'Do you remember what you were doing in this truck, Eva?'

I shake my head. 'No.'

'You see here, it's green, with a pest control logo on the side. Ring any bells?'

'No.'

'Do you know where you were before getting in the truck?'

'How can I, when I don't even remember being in it?'

'You were with Rosa and Lars earlier in the evening. Why didn't you leave when your friends did?'

'Leave where?'

Mac and Bern exchange a glance.

'Foxy Jack's bar,' Bern says. 'It was Valentine's night, and you'd been in the bar with Rosa and Lars. It was a busy night – well, busy by Foxy's standards.'

An image comes to me. 'Were there balloons?' I ask. 'Pink ones?'

Bern jots the detail down on his pad. 'I can check.'

'We'd been drinking,' I say, avoiding eye-contact with Mamma.

'That's right,' Mac says. 'That's certainly what your blood results said when you arrived in the emergency room. Anything else?'

I concentrate hard, only seeing those pink balloons and sensing the sickish swell of alcohol in my system. I can visualise a ring of moisture on a dark-stained wooden counter, feel the chill of a beer bottle held in my hand.

'Had you arranged to meet someone at the bar, perhaps? Someone other than Rosa or Lars? Maybe someone you'd spoken to on social media? On Facebook, or something like that?'

'Oh, no,' Mamma interrupts before I can speak. 'You know we don't use any of those things, Mac. We don't even have wifi out here.'

'Really?' Bern says, disbelief in his voice. 'I'm sure you could get it installed if you looked into it. Most of the town is connected now.'

'It's not that we can't,' Pappa says. 'We choose not to. Eva doesn't even have a mobile phone.'

Now Bern really does look surprised.

'It's a lifestyle choice,' Mamma says, and I feel my skin turning pink as I realise what a hippy she sounds when she says this out loud.

'So, you don't have any social media accounts, Eva?' Mac continues. 'What about an email address? You must be able to access emails at school.'

'Well, yes,' I say, 'but I don't bother with Facebook and all that. My friends all have it, but I can't see the point. Rosa and Lars only live a few minutes away. If I want to talk to them, I can just walk through the woods and knock on their door. I don't need social media to do that.' I sound like Mamma, I realise, and I wonder if these are her words I'm using.

'Rosa and Lars do use social media, though, don't they?' Mac says, speaking of his niece and nephew, addressing the comment to Bern. 'I suppose I just assumed everyone of your generation does.'

'How are they?' I ask with a pang of loss, feeling as though I haven't seen my best friends for months, or years. 'Can I see them? Maybe they remember something from that night? Maybe they saw who I got in the truck with?'

'No, they left the bar before you, apparently.'

Is it my imagination, or did Mamma just tut? Something's not adding up. I may not be able to remember anything from that evening, but one thing I do know is that my friends would never leave me in the bar to get home alone. Never.

I see another of those secret looks pass between Mamma and Pappa and a voice screams at the back of my head. *Don't trust them!* it says. *They're keeping things from you!*

'Did you know my parents are keeping me locked in here?' I blurt out, with no thought at all. I point towards the doorway, and my arm shakes with the fear I feel. 'There's a bolt on the outside of that door!'

My parents look apologetic, and to my shock Mac smiles kindly and nods.

'Oh, course – Tobias told us you've been sleepwalking, Eva. Your mamma found you out by the lake the night before last. You could have drowned, or frozen to death out there in these temperatures.'

Sleepwalking? I don't even know how to answer this. I've never sleepwalked in my life. And if that's the reason, why keep me up here – why not put a bolt on the outside of my regular bedroom door instead? 'Mamma?' I say, and the word emerges slurred, and all I want to do is close my eyes. 'Mamma?' I try a second time.

'I think you need some sleep, darling,' she says, squeezing my foot again, to shut me up. 'Mac?'

Mac looks over at Bern, who snaps his notebook shut, showing no signs of surprise at what I've just said. Oh, God, are they all in on it? What is this?

20

'Right, Deputy!' Mac says to him, 'I think we ought to leave these good folk in peace, don't you?'

As Mamma and Pappa follow Chief Mac down the stairs, Bern hangs back a second, looking as though he has something he wants to say.

'I'll pop back in a day or two, Eva,' he says. 'See if you remember anything else?' He slides a contact card on to my bedside table and taps it once with the pad of his finger. 'Here's my number, just in case.'

And what am I supposed to call him on? There's no phone up here, no way for me to contact the outside world. I'm so wiped, it takes all my effort to form the words I want to speak.

'Bern, I don't understand– the article said the driver is being prosecuted. Who was it?'

Bern stares at me for a second, confused. 'Oh, no,' he says, picking up the newspaper cutting Mac has left at the foot of my bed. 'It says he *faces* prosecution.'

There's a pause, while he waits for me to respond, but I find I can't. I can barely hold my eyelids open.

'He's still on the loose. He faces prosecution if we catch him. *When* we catch him, that is,' he says. 'And we will catch him, Eva. We've got reason to believe he's still in the area, so it's just a matter of time.'

I can sense Bern waiting for me to reply, and when I don't even open my eyes I feel the weight of his hand on my shoulder, a brief gesture of reassurance before it lifts and disappears. 'Don't hesitate to call us if you're worried,' he says, and then there's the sound of the door closing softly behind him.

Bern's words linger as my mind and body slide deep into sleep. Is that the real reason they've got me locked up here? Because there's someone out there who means me harm? *He's still on the loose.*

21

4

Eva

Through the murky waters of sleep, I am starting to wonder what it is that Mamma and Pappa are feeding me, what it is that tethers me to my nightmares, so tightly entwined with the threads of memories that float around the edges of everything I do and think. Tonight, I know I am deep in sleep, or nearing it, and despite my instinctive resistance there's something comforting about medicated slumber, the soft, dense fullness of it. As I sink, slowly, like a pebble through treacle, I return, as I do now each night, to the scene of the accident. I don't know if I have any real memories of it, and so this version is a mirror of the one I saw in that newspaper cutting, the image of which I've returned to so often that it has almost become my own. In my sleeping version, I'm like some astral projector, an observer, always separate from and invisible to the real people on the ground, to the police officers and paramedics at work trying to cut me free. From my high vantage point, I can clearly see my captor's truck, its green bonnet buried deep in the snowy bank; I see Chief Mac in his hooded police overcoat; the flashing lights of the patrol cars and the ambulance lighting up the figures who stand around, measuring footprints and tyre marks and speaking into their mobile phones as they scale up the manhunt. There are some regulars from Foxy Jack's bar there too, standing around, observing the unfolding scene: there's Foxy, wearing his grubby bar apron, hands on hips as though he owns the road, and Creepy Gurt, leering and stupid, knitted hat pulled down over his eyebrows, muttering to Mad Eric – all of them with Valentine roses behind their ears like flamenco dancers. None of them speaks, they just stand about, casually watching, beer jugs still in hand. I scan the landscape all around, casting my gaze across the snowbound fields and roads, looking for Rosa and Lars, for some evidence that they are near. But they're entirely absent from the scene, all trace of them gone. As I draw closer, the figures fade into the background and it feels as though the cogs of time are moving in reverse, because the astral me – the undamaged, all-seeing me – is tugged violently back towards the passenger seat, snapped back into the broken carcass of my body. Through sleep, I gasp at the pain of it, and I know the hurt is everywhere; but then it fades, and the car is moving along the dark road out of town and I'm turning towards the driver just as he's about to open his mouth to speak. It's pitch black inside the truck and out, but when he looks at me there are his amber eyes, so deep and clear. Every time I dream this, the eyes change, but always I know those eyes, until I focus hard on them, and under the light of my concentration they are gone, far from reach. When the eyes have disappeared, though, there's still the voice and those words which are meaningless, and yet so weighted with meaning.

'Eva,' the voice says urgently, as we hurtle along that white-out road in the nightmare darkness. *'Eva, do you trust me?'*

In the gloom of the attic room, Pappa quietly places my breakfast tray on the desk beneath the eaves. He turns the dial of the dimmer switch, so we're bathed in a soft vanilla light, and approaches the bed, looking down at me, his arms hanging at his sides.

'Oh, good, you're awake.'

I want to speak but the words won't come, only tears, which stream from my eyes and dampen my pillow. I tell myself to make them stop, but they keep coming, heavy and hot, running down my sharp cheekbones like little traitors. My body, sluggish with pain, just won't do what it's told.

'Come now, sweetheart,' Pappa says, reaching for a tissue and dabbing at my face. And then I notice a tear running the length of *his* face, disappearing into the thicket of his dark beard, and it's no use, I can't turn off the taps. 'Don't cry, Eva,' he says, 'please don't cry.'

I turn away from him and fix my attention on the wooden slats that conceal the outside view. Light motes move listlessly against the hinted daylight, disturbed by Pappa's presence, and I imagine my fist puncturing a hole in the shutters, splintering them wide. My skin would be unbroken, and I would soar through that window like a bird. There's a long pause, while Pappa stands at my bedside in his sunbleached gardening clothes, an oversized child trying to decide what to do next. The bruising around his right eye has faded to a yellowy-brown now, and I won't ask about it, because he'll only tell me again that he bashed it on the kitchen cupboard, when I know it appeared right after I heard him shouting a few nights ago, at the front of the house, way down below my window. There'd been the sound of heavy feet kicking up the gravel – like two people wrestling – and then my mother's screech of fear before the silence of the forest was reclaimed. If it hadn't been for my medication dragging me down I would have been scared out of my mind. By the next morning, I'd wondered if it was only a dream, until Pappa appeared with a livid swelling beneath his eye.

I should say something to him – thank him for my breakfast, anything – but I don't want to. I can tell he's hurting inside, but, right now, silence is the only power I wield.

'Eva, you have to try to eat something,' he says, making a show of checking the medical chart on my bedside table. He pulls the thermometer from its hygiene sleeve and asks me to open wide. Why isn't he at work? He should be out in his gardener's van, keeping his business running, not here nursing me.

There's a beaker of water on my bedside cabinet, tepid and untouched from the night before. Without thinking, I let my hand shoot out, knocking the water across the floorboards, soaking my father's slippered feet.

'I'm a prisoner,' I hiss. 'You're keeping me prisoner up here.'

'Oh, Eva,' he says, rushing to mop it up with a napkin from the tray. 'We've been through this.' Clearly trying to ignore my defiance, he crosses the room to open the shutters, and white light floods the room. 'The doctors say you're to have complete bed rest. You've only been home a fortnight! For now, you're to do nothing more than sleep and recover. Your mother's an expert in this, you know? People travel from miles around to be treated by her – she's the best in her field. If your mamma says you're to rest, you should listen.'

I narrow my eyes at him, despising the sense of what he says. 'I get that,' I tell him. 'But why *here*? Why in this room, with a *lock* on the door?'

'Sweetheart, you know about the sleepwalking – we have to keep it locked until we're sure you're past all that. And anyway, if you come downstairs, you'll only try to get up and about before you're ready. Mamma doesn't want you to exert yourself. You know what you're like, Eva, you can't sit still for five minutes!' He says this as if it's a joke.

I clamp my mouth shut, shrugging his fingers off me as he feels around the glands in my neck. When it's clear he's not going to give up, I let my lower lip drop just enough for him to pop the thermometer in and, with my eyes resolutely averted, I wait as he counts off the seconds before removing it again, checking it, and returning it to the steriliser cup. Blocking him out, I gaze at the poster that has appeared overnight from my old bedroom, stuck neatly to the sloping eaves overhead. As a child, I was obsessed with the Arctic fox, having only ever seen one behind glass in Kristiansand Zoo, where we bought this poster, a now sunlight-faded montage of northern animals and birds, from eagles to elks, from mayflies to moose, all circling around a central image of the amber-eyed fox, my favourite of them all. I have no memory of them putting it up and can only assume they brought it last night as I slept, along with the CD player I now notice plugged in beside a pile of my favourite albums.

'Good, good,' Pappa murmurs, making notes, patronising me with an everything's-going-to-be-OK smile as he lifts his pen from the page. 'We'll have you up and about in no time.'

'*I can barely lift my legs*,' I spit in response, unable to remain silent a moment longer. I attempt to drag myself into a sitting position, feeling the scars tugging tightly at my legs and abdomen, along the length of one weak arm.

Pappa perches on the edge of the mattress, taking my hand in his, squeezing it tightly so I can't extract it, and I hate him for his caring demeanour, his gentle bedside manner. He stares at me a long while, his eyes soft, and I notice for the first time a streak of white running through the left-hand side of his dense black beard. When did that happen? Before, there were just a few white hairs, and now this, a solid stripe, like a brushstroke. He must notice me looking, because his fingers go to it, almost protectively, and he looks away.

'When can I come back downstairs?' I whisper. 'Pappa? I don't understand why I have to be kept locked away like this!' My voice is rising now, and my father takes my other hand in his, to steady me again, to make me focus. 'It's more than just the sleepwalking, isn't it? Are you scared that the driver is coming back for me? He'll have seen the papers, Pappa – he wouldn't risk coming back. Mac and Bern would arrest him in a second! He's gone.'

'*Eva*,' Pappa says, firmer now. 'We don't *know* that he's gone. Until the police work out who it was driving that night – until they've put him away – we can't be sure of anything. Listen, I didn't want to tell you this but only last week your mamma saw someone out in the woods after dark, and then—' He trails off, his hand betraying his thoughts as it drifts to his bruise.

'He was *here*?' I ask, my empty stomach lurching at the idea I could be in danger.

Pappa shakes his head, and I can see he regrets saying it. 'We've no idea if it was the driver. It could just be a coincidence – a vagrant passing through, maybe – but yes, I confronted a man on our property, and, well, I tried to stop him and he caught me off-guard.'

I have no answer for this; I'm too alarmed at the thought of this stranger on our land, out here in the middle of the woods. We have no direct neighbours, no one to hear our screams or cries for help. Mamma and Pappa have mobile phones, but I don't, stuck up here, locked away.

'What if he gets into the house?'

'He won't. This room is just a precaution. You think *I* want you up here? You think your mamma does? Everything we're doing is for your safety. We've no idea if the driver was just some lowlife who offered you a lift – an opportunist, if you like – or whether he targeted you. Until Chief Mac catches up with him, we have to be vigilant.'

'What if he *does* get in here? How would you even know?'

'He won't! That's why we rigged up the monitor – to reassure you that you're not alone, Eva. If you're worried about anything, for even a second, you shout and we'll hear you downstairs.'

I think of the baby monitor strapped to the back of my bed, my parents' makeshift spy.

'But I'm going *insane*,' I reply, suddenly exhausted again. I just want to be in my own bedroom, downstairs, with Mamma and Pappa along the corridor, with my books and my music and my view of the lake. From my own bedroom I can just make out the top window of the Bruns' cottage over the treeline; Rosa's room. We've had a signalling system ever since we were little, where we'd blink our flashlights on and off after dark, a series of brief messages sailing over the canopy of forest and lake. Two flashes: Goodnight. Three flashes: Lars says hi. Four flashes: See you tomorrow? Five flashes: Still awake? I swallow a sob.

Pappa scoops me into his arms, and I don't even care that my ribs burn with fire, that the scars throb afresh, because at least I'm feeling something, breathing in his Pappa-scent of lemon blossom soap and freshly ground coffee. I know he still loves me, just as he did when I was small and he told me bedtime stories of the trolls in the forest and the *Nøkken* in the lake, and I can't raise the strength or will to push him away. Beyond the window I hear that fox again, its cry sharp and pained as it trails away. The fox has entered my dreams in recent days, and as I home in on its image behind my sleep-soaked eyes I welcome the familiarity of it, feeling anchored in the knowledge that some things are just that: dreams.

Pappa holds my head close to his chest. 'I'm sorry,' he murmurs into my hair, and I whisper it back to him, because I *am* sorry. I wish I could be more patient; I wish I could just get better. We sit like that for several minutes, as my heart rate reduces, and my breathing slows. When he gently helps to prop me up against the pillows, I ask, 'Have they been in touch yet?'

Pappa looks down at his lap and I know he doesn't want to answer, doesn't want to talk about Rosa and Lars again, about why they haven't been to see me.

'Sorry, Eva,' he says, without looking up. 'No.'

He's lying. 'Look at me,' I say, and he does, and there's apology in his eyes. 'Have they?'

Without blinking he repeats his answer. 'No.' Flustered, he stands and begins pressing my tablets out on to the bedside table. Beyond the sealed window, I hear the sound of the car leaving, of Mamma heading off to work. I visualise her in her clinic room, hands folded on the desk in front of her, stethoscope around her neck, her fuzz of long fair hair tamed into a neat coil at the back of her head.

Pappa turns to fetch my tray from the desk, laden down with eggs and juice and pastries, and slides it on to my lap. 'Will you eat it today, Eva? You're losing so much weight. Promise me?'

I look down at the congealing egg, and grit my teeth. 'Promise,' I reply, and a steely resolve grows inside me.

I watch as Pappa crosses the room, and although I can no longer see his expression I feel his masked sadness, his self-loathing, see it in the slump of his usually broad shoulders. His hand reaches for the door, and he steps over the threshold.

'I'll be back at lunchtime, OK? In the meantime, try to get some rest.'

The moment I hear the bolt slotting into place, I crawl from my bed and stagger across the floorboards to my little bathroom, where I tip the contents of my breakfast tray into the toilet.

This evening I've forced myself to get out of bed, and I've been sitting up at my desk, just thinking. The room, I realise only now, has been freshly decorated in a soft greyish-white, and several new striped rugs cover the wooden floorboards, cosying the place up. Tucked away from the rest of the house, free from noise and distractions, it used to be Pappa's office, a place where he could concentrate on his work designing other people's gardens. Where his computer once sat, along with his library of plant books, there is now a simple vase of yellow roses and a raffia basket containing art supplies, Mamma's attempt, I suppose, at keeping me occupied.

During the past hour I've been going through my CDs, in the hope that they might trigger a memory or two. And you know what? They have. There's an old Simon and Garfunkel album of Pappa's that's got mixed in with my collection, and the moment the opening bars of 'Homeward Bound' begin to play, a recent orange-tinted image flashes into my mind, of me, Rosa and Lars sitting in the tatty wicker chairs at the back of their cottage, drinking Sprite from cans as their mamma, Ann, unpegs dry washing from the line. Could it be that Ann has this album too? I don't know if it was playing at the time, but somehow this track and the memory have become firmly intertwined. It's just the three of us, because their father, Magnus, was gone by this point, discovered at the mountainside out on the edge of Stein Farm Road when Rosa and Lars were just eleven or twelve, dead from hypothermia after a night's heavy drinking. I force my mind to push that thought aside, to turn back towards the garden scene, in which the sun is low in the sky beyond the trees and distant mountain range, and Ann is cast in silhouette, her long skirts giving her the appearance of being from another era altogether. Again I have a sense of separation, of looking down on us all – towards Ann at the washing line, then back to me and my friends – and knowing that this is a good time. The radiance of the sky, the light clothes we're wearing, the fact that Ann is taking washing from the line – all these elements suggest late summer. Things, it would seem, were good between us then. So, what could have changed so dramatically between then and mid-February, the night of the accident? What could have caused them to leave me alone in the bar like that?

Two floors down, the front door slams, causing the glass in my attic window to rattle. My room has grown dark in the hours I have been sitting here, the only light coming from the desk lamp at my side. I glance at the display on my illuminated bedside clock; it's almost seven, and I wonder who could be calling at the house at this time, when the evenings draw in so early. Is it Mac, with an update on the driver of the stolen truck? I didn't hear a car pulling up – the kick of gravel is always a giveaway. And I know Mamma's home from work because she brought me my supper an hour ago, and left after five minutes when I snubbed her because she still wouldn't give me a straight answer about my tablets. All I wanted to know was what was in them. 'Let me worry about that,' she'd replied dismissively, and I'd argued that I wasn't a child, before turning my back on her and refusing to say another word. Maybe it's just Pappa outside, heading to the woodpile to fetch logs.

Stiffly, I ease myself out of my desk chair and cross over to the window, every step a great effort of willpower. The hunger pains are a constant now, and I've passed the stage where my stomach growls and complains, as I eat just the bare minimum to get the tablets down me without burning my insides. Every day they bring me my food tray, and when they fetch it again they find I've barely touched it. I don't know what I'm doing, really, but their constant attempts at persuasion tell me they're worried, and that's good. When Mamma checked my scars this evening, her hands lingered over the jutting bone of my hip, and she bit down on her lip. Perhaps the sight of my fading body will get me out of here; perhaps I might get bad enough to prompt a follow-up visit to the hospital. I know how warped these thoughts sound, but this is the way I live now; this is the way I think.

At the window, I wipe away the condensation to see two figures closing the gate behind them and heading back out into the forest. Exhilaration rises through me, but the glass is smeared, and I have to tug at my sleeve to clear it properly, to press my face to the window, to know for certain, without a doubt, that the two figures disappearing into the darkness are my best friends, Rosa and Lars. Feebly I hammer on the glass, knowing even as I do it that there's no chance of them hearing: they're too far away. I fumble at the handle, knocking the tiny key out; it bounces over the hard floor and beneath the bed. By the time I've retrieved it and wrested the glass open, my friends are gone. Like ghosts in the night, they're nowhere to be seen. With the icy winter air whipping at my skin, I drop to the floor and weep. Why would my parents turn them away? They know that the only thing I want is to see my friends. I don't care about anything else.

Crawling on my hands and knees, I grab at the baby monitor strapped to the side of my bed. 'I hate you,' I growl into it, imagining my parents listening in from the warmth of our cosy living room downstairs. 'I hate you,' I repeat. 'I *hate* you. *I HATE YOU!*'

Mamma doesn't come to fetch my empty plate this evening. She knows that this time they've gone too far. And I know it's time I made a firm plan of escape. I've got to get out of here.

5

Eva

I'm floating, starfish-like, in the lake at the edge of our home; a suspended arrangement of face and hands and knees and feet. Above me the sun is high and bright, and it's early enough in the day that my breath makes light trails of vapour as I exhale deeply, tuning into the muffled hum of the underwater world. In my peripheral vision, there are the tall pines, before the snow-topped mountains and the vanishing glacier; and, nearer, something else, a dark mass silently moving through the water. All is quiet, bar the gentle plop of surfacing fish, or the light settling of leaves as they drift to the forest floor. All is still; all is silent. And yet my pulse is throbbing fast in my eardrums, as I focus on remaining calm, on staying horizontal, half-submerged – and on not losing my nerve.

In a rush, and with a gulp of air, I'm under, and arms and legs and hair and faces wrap around me, like rope weed, squeezing me, tugging me down. When I open my startled eyes, they're right in front of me, unmistakable in the sun-sliced murk of the lake water: Lars and Rosa, light and dark, yin and yang, hair trailing, eyes bright, Rosa counting to ten as in the space between us she releases her fingers from a fisted hand. One-two-three-four-five-six – I think my lungs might burst – seven-eight-nine-ten. And then we're breaking through the surface together, gasping for air, laughing, shouting, disagreeing about who won that round. Nøkken; that's the game. Rosa's dark curls lick about her face like tendrils, while Lars's smooth blond bowl-cut slicks against his head in a strangely fashioned helmet. I hurt with love for these two. I love their laughter and their daring – I love the way they bicker over me, and let me in. They're like my cousins and siblings and best friends all in one, and I don't know how I could ever live my life without them.

Clambering on to the grassy lakeside, we lie on a vast striped blanket, me in the middle, feeling the day's heat increase, as the sun's rays dry our skin. We might be the last people on earth, with the silence that surrounds us, and I take a hand, one in each of mine, and their cavernous pain passes into me, as I pray that I might take some of it away.

'Is it wrong to laugh – to keep on having fun?' Lars asks, his voice soft and scared.

Rosa doesn't reply.

I press my thumbs hard into the centres of their palms. 'No,' I say with certainty, and I'm choking up, because I've never known grief of the kind they're feeling. 'Maybe in front of your mamma. But not with me. If you want to laugh or cry or shout or swear – I don't mind. Because I think you'd go mad if you didn't.'

In a smooth, synchronised movement, they roll into me, their arms looping across one another's, and we stay like that for what feels like all time, a tangle of twelve-year-olds, slumbering anxiously, weeping for the loss of their father under an August sky.

We were always there for each other, through everything, good and bad. So where are they now? Rosa and Lars haven't been back since that first visit, and I'm driving myself mad trying to work out what my parents said to make them stay away – or what it is that I've done wrong. Thoughts of our times together dominate, and, unlike my memories of recent events, these are clear and sharp-edged. *Real.*

Rosa and Lars are my most trusted friends; I know that we'd do anything for each other, and I struggle to recall a time when we've been separated for longer than a week or two. Aren't they missing me at all? Why haven't they come back to try again? And what must their mother think – surely she wonders why her children haven't seen their best friend? Ann has been like an aunt to me – in fact, she's Mamma's best friend too – and it seems suddenly impossible that she hasn't been to visit me either, since I've been back home.

But perhaps she has – and perhaps Rosa and Lars have been here over and over, with no success. I mean, how would I even know, with my memories dropping out like they have? Have my parents been keeping *everyone* away? Ann always called us the Troublesome Trio, not meaning it, of course, because we weren't any trouble at all; when we were together, we were never happier. From the moment we met as babies we slotted together effortlessly, growing up on the edge of our forest, in this tiny community where friendships count for so much. Rosa was the youngest, with me in the middle and Lars older by just a few weeks. Thanks to our mothers' friendship, we'd been through so many firsts together – first steps, first days at school, first swimming lessons in the lake – always side-by-side, experiencing each new event together, cheering one another on, catching each other when we fell. They'd even let me join them on visits to their grandparents in Hamme, conscious as they were that I had none of my own, that I wanted to be part of their extended family. And they treated me like one of the family, they really did. By rights, Rosa should have been in the year below me and Lars, but from the outset it was clear she was bright, and with only ten months between them Ann had persuaded the school to let her kids stay together. 'They should have been twins,' I once heard her telling Mamma as they sat drinking wine at the kitchen table, while we three rolled out biscuit dough amid clouds of icing dust and flour. 'It would have been easier, that's for sure! One pregnancy – one lot of swollen ankles!' Mamma had laughed along with her, but I could see sadness in her expression, and I knew it was because she had longed for a sibling for me. We'd all wished for it, Mamma and Pappa and I, but I guess it wasn't meant to be. And so, Rosa and Lars became my family – so much more than just neighbours from across the way.

Which makes my separation from them all the worse, all the more painful. I don't feel as though I've lost a limb; I feel as though I've lost two.

As I drag myself from bed, the thread of an argument floats near my consciousness, of angry words between Rosa and me. I can see her face, with the light of Foxy's pool room behind her, her eyes moist with hurt, but the words are inaccessible, frozen in time. Now, from downstairs, a sound distracts me as I tread across the attic room towards my bathroom, and that thread of memory is snatched away. Pausing in the doorway, I feel suddenly faint from hunger, feeble. What *is* that noise? The click of a door? The sound of voices or crying – or singing perhaps? I know there's only Mamma in the house because

37

today is one of Pappa's work days, and I haven't heard anyone else arrive since I was woken by his truck driving off this morning. For a moment I think the noise is crying, until the clear sounds of a woman singing drifts beneath my locked door, and I realise my parents must have left the radio on at full blast in their bedroom below. The music lingers awhile before it's gone, and I'm left standing here in the silence, with only the sound of my racing pulse thumping in my ears. Over the past week, I've jumped at every creak and knock, certain it will be Rosa and Lars returning to rescue me from this hell, but Mamma tells me they only called to pick up some schoolbooks I'd borrowed, that they didn't want to stay. How is that even possible? There was a time when our loyalty to each other was everything. I don't know why, but I'm growing increasingly certain that I've done something to test that loyalty; something connected to the night of the accident. Something unforgivable.

In the tiny bathroom, I set the shower running, and for the first time I turn to face myself in the full-length mirror, my fingers clamped tightly at the neck of my robe. Until now, I have managed to avert my gaze as I step in and out of the shower, and have only looked at small areas of my broken body in isolation – never as a whole. The prospect terrifies me, and as I stare into my own dark eyes I wonder what damage my brain has really undergone, for me to willingly starve myself, to go to these lengths in my bid for escape. The thing is, I *want* to look as awful as possible; I want my parents to feel a fear so great that they have no choice but to take me out of here themselves – and I know I'm getting close.

Before I have the chance to talk myself out of it, I allow my robe to slip to the wooden floor, revealing my naked body in all its emaciated glory. I should be shocked, but instead my reaction is strangely detached, as I find comfort in the concrete nature of the damage reflected back at me, the indisputable reality of it. My body doesn't appear to be my own. I've always been slender – not skinny by any means, but lean and toned, and strong, I suppose. The body in the mirror is not the same body. It's pale and bony; my breasts have receded to almost nothing, and my skin hangs thinly over my skeletal frame. And then, of course, there are the scars. The worst of them is an angry red slash that runs from my sternum to my hipbone, like a trail left by an unsteady marker pen. Pappa has told me that when the truck crashed that night the windscreen shattered on impact and the dashboard splintered, causing most of the serious damage to me. Running at a right angle across this deepest scar are a series of smaller cuts, above and below my belly button, another snaking into the deep hollow of my pelvis, puckering the skin there. There's a scarlet line along the length of my left arm, where the doctors had to open it up and fix it with metal plates, and a matching one down the outer shin of my left leg. I can relate these physical marks to some of the information I've gleaned from my parents in recent weeks: that I suffered two broken ribs, a hairline fracture to the fibula, abrasions to my hands and feet, a full break to my left forearm and a ruptured appendix that presented itself in the days which followed. I lift my fringe to inspect the pink scar that still dominates my brow, trying to imagine the moment of impact that caused it, the moment my face smashed into the windscreen of that truck. Mamma says you'll hardly see the damage once I've grown my fringe out – but I feel the tightness which twists from my central hairline to the outer edge of my eyebrow, and I'm not sure I completely believe her. I close my eyes for a moment, and blink them open, trying to imagine how others might view me, and I see, without doubt, that I look appalling.

Now that I've confronted the reality of my injuries, I can't seem to tear myself away. I remain there for half an hour or more, letting the shower run and run, until the trapped heat of the room mists up the mirror and obliterates my image altogether. Reaching out through the fog, I run my finger over the glass of the mirror, to create three seven-bar gates. That's how long I've been in here: three weeks. The marks hold for a few seconds, until the weight of moisture causes them to trickle and obscure. Nothing is stable, I reflect, as I step beneath the scalding water of the shower head, my mind sharper than it has felt in a long time. There are so many questions which can't be answered while I'm shut away in this room. I have to see Rosa and Lars, to find out what really happened that night.

I have to get away from here, and, one way or another, today's the day.

At lunchtime, Mamma tries to engage me in conversation, as though there's no bad feeling between us at all, but I'm tight-lipped and in the end she has to give up and focus on the practical tasks at hand. The weighing, the measuring, the temperature-taking and pill-stuffing. Since the day I saw my friends come and go, she and Pappa have tiptoed around me, pretending they didn't hear my anger and pain through the baby monitor that night, or every night since. Yesterday evening, as I pulled my covers up and settled for sleep, I said a prayer aloud, in the certain knowledge that one of them would hear.

'Dear God,' I said. 'I pray to you to let me die in the night, to let my heart stop beating, to let my lungs stop breathing. Amen.' It gave me a vicious thrill to know the upset this would cause them, because I want them to feel it. I want them to

40

know the suffering they are causing me by keeping me locked up here, away from my friends. Away from the truth.

'Are you hungry?' Mamma asks now, as she places a set of bathroom scales on the wooden floorboards. 'Nettie came by this morning and made some lamb stew especially. Your favourite.'

'Why didn't she come up to visit me?' I ask.

'She had a cold,' Mum says, without hesitation. 'Didn't want to pass it on to you.'

I don't believe her, of course. Nettie would have wanted to see me, cold or not. But Mamma stopped her, kept her away from me, like she does everyone else. I step on to the scales, not looking at the dial.

There's a pause, as Mamma's pencil hovers over her chart. 'Step off,' she says, and she bends down to it, fiddling with the reset button. 'And again.'

I step on and stand quite still. It's got to be a lot lighter than last week. I've barely eaten a thing, and anything I have been forced to eat has come straight back up again, the moment I know it's safe to purge. I glance at Mamma's face, and I see what I hoped for – shock and concern – and I step off the scales and return to sit at the edge of my bed, careful to keep my expression neutral.

'How am I doing?' I ask.

She has her back to me, as she stands beside my desk, pressing out more tablets and making notes on her chart. 'It won't be long now, Eva,' she replies in a practised, level voice. 'We've just got to get a few more pounds on you, strengthen you up a bit. Your immune system has been compromised—'

It's all bullshit, of course. I've heard these stock phrases a dozen times or more.

'Any news from the police?' I ask, and she looks round sharply.

'Er, not that I know of.'

'So, they haven't caught anyone yet? They don't have a suspect? Maybe you could call Chief Mac, ask him for an update?'

Mamma bobs her head, once. 'Good idea. I'll phone him this afternoon.'

'While you're at it, tell him to send my love to Rosa and Lars.' I stare at her, unblinking, and I can see in her face that she knows I'm on to her. Whatever it is she's hiding, I'm on to her.

'I will,' she replies, breaking our awkward eye-contact and scooping up the scales as she heads for the door. 'I'll bring your lunch in half an hour.'

I watch her stoop beneath the eaves and step through the door.

'Oh, and Mamma?' I call over, causing her to halt one step down, her fingers still on the handle.

'Yes?'

'Can you bring the salt up? I'm finding everything a bit bland these days.'

Another pause. 'Sure. OK, darling, I'll see you in a while.'

'You won't forget? I'm not sure I can bring myself to eat anything otherwise.'

She pulls the door shut, drawing the bolt. 'I won't forget,' she calls back as she descends the stairs.

And I know she won't; she'll do anything to get me eating again.

It's several hours since Mamma brought me lunch, and it's now dark outside, the sun having dropped low behind the distant snow-capped mountains. We're having one of the coldest, longest winters in seventy years, Pappa says, and I fantasise about being out there, my boots crunching over the last deep drifts, before spring starts to show itself in the coming weeks, breaking through the frosted surfaces in tiny bursts of emerald. I'm lying curled up on my bed, fighting nausea, holding back for as long as I can, just long enough for my parents to enter the room and witness the state of me. A cold sweat has broken out over my entire body. The window is open wide and I'm freezing, stripped down to just my vest and knickers, the better to showcase the horror of my skeletal frame. I'm desperate to run to the bathroom right now, to throw up, but I mustn't. I have to stay focused.

I home in on a summer memory, in which Pappa is standing beside me on a plateau high up in the mountains, as we pause to take in the blue skies and heather-festooned panorama of Nordfjord. Buzzards fly overhead, or eagles perhaps, their shrill cries echoing across the valley. Far below us, sitting on a rock at the edge of Grønnfoss waterfall, is Mamma, bare feet dangling, the picnic blanket behind her laden with drinks and sandwiches and treats; and further still, further than my mountaintop view could really allow, I see the Bruns – Rosa, Lars and Ann – making their way through the forest to join us, a fairytale hamper swinging between them.

Reluctantly my mind drifts back to the present, to the vile gurgling of my stomach, and I pray for the sound of Pappa's car pulling up outside the window, home from his day's work. Back to that summer day I go, swallowing hard, clamping my teeth together, forcing the memories to the front of my mind, like a meditation. How different life felt back then – how altered is the way I now view my parents. My jailors. Back then, we were tight, Mamma and I, communicating almost without words; just a look here, a stifled smile there, a slow wink of an eye from across the room, to signify a secret. On those picnic weekends, we'd cook together, baking *skolebrød* and cinnamon *bolles*, salted ribs and herring bites. Mamma would pare apples from our own trees, while I rolled the gingerbread, fashioning it into new shapes to unveil at the picnic. One time the biscuits were doctor-themed, for Mamma: little crosses and ambulances and sticking plasters that looked more like bricks. Another time, it was the animals of Norway. But the best batch I made was the one which caused Pappa to roar with laughter, throwing his head back with the force of it and dropping gingerbread crumbs into his thick black beard. *Vikings*. There were longships, Viking men and women, shields and hammers and helmets and swords. I fashioned tiny Norse gods in the shape of Odin and Freyja, and Pappa – the finest Viking of them all – couldn't have been more pleased.

A fierce wave of queasiness reminds me of the salt water I swallowed nearly an hour ago, and I shift on the bed, feeling the swill of it in my gut, as the sound of tyres on gravel tells me Pappa must be home. *Focus, focus*, I tell myself, forcing my mind's eye back to that summer picnic blanket. Mamma is wearing a chain of bluebells about her neck, and the sun beyond the distant lake creates a halo around her strawberry blonde hair. The crisp mountain air paints the tip of her nose a pinky red, and her green-blue eyes sparkle with life beneath pale lashes. Where are those people now? Where are my mamma and pappa, the people who loved me to distraction, who loved each other with such powerful force that they could hardly pass each other without a gentle touch or embrace? It strikes me that they barely look at each other these days, and my suspicion of them morphs into guilt, as I doubt myself and wonder if I am the cause of their division. Me and my stupidity; me and my recklessness. *What* did I do to cause all of this? What did I do to drive away my best friends, Rosa and Lars?

At last, the attic door swings open, and my parents tumble in, looking as though they've run all the way.

'Eva! Your window is wide open! It's the depths of winter! What are you thinking?' Mamma doesn't even look at me as she rushes past my bed to close it.

But Pappa remains in the doorway, shock-faced. His eyes are on me, on the sallow sheen of my skin, on the stick-like appearance of my scarred limbs. *Now*, I tell myself, unfolding my legs from the bed, shakily forcing myself to stand. *Now's the moment.*

'I needed some air. I'm not feeling so good,' I say in a weak voice, and I vomit on to the floor, once, twice, again and again and again.

Within seconds my mother is at my side with a bath towel, holding back my hair, screaming instructions to my father, who punches numbers into his phone with shaking hands.

'Hello?' he says when eventually they answer. 'Hello? It's my daughter, Eva – she's seventeen. She's throwing up – oh, God, *there's so much of it*. What? No, it's not a bug, I'm sure! She was in a serious road accident, she only came out of intensive care three weeks ago and she's on a lot of medication – yes, it's Eva Olsen – Dr Olsen's daughter!' There's a pause as he listens to the emergency operator at the other end of the line. 'Jesus, can you just get an ambulance out here? Please hurry,' he says. 'I think she's dying!'

He sinks to the floor at my side, his breathing laboured, and I feel the touch of his fingers, light on my bony spine.

I can't look up; I'm still heaving, the muscles in my stomach having gone into some kind of grotesque spasm. They think I'm dying, but beneath the curtain of my lank, sweaty hair I feel light-headed, euphoric. There's an ambulance coming, I tell myself, and I'm getting out.

As my mother gathers up wet towels and rushes back and forth to the bathroom, I hear a sob escape from my father beside me.

'What have we done, Ingrid?' he murmurs. 'What the hell have we done?'

6

Eva

I'm dying. I'm in the car again, on the dark and icy road, and I hear the driver's words, clear and soft: 'Eva, I'm not going to hurt you, I promise. You do believe me, don't you?' And I do believe him; I know he means me no harm, and yet it seems that his is a stranger's face. But now the scene shifts and there are hands on me. I can't see them, not with my eyes; I'm somewhere far beyond or far below the reach of the place that my body inhabits. But I feel them. I hear the muted buzz and whirr of engines and the sharp scent of a man as he leans across me, fingers pushing back my dress, running across my torso, slow like a lover, lingering over my ribs. He lifts my arm, cradles my wrist, murmurs softly as he lets it drop to my side. Is he mocking me? A female voice gasps in response, and I wonder what it is that they see. Am I hot or cold? Inside a building or out in the open air? I have no sense of it, no gauge, no concrete sensory perception other than this remote notion of being manhandled. For a moment there is nothing but those engines running, and I think perhaps the people have left me, let me be, but with that thought I'm assaulted by another set of hands, cool and purposeful, pawing at me without permission. The fingertips are smooth, and I detect neat nails as she moves the hair from my face, drifting past the hollows of my collarbone and under my neck. I pray that my mind is merely muddled, that it's just Mamma and Pappa at my side, that this is all a dream or a hangover or an accident. I imagine it's Rosa and Lars, tending to me after a heavy night out together, that I'm wasted but safe, that I'll be just A-OK come morning, in the cold light of day. 'Jesus,' says one of them, and it's a voice unfamiliar to me. 'You've heard the story, right?' There's more murmuring, and I think perhaps I'm listening to a TV show or a radio turned down low, that these voices aren't real at all. 'Do you think she knows?' asks another, and it's so close to my ear that I know they are real and I try to turn my head, to open my eyes, to tell them to back off, get out of my space – but I'm just not here. My circuits have been cut. I'm deep in the darkness, but some connection remains, because, just as a third voice breaks through, I feel them again and they're pressing down on me, all of them at once, pushing me where I don't want to be pushed, tugging at me, squeezing the life from me. I scream at them, NO-NO-NO-NO-NO! But they don't hear me, can't hear me, and still they push and touch and there's nothing I can do because I'm shut inside . . .

'You've had a light sedative,' Mamma says, the touch of her fingers cool on the back of my hand.

I'm in a private room, with familiar green and white striped blinds, and an overhead strip light which is too bright. I realise I'm missing a chunk of time, and my hollow stomach turns nervously as I try to piece it together. I can clearly remember

Pappa carrying me down the stairs in a blanket, and the paramedics strapping me to a gurney the way you see in films. As they wheeled me into the back of the ambulance, I was shaking uncontrollably, and it frightened me at the time, because, unlike my sickness, the tremors weren't planned. Outside it was pitch black, but the red wooden cladding of our home was lit up by the spinning lamp of the emergency vehicle, and our house lights shone out from the windows, as though everyone was still home. The vehicle doors closed with a clunk, and I wondered if it was the last time I'd ever see the place. From my prone position, I turned my head to see Mamma sitting beside me in the confined space, while the paramedic asked me questions, checked my pulse, administered a sharp pinprick to my arm.

But there's someone missing from the picture.

'Where's Pappa?' I ask now, attempting to reach for the jug of water at my bedside, only to find my hand is attached to a drip.

Mamma pours me a drink and brings it to me, carefully guiding the straw to my lips, as though I'm incapable. 'Someone had to stay behind—' she starts to say, and when I frown she adds, 'They only allow one extra person in the ambulance.'

'Is he coming? Can he bring me some things? I need some stuff, like my nightgown and a hairbrush – my toothbrush. Can you phone him?'

'I managed to grab a few clothes as we left,' she says, indicating towards a carrier bag and my snow boots in the corner of the room. 'But I'll send him a text,' she says, and she picks up her phone and taps out a message. 'If he calls back, I'll have to take it outside – the signal's a bit patchy in this room.'

The door to our room is slightly ajar, and it seems that the hospital is busy tonight. Doctors and nurses rush by, and as

I sip at my water I try to work out what my next move will be. The wall clock tells me it's coming up for seven, and I wonder what is taking Pappa so long to get here. He seemed so worried back in the attic; he said he thought I was dying, for God's sake. If that was the case, you'd think he'd want to be here for my final breath.

'What did the doctors say?' I ask. 'When they brought me in?' I have a faint recollection of their discussion, little wisps of a conversation held at my bedside while they thought I was out cold. Certain words stand out: *alarming; deficient; underweight.* 'They think I have an eating disorder, don't they?'

'You heard us?' she says, looking down at her lap.

I nod. 'The doctor said he was surprised you hadn't brought me in earlier.'

She looks up, instantly defensive. 'Eva, you were so weak – I could see your weight dropping on the scales, but I thought if we could just get you to rest and increase your appetite – I've even been putting protein powder in your cocoa.'

'I flushed it down the toilet,' I tell her.

The expression on her face says it all. She didn't have a clue.

'But, but – why?' she asks, drawing her chair closer.

'Because I was out of ideas, Mamma! Because you've been lying to me. Because you've kept me locked away up there, with no real explanation, no real *reason.*'

'That's not true!' she says. 'We had every reason! God, you've made yourself so ill, Eva, starving yourself like this. Everything your pappa and I have done has been for your protection – all we want is to keep you safe. You have to believe me. Ask me anything! I promise, I'll tell you the truth.' Her expression is earnest, and in that moment, I believe her.

'Tell me about Rosa and Lars,' I say, not missing a beat. 'Tell me why you sent them away last week.'

We're interrupted as the door to the room opens fully, and a nurse enters with a tray of food, placing it on the lap table and sliding it over the bed for me.

'Ah, you're awake!' she says, brightly. 'You must be hungry? I managed to rustle up a late supper for you.' She taps the side of her nose. 'Your mamma here knows how to pull a string or two!'

'Perk of the job,' my mother replies, and she touches the woman's arm lightly. 'Thanks, Allie.'

As the nurse leaves the room, my eyes fall on a garland of silver snowflakes hanging in the corridor outside. 'It's a bit late for Christmas,' I say, pointing them out as I pick up my fork. I'm ravenous, and for the first time in weeks I have no reason to starve myself. I'm out of the attic, and, it would seem, my mother is starting to talk.

She rises from her chair to close the door again. 'Now, you wanted to know about Rosa and Lars?'

I take a small mouthful of pie, and nod, chewing it slowly, deliberately. This is your reward, I'm telling her: if you give me the truth, I'll eat.

'OK,' she begins. 'The first we knew about your accident was when Mac called at the house just after midnight, to tell us you'd been airlifted here, to hospital. That night was a virtual white-out, and there'd been heavy snowfall all week, so the roads out of town were inaccessible. We were in bed, but still awake – waiting for you to arrive home. I wasn't too worried, I knew Rosa and Lars would see you home first as always, but I'd just started thinking about phoning to check with Ann when Mac arrived with the news.' She pauses, silently inviting my questions. 'There was a terrible two-hour wait before we could do anything, until Mac received a call to say they'd cleared the main road, and we jumped in the squad car with him and headed straight over to Hamme.'

I put down my fork. 'Mamma, I know all this. What I want to know is why Rosa and Lars haven't been to see me – why Ann hasn't been? She's your best friend. Have you heard from her lately?'

'I was getting to that.' Mamma's fingers worry at her wedding band, turning it this way and that. 'We fell out,' she says eventually.

'You and Ann? You've never fallen out!'

'I know,' she replies. 'When we realised how badly injured you were, we were desperate for answers. Mac told us the driver of the car had got away, that there were no witnesses, no explanation as to what you were doing in that truck with a stranger. So naturally we called on the Bruns – to ask them what they knew. To see if they could remember anything they hadn't already told their Uncle Mac.'

Mamma hesitates, choosing her words carefully.

'They weren't very helpful.'

'In what way?'

'From the outset, it seemed clear to both me and your pappa that they *did* know something about that night. I couldn't say what – but I've known them all their lives and I knew they were holding back. We asked them about the stranger in the bar, the person Mac thinks was driving, and they have no recollection of him at all. Doesn't that seem odd to you? I mean, everyone knows everyone around here – I find it hard to believe they wouldn't have noticed a stranger, especially on Valentine's night. When we asked them why they'd left you in the bar alone, they said you'd told them to go on ahead, that you'd get your father to pick you up.'

'But I don't have a mobile phone – and, anyway I'd never call you or Pappa out at that time of night.'

'Exactly! I asked them if you'd arranged to meet someone, a boy, perhaps, and Lars started to say yes before Rosa shushed him, and he clammed up and changed his mind. The pair of them were shifty, and I know they weren't telling us everything, Eva. I was upset, I said I blamed them for the state you were in – told them they might as well have been driving that truck themselves, for all the care they took of you. Of course, Ann reared up then, telling me I was the one who should feel guilty for not knowing what my own daughter was up to. I saw red, and, well, it got heated to say the least. I still can't believe it now, that they just left you there like that.'

I'm trying to process all this, to understand how it is possible my friends would have left me at a bar, especially if I *was* planning to meet a complete stranger. It seems inconceivable. Rosa would have interrogated me for the full story, without a doubt. She's like a terrier in that way; once she's got a sniff of something, there's no distracting her.

'Do you still feel like that, Mamma – do you still blame Rosa and Lars?'

She nods, grim-faced. 'I do. You might think it's irrational, Eva – I know your pappa does – but I do blame them. They're meant to be your best friends, and everything I've heard from them makes me think they're hiding something. And even if they're not, they're guilty of putting you at risk. Would you ever have left Rosa like that? To meet a stranger – to take her chances in that bar full of lowlifes like Gurt and Foxy, after drinking God knows how much? No! I've tried, Eva. But I just can't forgive them – and that's why I've stopped them from visiting. They let you down. They've let us all down.'

Something shifts in my memory; something connected to Gurt. I see his coarse bony face as he stands at Foxy's bar, watching me, watching Rosa, his leering thoughts right there on the surface.

'Well, I want to see them,' I say. 'They might tell me something they wouldn't tell you.'

The nurse breezes back in again, and this time she's wearing a party crown and offering us a plate of Christmas *julekake*. She smiles wickedly, urging me to take a big piece. 'Don't tell the other patients!'

I stare at the cake, and back at the nurse in her festive crown. I'm so stunned that for a moment, I can't even speak.

'Is everything alright, Ingrid?' Allie asks, looking suddenly concerned, and turning from me to Mamma.

'Fine, thanks, Allie,' Mamma says, taking a piece of cake herself and attempting to wave away my confusion. 'Eva's just—'

'Mamma, what date is it?' I ask.

She doesn't answer, simply frowns.

Nurse Allie stands between us, uncomfortably hanging on to that plate.

'Can *you* tell me?' I ask her. 'What date is it?'

Allie's frown turns into a hesitant smile. 'It's the seventeenth of December,' she replies, and she reverses out of the room with her cakes, leaving the door open in her haste to get away.

Before I have the chance to confront Mamma, her phone rings and it's Pappa, and she holds up a finger to silence me as she steps outside the room. As my mind desperately attempts to put this information into some kind of order, I'm left staring at those peppermint-striped blinds that now seem so familiar to me that I wonder if I've stayed in this room before.

It's December. *December.* The accident was in February, and everything my parents have told me suggests I've only been home for the past three weeks. I know I was in hospital for a while too, but, if it really *is* December, what on earth happened to the rest of the year in between? I think of the snow-cloaked landscape beyond my attic window, only now understanding with absolute certainty that I was not looking out on the landscape of winter retreating, but of winter in full swing.

If my parents are capable of concealing this, this most fundamental of details, what else aren't they telling me? The absence of those months sends a jolt of terror through me, and before I know it I'm out of my bed, tearing the drip needle from the back of my hand, pulling on my ill-fitting jeans, my sweater, my fur-lined boots. Without a backward glance, I open the door, spot Mamma at the far end of the corridor – on the phone still, her back to me – and move in the opposite direction as fast as my frail legs will carry me, keeping my head down, avoiding all human contact. Out along the bright, bleached corridors of the hospital I run, wild with fear, not knowing where I'm going, thinking only of escape.

In the lamplit hospital car park, dressed in only a single layer, I'm immediately struck by the blizzard conditions of the night. I make my way towards the main road, with no coat, no hat, no gloves – and no plan. I could die out here in these sub-zero conditions, but that thought is not enough to stop me or to make me turn back. Onwards I go, through the hospital gates, keeping my head down against the biting wind, arms wrapped around myself, braced against the excruciating sting of snowfall. The glow of streetlamps leads me out on to the main highway, where snowploughs chunter along on either side, fog lights creating halos in the darkness as they clear the way for the few slow-moving vehicles following steadily in their wake. As profound cold begins to take hold of me, some kind of primal instinct kicks in, and I know I have to act now. Going against everything my parents ever taught me about safety, about sense, I turn to face the oncoming traffic and stick my thumb out.

It's getting late, and the traffic is sparse. A few cars and heavy-goods vehicles pass by, perhaps not seeing me, or maybe not trusting my crazy, underdressed appearance at the roadside. I doubt I would stop to pick me up either. The drifts at the bankside are getting rapidly deeper, and my ability to see the path ahead is diminishing by the second. I've lost all sensation in my feet, sockless inside my snow boots, and my jaw judders uncontrollably. Another vehicle swishes by, horn blaring as I stagger weakly, desperately trying to hold my focus and strength. Will no one take mercy on me? I step closer to the road's edge, and with more determination I hold out my arm, ramrod-straight, thumb firmly cocked, and clamp my eyes shut against the slicing pain of ice on my skin. Finally there's a shunting vibration beneath my feet, and when I open my eyes, to my wonder I'm met by twin headlamps. A pickup has come to stop several metres before me. I blink, my arm still stuck out, as though the weather conditions have finally got the better of me and frozen me to the spot.

'Eva?' a man's voice calls out, as a figure emerges from the driver side, a black silhouette against the oncoming glare. 'Eva Olsen?'

My heart sinks. I'm not half a mile from the hospital, and they've caught up with me already. I bow my head, broken.

'Eva?' the voice repeats, louder, and I recognise it. The man is closer now, his pace quickening as he registers my frail condition. 'Get in the car, girl – are you nuts?'

Grabbing at my upper arm, he manhandles me into the passenger seat, before ducking round to the driver's side and climbing in himself. I'm almost blind with cold, and it's all I can do to tuck my chin into my chest and try to control the shudders that have gripped my entire body. He turns towards me and reaches over to the back seat, pressing his chest again my shoulder in his effort; he smells of stale tobacco and engine oil, and something else, an unpleasant animal scent. After a few seconds of rummaging about, he draws back with a blanket, which he wraps around me, tucking it against the seat, before pulling the safety belt across my body, pinning my arms down.

'What the hell are you doing out here, girl?' he asks me. Only now do I look up, as I realise the voice belongs to Gurt, and my blood runs colder still. Creepy Gurt.

I glance at him side-on, at the greasy black hair that sprouts from beneath his knitted hat, at the ancient oil streaks on the knees of his filthy orange boiler suit. He narrows his eyes, waiting for my answer, and I look away. *Oh, Jesus, oh, lord, what the hell is Gurt doing out here?* Something unspoken takes me back to that night in Foxy Jack's – something ominous and out of reach. Was *he* the driver? He was certainly there, I know that much; he's always there – he's Foxy's lodger, after all. But was he responsible for my accident in some way? Is *he* the person who's been watching our house?

'Where were you heading?' he asks now, fiddling with the heating dial, turning it up to full blast. He manoeuvres the vents to point them towards me.

The sensation is sublime; all at once I feel the heat rushing up over my lap, brushing beneath my face, warming my skin. I'm so relieved to be alive that for a moment I can't answer him, can't respond to my instinctive fear of him in any sensible way. If I had my wits about me I'd be out of that truck like a shot, to take my chances back on the roadside. But the warmth holds me captive.

'Where are you going, Eva?' he asks again, slotting his own safety belt into place, and flipping the indicator as he drops back onto the highway.

'To Rosa and Lars's house,' I reply, quite unexpectedly, and to my surprise he simply nods.

For a while, we drive in silence, and it occurs to me that he has never been much of a talker. To me Gurt's silence seems furtive, a way of concealing all the creepy things he's undoubtedly thinking, but Pappa puts it down to shyness, saying I shouldn't be so unkind, as Gurt's never done anything to harm me. My father looks for the good in people; it's one of his best, and worst, features. For some reason, he's always taken pity on Gurt, saying he just needs a break or two, his mother having died young and his father being a bit handy with his fists. When he was a teenager, four or five years older than me, Pappa used to let him fish on our land, and from time to time he'd knock on our door with a fish, by way of thanks. Mamma didn't like him much, though, and I guess that's where I got the idea. But the fact remains that although he's never actually done anything, he *is* creepy, and there aren't many around here who want to spend time alone in his company. It's a good job he's got his hunting buddies, Foxy and the like, otherwise he'd be pretty much on his own.

My thoughts return to the idea that he's been watching my house, and I wriggle my hands from beneath the blanket, readjusting the seatbelt to free my arms.

'What are you doing out here, Gurt?' I ask, sensation now having returned to my face. We pass by a road sign for Valden, telling us we're less than half an hour from home.

'Been at the hospital,' he replies. There's a pause, before he says, 'Old man's had a heart attack. Been visitin'.'

58

'Oh,' I reply, not believing him. My heart starts to drum beneath my ribcage.

'You?' he says.

I pull my blanket closer again. 'Check-up,' I reply. 'After the accident.'

The blizzard is growing heavier, and I feel certain Gurt hasn't been visiting his father at all. What if he's been stalking me, watching my every movement, following me to the hospital and leaping at the opportunity I presented him with when I fled into the open?

He clucks his tongue between his lower lip and teeth, making a horrible moist sound. 'That was pretty bad, wasn't it?' he says. 'The accident. We all thought you was dead, for sure. Most would've froze in that time. Specially with, you know, how bad you got hurt. Mac said you broke loads of bones – that you got scars all over you.'

I nod, too scared not to answer. 'It was bad.'

A few more miles pass, before he asks, 'I was wonderin', d'you remember much about it?'

'Not much,' I reply. *Why is he asking me this?*

'Huh,' he grunts, reaching into his glove box for a cigarette.

He rests one on his wet lower lip, before lighting it with the dashboard lighter. I could hurt him with that, I think, if I needed to. I could press it into his face, burn a dirty great hole in him and throw myself from the truck while he's caught off-guard. But I won't do that; I'd only snap into a hundred pieces on the roadside, or disappear down a ravine and die of exposure.

'That's good,' he says.

'Good that I don't remember anything?' I say. 'Why?'

He doesn't answer straight away, instead takes a deep draw on his cigarette, filling the truck with dirty white smoke.

'The shock, you know? That's what the brain does, to stop us from losin' it. People forget stuff when other people do bad things to 'em.' Somehow, Gurt manages to make everything sound sordid.

'It was a car crash.'

'Yeah, but – some fella had you, didn't he? You know? Some pervert. You prob'ly wouldn'ta known a thing about it.'

I feel sick, and in silence I watch the road and wish away the miles, praying that Gurt means to take me to my friends as I asked, that he doesn't have some other terrible fate in mind. Rosa and Lars, I remind myself: soon I'll be safe in the warmth of their little woodland cottage, swaddled beside their fire, drinking cocoa and eating one of Ann's famous butter cookies. I have no idea what I want to say when I get there, but Rosa will know what to do next. Rosa always has a plan.

'D'you remember anything about him? The fella?' Gurt opens his window a crack, sending his cigarette stub sparking out into the night.

'No,' I say, even more alarmed now, and my fears are realised when at the main junction to Valden Gurt turns the truck into a tree-shrouded lay-by and without a word steps out, slams the door, and activates the central locking. *What does he want with me?* My breath comes short and fast in the cocooned space of the truck. *Shit.* Where is he going? I watch as he hesitates beneath a tree, lights another cigarette, and takes out his phone, turning his back to me as he brings it to his ear. Who is he calling? Foxy? His hunting buddies? Was that his plan all along? You hear about it, don't you – girls taken and locked away and used and abused and – my mind is so confused, I no longer trust my own judgement. From here, I can see him in the shadows talking still, nodding his head every now and then, glancing back towards the truck, checking his wristwatch. I feel certain that I'm under threat, but there's no one else here on the edge of the road, no one to see me or hear me; no point in banging on the windows, and no point in screaming for help. By the time he returns to the truck, I'm entirely convinced Gurt means me harm. I stiffen, eyes on that cigarette lighter in the dashboard, wondering how I can press it in to heat up, without him seeing me and taking it away.

'Bit of business,' he says as he slams the driver's door shut, and I think even now he's trying to impress me, trying to seem the big man. He's an odd-jobber with a crappy van and a bag of his pappa's old tools. What kind of business could he possibly be involved in?

'Why did you lock the doors?' I ask, my voice shaky.

He starts the engine and sets off again. 'Force of habit.'

Another pause. 'How long will it take us to get to the Bruns'?'

'Ten minutes. Five if I put my foot down.' With this, his face splits into a wide grin, and he accelerates so that we're hurtling dangerously along the icy main road, his lights on full beam, as I pray that I live long enough to fight him off. The snow keeps driving at us, and even with the windscreen wipers on full power I have no idea how Gurt is able to keep this truck on the road, how he can make out where the highway ends and the lakeside begins. I reach out and push the cigarette lighter into its hole with a click, imagining the burning red heat he will feel when it scorches into his skin.

Gurt glances at me; at the lighter. 'Want a ciggie?' he asks, pleased-looking, and I bob my head, swallowing a scream as he chucks the packet into my lap.

With screeching tyres he swings the truck off the main road, and I think, this is it: he's taking me to some terrible cabin in the forest, to shackle me, to keep me his prisoner for God only knows what – when, sheltered beneath the canopy of trees, the snowstorm clears, and I see we're on the single farm track that leads to the Bruns' home and forest, that he's really taking me where I want to go. As the lights of their little cottage come into view, all fears I had about Gurt's intentions evaporate. *I'm here*, I want to cry out! *Rosa! Lars! I'm here!* But then, as we draw level with their front door, instead of stopping Gurt accelerates again, plunging his truck into the darkness of the forest, following the tree-lined path by the light of his headlamps, bumping over snowy tree roots and leaf mulch until the open gates and the imposing red boards of my own home appear.

'What are you doing?' I scream at him, again and again. 'Gurt!'

When he drives through the gates I see them waiting for me: Chief Mac and my pappa, standing beside the squad car, bathed in the yellow glow of the house lights, an unwelcome welcoming committee of two. And is that old Nettie I see at the first-floor window, looking out at me, her neatly rolled hair as white as the snow? I blink and her face is gone, a strange figment of my spent imagination. In a final show of bravado, Gurt slams on the brakes, spinning the wheels so that they kick up gravel and snow, winding down his window so he can holler over. 'Delivery for Olsen,' he calls out, and Mac shakes his head at the bad joke and ambles over, hand extended, thanking Gurt for his phone call.

Drained, I shirk off Gurt's stinky blanket and stumble out, throwing him one last glance as I summon up the strength to push the door closed behind me. And bang, there it is, a vision – a memory – slamming to the front of my mind, crystal clear. A still of Gurt's face through the glass of that stolen truck on Valentine's night, of him beyond the driver's side window and me on the other side, opening the passenger door, willingly getting in. Speechless, I watch his tail lights disappear, as it finally dawns on me: Gurt was the driver.

Without a thought, I fall into the open arms of my father, collapsing with weakness and relief, and in spite of my failed bid for escape I'm grateful to be home, alive. Without a word, Mac pats Pappa on the back and climbs into his police car, driving out into the darkness, disappearing before I'm able to say a word.

'Let's get you to bed, Eva-boo,' Pappa says, lifting me into his arms and carrying me inside, where warmth wraps itself around me with the comforting aroma of wood smoke and pine. Even before he reaches the foot of the stairs, I'm sliding helplessly into sleep.

'It was Gurt,' I murmur through the fog of collapse.

'I know,' Pappa replies. 'I'll thank him tomorrow. I told you he's alright.'

I'm too tired to respond; too tired to disagree. Too tired to put up a fight when, on the landing outside my old bedroom, I sense my father pause, before he continues along the carpeted hallway, out through the master bedroom and up the attic stairs.

7

Eva

I'm in hospital again, in a private room with green striped blinds across the windows, and Rosa and Lars at my bedside. The stripes make me think of the boiled mint toffees Mrs Halvorsen used to keep in a jar behind the counter in the bakery when I was small. But the detail of the blinds must be wrong, because, while I know they're there, I can't really see them, just as I'm unable to see my friends. With horror, I realise I can neither move nor speak to them. But I can hear them. 'Do you think they know?' Rosa is whispering. I feel the touch of cool fingers, pressing my hand tenderly as though testing me for life, and I'm certain those fingers belong to Lars, and I yearn to reach out to him, to pull him close. The scene shifts, and I am free of those invisible chains, free of the humming buzz and the bleachy sting of that place; the strangeness of my own legs is a wonder. I can see them moving beneath me, transporting my body to the lakeside, my white feet gliding over fallen fir and snow-crisped leaf, with not a stumble, not a moment's pain at all. And at the water's edge

I think perhaps the world has flipped, because the moon's reflection in the black water is a perfect orb of white, so sharp that I might instead be gazing at the sky. A night bird lands on the lake's still surface, breaking the illusion, sending ripples circling outwards across the water, forever and ever. In the forest that edges Lake Barn, nothing stirs. From here the blackness of the forest appears total, and yet, when I step beneath the canopy, the moon's bright light filters through in tiny beams of dust-light and the fox appears on the path ahead, white as the moon, and I know her. I drop to my haunches, extending a hand to beckon her close, but as she takes a first step towards me I'm seized by rough hands, and ripped from the beautiful dream.

'They have Gurt in custody,' Mamma tells me at suppertime, and she pulls me into a fierce hug, which I resist. 'Mac just phoned. Isn't that a relief, Eva? They found him at Foxy's a couple of hours ago.'

My sense of relief is subdued, less complete than I had imagined it might be. Gurt's no longer out there; he's no longer a threat to me. My abductor is caught, and the mystery of my accident is on the way to being solved. I *should* feel overjoyed. I'm standing at the attic window, looking out into the dark night, the moon in the sky overhead lighting up the snow-topped trees and casting a silver shimmer across the lake. On nights like these, Lars, Rosa and I would often stay over at each other's, swaddling up in our winter gear to take midnight excursions down to the pontoon, to smoke roll-ups and drink snaffled lager, and talk until the cold was too much to bear. En route, we'd gather small rocks from along the path, to cast out into the silent water, sending mercury circles undulating across the surface. The last time we did that must have been January; more than a year ago. I wonder again what that argument with Rosa was all about, and in some ways I'm relieved Gurt didn't drop me at their house as I'd asked him to. What if they'd turned me away? What if they'd told me they never wanted to see me again?

Strangely, I've grown increasingly sure that it was Gurt we argued about, or that at least he was responsible for the argument – or witness to it. After getting home the other night, after my nightmare journey with him, I slept like the dead, right through to midday the next day when I told my parents what I'd remembered, setting in motion the chain of events that brings us to now. Despite the stress and revelation of those previous twenty-four hours, on waking, my mind had felt still. I'd found a full breakfast tray at my bedside, and with absolute clarity I knew I had to eat it all, to focus on getting strong. Making myself weaker was no longer an option. In the couple of days since, I have slept for long hours, waking only to eat my meals and, when my parents are out of the room, to exercise a little, walking circuits of the room and stretching out my aching limbs, challenging tendons and muscles grown tight through months of inactivity.

More and more memories have risen to the surface, and, while my parents seem to be putting on a good show of being honest, the fact is, I'm still locked in this attic – and they're still holding back on the truth. I have so many questions to ask them, and I've been storing them up for the right time, and I think that time is now.

'Do the police think Gurt did it?' I ask.

Mamma pinches the top of her nose, as though trying to stem a headache. 'Who knows? They'll be interviewing him tonight, and Mac seems to think your statement is sufficient to keep him for at least a couple of days – to see if they have enough evidence to charge him.'

When Mac and Bern came to take my statement, I'd told them as much as I could, which, when I started talking, hadn't sounded like that much at all. They'd wanted to know what Gurt had said to me that Valentine's night, if he'd forced me into the truck, if anyone else was there. But my memory bank had remained sealed: all I could tell them was that I remembered getting into the truck on one side, while Gurt got in on the other.

'He had a flower behind his ear,' I'd added before they left to go and find him. 'They all did: Foxy, Gurt, Mad Eric. It was some stupid Valentine thing – Foxy was giving out roses to all the single people in the bar, and Gurt still had a pink rose behind his ear when he got in the truck.' I had tried so hard to zone in on that scene, but there was almost nothing else there. 'And I can remember sitting in the passenger seat too. I remember looking down at the clods of melting snow in the footwell, as they slid off my boots.'

'Were you afraid?' Bern had asked, and I'd said no.

Bern had jotted the detail down in his notebook, as though it was important, but it's not, of course. It's not evidence or proof or any of those other things they need if they want to charge Gurt. Me getting my bloody memory back is what we really need. Or a witness, someone who actually saw us leaving together.

'Eva?' Mamma says now, fetching my supper tray from the desk and carrying it to the bed. She sits and pats the space beside her. 'We need to talk, don't we?'

I turn away from my window view, as a pale streak of movement weaves through the nearest treeline. 'Do we get Arctic foxes around here?' I ask.

'No,' she replies, glancing at the poster stuck to my eaves. 'Very rarely, anyway. They're endangered – you'd have to go further north to see one in the wild.'

'I hear foxes crying at night, all the time – and I just wondered, you know, if maybe some of them were Arctics.'

She smiles. 'No, just regular foxes, I'd guess. You always were obsessed with seeing a white one, ever since you were tiny.' And then she trails off, covering her mouth with a hand. Is she about to cry? For a moment we just gaze at each other across the room. 'I promise you, Eva, once we get you up and about, we'll go on a trip together. The three of us, you, me and Pappa – we'll do one of those wildlife tours. See the Arctic foxes up close.'

I cross the room and sit beside her on the bed.

'It's nearly a *whole year* since the accident, Mamma,' I say, coldly. 'Why did you lie to me about how much time has passed?'

She takes my hand in hers. 'We didn't, darling, I promise. We told you the details so many times, and you'd just forget, day after day. After a while, we just stopped going over the story. We figured once you started remembering things properly, *retaining* things, we'd give you the full story again.'

'And what *is* the full story?'

She shifts position, so that she can look at me, and I slide the supper tray from her lap to mine and start to work my way through the fish salad she's brought me, thankful of the distraction. If I'm not careful, if I look at her for too long, I'll soften at her sad, gentle tone, and lose the resolve I've worked so hard to reach.

'Oh,' she says, noticing I'm clumsily hacking at the fish with the side of my fork. 'Your pappa didn't put a knife on the tray – do you want one?'

I shake my head and continue eating. 'It's fine – carry on.'

'After the accident you were in intensive care for a few weeks, and for some of that time you were conscious.' She

68

hesitates a moment, waiting for my response, but I'm focused on my plate. 'Just as we thought things were improving, you suffered a series of seizures, and you were put into an induced coma to protect your brain from long-term damage.'

'I was in a coma for the whole of that time?'

'Not all of it,' she says, 'but most. When they brought you back to consciousness we had you with us for almost a week, but then you slipped back under, and you stayed in that condition – stable but unresponsive – until early November, when, miraculously, you started to wake of your own accord. Because I'm a neurologist, two weeks later they let us bring you home.'

'*Home*,' I say, allowing my bitterness to spill over. 'To the attic.'

'You make it sound like a prison.' She sighs, and it takes all I've got not to fling my supper tray to the floor. 'We decided to put you up here for a number of reasons, Eva – but I swear, it really was mainly because it's the quietest room.'

It *is* the quietest place in the house; that's why Pappa set up his office here when his garden business really started to take off. You can barely hear there's another person in the house most of the time, because to get up here you have to pass through their bedroom and into what looks like a storage cupboard but is in fact a stairwell. It's effectively a secret room; a *perfect* prison.

'We also thought it would be safer – your immune system took a beating, and up here you were away from the germs and everyday bacteria that could impede your recovery. There was no bolt on the door then, Eva.'

'Pappa said the lock was because of the sleepwalking,' I say, and she nods. 'And what about the tablets? There are so many of them, Mamma. You know I stopped taking them, don't you?'

69

Again, she nods. 'Pappa found a stash of them in your sock drawer when he was packing your hospital bag the other night. You know you can't just stop like that, don't you? Your body won't like it. That's probably what caused your vomiting episode. That and your lack of eating.'

'Really?' I reply, relishing my secret. 'But what are they? And don't lie. I know you've been sedating me, Mamma. I'm not an idiot.'

'The sedatives were your doctor's idea – we started you on them soon after the sleepwalking became a problem. He thought a few weeks on them might help to calm your anxiety levels and allow you to sleep. To rest that part of your brain which is making you active at night time.'

'Well, I'm not taking those any more. And the others?'

'Painkillers and anti-spasmodics – for your seizures – and anti-inflammatories.'

Beyond the window, the foxes start up their nightly cry, a faint wail in the distance.

'What can't I do without?' I ask.

'The seizure drugs. That's the one I gave you this morning, with your breakfast. Until you've had your follow-up with one of my colleagues and had the all-clear, you *must* keep taking them. A fit could kill you, Eva. Or leave you permanently brain-damaged.'

Those words, *brain-damaged*, spark fear in me. I look up from my plate, at her earnest, fretful face, and on this matter alone I decide to trust her.

'I'll take that one, then – but as for the others, I don't want them. I won't take them.'

Mamma brings her hands together decisively. 'We'll reduce your doses this week, then, and have you off them the next. OK?'

I lower my plate to the floor and turn to hug her. She holds me so tightly, burying her face in my hair, and telling me she loves me, that it occurs me that she needs me now so much more than I need her. The ache I feel for my old way of life – for the love and trust I had in my parents – is profound, but I can't allow the hard shell I'm forming to crack. It's the one thing that will get me out of here. I think of all the other questions I have: I think of Gurt locked up in the police station in Valden town; of Lars and Rosa and that bewildering argument; and of Mamma, unable to forgive my friends for letting me down. I think of all these things and more, and I tell myself the questions can wait, because when I hand my mamma the supper tray and she kisses me good-night she has no idea that there's a knife concealed between my mattress and the bed frame – and she has no idea that I have another plan.

Tomorrow will be Christmas Eve, and my day has started with purpose and resolve. I rise at first light, clearing my breakfast tray at speed, and greeting Pappa warmly when he comes to take it away, careful to maintain my agreeable veneer. The moment he leaves again, I wrap a towel around the baby monitor at the back of my bed, to muffle any giveaway sounds, and set to work with the dinner knife.

It's now early afternoon and I'm busy working away at loosening the screws on my door frame when I'm distracted by the sound of a dog barking outside. Stashing my knife back beneath the mattress, I rush to the window to investigate. The light fades early in these winter months, and already the trees are casting deep shadows at the lake's edge. Chief Mac stands there, calf-deep in snow, his police dog at his side. He brought the Golden Shepherd in to school last year, to talk about the

71

dangers of drugs and the role of canines in the police force's war against crime. Lars had sniggered at his uncle's warnings at the time, what with Valden being one of the sleepiest, least threatening places in the Western world.

Below me, the slamming of the front door vibrates through the wooden frame of the house, dislodging snow from the roof, causing it to slide and fall to the ground with a familiar soft thud. I watch as Pappa crosses our drive at a brisk pace, pulling up the hood of his coat as he pushes through the wide gate and out on to the forest path beyond. Easing the window open a crack, I can just about make out their words.

'Hello!' Pappa calls over to the chief. He breaks into a light jog. 'Hey, Mac!'

'Hey, Tobias!' Chief Mac replies, releasing his focus on the lake's edge, where the dog – Innes, I remember now – is nosing the ground enthusiastically. 'Almost Christmas!' he calls over, with a cheery lift of his gloved hand.

As Pappa joins him at the water's edge, their voices drop to a conversational level, and their words are now impossible to hear, but their body language and gestures are fascinating. From behind the first line of trees, Bern appears, and the three men stand casually chatting, Innes now sitting calmly at the chief's side. Pappa looks freezing, hood up, hands thrust deep in his pockets, his shoulders slightly hunched against the cold. Next to Bern, who is dressed in his full police uniform, I notice that Mac's trousers and boots are scruffy, as though he was called out in the middle of digging his garden or fetching logs, although he's wearing his heavy police-issue coat over the top. Mac is doing most of the talking while Pappa nods throughout, following the direction of the chief's arm as it points in a sweeping direction from the edge of the lake and around the forest which borders it. After a while, Pappa raises his hand in a 'cuppa?' kind of gesture, and Mac nods towards the house. I take a small step backwards, not wanting to be seen spying, as Pappa pats the chief on the arm and jogs back the way he came.

For a while, nothing much happens, as Bern and Mac walk back along the lake's edge towards the pontoon and boathouse, before disappearing, and reappearing on the path at the other side of the trees. They head up the path again, through the gate and towards the house. Bern waves and smiles at me when he spots me at the window.

'Shit,' I mutter, hating that they saw me, and feeling suddenly as though I have something to hide.

I check my room over, to ensure I've left no signs of my morning's labour at the threshold to the door, and swiftly I straighten out my bedspread before running a brush through my unruly hair. As a last-minute thought, I pump a single spray of rosewater into the air and try to arrange myself casually at the window.

A few minutes later, my attic room is crowded, and I'm feeling like a circus freak all over again. Mac pulls out my desk chair and sits; Mamma and Pappa stand like guards on the other side of my bed, arms folded; Bern perches on his spot at the corner of the desk, close to me where I lean against the window. His proximity is unsettling, and I realise how unaccustomed I have grown to physical contact. Rosa and Lars and I were constantly hugging or bundling about together, joking and slapping hands off each other's plates, or simply sitting cross-legged, knees touching, barely noticing the warmth of one another's bodies.

'Mac and Bern want to go over a few details again,' Pappa says. 'Now that they've got Gurt in custody.'

I point my thumb to the window behind me. 'What were you looking for out there?'

Mamma and Pappa look to Mac for an answer.

'Oh, Ann reported seeing a prowler round her workshop last night. We were just following up.'

'With a police dog?' I ask.

Mac gives a little laugh. 'Just to be on the safe side. Ann wouldn't have called it in if she wasn't worried.'

Sometimes it's easy to forget that he and Ann are brother and sister, so different are they in temperament. Rosa says her Uncle Mac calls Ann 'the old hippy', while she calls him 'the golden boy', because he took the sensible route and got a proper job.

'Now, Eva,' he says, his expression suddenly grave. 'We've established you remembered Gurt Poulsen getting in on the other side of the green truck on the night of the accident?'

'Yes. You said you were going to see if his fingerprints matched up to the ones you found there.'

Bern nods. 'Yep, we checked, but the ones we found inside the truck weren't Gurt's. Was he driving?'

'I couldn't say, not one hundred per cent,' I reply. 'I was about to get in the passenger side, and he was on the other side, with his face right up close to the driver's window.'

Bern jots this down, the corners of his mouth dipping in concentration. 'Did you see him *actually* get in, Eva?'

I can't answer. I can see the door opening, can sense a body inhabiting the driver's space, but can I swear it was Gurt? I can't.

'You'd been drinking,' Mac says. He already knows this.

'Yes.' When Chief Mac doesn't react, I add, 'Quite a bit. We all had.'

Bern raises his eyebrows knowingly. 'Naturally, Foxy denied you'd been drinking alcohol – scared he'll lose his licence for serving sixteen-year-olds, no doubt.'

'I hope you've dealt with that, Mac,' my mamma says. 'None of this would have happened if Foxy had sent those kids packing when they came in looking for alcohol.'

Pappa raises a palm. 'We need to stop looking for people to blame – I'm sure Mac is handling Foxy in his own way.'

'I am,' Mac says, deftly silencing them, and returning to focus on me. 'And where were Rosa and Lars at this point, Eva? You'd arrived at the bar together, hadn't you?' He's talking about his own niece and nephew, but he maintains his professional tone. 'Where were your friends?'

I press my palms to my eyes, trying to access that memory again. They were there for much of the evening, and I can now remember the early part where we bought a few rounds and chatted with a couple of locals, moaning about the way the older lads always hogged the pool table – but I can't recall when Lars and Rosa left or where they were going. All I know was I wasn't happy about it; that I was upset and angry. 'I'm sorry, I just can't remember. They wouldn't have left without me, I'm certain. Maybe they were still in the bar?'

Mac muses on this a moment. 'Apparently not. Do you have any reason to think you might have gone off with Gurt of your own free will?'

'No!' I reply, my voice rising high into the room. I flush hotly at the suggestion. '*No* – I wouldn't touch Gurt with a bargepole! He's creepy.'

'Eva,' my father says softly. He's still not convinced that Gurt is responsible for all this.

'Well, he is! Mamma – you agree, don't you?' I know she does, because a few years back she made Pappa tell Gurt he couldn't fish at our lake any more. She didn't want me bumping into him when I walked back through the forest after school.

She glares at Pappa. 'He is, Tobias. If you're a girl, he *is* creepy.'

'Rosa says the same,' Bern agrees, rubbing his chin thoughtfully. 'And before that night, Eva, did you have much to do with Gurt – or any of the other regulars at Foxy's?'

I shake my head. 'I don't know why we even go down there.' An old image comes to me, of Foxy passing Lars his drink across the bar: a bottle of beer with a cocktail umbrella stuck in the top. *There you go, sweetie*, Foxy says with a wink, and the regulars fall about. They were always making stupid jokes like that, putting on camp voices when Lars was near.

'Did you talk to him, or anyone else there that night? Or did anything about Gurt unsettle you at all?'

'I definitely spoke to Gurt and Foxy,' I reply, but I've no idea why I'm so certain. I stare at Bern, feeling like a fraud.

'Go on,' he says with a small nod.

'I think Rosa had got talking to Foxy before I did . . .' I say, and as quickly as the answer comes to me it is gone. 'I was getting a drink, and . . .' Without warning, tears spring to my eyes, and I clamp my hand over my mouth to stifle a sob. 'I'm sorry,' I say again, waving a pathetic hand towards my head. All the power and determination I woke with seems to be draining from me as we speak. 'My mind, it just doesn't work.'

'Don't worry, Eva,' Bern says, gently touching my elbow. 'You're doing fine.'

A strong desire to be held by him possesses me, and I blush deeply, embarrassed at myself.

'There were a few out-of-towners in the bar that night,' Bern says, turning the pages of his notebook and pretending not to notice my high colour. 'Only this week Mad Eric remembered a particular stranger, a young man who arrived late in the evening and kept to himself on the far side. Do you recall him at all, Eva?'

I shake my head; this is the first I've heard of him.

'Hmm,' Mac muses. 'It seems no one else could remember much about him either. We're not taking it all that seriously, if I'm honest.'

'Why not?' Mamma asks.

'Because Mad Eric, as the name suggests, is a bit mad, and a hopeless alcoholic. He's not what you'd call a very reliable witness. Add to that the fact that it took him ten months to come forward with this information. Apparently he's been on the wagon since September, but just because he's sober now, it doesn't mean this new claim can be trusted.'

'What about Ann's prowler? And the guy we chased off our property? It could be the same man – it *could* be the person who took Eva that night,' Pappa says impatiently. 'Are you saying you've ruled Eric's man out completely?'

He so wants the driver to not be Gurt; he wants to believe Gurt is still that simple kid with his fishing rod, a bit grubby, neglected, but harmless all the same.

'No, not completely, Tobias,' Bern says. 'We circulated the description Eric gave us to surrounding police forces, just in case he turns up nearby. Eric was actually fairly lucid when he gave his statement – I was there. He said the stranger was between eighteen and thirty, of average height and build, and wearing a heavy winter parka, jeans and snow boots.'

'He certainly sounds like that guy we saw,' Mamma says.

'He does,' Pappa murmurs.

'He also sounds like fifty per cent of the men living in or passing through this area on any given day in winter,' I say, with a deep sigh.

'And what about Gurt?' Mamma asks, sitting down on the bed so that she's eye level with Mac. 'Have you got anywhere with him?'

'Yes and no,' Mac replies. He looks at Bern. 'We've been over the forensic records for the truck again, and even though, as Bern said, there are no matching prints inside the truck, there was a partial match to a single handprint on the driver's-side window. So we've been granted an extension to keep him a bit longer. His alibi was fairly patchy around the time Eva left the bar, so we have grounds, although what he'd want with this truck when his own was parked a few yards away is anyone's guess. We're expecting more test results back shortly after Christmas Day. The bloody holidays slow it all down.'

'Test results?' I ask, feeling nauseous. 'You mean like DNA? Did you find his DNA, in the truck?'

The pause which follows is brief but loaded.

'No, no, not as such,' Mac replies, smiling too brightly. 'It's just routine stuff. When we're dealing with a serious crime like this, we like to cover everything.'

Pappa shifts from foot to foot; he's getting impatient.

'Listen, I really need to speak to Rosa and Lars, don't I, surely?' I blurt out in the silence which follows. 'They might remember something about the person from the bar – we might jog each other's memories?' I cast my eyes about the room, hoping someone will jump in and support me.

When neither of my parents replies, Mac does. 'We've already taken their statements, Eva. They don't remember this stranger either, and we've been over their account of the evening with a fine-tooth comb, believe me.'

'But all this – you've basically got nothing.' I can feel myself losing control, and I despise myself for it. 'Gurt's going to walk free. You've got no real evidence!'

'We don't even know if Gurt did it, Eva!' Pappa snaps. 'You can't charge a man without evidence.'

78

'Well,' Mac replies in a soothing tone, 'what we do know is that following the crash the driver fled from the scene, and we're assuming he had a conscience of sorts, because the accident was called in on a mobile phone, Eva, just moments after it happened. Which could suggest it was someone known to you – possibly someone who cared enough not to just let you die out there.'

Mamma releases a disgusted little cough and runs a hand through her hair.

'And was it Gurt's phone?' I ask.

'I'm afraid not,' Mac replies. 'It was an untraceable number. When Bern responded, the only signs of the driver were his boot marks retreating through the snow and into the forest.'

'Bern was the first on the scene?' I ask.

'Yep,' he replies. 'I just managed to take photographs and measurements of the footprints before the snow obliterated them – size 43, Dr Martens by all accounts.'

'What shoe size is Gurt?' I ask, though really, I think I know the answer.

'He's a 43,' Bern says. 'But then so are a large proportion of the male population. It's the most common shoe size.'

Mamma shakes her head again. 'It's not much to go on, is it?'

Mac chews at his bottom lip purposefully. 'It's not, Ingrid. I'm afraid. But it's all we've got right now, apart from Eva's statement. Obviously, if we'd been able to speak with you sooner—' he says, but Mamma cuts him off.

'Well, she's not really been up to giving a statement before now, has she, Mac?'

'Comas are a bit annoying like that,' I add glibly, and I feel Pappa's disapproval from across the room.

'Is there anything else you can remember about Gurt from that night?' Bern asks.

'Because, you know,' Mac says, 'it's a very serious allegation you're making, Eva.'

Pappa clears his throat.

'And right now,' Mac goes on, 'as much as I'd like to keep Gurt in, we've got very little evidence to put him in that truck with you.'

'I haven't . . .' I start to say. 'I mean, I do remember him on the other side of the truck. I do remember him saying something creepy to me. But I just can't seem to get any further than the car park – I can't . . .'

'It's OK, Eva,' Bern says, 'it's OK. But it's also very important you let us know the minute you do remember anything else, OK?'

'I'm tired,' I say, turning to Mamma, and she stands, signalling an end to the interrogation. They file out one after the other, but Bern hangs back. We're standing beside the window, close, as the afternoon sun dips behind the distant mountains, painting the sky orange. Mamma is saying goodbye to Mac at the foot of my stairs; she'll be back up here any second.

'Bern, they're keeping me prisoner up here,' I tell him, my voice low and urgent.

He reaches out and rubs my upper arm, much like Lars would do. 'They're worried about you, Eva. They're just being extra-cautious, waiting to see how we get on with Gurt – we can't be sure we've got the right man yet, can we?'

'But—'

'Look, don't overthink it. Mac says if anyone breaks into your home this room is well hidden away, and they're unlikely to find you. This is the safest place.'

'They won't even let me see Rosa and Lars,' I say. 'Mamma's got this crazy idea that they abandoned me that night – she blames them, but I *know* they wouldn't have just left like that without a good reason. You're their cousin, Bern – they must have said something to you?'

For a chilling moment he looks caught out, and just as I'm starting to think they're all in on some terrible conspiracy he glances furtively towards the attic door. Suddenly, he grasps my hand in his, and the warmth of his skin is dizzying.

'If I tell you something, Eva, promise me you won't tell your parents?'

Silently, I nod, hope rising in me.

'That night, I saw Rosa and Lars coming from the bar, as I was pulling up in the car park outside, and they asked me for a lift home as the weather was coming in bad. Rosa told me you'd had an argument and that you'd stayed on. I asked if I should go back to give you a lift too, but they said you were fine and had a ride sorted with your pappa.'

'But that's not true, is it?'

'Not according to your parents. When we challenged Rosa and Lars on it, they swore that's what you'd said, and that you'd been insistent that they should go on without you. On reflection, Lars thought maybe you'd only said it to get rid of them, because you were upset.' He hesitates a moment. 'I hate myself for not going back and checking you were alright that night, Eva. If I had . . .'

'But why won't Mamma let me see them?'

Bern takes a deep breath. 'When we asked what your argument was about, Rosa refused to tell us, and she's remained tight-lipped ever since. Ingrid thinks she's hiding something.'

'And what do you think?'

'I don't know.'

'If I got to speak to her, she'd tell me, Bern! I'm sure of it.'

He shakes his head. 'Ingrid won't hear of it. She's told Mac that until Rosa comes clean about that argument, she and Lars aren't setting foot in your house.'

I can feel the rage bubbling away in the pit of my stomach. My hand, I notice, is still in Bern's. 'Will you talk to Rosa for me?' I ask him. 'Tell her I don't care about some stupid argument – that I'll come and find her as soon as I'm out of this bloody prison. Please? Will you do that for me, Bern?'

Bern sighs, and squeezes my fingers, and I rise up on my tiptoes to kiss him on the cheek. He looks shocked, and pleased. But then the chief calls his name from the room below, and Bern gives a brief nod and is gone, trotting down the stairs as Mamma bolts the door, leaving me staring at the wintry landscape outside.

Loyal forever. It's nearing midnight when I wake thinking about an oath my friends and I made when we were younger, as we sat at the pontoon beneath a springtime sun, pricking our skin with a fishing hook and pressing our three thumbs together in ritual. As innocent as it sounds now, it was real – we really meant it, and *I* still do.

I rise and go to the window, opening it wide and feeling the sharp bite of cold against my skin. In the far distance, I can just make out the twinkling festive lights of the enormous tree in the town square, where they erect it every year, just a few days before Christmas. Soon they'll be handing out *gløgg* and gingerbread rabbits outside Lapin's coffee shop, piping traditional carols into the snow-swept high street while everyone bustles about, swaddled in their knitted hats and gloves, stopping longer to chat with one another as the holiday spirit takes hold. I try to get my head around the idea that it is deepest winter *again* – almost Christmas – and the shock of the missing seasons makes my heart race. I saw nothing of spring, and I have no recollection of summer at all. Nothing. In my mind's eye, I try to recall more of what happened on Valentine's evening after I'd left Foxy Jack's, but all I can see is the white fox standing on the road, the one from my dreams, the one from my poster. The surreal quality of it tells me it's not a real memory, but it's the closest thing I've got. I'm relieved that my memories from before the accident are returning, but what of the time between then and now? Nothing. It's as though I died for the best part of a year.

Outside the window is something close to silence, but for the muffled creak of snow-laden branches, the soft and stealthy movement of night creatures as they go about their nocturnal labours. The landscape appears peaceful; in Lars and Rosa's direction, through the forest, I can make out fine wisps of chimney smoke lifting up over the trees and, much further, the distant lights of faraway towns and villages. Rosa and Lars will have finished school for the Christmas holidays; are they there, at home now, I wonder?

At the lakeside, a figure moves, stepping out from the dark cover of the treeline. I can't see his face, but, as he draws on a cigarette, for the briefest moment I think it's Pappa. But Pappa doesn't smoke. It's *not* Pappa, yet still I have the strongest sensation that I know this person, and at the same time I'm certain he is a stranger to me. Without shifting my gaze, I reach out blindly for my desk and click the switch on my side lamp – on-off-on-off – a reckless message to him through the darkness. As though in reply, he raises a hand to me, before he steps back into the forest, and is gone. A vision punches through the front of my mind – *a memory* – of this stranger standing in the corner of Foxy Jack's bar, watching me. I'm alone, no Rosa or Lars to be seen, and I'm upset. I'm leaning against the bar top, my elbows hooked back on the wooden counter, a beer bottle held loosely in my hand. To my left is Mad Eric, droop-eyed, gazing into his pint, oblivious to the rest of us as he slumps in his corner spot. And to my right, in the darkened far corner, is this figure. His gaze on me is intense and serious, and it's impossible for me to tell his age. He seems to be neither a man nor a boy. To an outsider, his intensity might be interpreted as menace, but I know it's not – it's more than that, it's . . . it's – is it *love*? Was I involved with someone, before all this happened? *Had* I planned to meet someone that night – someone who cared for me?

Just like the man-boy himself, the memory of this conjured emotion threatens to pull back into the shadows. This time, though, I've grabbed it with both hands, and I'm not letting it go. Stepping away from the window, I slip back into bed, thankful for the residual heat I find there as I pull my covers tight around me. In the darkness, my fingers feel along the gap beneath the mattress, locating my knife.

Taking a deep, slow breath, I anchor my thoughts and steady my resolve. I have my plan, I tell myself, I have my knife, and now, I think, I have Bern on my side. *You're not the only ones with secrets, Mamma and Pappa.* I roll over and let sleep take me.

I can play at that game too.

8

Eva

There's a baby crying. I know I'm sleeping – I'm sleeping so heavily, there's no way I could possibly draw myself up out of it, so I just run with the dream, though I know it's heading to places I don't want to go. At first there's darkness all around, and just the sound of that baby in the distance, so muffled and far away that I wonder if it's a cat or a fox wandering through the forest, crying for its mate. But soon the images start to show themselves and the horror of the moment grips me because I'm there, standing at the edge of the road – peering through the windscreen of an abandoned green truck, and I know the crying baby is trapped inside. The road is dark, shimmering with new frost, snow piled up along the verge and bright on the distant mountain peaks. 'Pest Control' is written on the side of the van, and I think about the things that might be found in its locked trunk, the mousetraps and poisons and ingenious tools of death. The wind roars around me, whipping my hair high and wild, and, when I look down, all I'm wearing is my summer dress, but it's not possible because it's the daisy-print one I had when I was tiny. It's the dress I wore for my tenth birthday party when Rosa and Lars bought me a Moomins lunchbox and flask. The dress is yellow and sunny and so special and new, and I know it's not right that I'm wearing it here, on an abandoned road in midwinter. Again I remind myself, this is only a dream. The dress is not real – the baby is not real. The truck doesn't exist; the road is a fiction. I should be icy cold, but I'm not. The baby's cries grow ever more insistent and I reach out a hand for the passenger door, snatching it away as the skin on my fingertips burns against hot metal. That's when I smell it – and then I see it: smoke rising up and out through the seal of the door. It snakes in the air between me and the truck, elegant as cigarette smoke, dark as soot. I fumble for a cuff to pull down to shield my hands against the heat, but I find none on this tiny little sleeveless dress. In one swift movement, I pull the dress up and over my head, wrapping it round my fist like a glove, and I reach again for that door handle, but the truck, screaming baby and all, bursts into flames. I stand in the road, naked and helpless, watching the truck burn as sobs rack my body. A tiny face appears at the burning window, and I see it's not a baby at all – it's the white fox, her amber eyes alert with fear, and she's crying for me to help her, and there's nothing I can do.

Although the valley is sleeping and all outside my window is in darkness, I feel more alert this morning than I have done in months. There's something in the air this morning – an electricity or energy beyond me and my attic bedroom. I breathe deeply, tuning in to the taut silence beyond my window, and the stomach-churning feel of it is worrying and pleasing all at once. It feels a little like the simultaneously nice and nasty feel

86

of picking at a scab: a conflicting blend of anxiety and calm, and of *something* about to be revealed. But it is only natural I should feel this way, because today is the day of my escape.

Tonight, it is Christmas Eve, when the midnight candle procession through town takes place, an old tradition in Valden, which starts with a feast in the town hall and, for some, ends with a boozy late session in Foxy's bar. Chief Mac and his wife Berit are the main organisers, and from experience I know you have to be near death before they'll let you get away with missing it. We've not skipped one yet, not in the seventeen years since we moved here, and, from what Mac said as he was leaving my room yesterday, even my incapacitation isn't a good enough excuse for my parents not to attend. 'Trust we'll see you tomorrow, Ingrid?' he'd said, making a statement of the question, and Mamma had done her best to sound positive. 'Oh, yes,' she'd replied, upbeat enough, but I knew what was going through her head. *How can we leave Eva?* Later that day, I'd asked her about it, and told her she was worrying unnecessarily – that she and Pappa deserved a night out together. '*Please*,' I'd wheedled. 'You both seem so tired these days, Mamma. It would make me really happy to see you go off and have a bit of fun. You can take some photos and tell me all about it on Christmas Day!' I could see she was moved by my warmth, and she agreed to attend the late part of the evening, for the procession only, so they could be back by half-twelve at the latest. 'No need to rush, Mamma,' I'd reassured her. 'If you do decide to stay on, I'll be just fine.'

When they set off tonight, I'll be completely alone in the house, and then I'll start work on getting out of this room. For the past forty-eight hours I've been practising with my pilfered dinner knife, loosening the screws of the door back and forth,

87

and I've done it so many times now, I'm confident they'll drop out with ease. The only unknown factor is whether, once the screws are out, I'll be able to get any further. Will my knife be strong enough to take the strain? Will *I* have the strength? God, help me, though, if that doesn't work, I'll find a way. I'm going to do everything in my power to make it happen. I can barely believe it myself: I'm planning to get out of this room, out of this house and far away from my lying parents.

My daylight clock is just lighting up, and I see I have half an hour or so before my parents bring me breakfast, so I set about my exercise routine early, starting with a pacing warm-up, and ten minutes of careful sit-ups and squats. I'm still weak, but my muscles are responding, and every day I ache a little less; the digits on my bathroom scales show I've gained nearly half a stone in the past week alone. My mind is rapidly growing stronger; my body just needs a little more time. By nine-thirty, I am perched on the edge of my desk at the window, making a mental list of the things I must pack to take with me, and watching the sun begin its ascent beyond the treeline. People always talk about the reduced hours of daylight in Norway's winters as though our climate is an unfortunate geographical blip we must endure – but the truth is, I love the wild variations we experience here. The seasons are so defined; none of that blurring of weather you read about in other parts of Europe, where you'd have to get up hours earlier to see a sunrise as beautiful as those we witness almost daily at this time of year. Will I leave Norway altogether, when I get out of here? Surely not; I can't imagine never seeing that skyline again. But perhaps, after tonight, I'll be viewing it from a different angle.

I glance back towards the door I must break through, my mental list acting as a steadying mantra: snow boots, parka, rucksack, gloves. Spare bra, thermals, knickers, socks. Bank card, hairbrush, passport, cash. I know exactly where Pappa keeps his emergency stash, five thousand krone, rolled up inside an old oil can on a shelf at the back of the big shed. Enough, if I'm careful, to keep me fed for a few weeks. And then there's the card for my own savings account, which from memory has at least ten times that amount, so any transport tickets or hostel costs can come out of that until I find myself a job somewhere. *Somewhere.* If I can hide myself away in one of the empty lakeside cabins tonight, I'll just have to get as far as the main Valden road at daybreak, and pray that someone picks me up. Will anyone be on the road on Christmas Day? The odd long-distance driver, perhaps, or a family on their way to visit relatives? I can only hope.

On the horizon, the emerging sun lights up a vast bank of clouds, painting them a fiery orange. Can I really do this? I stare into the glass of the window, into my own sunlit reflection. The truth is, I don't know. But what I do know is, my body and my determination are stronger than ever before, and tonight is the night.

After breakfast, the morning is a flurry of activity, as together we decorate my bedroom for the Christmas Eve lunch we have planned to make up for my missing this year's town feast. In the corner of the room is a small potted fir tree that Pappa has transferred from the garden, and which Mamma and I have decorated with hand-cut paper snowflakes and cinnamon biscuits, freshly baked this morning. My conscience is pricked at the scent of them, at the effort she's putting into trying to be normal and festive-jolly, and I can't stand that my love for them just won't go away. This would all be so much easier if I simply hated them, if they'd done something tangibly wrong, but what I'm accusing them of is so subtle and fluid, it's hard to articulate even to myself what it is that I'm escaping. They're lying to me, I'm certain. But what about exactly? They're shielding me from my best friends, but they tell me it's because they can't forgive them for putting me in harm's way. They're keeping me locked up, but they insist it's for my recovery, and for my safety, for just a week or two more. But that week or two keeps sliding, doesn't it? One week becomes two, two becomes three, three becomes four – and then what? Perhaps they'll never let me go.

As Pappa's compilation of cheesy Christmas love songs rings out in the room, I sing along and help to move the desk from the eaves, smiling as I light the candles of the chipped red holder we've had for as long as I can remember. By the time we sit down for our salmon lunch the table is transformed, the main platter swathed in fresh foliage and white berries, potatoes and vegetables carefully laid out in red and white bowls. A garland of tiny fairy lights now hangs in my window, and the three small glasses of red wine that Mamma has allowed us gleam warmly, reflecting colour, gem-like. At this moment, in this tiny encapsulated twinkling of time, I could almost be happy. Beyond the window, the sky is an eerie pinkish hue, and fleetingly I feel as though I'm outside my body, looking in through the window at this happy scene, of a family celebrating a simple Christmas in a loft room in Norway. But, up close, the dark circles beneath Pappa's eyes are still there, and Mamma's too, and I can't even imagine how much of a strain I must be putting on them.

We eat and chat throughout lunch, never once straying to the subjects of my accident, or Gurt, or my wish to be released. Every now and then, one of them jumps up, remembering something they've forgotten for the table, and they'll disappear back down the stairwell to fetch up the pepper or napkins or the little pile of Christmas Eve gifts Pappa reappears with on his final trip.

'I bet you hadn't banked on this at your age,' I say, placing my knife and fork down, as he takes his seat again, opposite me.

'What do you mean?' Mamma asks, caution in her tone.

'Well, by your time of life you shouldn't expect to be running around after a child day and night, should you?'

Just like that, Mamma's eyes fill with tears.

'What do you mean . . .?' Pappa says, and his anxious expression makes me feel as though I've said something really wrong.

'I mean, I haven't exactly been easy, have I?'

Now Pappa laughs, and at the same time Mamma cries.

'I – well, I just wanted to say I'm sorry. I'm really sorry for everything I'm putting you through.'

'Oh, Eva,' Mamma says and they're both on their feet, and I'm smothered by their embrace as they tell me over and over again that there's nothing to apologise for.

'I do love you,' I say. I realise it's the first time they've heard it from me in a long time, and I feel bad that it's probably the last time they'll hear it, too.

After we've stacked the plates, we all open a small early gift. Mamma's is a box of her favourite chocolate-covered dates, and, once she's opened the cellophane and we've all had one, Pappa passes me my gift. It's a photo album, containing pictures not only of us as a family, but also some grainy older ones of their own parents, who I've never met, all four of them having died long ago, before I was born.

'Before your accident, you'd been asking about family a lot,' he says.

91

'I had?' I reply.

He nods. 'And now that you're on the mend I thought you might enjoy looking through a few old snapshots.'

I turn the pages of the photo album, reaching a picture of my parents holding me as a baby in their Oslo apartment, shortly before we moved here.

'Are you sad you didn't have more than one child?' I ask them, looking up.

Mamma and Pappa each wait for the other to answer.

'Of course, we'd hoped for another child,' Mamma says, after a pause. She reaches behind her and brings out three more parcels.

Pappa smiles wistfully. 'We'd been trying for years, and then, just when we thought we'd never have a child at all, you came along. You were our miracle baby.'

'Go on, then,' Mamma says, handing the gifts to me. 'I hope you like them.'

'So, you had fertility treatment?' I ask, pushing the unopened gifts to one side. 'I was a test tube baby?'

Now they look at one another. 'Yes and no,' Mamma replies. 'We'd been having treatment for a few years, but without any success. We'd given up, and, to be honest, it had put an enormous strain on our marriage. We nearly didn't make it, did we, Tobias?'

Pappa lays his hand over hers. 'But then Eva arrived, didn't she, and glued us back together again.'

As they look at me, I see the love between them is still there, deeply buried, but real.

I turn back to my album and I think of the photograph that hangs in the hallway of my best friends' little cottage on the other side of the forest, in which a tired, heavy-breasted Ann Brun sits propped up in a hospital bed, a chubby infant Lars tucked beneath one arm, a newborn Rosa flopped sleepily in the crook of the other. In my photo, Mamma and Pappa look tired, yes, but they also look remarkably unaltered. I *know* I have nothing to base this on – after all, I didn't know them before they had me – but there's something in their posture, in the stiff bearing of my mother's lean arms, in the sharp lines of her collarbones, that bothers me. Pappa is leaning in, smiling down at me, and she's smiling too, but there's something *off* in the picture it presents. Am I simply being paranoid? Is it just the fact that we're a small family that makes me feel we are so very different? Perhaps this is why I'd always felt closer to my parents than Rosa and Lars seem to be with Ann. Is our smallness the reason I need and miss my friends so much, now there's this huge chasm of mistrust between me and my parents?

I pick up my other gifts, and peel back the shiny wrapping to reveal a fancy skincare kit, a tray of Swiss nougat and a book of poems retelling the Norse myths. Already, my mind is one step ahead, working out if I can fit some of these things into my rucksack tonight. The book is too heavy, I decide, and will have to stay behind in the attic.

Pappa stands, his scraping chair legs interrupting my thoughts as he starts to clear the table. 'We'll be back later with a few more presents before we head off tonight. Before then, you get a little rest, OK?'

'If you get peckish,' Mamma says cheerily, 'you've got a tree full of cookies to snack on.' She gathers up the remaining bowls, kisses me on the top of the head and follows Pappa out of the room.

As I hear the bolt sliding into place, I leave the table to return to my window view, pushing it open just enough to feel the world outside. The icy December breeze on my skin reminds me how life felt when I was alive, when I was *really* alive – alive enough to trudge through the snow, to kick at frozen puddles and experience temperatures low enough to freeze the tears on your cheeks. On a normal Christmas holiday we'd have been out there together this week, me, Mamma and Pappa, clearing the path of snow, restacking the woodpile, sharpening the axe head to split kindling for the fireplace. Stocking up the log store in the living room, to keep us going through the festive week ahead. Is it just my weakened condition that makes me so nostalgic for these ordinary things? Was life really that perfect? I'm pretty sure we weren't a spotless family, but I know what I feel. I feel like we all loved each other. I feel like we were honest; I feel like we were *OK*.

I'm starting to feel jittery when, around nineish, I tune in to the sound of Pappa's truck returning through the forest, back from helping Mac set up the town hall ahead of this evening's celebrations. I try to imagine the faces of the locals milling about beneath the Christmas lights of the town square, the warmth of pastries and *gløgg* wafting on the breeze, and a small, enduring part of me feels sad to be missing out. Will my friends be there? I wonder. I head to the window and peer out into the darkness as Pappa's tail lights disappear around the side of the house, where he's taken to parking ever since Mac spooked him with his talk of prowlers and truck theft. *Prowlers*, I think with a sick lurch, visualising myself running through the forest alone in the darkness. I glance back at my clock and wish the next hour away.

At ten, after what seems like an endless wait, my parents finally come to say goodbye.

'We'll stay for the midnight procession,' Mamma says, 'but we'll head straight back afterwards. Your father promises he won't let Mac talk him into going on to the bar.'

'Promise,' Pappa agrees, and he places an armful of treats on my desk, next to the new knit-your-own-scarf set that Nettie sent along for me, a thoughtful gift which will now lie unopened after I've gone. 'We've brought you a ton of festive sugar to keep you going. Don't forget to brush your teeth.'

Good-humouredly I roll my eyes at him and hug them both, and then they are gone, sealing the door behind them and heading back down through the house to leave me all alone. For almost half an hour I stand at my attic window, impatiently waiting for them to leave. The forest sounds alive tonight, the woodland noises drifting clearly across the still lake; the screech of the owl, the snapping flap of night-time pigeons as they batter through the branches, the heartbreaking cry of the fox. *Come on*, I urge my parents. *Where are you? Why haven't you left yet?* I'm suddenly terrified that they've changed their minds, that my mother can't bring herself to leave me on my own, fearful that I'll have a fit and die while she's gone.

Just as I begin to give up hope, light from the front door floods the driveway, and they appear, wrapped in their warmest winter gear, in a rush to get to Mamma's car. I watch as she takes the driving seat, and when Pappa makes his way to the passenger side I wave to catch his attention. He blows me a kiss, before he gets in and the vehicle trundles off through the gate, on to the bumpy forest path where it's swallowed up by the dark forest. I exhale, at once conscious of the heavy thump of my heart, the cold, sweaty texture of my hands. Still I keep watch, my eyes fixed on the dark woods, waiting, waiting, waiting – until at last the faint light of their headlamps appears on the far side, beside the Brun cottage, turning left on to the farm track and out to the main road beyond.

The second those lights hit the highway I get to work, acutely conscious that I now have less than two hours to get out of this room, get packed and get to the far side of the forest before my parents return.

As anticipated, the screws holding the long black hinges drop out with ease, my earlier efforts to loosen them bearing fruit. One after the other, I remove the fixings, casting them aside and pushing the hinge bars towards the wall, until eventually I'm left with a door which appears to be held up by nothing but the handle. But the reality is, it *is* held up by something more – by a solid iron bolt, attached to the other side of the door and frame. I run my fingers along the gap between the vertical jamb and the door, digging my nails into the wood, trying to pull it towards me to test for signs of give. There is none. The door is as unyielding as it was while attached to those big hinges.

Outside, a first firework sounds out into the night, and tiny dots of light scatter across the view. Turning back to the door, I estimate the level of the bolt and slide the knife's blunt point into the crack opposite, leaning hard in the direction of the wall, and detecting the slightest pinch of movement, before the metal of the knife appears to soften and bend.

'*NO!*' I cry out in a strangled scream. '*No-no-no-no-no!*'

I step back to assess the damage, sweat breaking out along the base of my neck as another firework breaks through the black sky, followed by long, low whistle. Carefully taking hold of the knife handle and bending it back to something resembling its starting shape, I ease it out, praying it won't snap, and cast my eyes about the room in panic. Without thought,

I begin to open drawers, tipping the contents across the floor, searching for an implement – anything long enough, strong enough and thin enough to wedge down the side of that doorframe – to get that door open! There's nothing. Heaving my mattress up and off the bed, I run shaky hands over the struts and fixings of the frame, trying to find something that might be removed, or fashioned into the kind of implement I need. But the bed is rigid, any visible screws fixed so tightly that they only serve to shear chunks from the tip of my mangled knife. My bedside clock tells me it's now after eleven, and, giving up on my bedroom, I race to the bathroom with my knife, and start attacking the shower door. Those struts! Those long, thin metal struts! Surely, if I can get one of those free, I can fashion it into something useful, some kind of lever to get that door open. With my knife, I try to prise the first strut away from the edge of the shower door, but the glass is slippery, and the hinged door won't stay still as I wrestle with it. When I attempt to apply brute force, my bare heel slides on a wet patch, tossing me to the floor with a heavy thud.

'Shit. *Shit!*' I curse, as, winded and bruised, I get to my feet, and try again. Hopelessness is threatening to overcome me, and I find myself stomping into my bedroom to snatch up the walking stick Mamma brought home from the hospital back in November. Not caring as I tear a fingernail to the quick, I rip away the rubber foot of the stick and take a running joust, through the bathroom doorway and into the shower screen. To the distant soundtrack of fireworks and celebration, the glass door shatters, leaving behind it an empty metal frame. I wrap my arms in bedsheets and hook them through the frame, heaving until it falls away, pulling plugs of plaster from the tiled wall. I drag the metalwork into the main bedroom, but, as I swing it round, it sideswipes the overhead light bulb, smashing it into a thousand pieces across my room. I'm plunged into darkness, not knowing where to tread for fear of cutting my feet to ribbons.

The sky fills with myriad bursts of colour, the radiance of the fireworks illuminating my room, lighting up the snow-covered canopy of trees that spreads far beyond my window.

A quarter past eleven.

Edging away from the bulb debris, I drag the metal frame to the room's threshold, and work at dismantling it by the crack of light shining beneath the door, until, at last, one of the struts breaks free.

'Yes!' I hiss, and when the next blast of fireworks lights up the room I move quickly, forcing one end of it into the space where a hinge had once been, saying a silent prayer as I lean against the jamb.

There's a slight movement, the lightest of creaks, and the metal snaps. I slide the new end of the strut into the crack just millimetres above, and do the same, with the same result. Breathing hard, I beg for another flash of light from the town's celebrations, as I repeat this process six, maybe seven times, until – *boom*! The sky, and my room, lights up under the full beam of a firework shower, its white spray bursting and holding for long seconds, and with one final, shoulder-bracing push there's a splintering sound on the other side and the door gives. It falls inwards against my waiting palms, flooding the doorway with the diffused light of the downstairs room.

I've done it.

With one last glance at the clock – eleven twenty-five – I descend the wooden steps from my attic prison, through my parents' bedroom and into the bright light of the landing. Pausing halfway along the corridor, I ease open the door to my old bedroom and my heart leaps into my throat. It looks exactly the same as I remember it: the forest-green bedding and leaf-print blinds, the books arranged tonally and the single wall of posters. I hover in the doorway; though nothing seems out of place, it doesn't take a genius to guess that they've been through every inch of this room, looking for answers to what happened.

When my gaze lands on the pinboard over my bed, I freeze. The board dominates the wall, and on it are pinned dozens of photographs, most of them taken with a Polaroid camera, of me and my parents and friends, of landscape views from our day trips to the mountains. A single image jumps out at me, an old favourite: it's a photo of me, wearing that daisy-print dress, standing at the lakeside with Rosa and Lars on his tenth birthday. We're squinting against the dazzling sunlight, me in the middle, an arm hooked over the shoulder of each of my friends, laughter in our expressions. Moments after this was taken, we'd stripped to our underwear and jumped from the pontoon, disrupting the peace of Lake Barn as we ducked and chased like water sprites. A rush of images comes at me, and I fight the urge to turn over my room in search of more pictures, but there's no time. My parents will be returning home straight after the parade, and by my estimate I've got an hour at most to get packed, take that money from the shed and get safely off the path before they drive back down it and discover me gone.

Wrenching open my wardrobe, I hurriedly discard my pyjamas and grab at the first pair of jeans I see, stepping into them and feeling their looseness around my hips. I'm going to need a belt. From beneath the bed I pull out my overnight bag, shaking the dust from it and grabbing items from around the room, stuffing them in: underwear, thermal tops, random cosmetics and a bunch of pens. My passport, the purse containing my bank card and a few loose coins. In the top drawer, my hand hovers over an old penknife Pappa gave me years ago, for our fishing trips down at the lake, and I wonder if I'd have the guts to use it if I needed to. I don't know how things will pan out once I get out of here, so I snatch it up and slide it into the front pocket of my baggy jeans, my mind racing over all the things I haven't packed or thought of – a toothbrush, my wristwatch, *a clear plan*. Seizing my old knitted sweater and a thick pair of socks, I head for the stairs.

On the landing, I stop. I can hear the low tones of a television, and all the lights are on downstairs. We don't usually leave the TV and lights on when we go out. Is this in response to Ann's prowler, as a deterrent to would-be burglars? I hear the faintest cough then, more like the clearing of a throat. There's somebody here! Did Mamma – still fearful of my safety alone – leave someone here to babysit me?

I strain to hear the sound again, but there's nothing. Still, I can't take any chances: adjusting the bag on my shoulder, I ready myself to make a dash for the front door, where I will slip straight into my snow boots, grab my parka and run. Sliding the penknife from my pocket, I release its blade. With one hand, I clutch the knife handle tight; with the other, I steady myself against the stair rail, adrenaline racing. Outside, beyond the solid wood panels of our lakeside home, another boom echoes out across the land, louder than any I've heard yet tonight, and I stifle a shriek. Again I listen out for signs of life from the living area, and in the silence which follows I take a single step down towards my escape. But at once I'm halted, because behind me, from beyond the closed door of our guest bedroom, I hear the keening cry of that fox again. Only, now it seems obvious – *startlingly* obvious – that it's not a fox at all.

The cry belongs to a baby.

PART TWO

9

Maxine, Neptune Court, Greenwich, England

Recorded interview between Alexa Evans, freelance writer, and Maxine Gregory, subject of A LIFE OF LOSS (Falun Publishing International).

MAXINE: I'm not really sure why you'd want to look at all these old photos, Alexa. A lot of them are from way before Lorna was even born – before Tara even. You'll be bored rigid, love. I'll just pick a few out for you, shall I?

ALEXA: Oh, no, I'd really like to see them all, if you don't mind, Maxine? You mustn't forget, this book is all about you. Of course the public are going to be interested in the story of Lorna's disappearance, but *your* history and *your* life, before and after that loss, is going to be equally important. We need to show them the real woman behind the tragedy. People will have seen you on their televisions or in magazines over the years, but then the focus has always been on Baby Lorna, hasn't it? Readers want to know who *you* are, Maxine. The photos will really help to build that picture.

MAXINE: That all sounds very fancy, but we were muck poor, you know. If you're looking for glamour in these photos you'll have a long wait! Still, I'll have a rummage as we chat, see what I can dig out. I suppose you'll want to put some in the book, will you – like they do in celebrity biographies?

ALEXA: Exactly.

MAXINE: Of course, there aren't all that many of me and my brothers when we were kids, 'cause we didn't have a camera back then. But one of my brother Ray's work friends down the dairy had one, so some of these old snaps are his. Quite the David Bailey, I recall.

ALEXA: Was the dairy in London?

MAXINE: Oh, yes. Ray had his own round for a good few years, before he met Rena. See that framed black and white picture next to the TV? That's me in the big cap, next to Ray in the milk float.

ALEXA: Look at you! What a sweetie. How old are you there?

MAXINE: Seven or eight, I'd guess. It would've been after my dad died. Lung cancer, poor bugger. Ray – he was the oldest – used to take me out on his milk round most mornings, you know, to give Mum a break. I think he must be about nineteen in that one, bless him. He'd let me sit up front with him, wearing his dairy cap all the way, and sometimes he'd even give me a few coins at the end of the week. I wasn't to let on to Mum about the money, though, Ray said, or she'd 'ave it off me in a flash! Mini Milk, that's what he used to call me.

(*pause*)

I was lucky to have him keeping an eye on me like that. I was the youngest, you know, and the only girl.

ALEXA: You were a big family. I guess things must have been hard after your dad passed away so young?

MAXINE: There were six of us kids – only two of us left now – and we lived in the dingiest bloody house you ever came across. Council knocked 'em down soon after we moved out. Honest, love, these days you wouldn't want to set foot in a place like that – eight of us crammed into three tiny bedrooms, with just the one lavvy and a coin meter for electrics we could hardly keep running. A proper London slum, they'd call it now! But you can't blame my mum and dad; they were hard workers – they just didn't have a pot to piss in. No one ever heard of a rich dock family, did they?

ALEXA: You've come a long way since then. This is a lovely little flat, Maxine.

MAXINE: It's not bad, is it? I never thought I'd see the day when I owned me own place! God only knows what Mum and Dad would've made of it; I like to think they might've been proud of me, in their own way. I know it's not much, but it's tidy and quiet, and a darn sight cleaner than Stone Street ever was.

ALEXA: I'm sure your family would all be *super*-proud of you, Maxine, if they could see you now. Where exactly was Stone Street?

MAXINE: Bermondsey. The street's not there any more. They knocked our place down not long after we'd moved on.

ALEXA: So, you're a real Londoner, then?

MAXINE: Through 'n' through!

ALEXA: That's really something, isn't it? Now, Maxine, as this is our first session, I've prepared a few starter questions to kick us off, and I thought we could just see where that takes us. Are you happy for me to dive straight in?

MAXINE: Fire away.

ALEXA: OK. I wonder if you can tell me a little bit about the morning your granddaughter was abducted from Dorset County Hospital? Where were you when you first heard the news?

10

Eva

When I push open the door, time seems to slow down, and at once the baby's cries are amplified, echoing the eerie calls of the fox that have haunted my days and nights. *You idiot*, I think now as the two sounds merge to become one and the same. There was no fox.

As I reach the edge of the cot, I'm aware of soft footsteps on the carpeted stairs behind me, and, reflected in the window facing me, I see a figure entering the room: old Nettie. Without a word, she joins me, her arm gently brushing mine, and we stand there for what feels like an age, gazing down at the now quiet infant.

'She's beautiful, isn't she?' Nettie says, her calm voice breaking the silence. 'I've quite fallen for the little mite.'

Beyond the window, another spray of fireworks lights up the sky, and the baby starts at the sound, her bottom lip trembling as though she might cry again. Nettie reaches in and strokes her neck, making soothing sounds, and it reminds me of being calmed by Nettie myself, when she used to care for me as a child, while Mamma and Pappa were working. *There, there*, she'd say, talking me out of some upset or other, smoothing away my tears with her silver-skinned hands. *Nothing to fret about, eh? All's good.*

I long to reach down to the child, to touch her cheek, to bring her to me, but somehow I don't believe I have the right, and I feel my fear and confusion threatening to spill over into madness.

'Nettie?' I ask, turning to look at her, questioning, and she simply bobs her white-bunned head, as though she's made some great decision.

'She was born on the first of November,' she tells me. 'There was a hellish snowstorm that night, when your mamma phoned from the maternity ward to say that the baby was coming earlier than we'd expected. She was in quite a panic, because she couldn't get through to your pappa who was working at the Gundersen house, down-valley. Thank the lord Ingrid was working late at the hospital that day, or she might never have got there in time. The roads closed for a while soon after, and your pappa didn't make it through till the next morning.'

Outside, a long, low whistle sails through the night air, followed by blooms of colour, lighting up the darkness like giant winter alliums.

'Why did she call you, Nettie?' Why not Ann, I'm wondering, but then I remember their rift, and it makes sense. In any case, if I ever had a baby, I'd want someone like Nettie beside me. 'Were you there when she was born?'

She rubs a knuckle lightly against the back of my hand. 'I was. It had been a planned caesarean, but this tiny one decided to start her journey a bit sooner than anyone had anticipated. By some miracle, I managed to get my old car through the snow and turned up just as little Bella here took her first breath.'

'*Bella*,' I repeat, the name strange on my lips.

The baby lies quite still now, chubby hands resting beside her head. Her blue eyes take us in steadily, moving from one face to the other, each shift of attention punctuated with a dark-lashed blink. Her skin is flawless, her cheeks round, and her head has a soft covering of white downy hair, flicking up at the forehead to form a tiny curling quiff. My heart clenches. Tentatively, I reach into the cot and press the pad of my forefinger into the infant's cupped palm. She closes her own tiny fingers around it, squeezing with surprising force before kicking her feet against the mattress with a gurgle. Warmth floods through me, and I'm suddenly aware of the weight of Nettie's arm around my shoulder, when I hear the solid thump of the front door closing on the floor below. I stiffen, one hand gripped to the top bar of the cot, the other clutching the neck of my sweater, as I tune in to the sounds of my parents removing their coats and boots in the hallway. I turn to look at Nettie, readying myself to beg her *please don't let them send me back upstairs* . . .

A few more seconds pass, and I hear Pappa's low tone telling Mamma, 'Nettie must be up with Bella.'

Nettie must be up with Bella. So casual; so ordinary. Here am I, shocked to the core at the bewildering presence of this small child – *my sister* – and yet, in those few words I under-stand how, in my absence, Bella has become a central part of their lives. Everyday life has simply carried on without me, but in a different shape. Everything has changed.

'Nettie?' Mamma calls softly from the bottom of the stairs. 'Nettie? Are you . . .'

I can't move. Nettie's fingers press against my upper arm, but I daren't turn my head in the direction of Mamma's voice. My mind is racing, and yet everything moves slowly, every sound and sensation muffled. A tide of questions rushes through my mind. Why would they hide this? I know they've always wanted a sibling for me, but surely they can't have planned Bella at their age? Was Bella a mistake?

'It'll be OK,' Nettie whispers, but I can't respond.

How did I miss all the signs? My parents have both looked exhausted lately, but I put that down to them worrying about *me*. Now I imagine them waking for Bella's night feeds in their one world down here, whilst all the time being carers for the fully grown invalid in the other world upstairs: the attic. And they've never complained about it – about me – not even once. Guilt jabs at me as Bella responds to the gentle stroke of Nettie's thumb against her cheek. Of course, this also explains why my parents were so seldom both in the room with me at the same time; why our Christmas meal was such a strangely disjointed affair, with one of them leaping up having 'forgotten' something every twenty minutes or so. Someone had to keep an eye on the baby.

'*Oh.*' I hear Mamma's quiet alarm on the landing behind me, and still I don't turn. 'Tobias,' she calls back down the stairs, her voice now rising to the level of a shouted whisper. '*Tobias!*'

In seconds, Pappa too is up the stairs, and Nettie grasps my hand and presses it to her own cheek, before stepping away. She is trembling, and that scares me more than anything. I still don't turn, and suddenly it's as though Nettie has vanished altogether, because some kind of second sight tells me it's just us here now, alone in this tiny little nursery. Mamma, Pappa, Bella and me.

On soft feet, my parents join me at the cot-side, Mamma sliding an arm around my waist, Pappa taking my hand, so that we stand connected, gazing down into the cot. Gently, Mamma plants a soft kiss on the top of my head, and her breathing is ragged.

'I've always wanted a sister,' I say, and the baby seems to crinkle her eyes at this, her dimpled hands grasping at the space around her.

'Oh, Eva,' Mamma says, and there's a sob caught in the back of her throat so that she can't continue with what she was about to say.

There it is again: that shift in atmosphere I've become so accustomed to – and ah, the lights in my brain flick on, and all at once I know the truth. My mind's eye zooms in on the scars which criss-cross my belly; on the looseness of the skin there. I think of the months I lost before I woke in my attic prison; and of that primal tug I felt – a keening ache from my breasts to my stomach – when I first laid eyes on this child. Pappa's fingers tighten around mine, and oh, God, oh, God, I think, please don't say it—

'Sweetheart,' Pappa says, and at once the air seems to be sucked from the room. 'Bella's not your sister, Eva. She's your daughter.'

The bleach-smelling room is full of people, but it's impossible for me to see them or to let them know I'm aware they're all here. There's Mamma and Pappa, Mac and Bern, and others whose voices I don't recognise, perhaps doctors or nurses? Sentences come to me in drifts, broken up and incomplete, and I flail internally as I try to untangle the riddle of their words.

'. . . boyfriends?' This is Mac.

'No, definitely not. No.' Mamma and Pappa, speaking at once.

111

'And she hasn't got a phone?' This comes more clearly from Bern, closer, as though he's sitting at my bedside. 'Are you sure?'

'So (blank) – social media? Facebook? Snapchat?'

'We don't (blank) – Eva shares our view on it.' Pappa.

'Really?' Bern again. 'Not many teenagers aren't using some form of social media.'

'Ask Rosa or Lars, they'll tell you. Eva doesn't use that stuff.' Mamma says, and she sounds clearer now too.

'Sure,' Bern replies, and I'm certain I feel his hand brush mine as he speaks, 'but say she wanted to, there are other ways she could access it. At school – or on a friend's PC. Just because she doesn't have a phone, we shouldn't rule it out. A lot of kids meet up that way these days. We'll get the school to check the browsing history on her PC account.'

'I'm certain you won't find anything,' Pappa says. 'She hates all that online stuff.'

'That may be so, Tobias, but we have to . . .' Mac's words are mangled as someone opens the door to the noise outside, and the sound of a trolley rattles through the room. '. . . everything points to our driver, but we still can't rule out the possibility that it wasn't him.'

Although I can't feel sensation, I'm aware of hands on me, a vibration of sorts, and a voice right up close. 'There we go. Let's just change this over, shall we?' a nurse murmurs, and I feel cool liquid entering my veins. How is it I can feel everything inside my body, and yet nothing on the outside?

'Let me talk to Rosa again.' Bern. 'I think she knows more than she's saying.'

'You think she knows? About . . .' Pappa again. 'About that?'

About what? I can visualise him indicating towards something, and his suppressed horror tells me it's a thing he fears.

112

What, Pappa, what? I long to scream at him, at all of them, to beg them to tell me what's going on, but then something chemical kicks in and the fight drains from me. When they leave the room, I'm left in a hell of silence and sleep.

'Bella,' I say, lowering my eyes to study my hands. Nettie has gone home, and we're at the kitchen table, my parents sitting across from me, Bella in Mamma's arms. It occurs to me that this is the first time I've seen our living space in almost a year. 'It's a pretty name.'

Mamma and Pappa nod, and I see their relief that I approve of their choice.

'What do you know about her?' I ask. 'About how she – you know . . .' I can't say it, I can't ask the questions that scream silently inside me, and to my gratitude Mamma steps in so I don't have to.

'Eva, you're already aware that we haven't been entirely honest with you.'

Still reeling from what I've just learned, I'm too stunned to reply with my normal sarcasm.

'And you finding out about Bella like this was not how we wanted it to happen.' She reaches across the table for my hand, and I give it to her, all fight having deserted me. 'We were so focused on getting you back to strength – hoping that you'd remember it all in your own time – and we didn't want to derail your recovery with something so hard to hear. We are so, so sorry, sweetheart. We love you more than anything. You know that, don't you?'

Again, I nod. The secrets burn from my parents like heat.

'Nettie seems to know Bella quite well,' I say, recalling how swiftly the baby calmed down on seeing the old woman's face at her cot side.

'She's been here a lot, to give us a hand with her,' Dad replies.

I think of all these weeks, when I craved human contact, when Nettie was just downstairs, looking after this baby, tending to her daily needs. I feel something close to jealousy.

'Nettie could've visited me, while she was here, couldn't she? She must have known I was up there all alone.'

There's a horrible pause, before Mamma shakes her head, with an expression that looks a lot like shame. 'I'm sorry, Eva, she asked to see you, but we didn't want to rock—'

'How come I never saw her from my window?' I interrupt.

Dad sighs. 'I always fetched her in my pickup, so you wouldn't spot her car in the drive and get upset.'

Of course, that's why he started parking down the side of the house – it's out of my view. I'm entirely wrung out. I shake my head, willing it all to stop. Mamma turns to look at my father, who nods resignedly, mirroring her as he reaches for my other hand.

'What we're about to tell you is going to be even tougher, sweetheart,' Pappa says, 'so I want you to be brave, and I want you to hear us out and save all your questions until the end, OK?'

I glance at the clock on the far wall and feel as though I've stepped into a parallel universe, in which nothing makes sense. It's one in the morning, and I'm sitting here as my parents calmly introduce me to the new baby across the table from me. My baby. *My. Baby.*

'OK,' I reply, and my mother begins.

As she speaks, a sense of subdued understanding comes over me, and I see myself as two entirely distinct individuals. There's the first me: carefree Eva, average student, loyal friend, casually rebellious and unremarkable in most ways. She loves to walk in the mountains in springtime, to swim in Lake Barn in high summer, to sneak forbidden cigarettes and bottles of beer with Rosa and Lars. She looks forward to meeting a boy, and to falling in love. She imagines motherhood one day – one far, far away day – and she will be good at it, just like her own mamma, and she will love her children to distraction. *That* Eva looks forward to adventures and travel and romance and comfort and lust and new tastes and new sights and new sounds.

And now, there's *this* Eva. This new Eva is a shell: pale and frightened and scarred. This version has no realistic vision of those future possibilities, no hunger for the new and unknown. She doesn't have to *imagine* those future babies; she has one.

'I was raped?' this Eva asks her parents in a whisper. *I* ask my parents in a whisper.

Pappa covers his mouth, as though all his worst fears might come spilling out at the sound of that one word.

Mamma swallows hard. 'Eva, we just don't know. But the dates seem to suggest it. When they found you at the scene of the accident, you were rushed into A&E and the doctors' sole focus was on saving your life. For a few weeks, we had no idea if you would make it at all – and it wasn't until you were much further on that the pregnancy was discovered. Those checks weren't done in the emergency room, because it just didn't occur to anyone that there'd been any other kind of foul play.'

I bring my palms down against the table in a tide of fury. 'Don't call it that! *Foul play*? "Foul play" doesn't even come close to what you're describing here! If you think the driver of that truck is the father of, of—' and suddenly I can't even remember her name, and I jerk my chin towards the baby in Mamma's arms '—then it has to be *rape*, doesn't it?'

My parents blink back at me, their horror at this conversation clear to see.

115

'Gurt?' I whisper.

An image of his leering face springs up in my mind, reminding me that he's still being held on suspicion of taking me that night, of driving that truck. I think I might throw up. Is he the one who did this to me?

'We don't know,' Pappa says. 'They're waiting for the test results. The DNA – they've taken samples from Bella and you, and, well, if Bella and Gurt match up—'

'I didn't give the police a sample,' I reply, confused.

'They took a mouth swab when you were—' Mamma stutters '—when you were asleep.'

'Asleep?'

'In your coma, Eva,' Pappa says. 'When the doctors found out you were pregnant, the police wanted to get a swab to put on record, for when they had a firm suspect.'

'Oh, *God*,' I gasp, running hands across my face, wiping away invisible grime. 'And if it's not Gurt?'

I think of the boy in the woods; the stranger in the bar. Could he have done this? I try to conjure up the lines of his face, the intensity of his expression. It can't be him; I don't want it to be him.

'If it's not,' Mamma says, glancing at Pappa for support, 'then we have to hope the police catch up with the guy Eric says he saw in Foxy's that night. He's their next best guess.'

Best guess? Is that as good as it gets?

'Look, I know I *don't* remember what happened that night, but it *is* starting to come back to me. If I had sex with someone that Valentine's, then I can be ninety-nine per cent sure it was not with my consent. Because if it wasn't someone I was serious about, if we weren't a couple, I would *never* do that. And that boy Eric saw in the bar – I think maybe we spoke that night, but I don't have a sense of romance between us – no

116

feeling that something of that kind was going to happen. I'd even started to think it was possible that I liked and trusted him, that he was a good person . . .'

I stare at the baby across the table from me, as a horrible thought presses to the front of my mind.

'Do you think he did it before or after we crashed? Surely he wouldn't have done that when I was so badly . . .' I trail off, depleted, and grieving for the old me.

A tear streaks down the length of Mamma's face. 'Oh, Eva, darling. You could drive yourself mad with all these questions. Believe me, we know.'

I lay my head down on the table and close my eyes, shutting my family out, too tired to weep any more. My friends are gone; my strength is gone; and now, with the arrival of this cuckoo baby, my freedom is gone too.

11

Maxine

Recorded interview between Alexa Evans, freelance writer, and Maxine Gregory, subject of A LIFE OF LOSS (Falun Publishing International).

MAXINE: I'll never forget that day as long as I live.

ALEXA: This was the day Lorna went missing?

MAXINE: It was the morning she was *noticed* missing. She was taken in the night.

ALEXA: And you were living in Dorset by this time, just a few miles from the hospital, is that right?

MAXINE: That's right. There'd been rain all week, but that morning we'd woken early to bright winter sunshine, and my first thought was, 'I'm a grandmother!' They had strict visiting hours at the maternity hospital, especially in the ward where my daughter Tara was, so to kill time I took the longer route from home, walking along the seafront and picking up the bus near the bay.

ALEXA: Tell me what happened when you arrived at the hospital? Who else was there?

MAXINE: I – sorry, love, it still upsets me to talk about it.

ALEXA: No, no, you take your time, Maxine, please.

MAXINE: (*pause*) It's fine. I'm alright, really. Let's carry on.

ALEXA: Who was the first person you saw at the hospital?

MAXINE: Well, at first, I was a bit confused. The day before, I'd just walked straight in through the main entrance, but this morning there were two policemen at the door, and a lot of other people milling about – and some of those TV cameras on legs, setting up on the pavement. It was so busy, and really, I had no idea what it was all about. The policeman at the entrance asked me why I was there, which seemed odd, and I said I was visiting my daughter – gave her name and everything – and his face changed, and he sent me in and right then I knew something was wrong. A mother knows, you know?

ALEXA: Mother's instinct?

MAXINE: Exactly. As soon as I got through the doors, I was hurried into a side room by another policeman, and there was Karl Gunn, sitting on the bench, white as a sheet, and my first thought was: Tara is dead.

ALEXA: How did Karl seem?

MAXINE: Scared. I asked him what was going on, and he just said, 'Lorna's gone – someone's taken her,' and I went numb. I sat down next to him, all the feeling gone from my knees, and the police officer explained that the hospital was in shutdown, while they searched for her and looked through the pictures from the security cameras. She'd just vanished, he said – snatched from the crib beside Tara as she slept. No one saw who took her, and no one even noticed her missing until the morning rounds at six a.m. 'Just Lorna?' I asked the

119

policeman, and he nodded. 'All the other babies are accounted for,' he said. And then one of the top dogs from the hospital arrived, and I can't even remember what she said, but she told me and Karl we could go and see Tara, who'd been moved to another room. When we got there – I swear to God, you never saw a more broken woman. She barely said a word to me.

(*pause*)

Do you mind if we talk about something else for a bit?

ALEXA: (*pause*) Of course, Maxine. Let's go back to your childhood again, if you're happy to. After your father died, how did the family make ends meet – I think you said your mother got herself a job? You were, what, seven? Your mum must have been a strong woman to keep going like that, with six mouths to feed.

MAXINE: She was tough as old boots, my mum. After the funeral, she took to her bed for a couple of days – but after that she was straight out, looking for a job. There was money coming in from my brother Ray's round, and before long the older boys started to add to the pot, so we coped, just about. My mother was out all hours then, but there was always food on the table at the end of the day, and for the first time in my life my collars weren't grubby!

ALEXA: Why's that?

MAXINE: Mum's job was at the laundry. She'd sneak our clothes in while she was at it – I'd never looked so smart!

ALEXA: Now, I've got copies of all your family births and deaths here, Maxine—

MAXINE: Where'd you get them?

ALEXA: Oh—

MAXINE: I didn't say you could have 'em.

ALEXA: They're public records. It's normal for us to access public records when writing biographies – it's due diligence, to ensure we don't get any of the important dates and details wrong. The publisher's lawyers always ask for it before they'll give a book the final sign-off.

MAXINE: (*pause*) So, who've you got there?

ALEXA: Your parents, you – this one's your daughter Tara's birth certificate.

(*pause*)

I notice the father's name has been left blank.

(*pause*)

Maxine?

(*pause*)

ALEXA: There's no father listed here, on Tara's birth certificate. That's not usual, is it, Maxine?

MAXINE: It is when you're not married.

ALEXA: But even then, most people still fill the father's name in – unless there are circumstances—

MAXINE: There weren't any 'circumstances'! I just didn't want to give a name.

ALEXA: (*pause*) Why was that, Maxine?

MAXINE: Because it was none of their poxy business, that's why. And it's none of—

(*pause*)

Sorry. I don't really like—

ALEXA: And when I did the maths, Maxine, I worked out that on the date you gave birth to Tara you were only fourteen.

MAXINE: Don't put that in there. Don't put that in the book.

(*pause*)

Can you make me sixteen, at least?

ALEXA: OK, but do you want to talk a little bit about life after Tara came along? It must have been hard for you, being so young—

MAXINE: I think I need a break.

12

Eva

The few days since I've been out of the attic – since I learned about the baby – have passed slowly, and I still feel as though we're living in a surreal bubble. My parents are going to great lengths to encourage me to bond with her, showing me how to warm up her milk, to change her nappy, to comfort her when she cries, and I'm going through the motions. 'She likes you,' is something my mother says a lot, and she's doing that thing she always did when I was little, going over the top with praise whenever I attempt something I don't want to do. I find myself staring at her, at that baby, wondering where she came from; wishing I could send her back.

This morning, we're sitting on the sofa by the glass doors at the back, overlooking the distant snowy mountain range, while Mamma shows me how to cut the baby's fingernails, to prevent her from scratching her delicate skin. It surprises me how sharp Bella's tiny nails are, and how helpless and uncoordinated she is, that she might accidentally harm herself. If I'm truthful I don't want to like her, or to feel anything for her, not when I remind myself of how she came into being. But the reality is, when I take those tiny fingers in mine, when her eyes fix on my face, something in my body responds, leading my emotions to follow. I hate myself for it.

Pappa joins us, shaking a bottle of warm milk and handing it to me along with a muslin cloth. I must be getting used to the routine, because without missing a beat I set to feeding her, propping her up in the crook of my left arm and tucking the edge of the cloth under the soft chub of her chin, to catch any leakage. She's getting sleepy, so I have to prod her lip a few times with the teat of the bottle, letting a drop of milk spill on to her mouth, which prompts her to latch on and glug.

'You're a natural,' Pappa says, and I roll my eyes at him, tired of his overuse of this phrase.

'I'll get you something to eat,' Mamma announces, and she crosses over to the breakfast bar, to slice me some walnut cake and pour me a glass of milk. She's on a mission to fatten me up again, and I find I'm not objecting.

Bella quickly drains her bottle, and as Pappa takes a seat on the sofa opposite I mop her face, flip the cloth over my shoulder and prop her up for winding. Pappa says she likes it best laid out on your lap, but my lap's not long enough, so I tend to hook her over my shoulder, patting her gently until she releases a satisfying wheeze of gas. Her soft head flops against mine, and I feel the warmth of her breath on my neck. Again, I feel that tugging sensation deep in my chest.

'So, I suppose I didn't breastfeed, then?' I say, when Mamma returns to sit beside me, placing my cake on the coffee table.

'No,' she replies, glancing across at Pappa. 'I – well, they suggested it, at the hospital, and I . . .'

She's struggling to continue and Pappa steps in. 'The midwife told us it would be best for Bella to have breast milk, and they had the idea that we could perhaps express your milk for her.'

'I couldn't bear the idea of it,' Mamma says. 'It seemed so wrong – you just lying there, unconscious, being milked like a cow.' She brings her hand to her mouth, horrified by what she's just said.

'We agreed to let her have one first feed – the most vital nutrients, the midwife said – but straight after, we insisted she was to go on to formula. And she's doing well on it, isn't she?'

'So, I *did* feed her myself? That one time?'

Mamma nods cautiously, and I almost break down in a wave of relief, a sense that my body was responding to Bella because perhaps we *did* make a physical bond at birth, with that one precious feed.

'Where did my milk go?' I ask, now lying Bella down on the sofa between us.

'There's a medication they prescribe to dry it up,' Mamma replies, and she smiles at me, apologetically. 'It's very effective.'

Outside, the sky is a fading blue, and for once, the snow has stopped falling. The house is warm, and the fire roars away, and Pappa's lunchtime stew bubbles gently on the stove. Despite all that has happened since Christmas Eve, it feels good not to be struggling; not to be fighting and plotting escape. I can't think of anything except for the present moment, because, right now, that's all there is.

A loud knock on the front door startles my mother as she places another log on the fire. 'Who can that be?' she asks irritably. She strides out into the front hall, and returns seconds later with Bern in tow, dressed in his full police uniform.

'Official business, Bern?' Pappa asks, by way of a greeting, and he stands, offering Bern his hand, as Mamma automatically fills the coffee pot.

'Yes and no,' Bern replies, turning to look at me. 'I'd been meaning to pop by anyway, to see how Eva was getting on. And I've got an update for you, so two birds with one stone and all that.'

He looks nervous to me.

'No Mac?' Mamma asks as Bern takes the seat beside Pappa and accepts a slice of cake.

'No,' Bern replies through a mouthful, 'he's been called out to look at some remains a hiker discovered over near Grønnfoss waterfall yesterday.'

'Remains?' I ask. 'Do you mean human remains?'

He grimaces. 'Been there a while, Pappa – Mac – reckons. Maybe a couple of years – they'll know more when they send it over to Oslo.'

'Good grief,' Mamma says. 'How horrible! Was it an accident?'

'Looks that way,' Bern replies, brushing crumbs from his fingers on to his plate. 'He was spotted in a crevasse by someone hiking high up the plateau there.' Bern points into the distance beyond the glass, to the great shelf of rock Pappa and I trek to each spring. It's our tradition. 'He was birdwatching, so he had binoculars on him, when a flash of fabric – a shirt – caught his eye. We were lucky. At first, he just thought it was pink fireweed, but he realised it's the wrong time of year for wildflowers and decided to clamber down for a closer look. Anyway . . .'

Pappa takes Bern's empty plate from him. 'Poor fellow. And . . . you said you had an update for us?'

Bern sits forward, bringing his hands together decisively. 'It's about Gurt Poulsen,' he says. 'I'm afraid we've had to let him go. We've dropped the charges.'

'What?' Mamma gasps. 'Why?'

'Because he didn't do it, Ingrid. Firstly, his DNA doesn't match Bella's.'

There's a long pause while we all take this in, relief and confusion sweeping through the room in equal measure.

'And we're now certain he wasn't the person who drove off with Eva. We've got him on CCTV at the back of Foxy's, and, while it does show him out in the car park around the time Eva left, he very clearly gets into a different van, where he appears to meet briefly with one of the other regulars, before they both return inside the bar. And then, two hours later, Gurt can be seen coming out again, after closing time. Eva's accident happened during those two hours – he couldn't have done it.'

'Why has this CCTV footage only just come to light?' Pappa demands. 'Shouldn't this have been looked at months ago?'

Bern clears his throat. 'Foxy kept quiet about it. It seems he and Gurt have been doing a bit of small-scale drug-dealing out the back there, and he was covering his own backside. Gurt tells us he remembers looking in the windows of a couple of other trucks that night, searching for his buyer, which would of course explain the presence of his handprint on the window of the one you were in. He says he didn't see you. Do you think perhaps you saw him through the vehicle, rather than from within it?'

I nod slowly. Yes, it makes sense as I focus in on the image. The perspective was off: I hadn't yet got in.

'So, who told you about the camera?' Mamma asks.

'No one. I just went and took another look around last week and spotted it over the back door. Unfortunately it only covers the back entrance, and there's no sign of you, Eva, or the green truck, so you must have been just outside the camera's range. You left through the front, didn't you?'

126

I nod again.

'The bad news is, if Gurt didn't do it, our man's still on the loose.'

Mamma is pacing now, and I can feel the rage radiating from her. 'What about Ann's trespasser?' she asks. 'The one she spotted around her workshop. And the guy who hit Tobias out front here – they must be one and the same? If he's the person who took Eva, we've got a bloody rapist prowling about, Bern! What are you and Mac doing about it?'

It's the first time I've heard her refer to the driver in those words, and it chills me to the core. There really is a man out there, a man who did me harm. Is he outside our window now, watching me? Could it really be the stranger I saw in the forest?

'Bern,' I say, my voice barely a whisper. 'I saw a man from my attic window – a week or so back.'

'What?' Pappa barks. 'Are you serious, Eva? You saw a man outside and you didn't think to tell us? What were you thinking?'

'I wasn't thinking,' I reply sharply. 'I was stuffed full of medication, off my head half the time, remember?' I hesitate, at once regretting having said anything at all. 'I thought he seemed – he looked so, so ordinary. I thought perhaps I knew him.'

'What did he look like?' Bern asks, ever calm, drawing out his notebook.

'Young,' I answer. 'Not all that much older than me. Shortish dark hair, a parka, jeans. He was smoking a cigarette. It was dark and I . . .' I trail off, because there's nothing else I can tell them.

'He sounds a lot like the guy you saw off a few weeks back, Tobias,' Mamma says now, calmer.

127

Pappa nods and stands. 'You'd better get back to it, Bern – see what Mac makes of all this. And ask him to pop by when he gets a chance, will you? I want to make sure you guys are giving this the priority it needs.'

Bern gets to his feet, and shakes Pappa's hand again. 'We are, Tobias, I promise you. If he's still out there, we'll find him.'

'I'll see you out,' I offer, and I leave Mamma and Pappa with Bella as I lead Bern to the front door.

'Are you worried?' Bern asks as he picks up his boots, leaving small pools of melted snow on the stone floor.

I nod.

'Don't be,' he says. 'We'll get him.'

I glance back through to the living room, where Mamma and Pappa are deep in conversation. 'I thought I'd have seen Rosa and Lars by now,' I say, keeping my voice low. 'Do they know I want to see them?'

'I haven't seen them either,' he replies. 'They were away at our grandparents' for Christmas – I think they get back today or tomorrow.'

'You'll tell them to get in touch, won't you?' I ask, helping him into his jacket. 'Promise?'

'Promise,' Bern says, and with a shy smile he steps outside, climbs on to his snowmobile and is gone.

For a moment I gaze out into the dimming light of the forest, and I wonder again if I am being watched. If Gurt didn't do this to me, who did?

I've not long put Bella to bed when I hear footsteps crossing the gravel outside, and my heart leaps as I rush to look out through my window, to catch a glimpse before they knock on the door. However, it's not my best friends who I see, but their mother, Ann, dressed in her heavy man's coat, the hem of it

128

clumped with snow from her walk through the dark forest. Her hair is hidden beneath a knitted hat, but in my mind's eye I see her without it, two thick braids hanging long, all the way down to her tiny little waist.

My heart leaps when I see her, but I'm at once seized by paranoia, unable to muster the courage to rush down the stairs to speak to her – to ask after Rosa and Lars. What can she want at this time of night? It must be important, for her to have trudged all this way after dark. Perhaps she's here to bring me a message from them? Hope rises in me, but the awkwardness and shame I feel about Bella and the circumstances of my accident is crippling, and instead of rushing down to see her I creep out on to the landing and listen as Mamma invites her in. The conversation is at first stilted and cool, but it sounds like the start of something, like the promise of reconciliation.

I sit up here in the darkness for half an hour or so, tuning in to the sounds of Ann and Mamma's voices in the kitchen, as Mamma offers drinks and food, and tries to act as though everything's fine. At one point, I hear Pappa's voice, announcing that he's heading out to the garage to work on his mower, I presume to give them some space. When the back door bangs shut Bella wakes in her room, and Mamma rushes up to fetch her, taking her downstairs to meet Ann for the first time, as I remain in the shadows, paralysed. From the sounds of Ann's pleased greeting, it seems Bella's role is as ice-breaker is a successful one, but then Mamma shuts the door to the living area, robbing me of any further insight.

It seems strange to me; unsettling. We almost never shut that door. Why all the secrecy? For a while I remain in the shadows at the top of the stairs, but it's impossible to hear their conversation and soon I give up and return to my room.

It feels as though Ann stays for a long time, and I lie on top of my bed in the darkness, not wanting to commit to sleep until she's gone. It's still so strange to me that there has been bad blood between Ann and Mamma, when once they were the best of friends. I think of the story my parents always tell, of their first meeting with her, way back when I was a baby, when they stood on this land under a summer sky, surveying their new home for the first time. As if from nowhere, Ann Brun had emerged from beneath the canopy of trees, waist-length hair twisted in a messy bun, long skirt flowing over red vegan shoes, a small baby swaddled tight against her body, another growing inside a rounded belly. *Woohoo!* she had called out to them in greeting, *Woohoo!* They had introduced their babies, Lars and me, to each other, and just like that the two women became instant friends. Ann has been like an aunt to me, and I'm certain that the old me would've been down those stairs in a flash, rushing in for a hug and asking after my friends – asking when I could see them. I don't know what's happened to my confidence in the time that's passed since my accident; it's as though some vital part of me died out on the road that Valentine's night.

My thoughts are broken by the slam of the front door downstairs, and the slide and fall of snow from my window frame. I rush to peek through the curtains, to see light illuminating Ann on the driveway below as the door is opened again, casting Mamma's shadow long across the gravel, the small mound of Bella visible in her arms.

'Ann!' she calls as her friend marches out towards the gate. 'Ann, come back! I didn't mean anything . . .'

Thanks to the triggered security lights, Ann is clearly visible, and I watch her spin on her heel, throwing an arm into the air to point accusingly back towards our house. 'Yes, you did,

Ingrid Olsen! Yes, you did! You have one version in your mind and you won't accept anything that disagrees with it. I could tell you a hundred times my children are not to blame for this, and you'd still not believe me.'

'I didn't say I don't believe you. I'm just saying, I think Rosa and Lars know more than they're letting on.'

'Why? Why would they keep quiet, if it meant not catching this man? They wouldn't! Lars even tried to talk Eva out of staying, but she wouldn't have it. If she'd arranged to meet someone in the bar, they didn't know anything about it, and as far as I'm concerned there was no way they could have prevented what happened. How dare you say they abandoned her?'

Mamma steps out, just far enough that I can see the top of her head. 'Ann, I just meant Eva's got a lot on her plate right now—'

'You *just meant* your Eva doesn't need them any more? Well, you should try telling Rosa that! You should try telling Lars. Does Eva even know they've been trying to make contact all this time? They're desperate to see her – and to meet Bella.' Ann turns to walk away, but then she hesitates and produces a yellow envelope from her pocket, striding back and holding it out towards Mamma.

Mamma doesn't answer her, nor does she step forward to take the card.

Exasperated, Ann flings it down in the snow. 'When the going gets tough, Ingrid, we should *stick together*. Isn't that what you once told me? Isn't that what you said when I lost my Magnus? Or when that Englishman came asking me questions about Eva – about you? I never said anything about that, kept your confidence, just like *friends* do. Ha!' She turns and continues on her way towards the heavy canopy of trees.

131

'Bullshit, Ingrid!' are her last words, and then she's swallowed up by the shadows. After a few moments, Mamma too disappears, and the front door closes with a soft thud.

I stand at my window, staring into the darkness of the forest where Ann now makes her way home, unseen, as I mentally try to pull together these invisible threads. Who is this Englishman Ann is talking about? And why did Mamma conceal the truth about Lars and Rosa's visits? They *haven't* forgotten me; all this time has passed, and I *have* been in their thoughts, in their hearts. I can hardly believe it's true. Just as I'd started to trust my parents again, to believe that their deceptions and actions really had been for my protection, I learn that they're still actively keeping me from my friends.

I snatch up my flashlight and angle it towards Rosa's window, blinking a message to her, as I have done every night for the past week, all the while not knowing she was away. I send her five flashes: Still awake? When a few seconds pass and there's no reply I know she hasn't seen me. Or she isn't there. With the invisible fortress my parents have built up around me, how could I possibly know?

But there's one thing I do know since Ann's visit, and I know it without a shadow of a doubt: my mother is a liar.

13

Maxine

Recorded interview between Alexa Evans, freelance writer, and Maxine Gregory, subject of A LIFE OF LOSS (Falun Publishing International).

MAXINE: Tell you what, let's sit out on the balcony today, now the sun's come out? I'll make us a cuppa.
(*break*)
ALEXA: This is nice, Maxine. You're lucky to have a little out-door space of your own.
MAXINE: It's a bit tatty, Alexa, if we're honest! I really should do something about those rust bubbles on the railings, and the walls could do with a lick of paint, but I do love it out here when it's fine. There's a communal garden down there by the fountain, but I prefer it up here. I like my privacy.
ALEXA: Your hanging baskets are pretty.
MAXINE: Nice, aren't they? I did 'em myself.

ALEXA: So, as agreed, Maxine, we'll make you *sixteen* when you had Tara, for the sake of the book. I talked with our editor, and she completely understands. So that's good, isn't it?

MAXINE: Yes.

ALEXA: And you still don't want to talk about Tara's father?

MAXINE: *No*. I don't know why you're so interested in all this. The book's meant to be about Tara's child, not mine. It's meant to be about Lorna going missing, isn't it?

ALEXA: It's your autobiography, Maxine. It's about you, your daughter Tara, your granddaughter Lorna – it's about all of you. It's about *family*. Who doesn't love reading about family?

MAXINE: I've told you, I didn't put his name on the certificate because I didn't want to. It's not important. And I wasn't some dirty floozy, if that's what you're thinking—

ALEXA: Not at all! You were only fourteen, weren't you? I was just wondering if, well, if perhaps you were a victim of circumstance?

MAXINE: A *victim*?

ALEXA: I mean—

MAXINE: I know what you mean, and I won't be tricked into talking about this, Alexa.

ALEXA: I'm not trying to trick you, Maxine. I'm here to work *with* you, not against you. It's just that I feel like we've got to know one another quite well over the past few weeks, and I suppose I'm curious, really.

MAXINE: (*pause*) Well, you know what curiosity did, don't you?

ALEXA: What? Oh, yes – ha, I get you. But seriously, the readers will want to know all about Tara – she was Lorna's mother, after all. Not having a father in her life will be of interest, in the way it affected her upbringing – both emotionally and financially.

MAXINE: We did just fine, thank you very much. I've always worked. Always put food on the table, sent Tara to school looking clean and tidy. What's there to know?

ALEXA: Well, for example, did Tara ever ask about her father?

MAXINE: Never.

ALEXA: Never? Really?

MAXINE: I know what you're doing Alexa, and I won't be led. Just put down that he was a boy from school. They'd believe that, wouldn't they?

ALEXA: So, I presume that's not the truth, then?

MAXINE: Per'aps we've done enough today—

ALEXA: (*pause*) Alright – alright, then, Maxine, let's move on to another subject. Can I ask you about your siblings instead? (*pause*)
Let's start with your oldest brother, Ray.

MAXINE: What about him?

ALEXA: From everything you've said, it sounds like he's been a major influence in your life. He took good care of you after your father died, didn't he?

MAXINE: I don't know what I would've done without him. My mother wasn't a very loving person, truth be told. Apart from when he married that Rena, Ray's the one person who stuck by me, through thick and thin.

ALEXA: Was he good with Tara?

MAXINE: Yes.

ALEXA: He was supportive?

MAXINE: Very.

ALEXA: (*pause*) Oh, and – sorry to keep jumping about, but I meant to ask you, how did your family react when you got pregnant so young? Your mother – your brothers? I know family members can react very differently about these things. Were there any negative feelings towards you?

135

MAXINE: My mum, she wasn't too pleased at first, and for a while some of my brothers wouldn't even speak to me— (*pause*)

ALEXA: What's the matter, Maxine?

MAXINE: (*pause*) I'm feeling a bit manipulated, if I'm honest, Alexa. I've made it clear I don't want to talk about this, and you won't leave it alone, will you?

ALEXA: God, I'm sorry, Maxine – really, I am. I'm being insensitive, aren't I? Listen, why don't you tell me what you'd like to talk about? Let's change the subject.

(*pause*)

Anything at all! A nice memory with Peter, perhaps?

MAXINE: (*pause*) Did I ever tell you about the time *Breakfast TV* paid for me and Peter to have tea at the Ritz? It was the fifth anniversary of Lorna's disappearance, and they thought we could do with a bit of a boost. Filmed it and everything – they were always doing things like that.

ALEXA: I bet Peter loved it – all those cakes!

MAXINE: I suppose you've been, Alexa? Well, I'd never been anywhere like it before. That tea room was like a fairytale palace. The telly people even bought me a posh frock, so I wouldn't feel out of place. I felt quite the lady!

ALEXA: The media hasn't been all bad, then?

MAXINE: Not all bad, no. There were some nice moments over the years, I suppose. No, it wasn't all bad.

14

Eva

Outside, beyond the glass doors of the living room, the landscape is still coated in a layer of white, and the temperatures won't really start to rise for another few months, until May arrives and springtime begins in earnest. This is the hardest feeling, having missed out on an entire year of seasons. Of course, Mamma, pragmatic as ever, puts my low mood down to my recovery, which is slow and steady, my exercise routine and free time now dictated by the needs of a baby.

Since Ann's visit a couple of weeks back, I find it hard to even look at Mamma, and she senses my distrust and calls it 'adjustment'. She is, I've recently come to realise, the master of reinvention. While my internal fury towards her rages on, externally I am complying, biding my time as I try to work out some kind of a plan for my future. Pappa's on my side, I think, though when it comes to the matter of Rosa and Lars he's no match for my mother, who won't shift in her opinion. Still there's no sign of my friends across the way, and their absence has robbed me of any sense of control. I'm paranoid about leaving the house, in case I bump into any locals who want to probe me about what happened, and so for now I remain here, in our house in the woods, living inside my strange lonely bubble. It is a small existence. These days I nap when Bella naps, eat my meals around hers, and watch TV with only half an eye, while I entertain her with brightly coloured toys on the playmat that dominates our once minimalist living space.

'So, is there any more news about Mac's mystery man?' I ask as Pappa carries a plate of sandwiches to the coffee table and joins me at the sofa. He's just got off his phone to Chief Mac, asking if there have been any further developments in my case, and I heard them discussing it. 'The body?' I add, when he looks at me blankly.

'Not really,' he replies. 'They haven't got much to go on, by the sounds of things. Mac reckons he's probably a vagrant, as they don't have a missing persons match on record.'

It's the weekend, but Mamma has been called into work, so she's dashing about the kitchen, trying to get out of the door, as Pappa and I are planning to watch a film together. When I ignore Bella grizzling on her playmat, Mamma scoops her up and holds her towards me, but I pretend not to notice, reaching for the local newspaper that's lying by my feet. Suppressing her annoyance, she hands the baby to Pappa instead.

'The local press seems to be enjoying it,' I say, pointing out a small update on the front cover. They're calling him 'The Grønnfoss Man', and in a way I feel grateful that it's a news item more interesting to the townsfolk than my unsolved 'abduction' a year ago. I wonder if they'll ever work out who the waterfall guy is, or if it will just be one of those things, a macabre discovery with no particular answer to be found. A bit like my accident: a horrible episode, best forgotten.

'Sandwich?' Pappa asks, rousing me from my thoughts, and when I look up I realise he's tricked me as he holds out Bella, so I have no choice but to take her.

She reaches up for my face, and I see love there, and although I *do* feel it for her too, I still don't know quite what to do with it. I catch Mamma's eye; she turns away quickly, and somehow I know she senses what I'm going through.

'She loves it when you play with her,' she says, concentrating on fixing a cheese roll to take for her lunch. 'You know you're her favourite.'

I scoff, repositioning myself to stop Bella from tugging at my hair.

Mamma looks up fleetingly, and away again, and I'm pleased because it means I'm making her mad.

Pappa fetches himself an apple, sniffing the air as he returns. 'Ooh, Eva, I think Bella wants changing.'

I raise my palms and wrinkle my nose.

With a good-humoured tut, Pappa disappears upstairs to deal with Bella, while Mamma casts me a withering look. But before she can get stuck into another lecture about taking responsibility she notices the time and drops the idea, rushing for the front door with her work bag and car keys. 'Bern's here!' she shouts as she steps outside, and then she's gone, leaving the front door ajar so he can make his own way in.

His arrival makes me instantly jittery, and in the moments before he enters I rake my fingers through my hair, wishing I'd known he was coming. Since leaving the attic I've barely set foot outside the house, save for one tentative shopping trip to the supermarket with Mamma, where on arrival a sudden panic seized me and I refused to leave the car, pulling my hood over my eyes to avoid being spotted by anyone I might know. It's pathetic, if I think of the power of my desire to escape before, when I would have done anything to be out of that attic room.

'Come on through,' Pappa is saying as he returns with Bella and settles her on the playmat. 'Look who it is, sweetheart. Bern's here for you.'

I rise from my seat, absently brushing off my top – I'm accustomed to being permanently crumpled or spilt on these days. I'm slightly alarmed to notice how neatly Bern's hair is combed, and that he's in his casual clothes, so he's clearly off duty.

'Hey!' Bern says, and after leaning in to stroke Bella's head he hovers by the kitchen units, not taking off his jacket. 'Ready?'

I turn to Pappa, bemused.

'Sorry, Bern, I haven't broken it to her yet.' He puts a hand on my shoulder. 'Now, I know your instinct will be to argue, Eva, so I want you to try to skip that bit, OK? I was telling Bern how you've hardly been outside since – well, since before Christmas, and he agreed to take you on a short hike into the mountains. What do you say?'

'I can't—' I start, but Bern jumps in.

'We don't have to go far. I mean, I know you've got to build up your stamina, so we'll only go as far as you like.'

'What if I see someone?' I ask.

Pappa laughs. 'You won't. No one else is stupid enough to go walking after all this snowfall, are they? Bern just thought it would do you some good to get a bit of fresh air.'

'And it would do *me* some good too,' Bern adds. 'I haven't had a day off in weeks, and I could do with some good company, to be honest.'

Good company. How can I argue, when Bern looks so keen, and Pappa so hopeful? I think of the whiteout landscape, of the eagles soaring high above the valley and the feel of sharp, clean air in my lungs, and I resolve to be brave. To be honest, some time away from Bella and her associated chores sounds like a tonic.

Ten minutes later, I'm togged up in my head-to-toe ski gear, crunching through the deep snow beyond our gate, thankful of the hiking poles Bern thought to bring with him. As we reach the path that leads to Grønnfoss waterfall, the horizon opens up and the low winter sun sends streaks of orange light across the white-coated fields and valleys. At the steep path behind the waterfall, the snow is compacted and icy, and Bern explains that it's the route the police used to access the dead man's remains a fortnight ago. He points in the direction of the crevasse where the body was found, and I feel sad that, for two years or more, no one cared enough about this person to notice him missing.

As we continue up the steep, rocky path, it doesn't take long for me to feel breathless, so out of condition am I, but Bern helps me up the tricky bits, and I let him do most of the talking as I conserve my energy, focusing on reaching the top without passing out. When the ground at last levels out, we stand for a while in silence, and I could weep for the relief I feel on seeing this view; at knowing some things have not changed. Some things have remained exactly, reassuringly the same.

'You're smiling,' Bern says, and I frown in response, making him laugh. 'It's just, I haven't seen you do that much lately and, well, you have a lovely smile.'

I look away, embarrassed, and focus on the horizon. What has happened to me, to my *joie de vivre*? I think perhaps it

141

was the discovery of Bella, and everything she represented, that was the final blow, robbing me of any remaining spirit I once possessed.

'Perhaps we could go into town together some time?' Bern suggests, scuffing his toe into a deep drift of snow. 'Not a big deal,' he says, when I don't answer immediately. 'Just a hot chocolate at Lapin's, maybe? Your pappa said you hadn't been out much, and I thought it might help – if you had a friend with you. You could bring Bella. I love kids, so it wouldn't faze me, you know?'

I'm so grateful to him for his kindness, and I shrug a little, to show I'm thinking it over. A small, lingering part of me wants to overcome this phobia, to venture into the world outside, while another, more dominant part has developed an acute fear: what if I find my universe entirely altered – what if no one remembers me, or even cares? My parents are worried, of course. I even heard Pappa use the word *agoraphobia* the other day, when he thought I was out of earshot, and Mamma keeps threatening to bring home a counsellor friend from work. But so far, I've refused. As my memories of hospital gradually return, I can't help feeling I've been prodded enough already, without inviting someone else to start poking around inside my head.

'That'd be nice,' I finally reply, a tight knot of panic already squeezing my chest at the thought of leaving the safety of home.

We continue further up the ridge, and when Bern asks me how my leg is I tell him I want to make it as far as the plateau, from where it's possible to see my house, and the Brun cottage, and the main road into town which passes Foxy Jack's bar. Eventually, we reach our destination, and I feel as though my legs might give way, pain screaming up the length of the bad one. Bern tells me to lean against him and catch my breath, which I do, glad of the support. From here, I can just make out Foxy's, where Gurt's orange van is parked, and I feel sick at the thought of them down there together, doing their dodgy deals, going about their grubby lives.

Bern sees me looking. 'We want to do a town-wide DNA sweep,' he tells me, and I draw away from him, shocked.

'The thing is,' he continues, 'the trail's gone cold. There've been no more sightings of our prowler since before Christmas, and the truck you were in gave us no forensic evidence, or at least none which matched anything on our database. So we're not left with many options, Eva.'

'How would the DNA help?' I ask, jamming my hiking stick hard into the snow.

'Well, I went on this forensics course a couple of months back. Our tutor was talking about the individual nature of DNA, the genetic "fingerprint" of us all, if you like, when I got thinking about Bella. She's our evidence – her DNA will not only contain your DNA, but also the father's DNA. That's why we tested Gurt, and it effectively ruled him out as Bella's father.'

'So?'

'So, what if we were to test all the males in town – everyone over the age of eighteen? And anyone who was known to have been in the area that night? It'll be time-consuming and costly, but ultimately it could give us some answers.'

My stomach churns as I think of all the men I know in Valden, good and bad. 'Can you make people take a test like that?'

Bern purses his lips. 'Make them, no. Encourage them, yes. As you know, Eva, there's no definitive evidence that you were raped, although everything you, your parents and best friends tell us suggests you weren't romantically involved with anyone before that night. So, we do have strong cause for suspicion. This sampling programme would be voluntary, and it would do two things – firstly, rule out certain men immediately, and secondly, highlight anyone who's not keen to come forward. It could narrow down the suspects significantly.'

'But once it gets under way, Bern,' I say breathlessly, 'everyone in the town will be talking about me; everyone will think I'm a victim.'

Bern places a hand on my arm. 'You can't think like that, Eva. People care about you – about our community. Honestly, I reckon most of our locals will come forward without much persuasion.'

What if they don't find him? What if they *do*?

'Will you agree to it?' Bern asks, his hand still holding me steady, and as our eyes meet I realise I have the power to say no, and the sense of it is intoxicating.

'Do you want to kiss me?' I ask him.

Overhead, a trio of buzzards turns in wide arcing circles, their cries eerie in the fading light. Bern brings his face close to mine, hesitating briefly, before our lips touch and we kiss softly, gently. It's over in seconds, and I'm left wanting more, and I like that.

'It's starting to get dark,' he says. 'Shall we head back?' He takes my hand in his, and leads me back down the way we came.

As the Brun cottage disappears from view, I tell him about Mamma's fight with Ann, and how Rosa and Lars still haven't visited me.

'They're away again,' he says, halting at the edge of the waterfall. 'Didn't you know? They've been on a foreign exchange since the start of the year. To England – they got a month's placement as part of their language programme.'

144

'So, they haven't been ignoring me?' I think of how, night after night, I've sat at my bedroom window, firing off fruitless torch flashes in Rosa's direction. My relief is vast.

'No!' Bern says, giving my hand a little tug and starting along the path again. 'I saw them at their New Year's Eve party, and they said they'd call for you as soon as they got back at the end of the month. Rosa's exact words were, "Sod Mamma and Ingrid, let them try and stop us." And you know what Rosa's like when she gets an idea into her head.'

I do. She's stubborn as a mule.

Bern's words suddenly sink in. 'They had a party at New Year?'

He nods, unlatching the gate to my home and gesturing for me to go first. 'It was a good one.'

'And they didn't invite me?' I say.

Bern takes my hiking pole and straps it with his to the back of the snowmobile. 'Oh, no – they did. I think that's why Ann was here that night, to give you your invitation. I asked Ingrid if you'd be there, but she told me you weren't feeling up to it.'

I shake my head, and watch his expression change as he realises Ingrid's been playing him too.

'I'd better get back indoors,' I say, at once impatient to get to the bottom of this.

'I'll call you about that hot chocolate?' he shouts over as I reach the front door.

'OK,' I call back, and I can't tell if the butterflies in my stomach are born out of my growing fondness for Bern or out of rage at my lying mother.

Once inside the front door, I almost collide with Pappa and the baby, who is already strapped into her car seat, swaddled so tightly that only her tiny pink face is visible.

'Oh, good, you're back,' he says, pecking me on the cheek. 'I suddenly remembered Bella's health check. You don't want to come, do you? I'm late as it is.'

I tell him no, waving him off as he loads the carrier into the back of the car and saying a silent prayer of thanks for this unforeseen opportunity. The moment they disappear beneath the trees, I set to work, on a hunt for I don't know what, all the while thanking my lucky stars that Mamma is out at work today too, that for once I have the place to myself. Starting in the living area, I turn out the kitchen drawers, the cupboards under the TV, the space beneath the footstool where Pappa stows all his work receipts. But I find nothing of interest or value to me down here; just recipe cards and invoices and instruction manuals for appliances. I hurry up the stairs, a sharp pain tugging at my weak abdomen, and head for my parents' room, where I crawl beneath the bed, pulling out boxes and suitcases, rummaging through the contents at speed, and finding only summer clothes and spare bedlinen.

My heart is hammering behind my ribcage as I get to my feet and scan the room. Their drawers contain only the things you'd expect: socks, underwear, T-shirts and jeans. Mamma's jewellery box and dressing table drawer contain the few pieces of silver she owns: a pendant, three pairs of simple earrings, a bangle she loves but never wears as it catches on everything. At the wardrobe, I search the bottom and find only shoes and boots, before reaching onto the top shelf to pull out two large boxes, which I set down on the bed. The first contains photograph albums, most of which I've seen before. I riffle through them, finding nothing new, until one solo photo slides out from the back of one. The photograph is colour, but of a faded quality, and even after the passing of time it is clear to see that the man and woman featured look to be from different places, different cultures. I recognise them as Pappa's parents, in a closer-cropped version of the photo Pappa had included in my Christmas gift album. His father is tall, conventionally dressed in a flannel shirt and flared jeans, his hair worn curly and short, a fine moustache adorning his lip. Even if I didn't already know, I'd guess this can only be Pappa's father, because he looks so much like him, in a more serious, perhaps more confident way. His mother, conversely, is tiny, like me, and I wonder if it is her I take after, my colouring and stature being so unlike Mamma's. She wears a traditional linen tunic and coloured wool tights, and her hair is dark and long, worn loose. She is looking away from the camera, her left hand shielding her eyes as she focuses on something out of view.

Beyond the window, the light has almost gone. All is quiet, except for the distant sound of the fox crying in the forest, and briefly I wonder how often it was Bella I heard from my attic room, and how many times it was actually the fox. Vehicle lights in the far distance remind me that I've got no time to lose, and I return the photograph and move on to the next box, which immediately bears fruit. Lifting away a bundle of old knitted baby blankets, my breath catches in my throat as I lay my hands on the yellow envelope I watched Ann fling at the snow, just before New Year's Eve. Sure enough, when I look inside, there is an invitation, with the simple hand-written words – in Rosa's unmistakable script – *Please come, Eva*, followed by a hundred kisses or more, filling the page, and breaking my heart.

I glance out at the view, and spot headlights drawing closer on the main road, turning left on to the top track. Quickly, I flip through the box, my fingers darting over letters, cards, old passports and tickets, and a thick wad of British press cuttings – the top one mysteriously headed *No More Clues in Baby Lorna Hunt.* I want to stay and keep looking, but can't risk it; I'm out of time. Sliding the invitation card into my pocket, I drop its yellow envelope back beneath the blankets and shut the lid, before returning the boxes to the wardrobe, and casting about the room to ensure I've left nothing out of place. I jog downstairs.

By the time Mamma walks in through the front door, I've positioned myself casually at the breakfast bar, and I afford her a smile as she drops her bag on the floor and asks me how my walk with Bern went.

'Do I detect romance in the air?' she asks, her face lighting up.

'Mind your own business,' I reply, looking away.

'Really? You're not going to tell your old mamma? I'm hurt.' She winks, to tell me she's joking.

I pull a face, teasing her, remaining quiet.

'It's a secret, is it?' she says, pinching my cheek as she fetches up the kettle and starts to fill it. 'That's alright, you don't have to tell me.'

Does she really believe everything's fine between the two of us, me and her, that we can simply return to our old joky, playful selves together? It's tiring playing out this charade with her day after day. I take a cookie from the tin, and snap it in half, spraying crumbs across the clean counter. 'Everyone needs secrets,' I say.

And she nods, entirely unaware that I'm on to her. Whatever it is she's got to hide, and I'm certain there's plenty more, I'm going to get to the bottom of it. I swear.

15

Maxine

Recorded interview between Alexa Evans, freelance writer, and Maxine Gregory, subject of A LIFE OF LOSS (Falun Publishing International).

ALEXA: You seem tired today, Maxine. Is everything OK?

MAXINE: I'm finding it all a bit much, Alexa, if I'm honest. We seem to go round and round in circles most of the time, and I can't see how half of it will be of any interest to anyone.

ALEXA: Oh, it really will be, believe me! If it reassures you at all, these emotions are normal. Autobiographies are notoriously hard-going in the writing stage – you have to revisit so much of your past, some good, some bad. And inevitably it means unearthing all sorts of unsettling emotions. But it really will be worth it in the end. I promise you'll be so proud of the final book.

MAXINE: (*pause*) It feels like I'm running out of steam. I don't know how many times I can keep going over all this – all your questions. It's upsetting, and I'm so tired all the time. I'm not as young as I used to be. How many more sessions do you think we'll need?

ALEXA: I think we're about halfway through. I *know* it can be tiring the way we jump about from one subject to the next, but it's only natural – we often don't know something's going to be interesting until we uncover it. That's why I ask so many questions, and certainly half of it won't make it into the book – but it's my job to winkle out everything the readers *will* be interested in. And I promise you we'll put it all into a sensible order before it goes to print.

MAXINE: I'll get to see it first? I'll get to say if anything's not right?

ALEXA: Of course! To the outside world, this is entirely written by you – it's your autobiography, Maxine – so whatever goes to print has to be with your blessing. We want it to be something you feel proud of!

MAXINE: Good, good. Thanks, love. I don't know, I've got a banging headache this week, and I'm finding it a bit hard, dredging up all this old stuff.

ALEXA: I *completely* understand, and I'm glad you told me how you're feeling, so I can be a bit more sensitive to it. Listen, why don't we make a start now and I'll get out of your hair as quickly as I can today? How's that sound?

MAXINE: You're a sweetie. Go on, then.

ALEXA: Now – after your mother died, you say the council moved you and Tara out to a new estate, is that right?

MAXINE: Miles away, it was. All the boys had moved on, got married, or gone off for jobs, so it was just me and Tara left in the old family home, and the council said we couldn't stay. They said it was a health hazard, what with the damp 'n' all, but I don't believe that. It was one of them programmes to move single mothers and poor families out, so they could tart up or bulldoze our old places and make a bob or two for the fat cats that ran it all. That's what Ray said, anyway. He told me, 'The nobs are moving in and cleaning up. You wouldn't want to be rubbing shoulders with the likes of them, sis!'

ALEXA: Ha, he was probably right! But were you and Tara happy in your new place?

MAXINE: Barnet? No! It was all brand new, like they promised – new cooker, new carpets, fridge – but I missed the old place like you wouldn't believe, damp 'n' all. In Stone Street everything was on the doorstep: the market, the laundry, the corner grocery. Tara was ten by the time we left. Back there, she could walk to school on her own, with friends. Up in Barnet she had to take a bus, and I couldn't keep a close eye on her like I could before.

ALEXA: Did Tara settle in, eventually?

MAXINE: Not in the way you'd hope. Ray said mixing with the wrong sort in Barnet was what sent Tara off the rails. She went through a bit of a bad patch. Rebellious, you know?

ALEXA: You said Ray was out of your lives for a few years, while he was married?

MAXINE: Ten years, it was. He met Rena at a dance, not long after I'd had Tara. After a couple of years' courting, they married, and I didn't see him again for a long time, not until Mum's funeral. They turned up late, breezing into the church looking like they owned the place – him in a natty suit that made him look like an Italian mobster, her doing her best to look like a film star. Ha!

ALEXA: You didn't like her?

MAXINE: I didn't like the way she looked down her nose at me, that's for sure! We chatted for a short while after the church service, and Rena invited us to visit them in Southend some time, but I could tell she didn't mean it. Ray was lovely to Tara, though. He gave her a bit of money when we said goodbye, and told her he was glad to see she'd inherited the family good looks. I'd never seen her look so chuffed!

ALEXA: Did you ever feel a bit jealous of Rena? I mean, in a way, she'd taken Ray away from the family, hadn't she?

MAXINE: Jealous of her? I don't think so. At any rate, it never lasted, did it, just like I said it wouldn't. When she kicked him out the following year, he moved in with me and Tara – and never saw Rena again. Now, she *was* a floozy. Dumped Ray the minute his business went belly-up, and shacked up with his best mate!

ALEXA: Poor Ray! But that must have been nice for you and Tara, wasn't it, having another adult about the house?

MAXINE: Oh, yes. Ray was still working back then, so the extra few quid coming in was a boon, and I was so happy to see my brother again. But then Tara started to play up, so things were a bit up and down for a while.

ALEXA: Tell me more about that. How did Tara 'play up'?

MAXINE: She'd always been a quiet little thing, but by the time Ray had been with us a few months she'd started to turn into a monster. Uncontrollable. I think she'd got so used to having me all to herself, she couldn't bear to share me with her uncle.

ALEXA: She rebelled, you say?

MAXINE: By thirteen she was out all hours, never saying where or who she was with, completely ignoring me, and Ray, no matter how kind he was. He was always giving her money or little presents, showing an interest in her school work, but it didn't make any difference. He stuck it out as long as he could, but then she got herself in trouble – *pregnant* –

and that was the last straw. She got her own way, in the end though, 'cause it drove him out. He said he didn't want to stick around if he wasn't welcome.

ALEXA: Oh – I don't have the details for Tara's first child here – that wasn't the pregnancy with Karl Gunn, then?

MAXINE: No, no – this was years earlier. Fifteen, she was. I didn't know what we were going to do about it, not having two pennies to rub together since Ray left us, but then when she was six months gone she lost the baby anyway. Stillborn, it was.

ALEXA: Oh, Maxine. It must have been a dreadful time.

MAXINE: I missed Ray terribly.

ALEXA: (*pause*) And losing the baby.

MAXINE: Oh, yes. Well, that was a blessing really, love. Tara would never have coped with a baby at her age. I'd been through it myself, I told her, and I wouldn't wish that on anyone.

ALEXA: (*pause*) So, what happened after Tara lost the baby?

MAXINE: Well, I wrote to Ray and told him all about it, hoping, I think, that he'd want to move back, now there wasn't a baby to worry about. Now that Tara had calmed down a bit.

ALEXA: Did he move back in?

MAXINE: No, not that time. But he did send us a few hundred quid, and we went on holiday – just Tara and me – our first holiday together.

ALEXA: And where did you go?

MAXINE: Dorset. I'd never been to the seaside, and one of my neighbours recommended a holiday cottage she'd stayed in the year before. So we ended up in Beaport, and by the time the fortnight was up we'd fallen in love with the place. Within a year, I'd wangled a council transfer and we were living there.

ALEXA: And it was there, in Dorset, that Tara met Karl?

MAXINE: Yes – years later, mind – but yes, that's where she met *him*. Karl Gunn.

16

Eva

Bern came for supper last night, and as we said goodbye on the front doorstep – neither of us bold enough to go in for a second kiss – he told me that Rosa and Lars are due back today. Their plane was due to land in Bergen in the early hours, and Bern was heading straight off from our place, to make the five-hour drive to meet his cousins at the airport.

Now, I stand at my bedroom window, looking out towards the forest and lakeside, scouting for signs of life behind the glass of Rosa's bedroom window, or for Bern's car turning in on the foggy top road. Over by the water, a strip of yellow crime tape – presumably blown loose from the site of that body at Grønnfoss – flaps from a branch, the wild movements of it suggesting a high wind. This view is the same one I had from the attic room, but with a more restricted aspect, being a floor lower. I have the strangest pang of longing for my old prison upstairs, something akin to nostalgia for a time when I knew nothing of the monumental shifts my life had taken while I slept. A thread of guilt tugs at me, that I should wish for a time when Bella was unknown to me, and I wonder at my ability to be a good mother. Am I selfless enough? Am I good enough?

I think of my baby, asleep in her room across the landing. I think of Mamma at work in her hospital clinic, her hair tamed into a fair twist at the back of her head, spectacles perched on her nose as she tends to her patients. And I think of Pappa labouring away in the back, clearing the path of snow and leaves, as he makes plans to build a playhouse for Bella, for when she's old enough to walk and run in the garden. These are my people, my family, and yet I ask myself, why, when I have so much, do I feel so alone?

The house is quiet, the only sounds coming from outside, where the tall young pines at the edge of the forest sway and snap in the wind, and the surface of the lake moves as though a body of fish are congregating beneath the water. On the top road, I spot the red post van turning on to the farm track, and I follow the vehicle's route as it trundles past the Brun cottage and disappears beneath the trees on its way here. Knowing Pappa is out back, I trot down the stairs and pull on my boots, daring myself to go outside to speak to the postman, Jonas, when he arrives. This is something I've been working on, ever since that first walk with Bern: setting myself daily challenges in a bid to regain my confidence, to be normal. I open the door as Jonas steps out of his van.

'Morning, Jonas!' I wave at him, and his face breaks into a wide smile.

'Morning, young lady! Long time no see!' He flips through a wad of letters and strides across the gravel drive, leaving large prints in last night's fresh snowfall. 'Are you on the mend?'

The wind tugs at the letters as I take them from his hand. 'Nearly good as new,' I reply, and I bring up an arm in a muscle pose, and he laughs.

As he returns to his van, Jonas calls over. 'I suppose your pappa's down with Mac and the relief team, is he?'

I shake my head. 'Should he be?'

'Haven't you heard? There's been another avalanche on the Briskpark road – they've closed the road, from what I hear. All the relief volunteers are down there – your pappa should have had a call.'

My pulse quickens. That's the road Bern will be returning along with Rosa and Lars. The road which leads us to the outside world, to the cities and transport links and food supplies and – and Mamma's hospital. 'Is anyone hurt?'

'Doesn't sound like it, but it's all hands on deck. I'm up there as soon as I've finished my shift. I'm surprised Mac hasn't called your pappa in.'

As though in answer, the sound of my father's chainsaw drifts high on the air, and Jonas raises his eyebrows. Pappa would never have heard his mobile over that noise; in any case, he'll be wearing his noise-cancelling headphones.

'You'd better go and tell him, love,' Jonas says. 'I'll probably see him down there later.'

And with that he gives me a little salute and drives back on to the forest path. Immediately, I cut through the house and out through the sliding doors to the garden, where I spot Pappa at the far end, cutting back the overgrown yew. I wave at him in wide sweeping arcs until I grab his attention, and he switches off his motor.

'What is it?' he yells over, removing his orange earphones and brushing cuttings from his beard with the cuff of his jacket.

'You need to phone Mac,' I shout back, 'Jonas says there's been another avalanche!'

Within moments, Pappa has stowed his equipment, loaded the pickup with ropes, picks, shovels and blankets and is speeding off along the forest path, leaving me alone, with only Bella upstairs for company. Still clutching the small pile of post, I tiptoe upstairs to check in on her, and find her sleeping.

As I wander back into my room, catching a glimpse of Pappa's distant truck turning out on to the highway, a flood of questions courses through my mind. Was anyone hurt? Is Mamma OK? Did Bern's car get through before the avalanche closed the road off, with his precious cargo of Rosa and Lars, or are they delayed on the other side of it? They should be back by now, I'm certain.

It's only when I fling the mail down on my bedspread that I notice one of the letters is addressed to me. I snatch it up again and study the handwriting, not recognising it at all as I tear at the paper and pull out a birthday card. *Happy birthday, Eva*, it says. *Lots of love, Px*

P? Who the hell is P? Whoever it is, they clearly don't know me all that well, because if they did, they would know it's not my birthday for another month yet. I turn the card over in my hands, willing my brain to fill in the gaps, as I try to recall someone, anyone with a name beginning with that letter. There's Piers in my class at school, but we've barely ever said two words to each other, and Penelope Lao from the year above, who's far too popular to bother with me. Petter Vale from the butchers, who's ninety if he's a day. P? I'm straining to think of anyone else – perhaps one of Lars's friends from film club, but I don't even know most of their names. And then, just as with enormous relief I spot Bern's car on the top road, the thought of Lars's friends brings a memory to the front of my mind, clear as day.

*

Lars and I are across from each other at the window seat over-looking the playing field, our lunch trays between us. There's no Rosa, and it occurs to me she must be off with Olaf again, smooching on the gym benches or mooning around the school grounds, holding hands. Rosie and the Hulk. That's what Lars and I call them, because Rosa is so tiny and Olaf, a star player in the school's American football team, is huge.

'So, how's your love life these days?' Lars asks me as he punctures his juice cartoon with a straw.

'Same as ever,' I reply, reaching over for one of his fried potatoes. 'Non-existent.'

'I don't know why,' Lars says, all matter-of-fact. 'I mean, you're not that bad-looking, and your personality is OK.'

'Thanks a lot.'

'When was the last time you had a date?'

I'm not even going to dignify that with an answer. Lars isn't exactly a sex god himself; I mean, he had one brief fumble with Nina Berg last summer – so he says – and here he is acting like a love guru. Recently some of the lads in our class have started taking the piss out of him for his lack of 'action', calling him Bender Brun and telling each other to 'watch your back' whenever he's near. It's been really getting to him.

I shrug. 'What about you?'

'Not much better,' he admits, and we eat for a while in silence.

'It would be quite nice to go out with someone, wouldn't it?' I say. 'I dunno, just for something different to do – for a change of scene.'

Lars nods. 'I'm so bored around here. I can't wait to leave. To travel the world. I'll get lucky then, I reckon. Everyone loves a Norwegian.'

I snort, reaching across to flip the straight blond hair off his face.

'Anyway, you've got nothing to worry about, Eva.' He narrows his eyes and chews thoughtfully. 'I've told you before, I've got friends queuing up to go out with you – I could set you up any time you wanted.'

I give him a sarcastic smile. 'Your friends are all dorks, Lars. I don't even know them. How awkward would that be?'

'Well, what kind of person would you go out with?'

'I don't know. Someone kind. Someone not too dorky, not too vain.' I reach in for another potato. 'Oh, and I'd have to not be too physically repulsed by them, I guess.'

Lars laughs, saying, 'Same,' and slaps my hand away from his plate.

After a pause, a strange look crosses his face.

'What?' I ask, intrigued.

Lars chews on his lip. 'Just an idea. I mean, you don't want to die a virgin, do you? Let me check it out with Rosa first and I'll let you know.'

'Ha!' I say, doing my best not to look interested. 'Just remember – I don't like surprises, Lars!'

He waggles his eyebrows. 'We'll have you fixed up by Valentine's Day.'

'That's only a fortnight away,' I reply with a scowl.

'I know,' he smiles mysteriously, clearing his plate and picking up his tray as the bell goes. 'Leave it with me.'

They're back. Rosa and Lars are back.

The last thing I think as I pull my snow boots on over my jogging bottoms is, Bella will be fine, I'll be back soon. I grab my padded parka, zipping it up as I yank open the front door, closing Bella's half-hearted grizzling behind it as I survey the snow-covered front drive to ensure that I really am alone.

With a sharp intake of breath, I set off at a run, immediately aware of the weakness in my legs, but continuing against the strong wind regardless. My exercises have strengthened my muscles to an extent, but my stamina is still woefully poor, and in no time at all my breathing grows laboured, made worse by a tightening corset of anxiety. It's been so long since I ventured this far alone, and the sheer scale of the world seems to press down on me, the sky vaster than ever before, the forest denser, fuller of menace. Part of me longs to just turn back, to forget the whole thing, to shut myself inside the safety of my warm, protected house, but I have to go on. Heart thumping, I dig my fingernails into the pads of my hands and command myself to stay focused. This is Rosa and Lars we're talking about; these are my best friends. There is nothing to fear.

At the opening to the forest I rest for a moment against a pine tree, fighting the tiny dots that play in my vision, anchoring my gaze on the churning lake and boathouse beyond the woods. The straight avenues of trees do almost nothing to protect me from the buffeting force of the elements and I press on, knowing it will take another five minutes of brisk walking before I reach Lars and Rosa's cottage. My pulse races with anticipation as I think of all the questions I want to ask them, all the news we have to share. They'll have heard about Bella. What will they think of me? Will they have answers – do they know what really happened that night?

Then I see them, far along the path, unaware of my presence ahead. My heart swells that they've come straight for me; they've returned home after a month away, and the first thing they thought to do is visit me. They're deep in conversation, not really taking in the swaying landscape of the forest as they stomp along, their steps in synchrony, Lars with his hands

161

thrust deep in his pockets, Rosa waving hers about, to punctuate her words. I could pick these two out from the furthest distance, from their body language alone. I know them as well as I know myself, and an unexpected sob threatens to escape me as their faces grow clearer and nearer. I only now realise I've stopped moving altogether, and I'm rooted to the path, my eyes locked on my friends. Everything else has vanished from my thoughts and all I can think is, this is it, this is the moment we come back together again.

Rosa's hand grips Lars's wrist, and there's an expression of shock on both of their faces. 'Eva!' I hear Rosa say, and then the bubble bursts and we're running at each other, and the only sound in the forest is the thud of boots on wet earth and the roar of pumping blood in my ears.

As Rosa and Lars wrap themselves around me, I have the sensation of being so small that I might slip through their embrace, to be whipped away, taken up by the wind. I cling to them, my tears a torrent, until eventually Rosa pulls back, holding me at arm's length so that she can inspect me closely. Why do I suddenly feel like a stranger to them? An uncomfortable shyness comes over me, and I rake about my soggy mind to think of something to say, something normal.

Lars speaks first. 'Eva – God, Eva – you're so *pale*.'

Without missing a beat, Rosa shoots him a fierce look, her eyebrows knitted. 'Nice, Lars. Just what she wants to hear!'

'Ah, fuck it,' he says, making me smile. 'Sorry, Eva, I'm a prat.'

I swipe at my wet face with the back of my sleeve and mutter, 'No change there, then,' and all at once we're laughing, grabbing one another's hands, and for a moment it feels just like we were before.

'We haven't got long,' I say, remembering Bella. 'Were you on your way to mine?'

They both nod. 'Bern just dropped us back. We were stuck in traffic for ages – another avalanche, but they've cleared it now.'

'Really? Pappa's down there, helping.' I glance over in the direction of the empty road; our time could be cut short at any minute.

'Bern said he thought your mamma would be out at work this morning. She hasn't exactly been welcoming . . .' Lars says, colour rising to his cheeks. Is it my imagination or is he more awkward than usual? Are they both? 'But we thought we'd give it another go.'

'How many times have you been over?' I ask.

'God, I've lost count,' Rosa says. 'We saw you in the hospital a few times, then we tried almost every week for the first month you were home – but we've been away for a month, you know?'

My head is pounding. 'I thought you'd forgotten me.'

'Never! Didn't your folks tell you we'd called?' Lars asks, and now he looks as though *he* might cry.

Waves of relief and anger and confusion rush over me. 'No!' I growl, stomping my heel against a hard clump of ice. 'No, they fucking didn't!' My heart is racing. 'Listen, can we walk down to the lake? I haven't got long, and we can't risk going back to my place.'

We turn into the trees, taking a direct route through the drifts of snow and snarls of winter bramble until we come out at the lakeside, where I cast a cautious eye at the red boards of my house at the far side. Ahead of us, the lake's surface continues to ripple under the constant buffeting of the wind, and we walk until we reach the old pontoon, close to the rotting boathouse – the same spot we so often dangled our feet from, to cool off in summer. We sit on the icy boards in a cross-legged row, Rosa then me then Lars. My leg is killing me, and I pull it tight to my chest, flexing my ankle this way and that to relax the muscles.

'What happened, Eva?' Rosa asks.

'Ha.' I laugh softly. 'I was hoping you could help me with that.'

'We've got so much to ask you,' Lars says. 'There've been all sorts of rumours going round.'

I look up, and when I meet his blue eyes the hurt of missing him and Rosa feels so raw. 'What kinds of rumours?'

'That you were running away with some guy,' Rosa says. 'With the driver of that truck.'

I blink at her. 'What else?'

'That Foxy and Gurt had something to do with it,' she continues. 'That me and Lars knew the kidnapper and have been withholding information from the police.'

I listen, but, try as I might, I can't get any words out.

'Not true, by the way.' Lars reaches into his pocket and pulls out a pack of cigarettes, lighting three and passing one down to each of us. 'Obviously.'

'That loser Foxy was shitting himself about getting done for serving underage drinkers,' Rosa says, 'so at first he tried denying we'd even been in the bar. He was more worried about his licence than he was about you nearly dying. I hate him,' she adds.

'Uncle Mac's thinking of doing him for wasting police time,' says Lars.

'I remember Foxy serving me a beer long after you'd left the bar,' I say. 'I was really hammered, granted, but I remember that clearly, because I was thinking what an idiot he was – and I remember him saying *something* that made me so mad . . .'

I can see Foxy now, in the gloom of the bar, snapping off the cap of my beer, slamming it down on the counter in front of me so that the foam rose and spilled over the bar. He squinted his piggy eyes at me and chewed on his lip, and in that moment he looked like someone trying to pick a fight.

'That night – did you see the driver of the truck?' I ask.

A look passes between them, and they both shake their heads. What is that? Sadness? Regret? 'Nobody did. Except Mad Eric, and no one believes him.'

'He said he saw a stranger, didn't he? A young man?'

'Yeah, but you know what he's like, Eva. He's barely standing by nine each night. No one's taking him seriously.'

Lars is exactly the same as I remember him, and so is Rosa for that matter. They're funny and sweary and straight-talking and bright, and I've missed them so much. I stub my cigarette out on the damp wood of the pontoon, feeling queasy. 'We argued that night, didn't we, Rosa?'

Rosa looks down at her lap. 'Well, yeah, there was an atmosphere, for sure.'

'We never argue,' I say and it's barely a whisper.

'Well, we did that night. You told me to fuck off, as it happens,' she says, holding up a hand to stop Lars from interrupting, 'and stupidly, Eva – I did.'

'*We* did,' Lars says. 'It's not just down to you, Rosa. I was there too. We should never have left you on your own, Eva. I tried to get you to come with us, but you wouldn't budge. You said you'd get your pappa to pick you up, and in the end we gave in and left you to it.'

I'm about to ask more about the disagreement we had, when it occurs me that they haven't even mentioned Bella. 'You said there were lots of rumours. What else?'

Rosa lets out a snort. 'You know what people are like around here. Your accident was the most thrilling event of the century – there were bound to be some bonkers theories doing the rounds.'

'Steinar Nord said he'd heard the crash left you brain-dead; that you'd be in a wheelchair for the rest of your life,' Lars says, breaking up a twig and flicking pieces out into the water like tiny missiles.

'Then there was the one about your parents locking you away in the attic!' Rosa laughs at this, then checks herself. 'Mind you, we did start to wonder after a while.'

I can't look at them. 'Anything else?'

'That you were – you were . . .' Lars trails off.

Rosa finishes his sentence for him. 'That you were raped.'

For a few moments, we're all silent.

'Did you hear the one about the baby?' I manage to say.

When I look up, they're both staring down into their hands, trying to form words.

Lars speaks finally, his expression anxious as he meets my gaze. 'Mamma told us she saw her. She said she's lovely.'

'She is,' I say. 'Her name's Bella.'

'I still can't get my head round it,' Rosa says. 'You're a mother, Eva.'

'*You* can't get your head round it?' I say, laughing despite myself. 'I still have to pinch myself every day to check I'm not in some weird . . . dream.' The word in my head is *nightmare*, but I don't say that out loud.

'The driver, whoever he was, he really, you know . . .' Lars stammers '. . . and you don't remember a thing about it?'

Rosa throws him another fierce glare and pulls me against her, nestling her chin in the crook of my shoulder. 'Mamma says she's beautiful. The baby. She says she's just like you.'

'Did she?' I whisper, and I'm grateful to hear that Ann thought that. I want Ann to like Bella. I want Ann to like *me*.

'It *is* like some weird dream, though, isn't it?' Lars says, our eyes meeting over Rosa's shoulder. 'It's like, one minute you were there, and everything was normal. And then you vanished – and had that accident – and then you came back, but with a baby. It doesn't seem real.'

Maybe it's not real, I think, and again I have the sense of leaving my body, of not really being there. I pull from Rosa's embrace, and ask, 'Lars, do you remember you were talking about setting me up with someone? One of your friends?'

His expression grows more serious, and he glances over at Rosa. 'Kinda.'

'We were in the canteen that time – Rosa was off with Olaf somewhere – '

'Urgh, that one's *totally* over and done with,' Rosa interjects, 'just to keep you up to speed.'

'And you were taking the piss out of me, Lars, about not having a boyfriend and all that. Remember? You said I'd die a virgin if I didn't get myself out there.'

Lars's mouth turns up at one corner. 'I s'pose so. Sounds like me.'

'You told me you'd thought of someone for me – you said you'd ask Rosa what she thought?'

'Yeah, but nothing came of it,' he says. 'I mean, Uncle Mac said the baby – the dates – the doctors told him it had to be the driver of that truck.'

I nod my head, exhausted, and I know he's right, but still, something doesn't fit. Lars stares at me, as though I might go on, and then he says, 'Don't you remember anything from before that night?'

167

My answer is interrupted by a sudden burst of sound from the far end of the lake. It's Mamma, and from our vantage point we see her clearly, standing at the boundary to our home, the yellow of her jacket vivid against the monochrome backdrop of snow and wood. When did she get home?

'Eeee-vah!' she calls through cupped hands, and the alarm in her voice is evident to us all. '*Eva!*'

We freeze, all three of us dropping into silence as we wait for her to shout again. Rosa covers her mouth with mittened hands, her eyes searching mine for instruction.

'I have to go,' I say, standing and stepping over Lars to make my way over to the bank, looking back only once I have reached the trees. 'I'm in so much trouble already,' I murmur.

My friends remain sitting on the old pontoon, staring at me. Of course, it sounds weird to them – wrong, even. Why on earth should I be so afraid? That's what they're thinking. They have no idea how it feels to be scared all the time, to be anxious and fearful of everything and nothing, every second of every day.

'I'm fine,' I say, even though neither of them asked the question.

Rosa nods slowly.

'I'll see you soon?'

Lars is frowning, looking at Rosa, nudging her. I don't know what to do to make them feel OK about this, so I turn to leave.

'Oh, we've still got your phone,' Rosa calls after me.

I turn back, confused.

'Your mobile?' Rosa says, as though she thinks I didn't hear properly. 'You didn't bother taking it with you that night, because you'd run out of credit, remember? You left it at mine.'

I shake my head.

'Don't worry, though – we didn't tell anyone about it. I just stuck it at the back of my drawer, to keep it safe. I know what your parents are like about social media.'

'Social media?'

'Yeah,' Rosa laughs. 'Don't tell me you've forgotten what that is!'

I want to ask her more, to tell her to run and fetch the phone for me, to power it up so that I might trawl through it for answers or clues. But Mamma's voice tears through me again.

'*Eeeee-vahhhh*!' She can't be far from us now. If I take the rough path, I might be able to avoid her and get back to the house first. Perhaps I could even pretend I never left?

'We'll call you,' Lars shouts after me, pushing himself up.

'They can't stop us, my friend!' Rosa yells, punching the air as she too gets to her feet. 'Revolution!'

I look at them standing at the pontoon's edge, my beautiful friends, and I can't find any words for them. Every step forward in my recovery seems to bring a new revelation, and my brain isn't big enough to take it all in.

'Just go,' Rosa says as Mamma's voice echoes louder still. '*Go*!'

I turn from them, and I run, back through the undergrowth, into the line of trees, back towards my prison of a home.

Tonight, I sleepwalk for the first time since I was allowed back downstairs, and it's only when I push the window open and feel the bitter rush of cold air that I wake to find myself in the attic again. Even in my waking state, I'm still stinging from the anger and disappointment meted out by my mother earlier, and from the guilt I felt at the sight of Bella's sweat-drenched face and puffy eyes. Mamma's words ring in my ears. 'She is your *daughter*, Eva,' she hissed at me while she soothed Bella possessively, as though she was hers not mine, holding her away from me to make her point. I hated her for being the one Bella wanted most. 'How could you have just left her like that? She *has* to be your priority now, Eva. *Nothing* else matters as much as Bella. Do you understand?'

I've never experienced shame like it. I spent the rest of the afternoon shut in my room, distractedly knitting, completing the scarf kit Nettie gave me, and which I'm surprised to find now in my hands. The full moon has come around again, and it seems to dominate the sky above the forest, casting a milky glow over the lake and surrounding land. I lean from the window, breathing in the clean white chill of night, and that's when I see him – stepping out from the forest shadows to show himself. He breaks into a run, leaving the cover of the trees and vaulting our gate effortlessly, coming to a halt a few metres away, close enough that I can hear the crunch of his boots on the snow. It occurs to me that he looks cold and vulnerable, and I lift the scarf high, propelling it into the space between us, watching it sail on the still air, to land at his feet. He bends to retrieve it, wrapping it around his neck, and I know he is no monster.

'Who are you?' I whisper down to him, as loudly as I dare.

He takes a step closer, but a flash of light flooding the driveway makes him halt: he's triggered the security lamps, the brilliance of them almost obliterating his features in the glare. The boy – because it's clear to me now that he is barely older than I am – brings a finger to his lips and holds up a folded piece of paper, which he slides beneath the log store before taking a backward step.

Alerted by movement on the floor below, I turn away, squinting into the dark shadows of the attic, but when I return my gaze to the window the boy is retreating, back into the trees. Now, in the round glow of the floodlit driveway, my father stands in his dressing gown, a shotgun in his grip. His posture is rigid, his feet planted wide as though poised for a fight, and, just as I think he's decided it's nothing, he points the gun towards the moon and fires off a warning round.

I start at the sound of Bella waking in the room downstairs, but I can't drag my eyes away from this scene. My gaze is locked on the dark space beneath our well-stocked woodpile, on the tiny corner of white paper which still protrudes, lit by the moonlight. That message is meant for me alone, and I won't risk losing it by rushing down there now. I settle on my old bed, and lie awake, waiting for long hours, until my parents' voices and movements fall silent, and I can sneak down through the house to snatch my message away.

17

Maxine

Recorded interview between Alexa Evans, freelance writer, and Maxine Gregory, subject of A LIFE OF LOSS (Falun Publishing International).

ALEXA: You say it was a good few years before Tara met Karl Gunn. What did she do in the meantime? If she was only fifteen when she lost the baby, I guess she would have been in the middle of her exams?

MAXINE: Tara missed out on those altogether. Her friends were all doing theirs while she getting ready to – well, I told you about all that. The stillbirth.

ALEXA: Didn't she do any retakes?

MAXINE: No, she couldn't face going back to school, what with all the gossip, so she took the next year off – worked in a local packing factory for a few months – and then, of course, we moved to Dorset. We got her in at the tech college there, and after a couple of years she landed a job on reception at the hospital.

ALEXA: At the same hospital where her daughter Lorna would be born – what, a decade or more later?

MAXINE: The very same. Tara was still working there when she fell pregnant.

ALEXA: And how did you like living in Dorset, Maxine? I mean, you said yourself that you're a Londoner through and through. Did you find it easy to adjust to the pace of seaside life?

MAXINE: I have to say, there were times when I missed the city. But it wasn't Barnet I missed – it was the old London of my childhood, and I knew that didn't really exist any more. Beaport was a nice little town, though. Not too big, not too small. We could walk to the beach if we wanted, and the supermarket was nearby too. There was a really good bus service.

ALEXA: Did you work?

MAXINE: Always. I had a lovely job in the local bakers for six or seven years, then, soon after it closed down, a big M&S opened near the bypass and I got a job there as a department manager. Baked goods, that was my department.

ALEXA: Were you surprised when Tara came home and told you she was expecting again?

MAXINE: Surprised? Shocked, more like, because there'd been no boyfriends – and I mean none at all – since we'd left all that business behind us in Barnet. She'd never talked about any lads at work, never been out on any dates or invited anyone home. Apart from that brief spell of trouble back in her early teens, Tara hadn't so much as shown an interest in boys. She'd been quiet as a mouse since we'd been in Beaport, and I thought perhaps she was just meant to be that way – on her own. Some people are, aren't they? I mean, she was thirty – a bit over-the-hill to start having babies.

(*pause*)

Anyway, first I knew about it, she announces that this fella, Karl, is coming to Sunday dinner, and could I please make a special effort to be nice for him! Well, I tried to press her for a bit more info – like what did he do for a living and where did they meet – but she wasn't having a bar of it, and told me to wait till Sunday, when I could ask him myself. She had me run ragged, cleaning the house from top to bottom and making two puddings, as if we was expecting royalty!

ALEXA: Ah, you must have been excited for her, though? Finally meeting someone – especially after everything she'd been through.

MAXINE: Oh, yes.

ALEXA: So, what were your first impressions of Karl Gunn?

MAXINE: (*pause*) Well, that morning Tara had been a nervous wreck, changing in and out of outfits, putting her hair up, then down, biting her nails to the quick – worse the nearer we got to midday. When the doorbell rang, she panicked and ran back upstairs, so I had to answer it and keep him talking for ten minutes while she got changed again. That's how I found out he was a junior doctor – I couldn't believe it!

ALEXA: What did he look like?

MAXINE: Tall, a bit on the skinny side for my liking. He was about her age, dark eyes and hair cut in a neat short-back-and-sides that I approved of. He was wearing a shirt and tie, which I thought showed a degree of respect. All in all, he was very presentable. Well spoken. Not from round those parts – I think he'd moved there for his job at the hospital.

ALEXA: Yes, that's right. I've got his details here.

MAXINE: Turns out he'd been to boarding school, would you believe, so there must've been a bit of money there too. I

174

know it's not nice to say, but I couldn't think what he'd want with Tara – she was so mousy and quiet, and, well, he was a bit of a catch, being a doctor an' all. He'd brought a little bunch of freesias for me, to say thank you for inviting him to lunch, and I remember the look of disappointment on Tara's face when she realised they weren't for her.

ALEXA: How did they seem together – Tara and Karl?

MAXINE: Awkward, to say the least. At lunch, I did most of the talking, all the while wondering why he looked so much like a fella heading for the gallows, and her barely uttering a word. Well, it all seemed a bit odd, if I'm honest, so I asked him, 'How long have you two been courting?' and he almost choked on his cabbage.

ALEXA: They *weren't* seeing each other?

MAXINE: Nope. He said, 'Sorry, Mrs Gregory – I don't know what Tara's told you, but she invited me here today saying she had something important to tell me.' I remember the way his Adam's apple moved slowly up and down his clean-shaven neck as he swallowed, and in hindsight I suppose he'd already guessed his fate.

ALEXA: His fate?

MAXINE: (*pause*) You know what I mean – that he'd been caught with his pants down. Well, at last, Tara found her voice. She said, 'Karl and me got together at the Spring Fundraiser, didn't we, Karl?' I tell you, he was white as a sheet. He put down his knife and fork and he started stammering. 'Tara, we've talked about this – we're *not* together. We'd both had too much to drink at that party, and it should never have happened.' Blah-blah-blah. He wasn't being unkind, as such, but I know it wasn't what Tara was hoping to hear.

ALEXA: What did Tara say?

MAXINE: Nothing. She just sat there, not a peep from her. So, I said, 'Are you married, Mr Gunn?' He opened his mouth to reply, and then seemed to think better of it and just nodded.

ALEXA: Tara had no idea? What happened then?

MAXINE: Then Tara said, 'But we're having a *baby*.' That was the first I'd heard of it – and, judging by the look on Karl Gunn's face, it was the first he'd heard of it too.

18

Eva

As February rolls on, heavy snowfall continues to gather in deep drifts across the land, and I find myself longing for springtime, when routes to the outside world open up, and escape from this place is imaginable. Valentine's Day comes and goes, and while my parents do their best to act normally I can tell they're as painfully aware of the date's significance as I am. Unlike previous years, there's no romantic gesture from Pappa to Mamma; no posy of flowers on the kitchen worktop, no breakfast in bed. It's not lost on me that I've even taken that from them.

It's now been a full fortnight since the boy left that note beneath the woodpile. When I fetched it, I found no words written on the little scrap of paper, only a solitary telephone number, and I tucked it away at the bottom of my wash bag, where it's remained ever since. I'm desperate to make the call, but he could be anyone, and, while I'm certain he doesn't mean me harm, my rational head urges caution. Soon I'll get my mobile phone back from Rosa and Lars, and then I can contact him without risk of my parents finding out. I just have to be patient. And let's face it, I've got good at employing patience over the past year or so.

Bella is nearly four months old now, and, while she can't be expected to talk yet, we have developed a communication, a language of sorts, and she's started to smile. Each morning, I set her down beside the sliding doors in the living room, to watch me through the glass as I fill the bird-feeders with suet pellets and sunflower hearts, cast aside the frozen disc of ice and replace it with a fresh top-up of lukewarm tap water. Together, from the warmth of the living room, we gaze out at the birds as they swoop in to feed, at bickering blackbirds and chittering finches, bobbing and diving and pecking in the snow. She understands I'm her mother, I'm sure, favouring me over Mamma when it comes to bedtime and baths, and in many ways I'm adjusting to my new role, as my love for her grows daily.

Today, we're off to the police station for an update with Chief Mac and Bern. As Mamma scrapes the windscreen clear, Pappa checks the house is secure while I strap Bella's carrier into the back seat of the car and slide in beside her. We pass the Brun cottage, where the lights are all on, and I glare at the back of Mamma's head, hating her for the clampdown she enforced after I ran off and left Bella on her own that day. I get it: my actions were unforgivable. But that's not Rosa's fault, is it? Or Lars's? When, after being sent away again several times, Rosa and Lars started phoning the house, Mamma unplugged the landline and stowed the handsets in the trunk of her car. Still, we've been flashlight messaging after dark, and I mean to see them in the next few days, one way or another. I've told Pappa how I feel, and he didn't disagree that my mother is overreacting, but at the same time he offered no solution. He's been so jumpy lately, not at all his normal steady self, and it worries me. I'm certain if he was OK he'd be wading in to defend me, to help me fight my corner.

At the station, Bern meets us in the car park, having seen us through the reception window as we arrived. He shakes Pappa's hand, and then Mamma's, and shifts self-consciously from one foot to the other, not knowing quite how to greet me.

'Hey, Bern,' I say, trying to mask how awkward I also feel. 'Give me a hand with Bella?'

I unclip her safety straps and lift her into his arms, grabbing her changing bag as I shut the car door. Bern rearranges Bella, so that her head is supported, and she blinks, astonished, up into his face.

'Oh, look! She likes you, Bern!' Mamma exclaims, and I jerk my chin towards the station door, mortified by her shameless attempts at matchmaking.

Inside, Chief Mac calls us straight in, and we sit around his desk. The pre-fab walls of Mac's office are covered in certificates and photographs, at least a dozen of them, taken of him with various officials or on team boat trips out on the lake. One wall is taken up with dented metal filing cabinets, and above Mac's head, behind the desk, is his father's old fishing rod, a family heirloom. I know this, because he told me that the last time we came in, when he was trying to put me at ease.

'Do you want her back?' Bern whispers from beside me, indicating Bella, whose little fingers are draped over his wrist.

I give him a sideways smile. 'Nah, you can keep her.'

He strokes the back of her hand, smiling.

'Right!' Chief Mac says, placing the thick wad of my file on the desk. 'First things first – how are you, Eva? Your mamma tells me you're hoping to get back to your studies next term? And how's this little bundle of joy doing?' He nods towards Bern. 'Looks like you've got yourself a babysitter if you want one!'

'I don't charge much,' Bern says, and Pappa tells him we might hold him to it.

I glance at the papers, just wanting this over with. 'I'm fine,' I reply. 'Getting better every day.'

'Bern says you've been on a few walks together lately. That's got to be a good thing, eh? Building up your stamina? There's nothing like a bit of mountain air to heal. And are you getting out much, apart from the walking?'

Mamma and Pappa exchange a glance, and I know they've been talking about me with Mac, and hate them for it.

'Not much. I mean, Rosa and Lars are only across the forest, but—'

'Actually, Mac,' Mamma interrupts, desperate as always to avoid a scene, 'we're going to have a little get-together to celebrate Eva's eighteenth next week. We'd love it if you and Berit, and of course you, Bern, would come along? Friday night, from sevenish.'

'A party?' Chief Mac replies, pushing his flat hands against the desk as though to steady himself. 'Wouldn't miss it for the world, would we, Bern?'

Trine from the front desk knocks, and enters with a tray of coffees, which she silently slides on to the desk, before shutting the door behind her. The mood shifts, as Mac passes out the mugs, indicates towards the sugar and milk, and opens my file.

'DNA results,' he says solidly, and my stomach tightens. 'Firstly, I'm glad to say that everyone we approached was happy to give a swab. However, now we've had the results in, Eva, the bad news – or good news, whichever way you look at it – is that none of our local men matches up with Bella.'

I look to Mamma and Pappa in turn, and it seems that, like me, they don't know how to react.

'I was really hopeful we'd get some answers,' Bern says.

The weight of silence hangs in the room for seconds on end.

'So, what now?' Pappa asks.

'Obviously we thought finding Bella's father might also lead us to finding the driver – the person responsible for your accident, Eva. But now, I think we have to turn our full attention to your stranger in the woods, Tobias.'

Again, that gut-clenching sensation. Why am I so fearful that he's clearly in the frame now? Why am I so certain he's not responsible for this?

'I'm not so sure,' I venture. 'I mean, I've seen him too, and he didn't look—'

'You don't *know* him, though, do you, Eva?' says Bern. 'You've said he *seems* harmless enough – but he's still a stranger, hanging around your house, and quite possibly – quite probably – the same guy Eric saw in the bar on the night of your accident.'

'I know . . .' I try, but I have nothing to add, nothing that I can articulate.

Mamma leans forward, propping her elbows on the edge of Mac's desk. 'You said no one else noticed him that night, Mac. Except for Eric?'

'Yes, but Foxy did say the bar was packed out. There was a big crowd in, so this lad could easily have gone unnoticed. If we could get a picture of him, Foxy might well be able to pick him out. Unfortunately we think the lad used the front entrance, because, like Eva, he doesn't appear on the CCTV at the back of the car park.'

'You said Margrete over the lake also reported something that night I chased him off, Mac?'

181

'That's right, Tobias,' Mac replies, turning a couple of pages in the file. 'You know we've got used to her reporting flashlights in the woods, out near your boathouse, over the years? We've never taken it too seriously – she's a bit of a worrier – and the few times we've checked it out in the past, it's only been the kids here, Eva and our two, doing no harm, down at the pontoon. But this time, she said she had a trespasser. A young white male, she said, hooded parka, short hair – could be the same man. It was late at night, and she only caught a brief glimpse from her window as he ran from the barn to the woods.'

The chief looks at me. 'Rest assured, we're treating this very seriously, Eva.'

Bern passes Bella back to me, then reaches into his inside pocket and brings out a scrap of paper, folded inside an evidence bag. He slides it into the centre of the table. Bella grizzles and shifts in my lap, as Pappa pulls the sealed note closer, and with a sick lurch I see my name and address written in neat block capitals. The writing style and pen matches that of the message the boy left for me beneath the woodpile, so there's no doubt this person is one and the same. *Say something*, my brain screams, but my mouth remains closed.

'Looks like he's been hiding out in Margrete's barn for a few days,' Bern says. 'There was a makeshift bed and evidence of recent use – food wrappers, cigarette stubs and so on – and this note, hidden in between the pages of a paperback.'

Mamma's pale eyes are fixed on the note. 'You think he's targeting Eva?' she asks. 'All these months, Mac – you think he's been here all this time?'

Mac purses his lips. 'Hard to say, Ingrid, but we don't think he's been using the barn for long. Margrete says her son moved his car out of there a fortnight ago, and there was nothing out of the ordinary then. If he has stuck around since the accident, I think he's been moving about. Or it's possible he went away for a few months after the accident, only returning when Eva was released from hospital in November.'

Mamma and Pappa stare at the evidence bag, processing their fear. I don't know what I'm meant to feel about this. The lad outside my window seemed so free of malice. Are my instincts completely off?

'What this does give us, Eva, is a very strong new line of enquiry.'

'How?' Mamma asks.

'Turn the paper over,' Mac says.

She does so, and there we see more jottings, detailing bus and train routes, fares and notes.

'Notice anything?' Bern asks. 'It's all in English – not Norwegian. And the book we found this in was a British edition too – *Never Let Me Go*.'

'I loved that book,' I murmur, although I'm not sure if I say it inside my head or out.

'Eva,' Mac says, closing the file and punctuating it with a thump of his closed fist, 'I think we're looking for an Englishman.'

As we leave the station, Mamma and I head into town with Bella as Pappa stays on to chat with Mac. I'm thinking about this new line of enquiry Mac mentioned, and just as we turn on to the high street I have a sudden jolt of recollection. I stop dead, staring in on the memory.

'Mamma?' I say, and she pauses a few steps on, turning back to me, squinting against the bright light of the sun. 'Do you remember the Englishman who stopped me on the forest path the year before last?'

'Um, not really,' she says, rummaging in her shoulder bag for her sunglasses. She jerks her head towards the hair salon, and we cross the road.

The memory of this encounter is suddenly so clear to me, I can't believe I'd ever forgotten it. 'Really?' I say. 'I was pretty shaken up about it at the time.'

'It was probably nothing,' Mamma replies. Her tone is casual, but I can't help noticing how the colour has drained from her skin.

'Mamma, you must remember it?' I insist. 'He was an Englishman, and he stopped me on my way home from the Bruns'. He knew my name.'

It's August, Friday of the first week of the new school term, and, as the day is warm and the sun still high in the sky, Rosa, Lars and I decide to take a detour on the way home, to dip our feet in Grønnfoss waterfall, a short walk from our forest. Mrs Larvik, our form tutor, handed out colas at the end of class – a rare treat – and we leave school in high spirits, drinking from our cans and chatting over each other. Lars is planning a party for his sixteenth birthday at the end of the month, and, as we walk, he and Rosa argue good-heartedly about who to invite and what music to play, and how they might convince Ann to let them hold it at theirs. Across the fields, wild fireweed is out in abundance, creating a pink haze over a landscape which was not so long ago a canvas of snow.

As we pass the Brun cottage to take the footpath to the waterfall, Lars looks back over his shoulder and halts. Out where the road narrows into dirt track, a car has stopped, and its driver appears to be looking in our direction.

'That car's been following us,' Lars says.

Rosa laughs and starts walking again. 'You've been watching too many films,' she replies.

'No, honestly – I noticed it earlier, outside school, because it's got a memorable number plate. See? 757575.'

The car is still sitting at the start of the dirt path, facing our way.

'I suppose it is a bit strange the way it's just parked up there,' I say. 'This road only goes to one of two places – yours and mine.'

The three of us continue to watch the car for a while, and when it starts to back up and turn around the way it had come we decide it was simply an out-of-towner who'd taken the wrong exit.

Later, when I say goodbye to my friends outside their cottage and take the forest trail home, I'm startled to spot a bright-shirted man walking towards me in the distance, his pale skin and clothing dappled by the sunlight which breaks through the trees above. He doesn't look like a walker; his clothes are too suburban for that, his walking boots too clean. Perhaps he's a visitor, a client of Pappa's? But no, my parents are both at work at this hour. As the distance between me and the man narrows, I remember the strange car and I begin to regret my slow thinking, and wish I'd turned to run back to the Brun house the moment I'd set eyes on him.

'Hi!' he says, as he approaches, and he waves one hand high in the air, I presume to signify that he is no danger.

Still, I am terrified.

'Eva, isn't it?' he says in English.

I stop, so that several metres still separate us, and nod cautiously.

'Thought so.' Now, he places his hands in his pockets. He looks delighted. 'I've just been up to your place, hoping to speak to your parents. You don't happen to know where they are, do you?'

'Er, no,' I reply, scrabbling for an answer, because I don't want to tell him they're out at work – that we are all alone together in these woods. 'They – they should be back any minute.' It

185

isn't true, of course, they'll be at least another hour but he doesn't know that.

He smiles again, broadly, and as the sunlight ripples through the canopy I can see the pink of his scalp shining through his thin, sandy hair. He isn't tall, but he's stocky with a small rounded belly, and an expression which suggests he doesn't realise he isn't handsome any more. His hands are now occupied, I notice, fiddling with a sturdy black camera, one eye on me, the other on the digital display. 'Don't suppose I could wait at your place, could I? Until they get home? I've come a really long way to speak to them.'

I look over my shoulder. I'm exactly halfway between my house and Rosa's. Is it better to run back to them, or forward to my own home, where I could barricade myself in until my parents return?

The man makes the decision for me.

'Look, I can see you're not sure, Eva. Don't worry, I'm not offended! You head on home, and I'll come back another time. Really! It's fine!' With that, he lifts the camera and fires off a burst of shots. The sound of the lens shutter echoes sharply through the quiet forest: ticker-ticker-ticker-ticker!

Adrenaline pumping, I pull my rucksack tight against my shoulder and run. I run past him, as fast as my legs will take me, all the way home until, with shaking hands, I turn the key in my front door and chain-lock it securely behind me. Seconds later, I'm on the phone to Rosa, breathlessly telling her what's just happened.

'Oh, my God, Eva. He sounds really creepy. Thank God—' She stops speaking, and I hear the rustle of her shifting on her bed to look out of the window. 'Jeez,' she hisses. 'You're never going to believe this. He's just knocked on our front door. I can see him now, out on our footpath. He's talking to Mamma.'

At the hair salon, we bump into Nettie booking in to have hers done too, and she manages to persuade my mother to leave Bella's carry seat with me, so I can get a lift home from her when I'm done. Mamma seems happy to head off, promising me she'll call Mac straight away, pulling out her phone before she's even out of the salon. While Sophie the hairdresser washes my hair, Nettie sits with Bella on her lap, cooing and sighing, and chatting to me over the rushing hiss of water, telling me what a beautiful baby I have. By the time I'm sitting in front of the mirrored wall beside Nettie, she's engaged the whole salon in her conversation, and Bella is being passed around, an expression of calm bemusement on her face.

'How are you doing, lovely?' Nettie asks as Sophie combs through my hair, pretending not to listen in. 'I'm glad to see you out of the house.'

I blink at my own reflection, as Sophie pulls the hair straight at the front, assessing the wonky shape of it. The shorn area behind my ear must be nearly six inches long now, still way shorter than the rest, causing the top layers to stick out at a clumsy angle. 'Cut it off,' I say, eyeing up Sophie's neat pixie cut. 'I want to go short.'

Sophie looks at me askance, and then shakes her head. 'You will look gaunt,' she says in her heavy French accent. 'Don' do it.'

I glance around the salon, at the model pictures stuck up on the walls, and say, 'How about a bob, then?' and Sophie agrees, yes, that would look *chic*, and Nettie puts her hand over her heart and releases a sigh of relief.

'She's right,' she whispers.

'Mamma won't let me see Rosa and Lars,' I tell Nettie, when she asks me what I've been up to lately. 'She still blames them for my accident, and she's so overprotective of me and Bella. It's suffocating.'

'Don't be too hard on her,' she replies, tapping the edge of my chair with her fingertips. She wears a single ring on the middle finger of her right hand, a large black polished moonstone, set in silver. 'I know she can come across as hard-nosed sometimes, but I've never met a mother more devoted in all my life.'

'Really?' I say, surprised to hear Nettie speak so frankly about my mother. 'What makes you say that?'

'The trouble with people these days,' she continues, 'is that they think having a baby is like getting a pet. But you know now, don't you, Eva? It's no picnic, is it? It's hard work, and sometimes you have to be ruthless and brave – like a lioness. Did you ever see those wildlife programmes, with lions in the wild, seeing off the hyenas who're after their cubs? She's like that, your mamma; she's fierce as a lioness.'

'But she doesn't always know best,' I complain. 'She thinks she does, but she doesn't. If she did, she'd let me see Rosa and Lars.'

'Ah, she'll come round. She and Ann had a fight, didn't they? I think it's Ann she's punishing, not the kids. You know Ann told your mamma she should blame *herself* for your accident, don't you? She was only sticking up for her own kids, but she more or less called Ingrid a bad mother.'

Sophie lets her impassive mask slip and suppresses a gasp. 'Ouch. If she say zat to me, I would ponch 'er on ze noz!' she says, and her thick accent has us all laughing, and it feels good to be talking about this unspoken row so openly, and for the first time.

'Well, let me tell you, Sophie,' Nettie says, drawing the hairdresser in closer, 'Ingrid is anything but a bad mother, and what Ann said must have hurt her. I think maybe if she had punched her on the noz it would've done them both some good, but instead they're caught up in all this bad feeling and it's poor old Eva here who's suffering the most.'

Sophie sucks air over her teeth and shakes her head.

'Maybe you could talk to her for me, Nettie?' I venture. 'She might listen to you. She's so stubborn – she blocks me every time I bring it up, and Pappa doesn't stand a chance!'

'You know you get your stubborn streak from her, don't you?' Nettie says, and she chuckles as I fold my arms grumpily across my chest.

I miss this. I try to think back to my primary school days when Nettie was around so often she almost lived with us, picking me up from school, chatting with me, feeding me, making me laugh in the hour or two before my parents arrived home. She's the closest I've got to a grandmother, and I feel ungrateful when I think how little I've bothered with her since hitting my teens, always in a rush to leave the table when she comes for Sunday lunch, and never taking her up on her offers to meet me in town for a coffee.

'Ah, I had glossy dark locks just like that when I was young,' Nettie says wistfully, patting down her own neatly coiled white hair and nodding towards my reflection.

I look up, realising Sophie has finished, as she sprays a light mist of lacquer over my neat new bob. It looks so dark and shiny, I daren't touch it for fear of ruining the effect.

'This,' Sophie says, angling a hand mirror so I can see the back, 'is classy. *Très chic!*'

I smile inwardly, feeling as though perhaps I look something close to passable for the first time in months.

'I'll be another ten minutes, lovely,' Nettie says as Sophie starts to unpin her long snowy hair, combing it through. 'Do you need to do anything in town while you're waiting for me to finish?'

Riding on a sudden wave of independence, I pay the receptionist, and, while Sophie gets to work on Nettie's blow-dry, I take Bella along the high street to buy some chocolates from Lapin's, and pop into the bank on my way back to her car. It's a beaten-up old Land Rover she's had running for over twenty years, and she's just getting in as I arrive, her hair now rolled back into its customary bun at the back of her head. I wonder why she bothers going to the salon, when she always emerges looking exactly the same as when she went in.

'Where to?' Nettie asks once Bella is strapped in the back. She regards me meaningfully, then starts the engine, indicating out on to the high street. 'Or do I even need to ask?'

Five minutes later, we pull up outside Lars and Rosa's cottage, and Nettie asks me if I want her to wait. It's only early afternoon, but already it's getting dark.

'No, thank you,' I reply, and, as my friends appear at the front door with their mother, I cling to Nettie and tell her I love her, and she looks so happy I fear she might shed a tear.

'Go on,' she scolds with a jerk of her head. 'And don't forget to tell your parents it was your idea, or they'll never let me near you again!'

With a jerky U-turn and a toot of her horn, Nettie drives away and I'm left cradling Bella's car seat, a bag of chocolate pralines, and twenty thousand krone in crisp notes nestled at the bottom of Bella's changing bag.

19

Maxine

Recorded interview between Alexa Evans, freelance writer, and Maxine Gregory, subject of A LIFE OF LOSS (Falun Publishing International).

ALEXA: Over the years there have been a lot of different theories circulating about Lorna's disappearance, haven't there?

MAXINE: A lot.

ALEXA: I was following the case myself at the time she was taken – I told you, I was a junior reporter back then? Did I mention I covered Dorset?

MAXINE: Really? You weren't one of those bloody vultures hanging around outside my house at all hours, were you?

ALEXA: (*laughs*) No – as I say, I was only a junior, straight out of A-levels. I did run a piece or two, though, in the follow-up. My boss let me cover some of the smaller articles and I've been interested in the case ever since. I think that's why Olivia – at the publishers – thought I'd be a good fit as your ghost writer.

MAXINE: Small world.

ALEXA: Karl Gunn was a prime suspect early on, wasn't he?

MAXINE: They always think the parents did it, don't they? One of the papers reported that he had 'considerable debts', so it didn't take long for the media to start hinting that he'd 'sold' Lorna to clear them. The 'debts' turned out to be student loans, from medical school – nothing major for someone on a doctor's salary, I'd think.

ALEXA: Yes, I remember reading that. The theory went that he'd arranged her abduction as part of an illegal adoption deal – that Lorna was being sold on to a childless couple elsewhere in the world. One of the papers reckoned she'd been trafficked to Norway, didn't they?

MAXINE: A porter at the hospital told the police he'd seen a doctor the night Lorna got snatched, talking to a woman in the corridor, in a foreign language. The porter only really noticed them because he was Swedish himself – recognised it was Norwegian they were talking in.

ALEXA: Did he hear what they were saying?

MAXINE: He said the woman was admiring the baby, stroking its cheek, and the doctor was holding the baby like it was his own – but the language thing didn't add up till they dug a bit deeper and found out Karl was half-Norwegian. You'd never've known it to talk to him. Sounded English as you and me.

ALEXA: Didn't they catch them on CCTV at all, so they could confirm it was him?

MAXINE: No, the security camera in that corridor was out of action that night. One of the nurses told me they thought whoever took Lorna had fixed it that way, so they could get away without being seen.

ALEXA: So, the whole thing really must have been premeditated – carefully planned out.

MAXINE: Must've been, 'cause whoever took her didn't leave a trace. It was like that baby just disappeared into thin air.

ALEXA: (*pause*) Now, this is a horrible question, but I have to ask it, Maxine – it must have been awful to read the speculation about paedophile networks. A lot of people seemed to think she'd been trafficked through a network of that kind, quite unrelated to Karl.

MAXINE: I can't even think about it, Alexa.

ALEXA: And – there was also a theory that – I'm sorry, because I really do know this is hard – that Tara may have killed the baby herself, suffering from some kind of post-natal mania or depression.

MAXINE: (*pause*) Disgusting, isn't it? Something like this happens, and in no time at all the gutter press starts flinging mud like that.

ALEXA: Apparently there were other CCTV black spots in the hospital, and Tara went off screen for over twenty minutes that night.

MAXINE: So, what? She was probably in the shower – or, you know, in the lav. I mean, what do they reckon she did with the baby, once she'd killed it? You can't just *vanish* a dead baby, can you? Not in a place like that. Anyway, Tara couldn't hurt a fly, I can tell you that much. She wasn't always right in the head, but—

ALEXA: What do you mean, not right in the head?

MAXINE: Oh, you know, since she lost that first baby – she was on the pills, wasn't she? Anti-depressants.

ALEXA: A lot of people take anti-depressants – a lot of people get depressed. It doesn't mean—

MAXINE: Yeah, but Tara was always a bit odd. I'd rather you didn't put it in the book, but between you and me, even as a child she was taken by strange moods – making awful stuff up – terrible lies – and refusing to speak for weeks on end, even running away once or twice. I mean, she killed herself in the end, didn't she, more or less? You'd have to be a bit, you know, touched, to run out into the road like that, wouldn't you?

ALEXA: The way Tara died was reported as a road accident – are you saying she *intended* to kill herself, Maxine?

MAXINE: I couldn't really say, but she was certainly in a right state that day – the day she was released from hospital – and it seemed to me the minute we got out through the front entrance she practically threw herself under that van. TV crew, it was, come to film us leaving the hospital, bloody vultures. And my poor Ray. He was parked in the car over the road, waiting to give us a lift home – he had to witness the whole thing. Can you imagine? If she *did* mean to do it, it was a terrible, selfish thing to do.

ALEXA: I . . .

(*pause*)

But surely it's possible Tara was beside herself with grief, not concentrating – that when she stepped into the road it really was just an awful accident? If she'd suffered from depression for a long time, the trauma she was going through, losing Lorna, might have affected her judgment?

MAXINE: Per'aps. Anyway, my main point is, she might have been a bit 'depressed' as you put it, but I know she would never have touched a hair on that baby's head. So, the police were barking up the wrong tree with that theory.

ALEXA: You and Ray even had the finger pointed at you, didn't you, Maxine?

MAXINE: (*pause*) That was a dreadful time. Ray had only just arrived the week before – he was moving down to Beaport to stay with us for a while, because his GP thought the sea air might be better for his lungs.

ALEXA: What was wrong with his lungs?

MAXINE: Smoker. He'd been on forty a day since his teens – just like our old dad.

ALEXA: How long was it since he'd last lived with you?

MAXINE: Oh, fifteen or sixteen years – we hadn't seen much of him since before all that bother with Tara when she was younger.

ALEXA: (*pause*) And how did Tara feel about Ray moving in? Being a new mother, you'd have thought she might have wanted a bit of space.

MAXINE: Not at all. I knew she'd be happy about it once she got used to the idea.

ALEXA: (*pause*) And what about Karl – what was the arrangement there?

MAXINE: Right from the start, Karl made it clear that him and Tara would never work out. He agreed to support her financially and to 'be involved', but that was it. When Ray heard about everything, he offered to move in and lend a hand – he was always good with kids.

ALEXA: It's just – well, one of these news articles from the time quoted a member of staff from the maternity ward, who said that 'Tara seemed very distressed that her uncle was moving back into the family home'. The piece goes on to say that Ray had also been questioned by the police in regard to Lorna's disappearance, but had for the time being been ruled out of the investigation.

MAXINE: Of course he was ruled out! That poor man had barely unpacked his bags when that baby went missing! The police – quite rightly – worked out that the nurse or whatever she was, was talking bullshit. *Excuse* my French.

ALEXA: (*pause*) So, Tara *wasn't* distressed about Ray moving in?

MAXINE: No. She was not.

ALEXA: Maxine, do you believe Lorna is still alive?

MAXINE: I do. I really do – I can feel it. A grandmother knows these things. That's why I'm doing this book, Alexa. Because I still believe that one day we might bring my beautiful granddaughter home.

20

Eva

Today, it is my eighteenth birthday, and Mamma, Pappa and Nettie are downstairs preparing food for tonight's celebrations. My parents whisked Bella away this morning, to give me a break, and I'm watching the sun come up behind the curtains, allowing my mind to drift and travel over recent events. Since seeing Rosa and Lars last week, I feel as though a new door has cracked open, as though perhaps normal life here in the valley might resume after all. There's still no news on the driver, but Mamma says she's passed my description of the Englishman to Mac, and he's taking it seriously. I'm hoping it could be an important lead. I'm leaving nothing to chance, though, and am still suspicious of my parents, taking certain precautions – starting to gain control of my life in all sorts of ways. My hidden cash store has grown, as I've now made two large withdrawals from my savings account, and I plan to do the same every week from now until the account is clear. If things here take a bad turn again, I want to be in control of my destiny, to be able to escape if the need or desire takes me. To where, I don't know, but to *be able to* is the vital thing; knowing I can is as important as the act itself.

The other change is that I now also have possession of my old secret phone. That day Nettie dropped me at the Bruns, Rosa handed it to me when we got to her bedroom, together with a two hundred krone phone voucher, and I felt my world expand. But the good feeling was short-lived, because, when I got back to my own room that night and went to apply the credit, I found I couldn't remember my handset's passcode.

The phone has been stashed at the back of my sweater drawer ever since, and now, like a birthday present from the gods, the PIN number appears to me, clear and sharp. In a flash, I leap up to locate the handset, plugging it in at my bedside and cursing its lack of speed as I wait for the charging bars to appear. Once it pings into life and I've loaded the credit, I get back into bed, switch the volume to mute and scroll through the phone, looking for clues to my recent past.

In the texts folder, the only messages are between me and Rosa and Lars, the last one from my Sent folder, saying I'd be at their place in ten minutes – delivered at seven thirty-two p.m. on that Valentine's night. On the home screen, there are a number of apps, including YouTube, Snapchat, Instagram and Facebook, all of which my parents would be horrified to see. I click on the YouTube app and am reminded of the hours my friends and I would waste watching the kinds of funny videos my parents had never seen but would describe as garbage. The Snapchat and Instagram accounts appear to be inactive – but when I click through to Facebook I'm surprised to see I have a live account, and posted on my timeline I find dozens of well-wishing messages from school friends and acquaintances, all sent soon after my well-documented car crash. I scan them, moved by the strength of feeling I see there, and then my heart rate accelerates, as I notice the red alert button in the top right-hand corner, telling me I have messages. I click on the icon and I find unread messages dating back to November, when I was first released from hospital, all of them from the same person.

It's him. The profile image is unmistakably that of the boy from the forest; the boy from the bar. And his name is Peter Gregory. *P*.

The latest message, dated yesterday, reads: *Call me. I have to go back to England on Friday – please call or message me before then!*

Without hesitation, I type out a response: *What do you want?*

In the few seconds it takes me to throw back my covers and pull on my dressing gown, an alert arrives onscreen.

Peter: *To meet again.*

Again? We've met before? I hesitate, foreboding looming darkly; if I continue this conversation, there is no way of knowing where it might lead me. I tap out my reply.

Me: *Why?*

Peter: *Seriously? We can't leave it like this, can we? After what I told you that night – you must want to know more? There's so much you don't know.*

Suddenly, I'm certain it was him driving, him beside me in the front of that truck. He'd said something to me – something shocking – something that's still, even now, just out of my grasp . . .

Peter: *Are you still there?*

Is he a monster, as Mamma and Pappa and Mac and Bern all think?

Peter: *Please, Eva? I can't stand to go without seeing you again. I'm so sorry about what happened that night – will you just let me explain?*

Me: *Where?*

Peter: *Tonight, at the boathouse near yours.*

Me: *I can't. We're having a party for my birthday. I can't come tonight.*

A pause; a few horrible seconds where I think perhaps, he's given up on me.

Peter: *I'll be there at midnight. It's up to you.*

I'm back on the quiet road between Foxy Jack's and the main highway, and it must be late because there's no other traffic, either up ahead or behind. I'm in the passenger seat, as always, and I don't know the vehicle; I don't recognise the sherbet lemon scent of it or the black driving gloves that balance on the dashboard and land on my lap as we steer sharply left. 'Ice,' the driver says distractedly in English, and it's his voice again, and although I can't see him I know that I trust him. He's about my age, and his vibe is good, and I laugh, simply because I'm drunk, before asking, 'Don't they have ice where you come from?' He laughs too and reaches across to turn up the heating. His hand brushes my knee, and suddenly Creepy Gurt is in my head, and I wonder if they're all the same – men – are they all just the same, beneath the surface? I think of the way Foxy leered at me from behind the bar as I left, and the filthy way he spoke to me, and for the first time that evening it occurs to me that I could be in real danger, that I may have just made the biggest mistake of my life, climbing into this truck with a complete stranger. 'Who are you, really?' I ask him, and the vehicle swerves again, and although I still can't see his face I realise with a lurch that he's struggling to keep control on the ice. He tells me then, but his words are lost, because the last thing I remember is those amber eyes on the road ahead, and then nothing. Nothing but white.

By nine o'clock the house is full, Mamma and Pappa having invited every neighbour and shopkeeper they've bumped into in the fortnight since they decided to throw this party for my eighteenth. They're compensating for the fact that, with the exception of the Bruns, I've said they're not to invite any of my old school friends, who I haven't seen in over a year. Pappa's gone overboard decorating the place with hundreds of tiny white fairy lights he picked up at the hardware store this week, and in the black of the winter forest they are mesmerising. There are metres and metres of them, strung all the way from the gated entrance to the front door, garlanded throughout the house, and snaking up and over the branches and shrubs of the back garden so that the place looks like a fairy palace. I feel embarrassed about the pile of presents on the sideboard, which grows every time a new visitor arrives, while at the same time, I wonder what people have chosen for me, now that I'm officially an adult. I scan the room as the volume of chatter and music rises. Chief Mac and his wife Berit were the first to arrive, giving a lift to old Mrs Halvorsen from the bakery and her next-door neighbour who was widowed late last year, and the four of them sit around the kitchen table on the upright chairs. I can tell that Mac is now itching to get up and join the men on the far side of the room, where the drinks are flowing faster. There's Sophie from the salon too, and the girl who sweeps up for her, leaning up against the fridge in conversation with postman Jonas. Margrete from the farm and her son Geir have popped in, and I'm hoping he didn't mention the party to Foxy or Gurt, who he regularly goes

201

hunting with down-country. I can tell from their gestures that Pappa is comparing fishing stories with Geir, and it's good to see him smiling again. He's trimmed his beard a little for the occasion and put on his smart tan cords and his best *lusekofte* waistcoat, and he looks like a handsome woodcutter, a man of the forest. Mamma has her fair hair curled and piled high upon her head, and she's wearing my favourite of all her outfits, a flowing red linen dress which almost reaches her ankles and makes her stand out in the room like some pale and mystical woodland creature. If only I could forget the events of this past year; if only I could let my residual love for them blossom to its full strength, and return us to the way we were before. Mamma glances across at me, as though hearing my thoughts, and she smiles gently, pride in her eyes, before she's torn away again, diverted by one of our guests.

Some of her colleagues are here too, with their partners and children, and right now I'm grateful to the younger ones for the attention they're showering on Bella, giving me the perfect excuse not to interact with the adults as I sit cross-legged on the mat beside the fire, 'entertaining' them. It strikes me how wonderfully uncomplicated small children are. These young-sters have no doubt heard about my accident, but their interest will have been fleeting, lacking in that analytical curiosity everyone else seems to possess. From here, I can see Nettie circulating with drinks and nibbles, and when the doorbell goes again she sets down her tray and bustles across the room, out into the hall. Seconds later, she returns, with not only Rosa and Lars, but Ann too. Nettie has Ann by the hand and she waves to Mamma, beckoning her over, and after just a few words the two women are embracing. I abandon the children and rush to be with my friends, foisting Bella on a delighted Nettie, and allowing myself to be enfolded in Lars' and Rosa's hugs.

'Where's Bern?' I ask, knowing that their cousin had planned to arrive with them.

'Oooh, where's Bern?' Lars mimics, and I thump him lightly.

'He thought he saw a light in the woods, so he's just checking it out,' Rosa replies, 'Ever the policeman.' She taps the breast pocket of her coat, code to tell me she's got cigarettes.

As though no time has passed at all, we disappear through the growing wall of people, surreptitiously fixing ourselves Cokes with a decent dash of rum from Lars's pocket, and, grabbing my coat, we head outside to smoke beneath the snow-laden trees at the bottom of the garden.

'What about Mamma and Ingrid?' Lars says, taking the rum from his pocket and topping up our glasses. 'Friends again, just like that.'

'Yeah,' Rosa scoffs. 'Took them long enough. It was Nettie, you know? I think she had a word with Ingrid first, then she came round to ours last night and told Mamma that Ingrid wanted to bury the hatchet.'

'Good old Nettie,' I sigh, exhaling smoke and feeling instantly light-headed. I stomp the half-finished stub into the ground. 'I don't think I like smoking any more,' I say. 'Since the accident.'

Rosa takes another drag. 'I once read about this bloke who had a bump on the head and lost his sense of taste. Or was it smell? Anyway, it changed something in his brain.'

'There was that other one who lost his – what d'you call it?' Lars says. 'Empathy. He was a kind of psychopath after his brain got injured – not like a serial killer or anything, more like he didn't care what people thought or how they felt. It was creepy.'

'Mine's not like that,' I say, instantly paranoid that my friends think I'm damaged in some irreparable way.

'Of course not, silly,' Rosa says, grabbing an arm around me. 'You just can't remember much, can you?'

Through the glass doors, I see Bern in the living room, clearly searching for me, looking over heads, a gift in his hands.

'Oh, there he is,' Lars says. 'You know he's smitten, don't you, Eva?'

'No, he's not,' I say, as nerves dance in my stomach. 'Back in a sec, OK?'

Rosa wolf-whistles as I sprint across the garden towards the house. Bern spots me through the glass, and I return his pleased wide smile, noticing he now has Bella in his arms.

'Ha,' I say as I step inside, kicking off my boots and feeling the warmth of the house turning my cheeks rosy. 'Did Nettie palm her off on you?'

Bern sweeps his free arm around me in a warm embrace, kissing me on the cheek with a new confidence.

'No, it was Ingrid. I think your mamma's taken a shine to me – for you, I mean.'

I blush and follow Bern as he leads me to a space on the sofa, where he's left his gift.

'Here,' he says, wedging Bella between us. 'Happy birthday.'

Inside the bright yellow tissue paper is a shoe box, containing a pair of size 37 walking boots. Good ones.

'I thought about getting you a necklace or a pair of earrings,' he says, taking my ankle in his hand as he slips a boot on to one foot and then the other, lacing them up and nodding with approval. 'But I decided to be selfish and get you something we could both enjoy.'

I laugh, more pleased with this gift than I can begin to express.

'Will you, Eva Olsen,' he says ceremoniously, 'go walking with me on a regular basis?'

'I will,' I whisper, kissing Bella's head, my eyes fixed on Bern's face.

At the centre of the room, Pappa stands on a chair and chinks a spoon on the side of a glass.

'Everyone!' he calls, reducing the room to a low babble. 'I promised Eva there'd be no speeches, so all I'm going to say is this: there's cake on the kitchen counter – and happy birthday – to Eva!'

'To Eva!' the crowd choruses, and everyone raises a glass, and the party continues, and I'm relieved he kept it short.

Beside me on the sofa, I feel the warmth of Bella's little body as her fingers work at the fabric of my trousers, and I'm jolted by the thought that perhaps I've got everything wrong. I think about this morning's message from 'Peter' and I realise how insane it would be to go and meet him tonight, to put myself at risk like that. I have so much to lose. I'm not going anywhere, am I? If I were to run now, I'd be leaving all this behind. Mamma and Ann have reconciled; Rosa and Lars are back in my life. Bella is surrounded by all these people who love her, and now, here is Bern, showing me such tenderness and care that I can't even start to imagine life without him – without them all.

'Where are Rosa and Lars?' I ask, suddenly aware that they've missed out on Pappa's toast. I pass Bella back to Bern and ask him to fetch me a piece of cake as I head for the back door again, and peer out to see them unmoved, down at the end of the garden in the shadows where I left them. Still in my coat, I pass through the glass doors and jog over the snow-crisped grass to join them. But they have their backs to me, and I realise they're involved in a heated argument. I halt several feet away, not knowing whether to alert them to my presence or to retreat back to the house.

205

'But she doesn't remember a thing. Why rock the boat, Lars? If you tell her now it could ruin everything – for all of us.' Rosa is waving her hands around, the way she does when she's agitated. Smoke billows, and I hear her take a deep drag on her cigarette.

'How?' Lars asks.

'Because it would change things – just like I always said it would! You're drunk. You wouldn't even suggest it if you were sober!'

'I've been thinking about it for ages – not just tonight, Rosa! It's not up to you to say what people should or shouldn't know about their own lives. You're not God!'

'Oh, fuck off, Lars!' she hisses.

'No, you fuck off,' he retorts, and I almost laugh, because this is so like them, so much the Rosa and Lars I know.

'You won't even let me tell her who we'd set her up with that night—'

Now, I step out of the shadows. 'When?' I call over. 'Are you talking about Valentine's night?'

They both spin round, caught out.

'Yes,' Lars says, as Rosa replies a firm, 'No.'

'Who was I meant to meet in the bar, Lars?' I ask, my voice rising.

The whites of his eyes are bright, reflecting the shimmer of the fairy lights strung all around us. He glances towards the house, its glass wall a showcase to the crowd of guests inside.

'*Lars,*' Rosa warns him.

But he won't be silenced. 'It was Bern,' Lars says. 'You were meant to be meeting Bern.'

Across the garden, through the glass doors to the house I see Bern, chatting with Mamma and Pappa, Bella still in his arms. I think of the way he is with her, with me, and an image lights up in my mind, of Bern's figure, standing just outside the pink balloon-festooned doorway to Foxy Jack's bar that night, his gaze on me for only seconds, before he disappears into the darkness.

My pulse is racing, and I blink at my friends, watching Rosa's face shift in anger at Lars as he holds his hands up as though to ask, *what's the big deal*? Pulling my phone from my pocket, I check the time – eleven forty-eight – and, with one last glance at them, I turn and run.

I sprint through the garden in the darkness, along the fairy-lit side of the house, moving as fast as I can, to get away from them all. Is no one being honest with me? Can no one be trusted? Not even Rosa and Lars? Not Bern? Out through the gate I go, heading into the darkness, with only the light from my phone to guide me, moving too fast to question what it is I'm about to do, the risk I'm about to take. I cut across the forest path and jog down towards the pontoon, overhanging branches snagging at my coat, the vibrations of my thudding boots dislodging clumps of snow which fall like missiles from above. At the boathouse, I almost collapse with exhaustion, gasping and casting around for signs of Peter, my stranger, but there is none.

I'm panting, folding over, hands on my knees as I catch my breath. What the hell am I doing here? I must be insane.

In the darkness beyond the wooden walls, the snap of a fallen branch alerts me to the fact that I'm not alone, and drawing breath, I prepare to flee again, to cry out for help. But before I can utter a sound a hand clamps across my mouth and I'm pulled into the shadows of the boathouse, held firm by invisible arms.

'Eva,' his voice whispers, close up against my ear. 'It's me – *Peter*. Please don't scream. *Please?* If you do, they'll catch me, and it'll be the end. They'll put me inside. OK?'

I have a choice: I can scream and run back into the arms of known liars and cheats. Or I can trust this stranger, who may or may not be a rapist and a coward. Heart thumping, I nod slowly, and, true to his word, he loosens his grip and I step away, turning to look, for the first time, directly into his eyes.

For long seconds, all time stands still in the darkness, only the merest hint of light bouncing off the lake's surface from the farmhouse across the way, throwing a watery sheen over the boy's skin.

'I know you,' I say, replying in English, my voice low and calm. 'I *know* you.'

He nods, slowly, cautiously.

'You were driving that night?'

Again, he nods.

'Who are you?' I ask.

He hesitates, never looking away, before answering, 'You really don't remember? You don't remember what I told you that night – before we crashed?'

'No.' Even as I say it, fragments float in, resurrected by the familiar sound of his voice.

Peter reaches inside his jacket and brings out a folded newspaper cutting, which he hands to me. Turning the torch of my phone on it, I read the headline, recognising it as an exact match for the one I spied in my mother's secret box: *No More Clues in Baby Lorna Hunt.*

'It's not your birthday today,' he says. 'Your birthday was a month ago.'

I don't understand; he's speaking in riddles. 'What is this?' I demand, fear and impatience rising in me.

He points to the word *Lorna*. 'This,' he says, 'is you.'

'Lorna,' I read aloud. 'Lorna?'

'And this,' he continues, pointing to the small boy in the photograph, captioned *Peter and grandmother Maxine*, 'is me.'

From across the forest, I hear Bern's voice booming. 'Eva!' he calls out, the word echoing through the trees. Rosa and Lars must have alerted him. 'Eeee-va!'

'I don't know what to say,' I gasp, and Peter clutches my sleeve, his eyes wide and terrified.

'Eva, I'm your brother.'

I've heard these words before, I now realise with absolute clarity. I heard these words from the driver of that truck on Valentine's night, right before the white fox stepped out into the snowy road before us; right before everything went blank.

'Do you understand, Eva?' Peter's words bring me back to the moment with a jolt. 'Not just your brother – I'm your twin. Those people who call themselves your parents – Tobias and Ingrid? They're impostors. I don't know how they got you or why, but they're lying to you. Your mother – she said she'd kill me if she saw me again – she threatened to shoot me.'

'Eva!' Bern's voice is closer, and now it seems he has been joined by my parents too, because the cacophony of voices and calls is growing stronger and closer.

'You spoke to her?'

'When I told her I knew she'd abducted you in England, she asked me which paper I was working for – but I didn't even get a chance to say who I really was, because she pulled a rifle on me and told me to get off her property before she put a bullet in my head.'

'She said that? She said she'd shoot you?'

'I swear.'

I gasp at the sound of heavy feet crashing through the undergrowth.

'You have to go,' I tell Peter. 'Bern's a policeman – he'll have you locked up in a heartbeat.'

'You'll call me?' Peter asks, the urgency in his voice heartbreaking. 'I fly back to London tomorrow. You'll call me?'

'I'll call you,' I promise, and then he's gone; vanished.

Seconds later, what little light there is in the boathouse is swallowed up by the ominous figures of Bern, Mamma and Pappa, a three-strong posse to take me back home. I step out of my own accord, raising a hand to halt my parents' questions, as wearily, I trudge back home.

'You scared the life out of us!' Bern says, falling in step with me as I walk along the path, a few feet ahead of my parents. His gloved hand gently rubs my rigid shoulder. 'Rosa said you just took off. That you ran off into the woods without a word. What happened?'

'Nothing,' I reply, coming up with an answer I know will shut him up. 'I just got overwhelmed.'

The lights of the house are now in view, and, passing through our front gate, flanked by Bern, Mamma and Pappa, I feel more trapped than ever before, more even than I did during those weeks spent locked away in my family attic. Inside my pocket, my fingers run across a corner of Peter's old news article, and I think of the web of lies that grows daily in my life, stretching ever wider, wrapping itself around everything I hold true. Is Bern responsible for Bella? Could this outwardly gentle man, someone I've come to care about deeply, be the monster in the story of her creation? As I tramp up the stairs, leaving the party to carry on without me, I allow my mind to speak the words my lips cannot: if what Peter says is true, I have a brother. I have a *twin* brother.

It seems there is nothing I can be certain of any longer, except this: I have to get away.

PART THREE

21

Maxine

Recorded interview between Alexa Evans, freelance writer, and Maxine Gregory, subject of A LIFE OF LOSS (Falun Publishing International).

ALEXA: You received a lot of criticism about that first tabloid interview, didn't you, Maxine? It was less than a week after Baby Lorna had gone missing.

MAXINE: (*silence*)

ALEXA: How did Karl and Tara respond to it?

MAXINE: Karl was furious. Tara was still in hospital and I was there by her bedside as per usual, and I'll never forget how he came round shooting his mouth off, waving that newspaper in my face – accusing me of making a quick buck.

ALEXA: You *did* receive a payment from *The Sun*, didn't you?

MAXINE: Well, yes, but I wasn't going to just keep it for myself – Tara was going to need all the help she could get, and there was Ray to think about too, without any work . . .

ALEXA: What did Karl say to you?

MAXINE: He called me a leech – can you believe it? I told him, 'You men think you can go around sticking it in whoever takes your fancy, and not take the responsibility when it all goes belly-up?' I asked him how else we were meant to afford nappies and formula!

ALEXA: How did he take that?

MAXINE: He told me he *was* going to take responsibility – that before Lorna disappeared Tara had agreed to give him sole custody – that the legal papers were already being drawn up. I asked Tara if it was true, and she didn't say a bloody word, just sat there with her hands over her face.

ALEXA: She didn't deny it?

MAXINE: Well, no. But Ray stepped in then, and told Karl that when we got Lorna back she wasn't going anywhere. He said Tara wasn't fit to make that kind of decision on her own, that we'd fight it all the way – that the courts would favour us, for sure. She'd be staying right there with us, with her *real* family.

ALEXA: Was that the first time Karl and Ray had met?

MAXINE: Yes, and you should've seen the look on Karl's face. It was like he *hated* Ray, and I thought, what's that girl been saying? What poison has she been dripping in his ear?

ALEXA: What do you *think* she'd been telling him?

MAXINE: Oh, God knows. Karl was livid, at any rate. 'And what about Peter?' he yelled. 'He still needs a father!'

ALEXA: Of course, the joy of Peter's arrival must have been completely overshadowed by the disappearance of his twin. He was in a different room when Lorna was taken, wasn't he?

MAXINE: He had a touch of jaundice, so the doctors kept him under the lamps for a couple of days, under nurse supervision until he was OK to return to Tara's room.

ALEXA: What happened next, with Ray and Karl?

MAXINE: When Karl wouldn't back down, Ray squared up to him, and said, 'You think the courts would give *you* custody? You won't even get access, mate.' Karl lost it then – he punched Ray hard in the face, sent him flying. Split his lip, he did. One of the other doctors had to ask him to leave.

ALEXA: Karl *punched* Ray?

MAXINE: He did. Mind you, it was the best thing that could've happened, really, 'cause we reported Karl to the police.

ALEXA: Why was that a good thing?

MAXINE: Well, the police went to Karl's flat that evening and he was charged with assault. If he ended up with a criminal record, we'd have the upper hand, wouldn't we – if he was trying to take the baby off us? His job was on the line too, what with him being a doctor in that very hospital. I think maybe Ray pushed his buttons with that in mind. He was smart, our Ray.

(*pause*)

But it didn't really matter in the end, because they gave us custody without a fight.

ALEXA: Oh, hang on, we're jumping ahead a bit. What happened next?

MAXINE: The next day Karl came back to the maternity ward for Tara's final discharge – she wanted him there – and, well, the rest is history. She was knocked down in the road the second we set foot out of the place. I'll never get over seeing that. Killed by the press, God rest her soul. Just like Princess Diana.

ALEXA: You must have been heartbroken, Maxine.

MAXINE: I was.

ALEXA: And Karl? He must have been upset too? I know they weren't together, but she was the mother of his children, and they'd clearly been working together to sort out custody, and so on.

MAXINE: Ha! He was nothing but a coward, when it came down to it.

ALEXA: Was he?

MAXINE: Yes! Didn't stick around to face the music, did he? That very same night he took off to Beaport Bay and drowned himself.

22

Eva

By morning, I'm packed and ready to go.

With my parents distracted with the task of clearing up after last night's party, I convince Pappa that Bella and I are meeting Bern in town, and I ask him to drop us a little way down from Foxy's bar, on his way to the recycling bank. When you have a baby, I've learned, it's hard to go anywhere without a big bag of stuff, and today this works in my favour, as Pappa doesn't even question the full rucksack I'm carrying. He thinks it's full of nappies and muslin cloths; I know it's stuffed with clothes and cash.

'Have a nice time,' he tells me as I unstrap Bella from the back seat, and he reaches a hand out through the car window as we walk away. 'Look after that little poppet!'

As he drives off, I dismiss another text from Rosa, asking me why I'm not returning her calls. Taking a deep breath, I start to walk in the opposite direction from town, my breath billowing white clouds into the icy air, as I go in search of the last person on earth I want to ask a favour of.

Gurt's orange pickup is parked out the back, and when I see him at the top of his ladder, clearing out the gutters, I'm relieved I don't have to go knocking for him, when there's a chance I could bump into Foxy too. The car park is littered with rubbish, and one of the bins is on its side, knocked over by a fox or the wind, exaggerating the usual grubbiness of the place.

'Alright, Gurt?' I call, doing everything in my power to sound calm and controlled.

He turns his head slowly, looking down at me on the path below, Bella in my arms. Without a word, he descends, in no particular rush, until he's standing before me, oily hands planted on the hips of his boiler suit.

'You?' he says simply.

I shift Bella's weight, an excuse to break eye contact with him. 'Yep, me.'

'Still think I did it?' he asks with an uneasy smirk.

'No,' I reply. 'I know you didn't.'

He waits.

'I'm sorry,' I say. 'I don't know what else to say, Gurt. I got confused. I really am sorry, you know?' And now, I tap my head, and this seems to do the trick because his smirk turns into something altogether more friendly. 'I heard you're getting done for dealing,' I add, trying to keep the conversation going. 'I'm sorry if I caused that too.'

He puffs his chest a little, shifts from one foot to the other. 'Just a caution, solicitor reckons. First offence.' He laughs now, a short bark. 'That they know of!'

'Listen,' I say, lowering my voice, knowing he'd like to think I'm taking him into my confidence, 'how'd you like to earn some cash? I don't suppose you've got much work on at the moment.'

'How much cash?' he asks, not missing a beat. This is why I thought of Gurt – not because he's trustworthy, but because he's skint, and he can drive, and there's a good chance he'll keep quiet for the right price.

'Two thousand krone. I need a lift – it'll take most of the day – and you're not allowed to breathe a word about it to anyone.'

He raises an eyebrow. 'Two thousand? Where to?'

'I can't tell you till you agree. And we'd have to leave right away.' My pulse is racing as I wait for his reply, and he makes a chin-rubbing meal of mulling it over. 'I'd pay your petrol on top,' I add.

Moments later we're on the road, heading first for Nettie's house, where I tell Gurt to park some way up the street, so she doesn't see who brought me.

'Eva!' she says when she comes to the door, instantly opening her arms to me. 'Come in out of the cold.'

'I can't stay, Nettie,' I tell her, stepping into the front room of her little suburban house. 'But I do need your help. Can I trust you?'

Without a word, she takes Bella from me, and watches as I remove a small Peter Rabbit bag from my rucksack and place it on the seat of her armchair.

'There are enough nappies and milk there to last for today at least, but you'll need to pick up some more tomorrow. Oh, you'll want money for that—'

Nettie waves my cash away, impatient for me to explain. 'What's this all about, Eva?' she asks, her dark eyes studying me carefully.

'Mamma and Pappa – they've been lying to me. For years.' I wait for her shocked response, but it doesn't come. 'They're not really my parents, Nettie.'

'And what makes you say that?' she asks calmly, and I guess she must be thinking this is all down to my head injury, that I'm getting confused again, that I'm still unwell. I mean, the accusation is so far-fetched, who wouldn't think it? 'Did they tell you that?'

'No! I – someone else did – someone,' I reply, cautioning myself to not give too much away, 'someone from England. He says I was abducted – that Mamma's not my mother. And Pappa's not my real father.'

'That's not true,' Nettie objects, but I don't have the time to argue this out with her, to risk not getting away. How can I persuade her not to go straight to my parents?

'You have to help me, Nettie. You're the only person I can turn to – the only person I really trust! Promise me you'll look after Bella? If you can just wait until this evening before telling them, it'll give me a chance to go looking for some real answers.' I gather up my rucksack, refastening the catch.

'But where are you going, lovely?' Now, she looks scared, and she reaches out a hand to grab my wrist. Her fingers are silvery with age, but her grip is firm.

'I won't be long – maybe just a few days. But I have to find out more, Nettie. I have to know where I come from. And my parents, they're never going to tell me the truth, are they? That much I do know.'

Without waiting for her reply, I kiss her on the cheek, then Bella, and I pull the door closed behind me as I jog back down the street to Gurt's waiting truck, forcibly swallowing the anguish I feel at leaving Bella behind. I can't cry now; I have to hold it together, for her sake, as much as mine.

I count out a thousand krone and press the notes into Gurt's palm. 'You'll get the other half when we arrive.'

'Where are we going?' he asks as he drives out towards the highway.

'Bergen airport,' I reply, and then I close my eyes, and we drive in silence for the rest of the five-hour journey.

23

Maxine

Recorded interview between Alexa Evans, freelance writer, and Maxine Gregory, subject of A LIFE OF LOSS (Falun Publishing International).

MAXINE: When it happened, the press got wind of Karl's suicide before the police had a chance to tell us themselves. The cameras were outside before I was even up and dressed – I think some of them had been there all night, camped out hoping to get a free scoop on our grief after Tara's death.

ALEXA: The police called at your house to tell you about Karl, did they?

MAXINE: It was early, and I was still in my dressing gown, putting the kettle on for me and Ray. We'd hardly slept a wink, with Peter keeping us up most of the night, crying and wanting his bottle. I could already hear the racket of reporters out the front, and when I peeked through the curtains I saw there were even more of them than before.

And then I saw the headlights of the police car pulling up outside, and all the cameramen shifting out of the road to let them through. Two officers came to the door, and their faces were set so grim, I had a terrible feeling. What now? I thought.

ALEXA: And what did the police say to you?

MAXINE: I opened the door and the older copper put his arm across the doorframe, to block me from the cameras. It felt like something from a film. 'Can we come in?' he asked, and it was then that I saw it.

ALEXA: Saw what?

MAXINE: Karl's medical badge, wrapped in a clear plastic sleeve, still damp with sea water.

ALEXA: I know you weren't on good terms, but still, it must have been a terrible shock.

MAXINE: I'll never forget the young officer's words. 'Mrs Gregory,' she said. 'It's bad news, I'm afraid.'

(*pause*)

Sorry, I—

ALEXA: It's OK, take your time, Maxine. There's no rush. Karl's belongings had been discovered by a walker, down on the beach that morning, is that right?

MAXINE: Yes. Not a ten-minute walk from our house.

ALEXA: And the police reached a quick verdict of death by drowning, didn't they? They found a suicide note at his home, I believe.

MAXINE: They did. One of the officers told me they'd been to Karl's flat that morning, and found a letter, protesting his innocence over Lorna's abduction – saying that he couldn't take the 'burden of suspicion' any longer.

ALEXA: What did you think when you heard Karl had killed himself?

MAXINE: I thought the same of Karl dead as I'd thought of him alive. He was a bloody coward. Taking the easy way out. Running away from his responsibilities, again.

ALEXA: His responsibilities? You're talking about Peter?

24

Eva, Bergen Airport, Norway

At the airport, I follow Peter's instructions, effortlessly buying a ticket for the 19.10 flight to London and moving through security and passport control with no problems at all, despite my acute fear that my every move is being monitored. There are CCTV cameras everywhere. I know that I've got four or five hours before Gurt reaches home again, and if he can keep quiet it could be days before anyone notices my passport is gone or considers the almost unimaginable idea that I've left the country. Even if Gurt does blab, there's no way any of them, my parents or Mac or Bern, could reach me before my flight takes off, and – as Peter has reassured me – even if they alerted security in England, they've got no grounds for stopping me: I'm an adult now, with the freedom to go wherever I please. Something tells me that the British police are the last people my parents will want to involve, and I remind myself to calm down and get a grip.

In the departures lounge I buy a large top-up for my phone, and stop off at the pharmacy to pick up the toothpaste, shower gel and deodorant I forgot to pack, along with some ibuprofen to take when my aching leg flares up again. I settle at a single table in a corner of the juice bar and nibble on a rye sandwich, picking out pieces of soggy tomato as I scroll through Peter's recent messages. I have a two-hour flight ahead of me in which to prepare myself, but still, I feel the need to read and re-read our plan, as though knowing it by heart will render it successful:

Me: *I'm coming to London.*

This I sent soon after we'd come face-to-face in the boathouse at midnight last night, the message tapped out with shaking fingers, not really believing my own words at the time. But when Peter's reply came, in the form of one simple word, a question showing faith in my ability to act, I knew I would do it.

Peter: *When?*

Me: *Tomorrow. I don't know how, but I have to get away from these people. They're all liars. Every one of them.*

Peter: *What about your baby?*

Me: *I don't know. I'll think of something. There's only one person I can trust with Bella now. I'll work it out.*

Peter: *Have you looked up flights yet?*

Me: *Couldn't you wait for me? We could fly together.*

Peter: *No. I've got a return ticket, and tomorrow morning is my last chance to use it. I can't afford to get another. Don't worry. I'll look up flight times for you now.*

There was a gap of an hour while I waited for his next reply, and I paced my bedroom as the party continued downstairs without me, my parents having made my excuses for me, citing 'exhaustion' as the cause of my early departure. I

226

stuffed clothes into my school rucksack, endlessly changing my mind about what I would need, and trying to work out a plan for Bella, and for getting to Bergen. At just after one in the morning, Peter's reply came.

Peter: *If you can get to Bergen airport by 5pm, there's a 19.10 flight to London Gatwick. Can you do that?*

Me: *Yes.*

Peter: *And I'll try to book you a room – I think there's a cheap hotel on Bankside.*

I jot down the flight time and the name of the hotel.

Peter: *How will you get there?*

Me: *I don't know yet. How are you getting there?*

Peter: *I'm hitching. Right now I'm sitting in the front of a lorry, next to a bloke with a big white beard, called Thor. I'm not even kidding – though I think he might be bullshitting me about the name.*

Me: *Is he wielding a hammer? If so, he's telling the truth.*

Peter: *Haha. Well? How will you get to the airport?*

I stare at the exchange now, laid out on my screen, and it strikes me as extraordinary, the speed with which we connected. He even types his replies out in full, like me, none of that text talk. My responses to him – and his to me – are like those I would share with Rosa and Lars, who I've been friends with for eighteen years. Not like someone I hardly know.

Me: *I'll get there.*

Since then, after what felt like an endless wait, he's told me he landed safely in London, and in return I've sent him an update, telling him I'm in Bergen, ticket bought, waiting to board. Now, a new message pings onto the screen.

Peter: *When you get through arrivals, take the Gatwick Express to Victoria and go straight to the taxi rank. Ask them* to take you to the Budget Inn at Bankside – it's near Tate Modern, if they're not sure. You've got plenty of money, right?

Me: *OK – and yes, I've just changed some money up.*

Oh, God, this is real. This is really happening.

Peter: *I've booked you a room – I used my surname, so it's Eva Gregory, OK? You have to pay on arrival.*

Me: *Will you be there?*

Peter: *No, I'm booked into a cheap hostel close by. I'm there now. Drop me a message when you get to your hotel? It'll be late by then, so we'll meet in the morning, yeah?*

In the busy forecourt ahead of me the departures board blinks and changes.

Me: *My gate number's just come up on the board. I've got to go.*

Peter: *Safe journey, Eva.*

And that's it. A woman's voice repeats the flight announcement over the speaker and I'm picking up my rucksack and my feet are walking in the direction of that gate, and despite my racing heart I'm more focused than I have been in a very long time. I'm on my way to meet my brother. I'm on my way to discover my past.

And, quite possibly, I'm on my way to discover my future.

25

Maxine

Recorded interview between Alexa Evans, freelance writer, and Maxine Gregory, subject of A LIFE OF LOSS (Falun Publishing International).

ALEXA: I was hoping I might have met Peter by now. He still lives with you here, you say?

MAXINE: You know what teenagers are like. He's never bloody here! Work – friends – the skate park, I don't know. I'll try and make sure he's home next time.

ALEXA: It would be lovely to get an up-to-date photo of you both, to include in the book. Olivia said she'll organise a photoshoot in the next month or so – do you think Peter would be up for that?

MAXINE: I'm sure of it. He's a nice-looking lad. He'll have to ask for time off work, of course – he's an apprentice, you know? Mechanic.

ALEXA: Let's talk a bit more about Peter, shall we – about those early days after his twin sister was abducted. I can't begin to imagine how Tara must have felt, knowing one child had gone missing, and the other, well – what was wrong exactly, Maxine? You mentioned jaundice.

MAXINE: When the twins were born, Lorna was just fine, but Peter was a bit yellow. The midwife told us it was very common, that mostly it just goes away on its own, but the doctors decided Peter should be moved to the lamp room for a night or two, while Lorna stayed in her crib next to Tara. It was just a precaution really, but when they took him away she got frantic – she worked herself up into a real a state.

ALEXA: Was that common for Tara?

MAXINE: Oh, yes, very. She was always a worrier. I do remember Karl asking the registrar lots of questions about it – asking if it was really necessary to keep Peter in the lamp room. I thought that was a bit odd at the time, what with him being a doctor. You'd've thought he'd be all for it, to be on the safe side.

ALEXA: And they moved Tara and Lorna to a private room?

MAXINE: It seemed like a real perk at the time – until later, when the police said they reckon that's how Lorna was taken so easily, because her kidnapper didn't have to get past all those other women and babies on the main ward. Turned out that Karl had pulled a few strings to get her that room – which was the only one that didn't look straight out on to the nurses' desk.

ALEXA: Another reason for the police to suspect Karl had arranged the abduction himself? Do you think he did it, Maxine?

MAXINE: I don't know if it was Karl who took Lorna – I'm not sure he had it in him.

ALEXA: If it wasn't Karl, why do you think he killed himself, when he still had Peter?

MAXINE: Like I said, his suicide note said he couldn't take the suspicion any more. And anyway, he knew he'd blown his chances of getting Peter, after he'd thumped Ray like he did.

ALEXA: (*pause*) Such a tragedy. Peter grew up not knowing either of his parents. But it sounds like you've done a wonderful job of bringing him up, Maxine. I've seen all the press photos and television interviews of him over the years – it looks as though he was a lovely little boy.

MAXINE: He was.

ALEXA: It's heartbreaking to hear him saying how much he missed his sister, in those early TV appearances.

MAXINE: He was very photogenic, wasn't he?

ALEXA: Very. I don't think he's done any media appearances for a few years, has he? Why is that, Maxine?

MAXINE: (*pause*) Too busy being a teenager, I suppose.

ALEXA: Ray was your agent throughout, wasn't he – for all your media appointments?

MAXINE: And Peter's too.

ALEXA: Now, this is a sensitive one, so I don't want you to take offence, Maxine. But we have to cover it, because your readers will no doubt be wondering. It was reported that you were paid a great deal of money for those early exclusives, and that you've continued to make a fairly healthy living from your interviews over the years. What would you say to anyone who said you've made money from your daughter's tragedy?

MAXINE: I'll say they're wrong.

(*pause*)

ALEXA: And, what else?

MAXINE: I'd say, how the hell was I meant to support my grandson, when I had to give up work at that age, to bring him up? I didn't ask for it, that's for sure! Who do they

231

think had to clothe him? Feed him? Put a roof over his head? Everything I ever did was for Peter. I sacrificed a lot for that boy!

ALEXA: No, no, you're right. You've got to live, haven't you? I'm sure the majority of the reading public will see it that way too, Maxine.

(*pause*)

OK. Let's talk about your next move, from Dorset back to London. After a couple of years, you and Peter moved into this flat, here, didn't you? Was this the first property you'd ever owned?

MAXINE: Yes. Paid for it outright.

ALEXA: With money from your interviews?

(*pause*)

Look, Maxine, I'm not trying to trip you up – I promise. We just need to work out how to present this in a positive light. Perhaps you wanted to move Peter here because there were better opportunities for him in London?

MAXINE: Yes, I did.

ALEXA: And did Ray come with you?

MAXINE: Yes. We became Peter's legal guardians, together – when Peter was a year old.

ALEXA: Is Ray still your agent?

MAXINE: Oh, no – the cancer – that's him over there, in the big picture frame. He was just about to start his chemo when that one was taken, bless him.

ALEXA: I'm sorry. May I . . .? It's a lovely photograph. When was it taken?

MAXINE: Just last year.

(*pause*)

I don't want you making out I'm a money-grabber, Alexa. This book won't do that, will it? I mean, I can't have people getting the wrong idea about all this. You'll say we're doing it to find Lorna, won't you?

ALEXA: There's really nothing to worry about, Maxine. You'll get to see everything before the book goes to print, I promise. Let's go back to talking about Peter. The public know his face, they'll remember his heart-rending interviews, and they'll want to know he's doing well. Tell me, did he ever mind all the media attention?

MAXINE: Of course not. He was a good boy. Ray always said he was a natural.

ALEXA: And, when do you think it will be possible to speak to Peter? I'm dying to meet him.

MAXINE: Well, like I said earlier—

ALEXA: It would be really great to get his take on things – to hear what he thinks about the continuing search for his twin sister.

MAXINE: I thought this was my story.

ALEXA: Well, yes, of course—

MAXINE: Peter's a busy lad – he's hardly ever here, truth be told. Probably got his eye on some girl he doesn't want his old gran to know about. You know what boys are like.

ALEXA: Maybe he wouldn't mind making a point of being here when I next visit? It would be really helpful. I'd only want a few—

MAXINE: Will do. Right, are we done for now, then, Alexa? To be perfectly honest, I've got a lot to do, I can't sit here chatting all day.

(*pause*)

You'll make your own way out?

26

Eva, Bankside, London

As soon as I step out through the tinted doors of the hotel reception, I'm dazzled by the bright sunlight bouncing off the Thames, and by the noise and bustle of London's Bankside. Everything is different here, I'm reminded, and nothing – from this moment forward – will ever be the same again. It's a new day, and I marvel how much can change in twenty-four hours. This time yesterday I was standing at my bedroom window, looking out over lakes and snow-capped mountains, and now, here I am, in London, alone, walking beside the River Thames, under what feels like an entirely different sky. I feel another roll of anxiety as I think of Bella missing me, and I swallow the emotion down, telling myself that Nettie will care for her so well that she'll barely notice I'm gone. Everyone else in Valden *has* noticed I'm gone, it seems, as Lars and Rosa's texts and calls have continued through the night, unanswered, the last one telling me, to my shame, that Bella was found with Nettie yesterday evening, when the police were doing door-to-door enquiries. Bella's still there, Rosa's message said, and I'm unsettled to hear that my parents didn't rush straight round to fetch her back. Why not? I'm desperate to ask this question, and so many others, but for now I can't speak to anyone from back home, not yet, and instead I focus on this strange new world around me.

Even this early in the day, fragrant aromas waft from the open doors of cafés and restaurants along the way, as river-boats cut smoothly through sparkling water and men and women in City suits bump shoulders with buskers and sight-seers. I follow Peter's instructions, walking with the river to my right, too distracted by the enormity of what I'm about to discover to enjoy the novelty of my new surroundings. I pass a noisy gathering of tourists next to a billboard adver-tising Shakespeare's Globe theatre. This is too surreal: I'm in *London*, beside the Thames and Shakespeare's Globe, on my way to meet a brother I never knew existed. My parents have lied to me – betrayed me – my entire life, and, depending on what I discover today, I may never see them again. I may *never* see them again. The shock of this notion leaves me reeling, and as I find myself standing before the imposing entrance to Tate Modern, I think my life has never seemed so unreal.

Inside, I'm relieved to see that the level I'm looking for is free to enter – I guess this is why Peter chose the place – and I step on to the escalator, my heart rate increasing as the exhibition rooms come into view. He told me to find the metal man, and sure enough, after some false starts, I find the piece Peter described, a full-sized sculpture by Antony Gormley, just like the ones they have back in Norway, all around Stavanger. I stand with my back against a blank white wall, and I wait. The gallery is busy, with school groups and tourists passing through in great clusters, but, strangely, not many linger in this room with the dark grey man. In my anxiety I find myself anchored to the figure across the room, the smooth lines of his physique soothing, his featureless face turned gently skyward. The puncture to his heart, the wide-planted feet and open palms speak to me, and when I see the exhibit is called *Untitled* it makes a strange kind of sense to me.

'Eva,' Peter says, and before I know what's happening we are clinging to each other. 'Eva,' he says again as we break apart. In his eyes I see my own reflected, and I know there is no threat in them. And there is no doubt that he is my brother.

'Why here?' I ask, and we start walking towards the entrance to the next room.

'I came here once on a school trip. I thought maybe you'd feel safer, meeting in an open place?'

He's right, of course. All the way here I'd been talking myself in and out of the endless reasons I should or shouldn't meet him. What if, like everyone else, he's lying to me? What if I've risked everything – Bella, my family, my friends – and flown all the way here for nothing? What if he's dangerous? What if he's not who he says he is? All those fears have evaporated, in these few brief moments.

'You found it OK?' he asks me.

I glance at him fleetingly, and know he's as nervous as I am. He's tall and thin and dark-haired, and so familiar it nearly floors me. One hand is hooked in his jacket pocket, the other clasped around the black and white scarf I cast down to him that night from my attic room window. He appears somewhat ill at ease in this gallery setting, like a creature out of his natural habitat, and yet it seems right that he should have suggested we meet here.

I nod. 'You like art?'

'Yeah. I was always quite good at it, but my gran talked me out of doing it at college. She made me do an apprenticeship instead – I'm a mechanic.'

'Really?' It explains how he managed to break into and drive that truck. 'Do you like it?'

'It's not that bad,' he replies, tugging at the ends of his scarf. 'I want my own business one day, you know, a garage or something.'

We pass through a crowded room and stop in front of a huge painting entitled *Gothic Landscape*, a mass of chaotic black and white swirls and lines.

'Tell me everything, Peter,' I say, as we stand side-by-side, staring at the image. 'How did you find out about me? I mean, I'd never heard of this missing Lorna baby before.'

'In England,' he says, '*everyone* has heard of Baby Lorna. It was one of those cases the public never forgot about.'

'But children go missing all the time. What was so special about my case?'

His eyes stay fixed on the painting. 'No one ever forgot it, because both our parents died soon after you were abducted.'

'*Both* of them?' I ask, now turning to look at him directly.

He nods towards the next room, eyes fixed ahead as we continue to pass through the swelling crowd. 'When the news broke, the papers went mad, camping outside the hospital at all hours, waiting for a scoop. On the day our mum discharged herself, she left the building and was mobbed by reporters – and she made a run for it. She was hit by a press van, speeding in through the hospital grounds to report on the case. Killed on impact.'

I sink on to a large central seat, the weight of Peter's revelation almost unbearable. I feel suddenly tiny, insignificant; out of my depth.

'I can't believe this is happening,' I tell him. 'My mother and father, if you met them – well, they're so ordinary. I know you're telling me the truth, Peter, but I just can't take it all in. I love them – loved them – but everything they've ever told me is a lie. The pictures of my grandparents, the stories of my birth, even the way they compare me to each other.' I laugh, a hard, strangled sound. 'My mother's always telling me I've got my pappa's practical streak, like I inherited it from him, like it's in my genes. But all this time it was just lies!'

Beside me, Peter hangs his head; he doesn't know what to say. Why would he? We're complete strangers.

'What about you?' I ask. 'Where were you when your mother's accident happened?'

Peter sits beside me. 'My grandmother was holding me at the time. Otherwise – well, I wouldn't be here now, I suppose.'

The gallery space is disappearing behind the growing number of visitors, and yet it feels as though it's just me and him in the place.

'And our father?'

'Karl. They thought he had something to do with your abduction, because Tara and he were never actually a proper couple, so it was easy for people to say he hadn't wanted us in the first place. It'd been just a one-night stand, my gran says.'

All the romantic theories I'd started to imagine about my true birth parents are scattering.

'So, they never loved each other, then?'

'No. The thing is, as soon as Tara died, Karl went and killed himself too, so there was no way of getting to the bottom of what really happened, whether he was responsible for your abduction. After his suicide, the theories really took off – they're still speculating about it now, eighteen years later.'

238

'What kinds of theories?'

'The most popular one was that he sold you to some child trafficker to clear his debts, then fell apart with the guilt of it. Some people say he killed himself before the police closed in on him – others say he was completely innocent but couldn't take the accusations hanging over him.'

'What do you think?' I ask.

'About what happened? I dunno. Sometimes I hate him for leaving me, with *her* – Maxine, my grandmother – and other times, I get how it feels to want to take the easy way out. I s'pose the simple answer is, I just don't know.'

For a while we just sit there, silently watching the crowds pass by, side by side, strangers intrinsically linked.

'How did you find me?' I ask him.

'A couple of years back, a journalist – or investigator, I think he called himself – came to our place asking questions. He claimed to have some proof that you were alive and well in Norway. We've had crackpots calling us in the past, but this guy seemed different. And it kind of made sense that you could be there, because our real dad had been half-Norwegian.'

'Really?' I ask, and we rise, continuing through the exhibition. 'So, he was only half-English?'

'Yeah, but I think he mostly grew up here. P'raps that's why your English is so good? It's in the blood.'

'We pretty much all speak good English in Norway,' I reply.

Peter smiles self-consciously, stuffing his hands deeper inside his pockets. 'Yeah, I s'pose.'

'Sorry,' I say. 'You were telling me about Karl.'

'He was a doctor. That's what Maxine, my gran, told me, but much more than that I don't really know. Anyway, I managed to get a name and location from this investigator guy before he left – for the people he suspected in Norway – and when

Maxine refused to follow it up I swore I would. It took me nearly two years, but I got there in the end.'

We've come full circle and now stand on the wide landing, looking out through glass walls over the floors below. It feels like a scene from a science fiction movie, as people move serenely across a vast industrial landscape.

For a few minutes, neither of us speak and we stand side by side, gazing out over the scene.

Eventually, and to my stomach's gratitude, Peter says, 'Are you hungry? I know a great place for breakfast in Borough Market. We can walk from here.'

We head back along the river front, watching the tourist boats zipping up and down the Thames in the morning sunshine. On the far side, people stroll along the riverbank with dogs and children, making way for cyclists and pushchairs, living their normal lives. What's normal? I wonder. I don't know, and it seems Peter's never really known it either. As we walk, he tells me more about his childhood growing up with our maternal grandmother, Maxine, and her controlling brother Ray who moved in with them soon after Peter was born. I feel guilty hearing about the hard time he had while I was living in comparative peace and comfort hundreds of miles away, across the sea – yet it seems both of us were lonely, in our different ways. I always loved and envied what Rosa and Lars had together, always felt sad that I would never experience what they so easily took for granted. It feels extraordinary to me now to think that, like Rosa, I had a brother out there all along. It explains the incomplete feeling I'd always experienced, something I'd put down to being an only child. It wasn't that at all; my other half really *was* missing. If we'd had each other, I think as Peter leads us away from the river path and into busy winding streets, wouldn't life have been so much better, for both of us?

'Peter, why didn't you just go to the police, instead of going all the way to Norway yourself?'

We enter the noisy market square, and head for a breakfast stall at the far side, where Peter orders us tea and two 'full English'. We take our mugs and sit at the end of a wooden bench table, facing each other.

'At first, I couldn't do anything,' he says. 'The journalist – Dave Gander, he was called – asked me not to say a word until he'd been to Norway himself and gathered a bit more evidence. I told him we should go to the police, but he convinced me they wouldn't take it seriously until he had something more concrete. Until he'd found out more about you and your parents.'

'So, then what happened?'

'Nothing. He never called, and when I tried phoning his number a few months later it just went to voicemail every time. I assumed either the lead had gone cold, or more likely he didn't want anyone else getting in on it before he had a chance to make some money. When we'd seen him all those months earlier, he'd told Maxine that he was planning a book, and she was furious. You know *she's* writing a book? *A Life of Loss*, it's called. *Ha!*'

I'm shocked by his altered expression, by the bitterness that has replaced the previously open features.

'She's been squeezing the story for cash from the moment Lorna—' he shakes his head '—since the moment *you* disappeared. Maxine's bad enough, but then there's her brother Ray, who's been pulling her strings for years. He's her agent. He arranges all her TV interviews and contracts – has done for years. She even signed him up as my agent, back in the days when they used to wheel me out like some kind of performing pet.'

241

'What, you had to go on TV?'

'From about five onwards I was constantly on TV or in the papers, always with Maxine, the grieving grandmother. Ray would coach me on what to say, how to say it – I've watched some of the footage back and it makes my skin crawl. But I started refusing to go along with it when I was about thirteen, and that's when life at home really got bad.'

A dark shadow passes across Peter's face and I can't even begin to imagine what it is he's really been through. 'Did Ray beat you?' I ask.

'No, never. I mean, if you met him, you'd think he was quite the charmer. But he had a way of manipulating things, of kind of shutting you out if you didn't do what he said. I stopped bringing mates home, because he'd always put me down in front of them, taking the piss but making out it was all just a joke. One time, I woke up with the flu – I'd totally lost my voice – and Ray said he'd call my boss for me. But stupidly, I'd forgotten about a row we'd had the night before, and when he phoned up my boss he told him I wouldn't be in that morning because I was off for a job interview somewhere else. I was too sick to call in and put it straight. I didn't sleep that night, worrying the boss would sack me the next day.'

'Why would Ray do that?'

'It was always about power, about me not getting above myself. About him being the big man. He hadn't worked for years by then, and I know it wound him up to see me getting started – earning a bit of money, not having to ask him any more, especially as I'd stopped playing ball when it came to all those interviews. If you challenged his control, you were the enemy. Trouble is, Maxine worshipped the ground Ray walked on, so it was never any use complaining to her, 'cause she'd always take his side over anyone's.'

'Well, you're away from all that now, aren't you?' I say. 'You don't have to put up with Ray any more.'

'He was on his last legs when I left a year ago. He'd already started getting forgetful and coming out with all sorts of weird things, but then he got diagnosed with lung cancer too. Doctors reckoned he had six months, tops. With any luck, the old fucker is already dead. Maxine, on the other hand—' and now his face lights up, as he says, 'Man, she's gonna hate you turning up. This is going to really screw up her plans for world domination!' His former warmth returns, and when the woman behind the red market counter calls out our number he flashes her a smile and jogs over to fetch our plates.

A 'full English', it turns out, is a mountain of sausage, bacon, eggs, tomatoes, mushrooms, toast, and a strange potato cake called a 'hash brown'. We eat and talk, and when I can't manage my second egg Peter spears it from my plate and polishes it off. I can't remember when I last felt so alive; when I last felt so much a part of something. My guilt swells again as I think of Bella back home.

'Tell me about your baby,' Peter says tentatively, as though reading my mind. He pushes his clear plate away and reaches for a paper napkin.

I realise I've never had to explain this to anyone before, and I don't know where to begin.

'They're pretty sure it happened that night,' I say, meeting his eyes. 'After I was found in your truck in that state, everyone assumed that the driver must also be the father. They think I was raped, because I'd never – *you know*.'

Peter is speechless, and the shock that radiates from him is physical. 'I didn't – I wouldn't—'

'Oh, I know it wasn't you *now*!' I say in a rush, and the relief on his face is instant. 'God, no! But meeting you – knowing

243

who you really are, it does mean we now have no idea how I, you know . . .' I trail off, struggling to put this awful thing into words, trying to stop my mind from conjuring up Bern's image. 'To be honest, I've got enough new information to deal with right now. And you know, the truth about Bella might not be something I want to hear for a while.'

Neither of us speaks for a few moments, until I ask, 'Where were we going that night? Where were you taking me?'

'Nowhere,' he replies. 'That's the stupid thing. There was no grand plan, because although we'd started to talk on Facebook it was really low-key, just me kind of testing the water, if you like. I hadn't told you much about myself, and we hadn't arranged to meet yet. So that night, it was just a coincidence, me being in the bar at the same time as you – I'd been hiding out in one of the empty cabins near the lake, and I was freezing, so I'd gone into Foxy's for a drink, to warm up for an hour. And then I saw you there, across the room with your friends, and I thought it had to be fate. I honestly couldn't believe it.'

'Why didn't you come up to me in the bar, then?'

'I didn't want to tell you about all this in a public place, because I had no way of knowing how you'd react. You could've gone ballistic for all I know, learning you had a brother you'd never heard of – that your parents were frauds – it just didn't seem right, putting you on the spot in front of your friends.' He falls silent for a second or two. 'If only we'd never driven out on to that icy road, none of this would've happened, Eva. If I'd only told you in the car park.'

'Why didn't you?'

'There was this bloke hanging around – weaselly-looking guy with greasy hair, and a rose stuck behind his ear. He followed you out of the bar when you left – you looked upset – but after wandering about the car park for a bit he just headed around the back of the building and got in one of the vans there. You were over by my truck and, when I offered to give you a lift, you suddenly recognised me and asked if I was Peter – if I was the guy you'd been talking to on Facebook.'

'Was I scared? I mean, I didn't know you, did I?'

'Scared? No. You looked relieved – you said you didn't want to walk home alone with him lurking about. What was his name? Bert?'

'Gurt,' I murmur, at once remembering the moment I saw Gurt's face through the driver's side window of the truck – the memory which had made me report him to Chief Mac. He hadn't been getting *into* the green truck when I saw him; he'd just been on the other side of the glass, walking by. 'But on my phone,' I say, trying to piece it all together. 'There are no messages from you before these recent ones.'

He shakes his head. 'After the accident, I deleted our conversation, as well as deactivating my social media accounts. I thought if anyone had access to your account, it could have led the police straight to me.'

A girl in a red apron briskly clears the table, gathering up our plates in a single fluid motion. 'Go on,' I tell Peter.

'I waited, that night,' Peter says. 'After our accident. I called the emergency services and I waited in the trees until the ambulance arrived. I didn't abandon you, I want you to know that. I just couldn't risk getting caught – I'd stolen that truck, and I knew that if they banged me up for that they'd never let me anywhere near you. I had to hide out, until I could try to see you again. But that chance was a long time coming, and when you didn't come out of hospital I had to return to London for a few months, until I'd saved up enough money for another flight in the autumn.'

I'm still processing what Peter has just told me, as memories rise to the surface, confirming everything he has just said. My leg has started to throb, with all the walking we've done, and I search in my rucksack for painkillers, washing them down with the last of my tea.

'I'm sorry about the accident,' he says, gravely. 'I'm so sorry that I was the cause of all your suffering. I've thought about nothing else since it happened, Eva, and there's not a day when I haven't hated myself for what I did to you.'

I see pain in his eyes; it never once occurred to me that the driver – the monster we had all imagined – would be hurting too.

'Why did we crash?' I ask. 'I remember seeing the deep snowdrift along the verges, and you saying something that shocked me – and I thought there was an animal in the middle of the road.'

'That's right,' Peter replies.

'What was it?'

'It was a fox,' he replies.

'A white one?' The image of that Arctic fox has grown so clear to me over the past few months, but I know it's just another figment of my imagination. We don't get white foxes as far south as Valden, everyone knows that.

He frowns, remembering. 'I think it was a regular one, but you'd easily have mistaken it – its coat was covered in snow. But we swerved to avoid it – that's how we ended up in the snowbank.'

And then I see it, but this time as a hard-edged memory. I'm there, on that infernal journey again, and we're driving through darkness, the windscreen wipers struggling against the snowfall that now lands against the glass in large soft blobs. I know I'm drunk, and it suddenly occurs to me that we're headed in the wrong direction, and I turn to look at the stranger who's driving and there he is, Peter, clear as day. I turn back to the windscreen, squinting into the whirling, swirling white-out landscape and then I see her, the white fox on the road ahead, her misty fur whipping about like a wind-beaten cloud, the amber of her eyes set in fear as we hurtle towards her. And I know he tries to miss her, because I feel it, I feel the jerk of his wheel, and the crunching shunt of tyres on ice, and then we nosedive into the snowbank with the sickest of thuds, and my world shuts down.

I burst into tears now, covering my face with my hands in an attempt to stem my sobs.

'I'm sorry,' Peter says, reaching across to me.

'It's not your fault,' I reply, taking a breath, trying to regain control. 'It's the lies. You wouldn't even have been there if it weren't for all those lies. They've lied to me – to us – about *everything*.'

'What do you want to do?' Peter asks.

'I don't know,' I say, a sudden wave of strength coming over me. 'But one thing's for sure, I'm not going back to them. I've got Bella to think of now, and there's no way she's growing up in a house of lies, the way I did. I don't ever want to see them again.'

I glance at my mobile phone, as yet another message arrives from Rosa.

Eva, you have to phone me! Your parents took the nine a.m. flight to London today. They found a note in your bedroom – of the hotel where you're staying – and they're on their way!

27

Maxine

Recorded interview between Alexa Evans, freelance writer, and Maxine Gregory, subject of A LIFE OF LOSS (Falun Publishing International).

ALEXA: You've had your hopes raised over years, haven't you, Maxine? Reported sightings of little Lorna, lots of false leads. How did you stay positive?

MAXINE: It's been very hard. Every time the police called to say there was a fresh line of enquiry, we'd think, maybe this time it really will be her. There was one girl, a few years back, who walked into a police station in Dorset, claiming to be Lorna.

ALEXA: Really? I never heard about that one.

MAXINE: It never made it into the papers, 'cause it was just some nasty little cow who'd done it on a dare. The police took it seriously, what with it being right on the doorstep from where Lorna went missing – but it came to nothing.

ALEXA: There were letters too? Awful ones, saying they knew where her remains were buried?

MAXINE: Also bogus.

ALEXA: You seem very calm about it all. I suppose you have to shut off your feelings, to an extent?

MAXINE: Exactly. These people feed off pain. That's what a copper told me early on, and he was right. Don't give them the thrill of seeing you crumble, he said. So, I hold my head high and I rise above 'em.

ALEXA: It sounds like good advice. And you've clearly never given up hope of finding your granddaughter. Did you ever consider hiring a private detective? There are people who specialise in this kind of thing.

MAXINE: Ray did meet someone, a couple of years back. This fella was called Dave something-or-other – Gander, I think. He described himself as an ex-journalist-turned-investigator – and he bumped into Ray in one of the pubs around here. At first it seemed like a random meeting, but it was only later on we realised he must have found out where Ray drinks and got talking 'by chance'. Ray invited him back to the flat to meet me and Peter and talk terms.

ALEXA: Terms?

MAXINE: Well, at first, Ray thought Gander would be looking to get paid – like a regular private detective might, and we would've considered that. But as he got talking we saw he had something bigger in mind. He wanted to write a book about it – about Lorna.

ALEXA: So, he wasn't intending to charge you a fee?

MAXINE: No. But he *was* looking to make money from us. He said he'd been on Lorna's trail for a couple of years, that he wanted to *help*. He had this whole speech prepared, about how he'd followed the case since the start, and felt like he knew us after watching us on TV. He had 'strong evidence' that Lorna was alive and well – and living under a new identity. He went along with the theory that Karl had passed the baby on to a childless couple he knew in Norway.

ALEXA: Weren't you excited to think he might be on to something?

MAXINE: Nothing he said was anything new – the theory that Karl did it was an old one – the only new bit was this Norwegian couple, and that hardly took a lot of imagination to dream up, bearing in mind the police had already found out Karl was half-Norwegian. No, I saw Gander for the chancer he was the minute I clapped eyes on him.

ALEXA: What about Ray, what did he think? And Peter?

MAXINE: Ray agreed with me, he thought the man was a parasite. But Peter kept Gander talking out on the landing there, after he'd seen him to the door. He was sixteen by now, and the idea of finding his sister had grown into something of an obsession. He wanted to believe this man – he even took his business card and made him promise to get in touch if he found anything out. But I didn't want that man anywhere near us. And I sure as hell wasn't going to support his idea for a book!

ALEXA: Of course, the publishers had already approached you with the proposal for your own book by then, hadn't they?

MAXINE: (*silence*)

ALEXA: If this investigator was planning a book too, there would be something of a conflict, I suppose? I mean, it would be competition.

MAXINE: Who'd want to read his book? I wasn't worried in the slightest! I told you, he was a chancer.

ALEXA: Did you ever hear back from him again?

MAXINE: *No*. Like I said, he was nothing. Dave Gander was nothing but a time-waster.

ALEXA: (*pause*) I think this will probably be our last full session here, Maxine, before I go off and work up what we've got. Olivia wondered if we could meet at the publishing office tomorrow afternoon, for a bit of a round-up with her. She says she's got a mock-up of the book jacket to share with us – and she might have a few additional questions for you.

MAXINE: Additional questions? Like what?

ALEXA: Oh, just things I might not have thought of. It's always good to get another set of eyes on these things. She suggested midday? I expect she'll get some lunch in.

MAXINE: Lunch? Yes, I think I can do that. At the fancy offices by the river?

ALEXA: That's right – where we first met.

MAXINE: It'll be nice to see the book cover. Blimey, it's all getting a bit real now, isn't it? When's the release again?

ALEXA: Well, they want it on shelf pre-Christmas. The timings are pretty tight, but I'm confident we can do it, after all our brilliant sessions together. You've been amazing, Maxine. (*pause*)
Olivia thinks it's going to be a bestseller, you know, with all this renewed press interest since the twins' eighteenth birthday. I expect you've been inundated, haven't you?

MAXINE: I keep the phone unplugged while you're here, otherwise it'd be ringing off the wall! Most of them want to know if I think we'll ever find her. If I think Lorna is still alive.

ALEXA: What do you say?

MAXINE: I tell 'em we'll never give up hope of finding her – and I ask them to appeal for anyone who knows anything to come forward. All the usual stuff. I don't know why they bother calling me, really, I mean – what more is there to say?

ALEXA: (*pause*) It's a pity I didn't get to meet Peter after all, though. I thought he might have been here today.

MAXINE: I think he had an assessment this morning, down at the garage. He couldn't hang around. Another time, per'aps.

ALEXA: Maybe he'll come to the book launch?

MAXINE: I'm sure he will. You *will* let me read the book before it goes to print, won't you, Alexa?

ALEXA: Of course – it's written into your contract that you'll get to sign it off.

MAXINE: And there'll be some more money, when you've finished typing it all up?

ALEXA: You can talk to Olivia about that tomorrow – or ask your new agent? She'll know the exact terms of your agreement, but there's usually another payment on release, yes.

MAXINE: Good, good. Here's your coat, love. It's been good, this, hasn't it? Talking and all – you're ever so easy to chat to, so I'm glad Olivia chose you. You haven't forgotten about what we said – about making me sixteen when I had Tara, not fourteen?

ALEXA: Yes that's fine. Olivia knows about it, so for the purposes of the first draft, yes, I'm making you sixteen. I'm sorry I didn't get to meet Ray, either.

MAXINE: Yeah, well as I said—

ALEXA: (*pause*) Cancer's a terrible illness.

MAXINE: It is. Well, you'd better be off, then?

ALEXA: (*pause*) Oh, just one last thing, Maxine. We never really did get to talk about Tara's father, did we? I wondered if you'd stayed in contact with the father over the years. If Tara ever got to meet him at all?

MAXINE: (*pause*) Why'd you want to know about that?

ALEXA: People will want to know, Maxine, I'm certain. The readers will be interested.

MAXINE: (*pause*) Well the *readers* can – excuse my French – mind their own fuckin' business.

28

Eva, Neptune Court, Greenwich, London

By the time we reach Peter's flat, the ache in my leg has intensified to a screaming pain. While he fumbles for his keys, I rest against the wall of a shabby fountain at the edge of the entrance path, my eyes locked on the shadow cast by Neptune's trident, as I concentrate hard on not passing out. Once we're through the security door and up the dim stairwell into the apartment, I flop gratefully on to the sofa. Thankfully, Grandmother Maxine is out, and Peter checks the apartment for signs of activity, before heading for a wall calendar hanging above the kitchen counter. Their home is open-plan, with the kitchen, diner and living room all in one; doors lead off the main space to the bedrooms, a bathroom and a small balcony. It's tidy and conventional, with the occasional nod to tacky glamour here and there – a glass chandelier as centrepiece in the low ceiling, an Art Deco lampstand over by the old box TV, a crystal decanter on the shelf beside plastic beakers and cheap mugs.

For a few quiet moments Peter stands gazing out through the glass of the balcony doors, and I run my hands over my face, panicked at the thought of my parents following me to London.

'That flight gets in about now,' Peter says, glancing back at me. 'But you've got to allow at least another couple of hours for them to get through security and into London.'

'They couldn't possibly know where we are now, could they?' I've been frantic all the way here, cursing myself for my stupidity, for leaving that note in my room back in Valden – the scrap of paper detailing my flight times and hotel. I can only imagine I'd managed to sweep it to my bedroom floor in my rush to leave the house, not missing it, as the details I needed were all contained in my text conversations with Peter. 'I mean, the hotel aren't allowed to give out details, are they? I checked in under Eva Gregory, so they wouldn't know it was me.' I can hear the panic in my own voice, the rise of my anxiety. 'And Chief Mac or Bern wouldn't be able to pull strings with the British police, would they? You know, to work out where I am?'

'Nobody knows you're here,' Peter says firmly. 'They've no idea you're with me – they can't get to you. You're safe, Eva, OK? And we won't be here that long. I just need to collect my stuff together, get the last of my earnings from the cashpoint, and then we'll catch the train back to Gatwick. In a way, them being over here couldn't have worked out better. It means they won't be *there* to stop us when we go back for Bella – even if your folks do eventually work out where you are, we'll be well on our way back to Valden.' He hesitates, and regards me steadily. 'Are you sure you're up for this?'

I nod.

'Because once we're done with Valden, Eva, there'll be no going back. Your parents will be arrested – it'll be just you, me and Bella. Are you sure that's what you want?'

'I'm sure.' I exhale, wincing against my leg pain. Of course I'm not sure; how could I be? But, now I know the truth about my parents, what choice have I got? I'm so desperately tired, I just want to rest, to stop moving. 'How long have we got until your – until Maxine gets back?'

'We're OK for a bit, I think,' Peter replies, checking his watch and crossing back over to the wall calendar. 'This says she's got an appointment with her publisher at twelve. We've got at least a couple of hours before she'll be back.'

'Publisher?'

'I told you, she's writing a book – an "autobiography". Always banging on about it,' he scoffs. 'She's got a ghost writer, although I reckon she'll do her best to hide the fact, and claim it as all her own work. I bet the publishers didn't trust her to write it herself. She's a pathological liar. They've probably already sussed that out.'

'When's the book due out?'

'November. When she signed the deal, the year before last, they told her they expect it to be a Christmas bestseller, and she was already mentally totting up her fortune. Can you believe she even asked me to do a photoshoot for it?'

'To go inside the book?'

'Yeah. You can imagine what I told her do with her photoshoot. *And* her book.'

Peter scans the room and casually picks up a large silver-framed photograph of an elderly man, and he stares at the picture for a minute or more. 'This is new,' he says eventually, returning the picture to the kitchen counter, his eyes hard. '*Ray*. Maybe the old bastard finally croaked it.' Peter appears outwardly calm, but I can sense the torrent of emotions at work within. How must it feel, to be free of this man after all those years?

'Do you have any other photos?' I ask. 'Of family?'

He disappears into a bedroom, and returns with a large scrapbook, full of news cuttings and photos.

'This,' he says, placing it on my lap as I pull myself into a sitting position, 'is Maxine's bragging book. It's basically a diary of all the articles and interviews she did since the day you disappeared, eighteen years ago.'

I scan the first few pages, which headline with the abduction, stopping at one entitled *Tragic Lorna Mum's Paparazzi Death*. A few pages on and I find *Lorna Dad Drowned* and *Was Lorna Dad Guilty or Hounded to Suicide?* This article outlines the circumstances surrounding our parents' deaths, and shows two grainy photographs of the pair, both of poor quality and clearly cropped out of larger group photos. Another feature, from *Heat* magazine, leads with a glossy photograph of six-year-old Peter, flanked by his grandmother and uncle, with the headline *Lorna Twin's Heartache for Missing Sister*.

I stare at the picture for a long time, composing myself, feeling a rush of emotion stirred up by the thought of this tiny child left behind with these awful people.

'Why me?' I ask. 'Whoever it was that snatched me, why didn't they take you too – or instead?'

Peter shrugs. 'I was born a bit jaundiced, so I was in another room to start with – where there are nurses and doctors round the clock. Much easier to take you. Or maybe your parents wanted a girl.'

What a disturbing thought, that they might have requested a specific gender of child, much as you might choose an item from a mail order catalogue.

'Do you have any better pictures of our mother?' I ask, and it occurs to me that of course he would. He's grown up with his natural grandmother; there'll be pictures everywhere.

He takes his wallet from his back pocket and slides out a tatty-edged passport photograph of a young woman. 'She's about fourteen in this photo. It's the only one I've got. I think you look a bit like her.'

'Hasn't your gran got any more?'

He shakes his head. 'None.'

I gaze at my birth mother's young face, and I can see, yes, I'm quite like her. Her eyes are like Peter's; like mine. Any remnant of hope about Ingrid, my mum, evaporates, and I am devastated all over again. Can this really be happening to me?

'Where did you get this picture?' I ask.

Peter grimaces. 'I found it in Uncle Ray's room, in the back of his shirt drawer. The only reason I knew it was her was because it says so on the back.'

Sure enough, there on the reverse are the words, *Tara, aged 14*.

'There was all sorts in the drawer,' Peter continues, 'girls' knickers, lip balms, hair bobbles – and a whole load of photographs. Mostly just regular ones like this, but also a few horrible Polaroids of young girls with their faces offscreen.'

A chill run through me. 'What did you do, when you found them?'

'I showed them to my gran.'

'And what did she do?'

Peter slides the photo back into his wallet and returns it to his pocket. 'She beat me to within an inch of my life and made me swear to never repeat a word of it to anyone. And then she made me put the pictures back. I kept this one, though. I wasn't gonna let him have this one back.'

'I'm so sorry, Peter.' I shut the album and hand it back to him, sliding down against the cushions as a wave of exhaustion and sorrow overcomes me. That poor woman, our mother. What she must have endured. I close my eyes, only wanting sleep, barely noticing Peter's cool hand against my forehead.

'Jeez, Eva, you're burning up. Can you take a couple more tablets?'

I shake my head wearily. 'They were my last two. Can you find me some more?'

He slides open the balcony doors to let in some air, before rummaging through kitchen drawers and cupboards. When he fails to find any painkillers, he pulls on his jacket and checks his watch again.

'Don't go anywhere,' he says as he leaves the flat. 'The high street's only ten minutes away. I'll get some paracetamol, and pick us up a sandwich while I'm out.'

As the door clicks shut behind him, I ease my feet from my trainers and undo the top button of my shirt, relieved to feel the air from the open balcony as it cools my overheated skin. This is the hardest I've exerted myself in all the time that's passed since my accident, the longest period I've been away from home, and my limbs feel like lead.

Within moments, I'm sliding into a deep sleep.

29

Maxine, Falun Publishing International, London

Meeting Notes: Present – Olivia Finch, Editorial Director (Falun Publishing International), Monica Hart, Corporate Lawyer (Falun Publishing International), Alexa Evans, freelance writer, and Maxine Gregory, subject of A LIFE OF LOSS (Falun Publishing International).

ALEXA: Maxine, you remember Olivia? And this is Monica Hart, company lawyer – remember I said Legal would have a read-through at certain points in the process? To make sure we've got all our facts straight?

MAXINE: Oh. Oh, yes. How do you do?

MONICA: It's a pleasure to meet you, Maxine. I'll just be here to listen, to make a few notes – ask any questions that might be relevant, from a legal perspective.

ALEXA: (*pause*) You don't mind if I record us as usual, do you, Maxine? (*pause*) That's great.

OLIVIA: So! What do you think of the cover options, Maxine?

We took them into the sign-off meeting this week, and everyone absolutely loves them. This one's my favourite. That title's going to really jump off the shelves.

MAXINE: (*pause*) It looks very nice, thank you. Very eye-catching.

OLIVIA: As you know, we're keen to include a comprehensive photo segment in the centre. Alexa tells me you couldn't find many pictures of your daughter, Tara? That's a bit surprising.

MAXINE: We must have lost them in the move.

(*pause*)

You know we moved a few times over the years. Things got lost. Maybe they got mislaid when we came here from Dorset.

ALEXA: Do you think anyone else will have copies?

MAXINE: There's no one else left to ask, really. No other family.

OLIVIA: No one at all? What about Peter – he must have one or two pictures of his mother somewhere? Could you ask him?

MAXINE: (*pause*) I'll ask him when he gets home later.

OLIVIA: Alexa says she hasn't managed to meet him yet.

MAXINE: He's a teenager. You know what they're like – always out.

OLIVIA: It's just that Alexa said she couldn't help noticing there aren't many signs of him around the house. Isn't that right, Alexa?

ALEXA: Yes, I mean, I know teenagers are often out and about – but they're also notoriously messy. I guess I just expected to see more evidence of him. Shoes lying about, study books, earphones – that kind of thing. There were a couple of men's jackets on your coat hook, but they looked more like they belonged to an older man.

MAXINE: Flippin' 'eck, I didn't realise you were doing a full recce of my place, Alexa! I'll have you know Peter's a very tidy boy, and he keeps everything in his room where it belongs. I don't like his big shoes lying about the place, so they're all tucked away under his bed.

ALEXA: I wasn't snooping, Maxine – I just couldn't help noticing, that's all.

(*pause*)

OLIVIA: And what about Ray?

MAXINE: What about him?

OLIVIA: You don't think your brother Ray might be able to help with the photographs?

MAXINE: (*pause*) Ray? No – I don't – he's –

ALEXA: He's been battling cancer for years, hasn't he, Maxine? He sadly passed away, quite recently.

MONICA: Oh? I don't recall seeing a record for that in your due diligence file, Alexa.

ALEXA: No. I wanted to ask Maxine about that today—

(*pause*)

Is Ray really dead, Maxine?

MAXINE: He – well, yes, I mean I never said—

ALEXA: Didn't you?

MAXINE: Are you calling me a liar? I don't have to sit here and be insulted like this—

OLIVIA: Whoa, slow down there, Maxine – no one's insulting you! Come on, let's take a walk on the terrace, shall we? Come on, Alexa, you bring Maxine's tea. We'll go and sit in the fresh air and work this out, yes?

(*pause*)

Now, Maxine, tell us about Ray. All I know from Alexa is that she, she felt – *maybe incorrectly* – that you led her to believe Ray was dead.

ALEXA: But when I checked, there doesn't seem to be a listing for his death at the Records Office.

(*pause*)

MAXINE: He's not dead.

ALEXA: And the cancer?

MAXINE: That's true – he's had it for years, but – God knows how – he's still going.

ALEXA: I don't understand, Maxine, I tried asking you about him on at least two occasions and you gave me the strongest suggestion that he died some time last year. You certainly avoided talking about him.

MAXINE: (*pause*) I panicked.

OLIVIA: Why?

MAXINE: I thought if you knew he was alive you'd want to meet him.

ALEXA: Well, you're right there.

OLIVIA: And why would that be a problem, Maxine?

MAXINE: (*pause*) He – he's always had an eye for the ladies, has Ray. You know, he's a bit of a charmer. But recently, well, he's getting on a bit – and he can become a bit confused.

OLIVIA: Are we talking about dementia, Maxine?

MAXINE: That's what the doctors say it is, yes.

ALEXA: But I don't understand why—

MAXINE: (*crying*) He's lost all his – his *reserve*. No, that's the wrong word. What I mean is, everything that used to be inside his head – well, he just comes out and says it now. It's like he can't keep any of it in. He says the most terrible things, with no shame, and I didn't want you hearing it, Alexa. God forgive me, I'm ashamed of him, and I didn't want you hearing some of the horrible things he's capable of saying. The stuff he says to me—

ALEXA: Oh, you poor thing, Maxine. Come here, there's nothing to worry about now, is there, Olivia? Not now we know the truth. You know we're on your side, don't you? I'm sorry I was tough on you just now, but you must feel better that it's out?

OLIVIA: Of course, we sympathise, Maxine, but it's important we're all honest with each other, especially on a project as high-profile as this. We'll go back inside in a minute and update Monica on this little detail. But promise me that *is* everything? There's nothing else we need to know?

MAXINE: *Nothing*. That's all.

OLIVIA: That's good. That's really good.

ALEXA: So, where does he live these days? Is he in a nursing home?

MAXINE: Who, Ray? Oh, no, he lives with me in Greenwich – has done ever since we moved there when Peter was just a tot. He's still family, after all, and most of the time he's just fine. Family have to stick together, don't they? What's that saying? *Blood is thicker than water*. That's it, that's what Ray always says.

30

Eva

Even before I wake, I feel the presence of him beside me on the sofa, the weight of his hand on my leg. The smell of stale cigarette smoke threatens to choke me, to make me gag.

'Who's this, then?' he says, as I wake with a small scream, and with slow force he presses me back against the cushions with his other hand. He's perched on the edge, and he shifts closer, effectively trapping me between him and the sofa back. 'Hush, little baby.'

His voice is coarse, though his clothes hint at a taste for more refined things, and a full head of white hair is carefully combed in a neat side parting. For an old man, I can see he's strong, almost handsome, with cold grey eyes that tell me he's dangerous. For a moment he studies me with those eyes, and I wonder if he is in fact blind, because his focus drifts as though he's seeing something else altogether, something or someone outside of this room. I've never been more afraid in my life.

'Maxine?' he hollers, 'Maxie!' But there's no one else here. It's just me and him, alone in this flat. 'Always out, gallivanting,' he mutters to himself, reaching to run a rough finger along the line of my jaw. 'I knew you'd come back,' he says then, and he smirks, as though he's won an argument. 'You're still a pretty little thing, aren't ya? Haven't lost your looks.'

'We've never—' I protest, desperately trying to drag myself up to a sitting position. But he won't have it, and he blocks my movement by grabbing my wrist, twisting it painfully. When I shriek, he brings a finger to his mouth, shushing me as he lifts the hem of my shirt, pulling in his chin to peer underneath. My skin crawls, and my heart hammers, and all the while my eyes scan the room, looking for a way out of this, a way to outfox him. I'm barely breathing, as I realise that, against all odds, this is Ray – it's Uncle Ray, and he's not dead, and I'm lying here beneath his filthy hands, as helpless as a rabbit in a snare. Silently I pray for Peter to walk through the door and rescue me.

'How old are you now, doll? Sixteen? Seventeen?' He draws back momentarily, narrowing his eyes. 'You think I'm too old for you? You think a man of my age i'nt up to it? Is that it, eh?' He smiles widely to display straight teeth, ivory-white, and if you couldn't hear the words he's speaking his expression would suggest he's just a charming old man, having a nice chat. 'Fit as a fiddle, me!' he announces, and there's menace in his tone.

My mind is stumbling around for possible escape routes, but fear has me in its grip. What is it you're meant to do in these situations? I could ram him in the nose with the heel of my free hand, but his is right beside mine, poised to block me. I could try appealing to him – I could tell him Peter's just moments away, that I won't tell anyone if he'll just let me go. But I'm too slow, because with a single violent tug he rips my shirt to one side, sending buttons ricocheting across the floor. They lie, scattered like inky drops on the deep orange carpet, a trail between me and the door, my only possible exit from this place. Horrified, I watch the old man's mouth twist as he reaches for his belt, snapping the buckle back, his focus disappearing to some far-off place, arthritic fingers working at his fly. Surely I can overcome him? The old me would have done; the old me would have had the strength – the fight. As I struggle to sit up, he knocks me aside with a single sharp backhand slap to my ear, and the pain is excruciating. In a moment's clarity, I know that all I can do is stall him.

'You're Ray,' I say, my voice shaking.

His eyes soften, as though he's drifting back from that somewhere-else place, and he runs his knuckle along my throbbing jawline again, tender and threatening all at once.

'*Uncle* Ray to you, Tara, love,' he replies.

He thinks I'm *Tara*. My stomach pitches at the thought. He thinks I'm his niece, and yet he's behaving like this. Is this how it was for her? Is this what she had to suffer all those years ago?

Briefly, Ray's grip loosens, and, just as I believe I might escape, he reaches inside the front of his trousers and grabs my wrist tighter, trying to wrestle my hand into contact with his groin.

'No!' I shout, writhing to free myself from his grip, but he's so strong. 'No! I'm not Tara!' I yell, fighting with all my might, kicking out with my weak legs, landing a blow against his hip, only to be overcome again as his elbow lands clumsily in the scarred hollow beneath my ribs. I release a howl of pain, and, grabbing a handful of white hair, I shove him with all my strength. '*NO!*'

Now he does stop, and his face slackens as confusion appears, swiftly shifting into anger. 'You're not Tara!' he shouts, outraged. He bends to take a closer look at my face, his eyes trailing the length of my pale torso, disbelief taking the place of lust as he registers the fierce criss-cross of scars so visible there. 'Tara wouldn't *dare* say no.'

There's a thump, like the sound of something dropped, and a gasp – not his – and before I know what's happening Ray is shunted sideways, and there is an elderly woman now in the room, dressed in a neat tweedy wool coat, her face twisted in rage, her hands raised. Beyond her, the entrance to the flat stands open, and a large stack of printed paper lies strewn across the carpet. Ray is backing away now, tugging at his belt, trying to save his dignity, and that's all the advantage she needs to be able to batter him across the living room and out through the open doors to the balcony, where they come to an abrupt halt as he connects with the low rail. I watch, captivated, frozen, as Ray makes a big show of straightening out his shirt collar, waving her away as though swatting at a fly.

'*There* you are, Maxie,' he says with a half-smile. He runs fingers through his hair, pushing it up and away, like an old movie star.

'I *heard* you, Ray,' the woman – Maxine – hisses. 'I heard what you said! I heard what you said about *Tara*!'

As quietly as I can, I slide to the edge of the sofa, pulling together the sides of my wrecked shirt. My skin feels stained from that man's touch. *His own niece?*

'Tara?' she says again. 'You promised me, Ray, you filthy bastard. I asked you, and you promised me nothing had happened!'

From where I'm sitting, I can see him out beyond the glass doors, lighting a cigarette as he leans on the railings, studying his sister. The younger man in him seems to rise from the ashes, puffed up, confident, certain of his right to act just as he pleases. I fumble around at my feet, locating my trainers.

'Don't give me that, Maxie,' he says, smiling. '*You knew*. You *always* knew. Fuck me, she tried telling you often enough!'

Pulling on first one then the second trainer, I stealthily rise and head for the open door, but Maxine's voice stops me sharp. When I turn back, I see the same hard expression that I saw in her brother's face, and it sends a chill through me.

'*Oi*! Don't think you can just leave like that, missy! I wanna know what you're doing here. Are you something to do with that grandson of mine?'

I take a step backwards, readying myself to break into a run.

'What did he do to you?' she demands, darting an arm in Ray's direction. 'Did he touch you?'

I nod slowly, and the woman's face grows more terrifying still, as her anger shifts to disgust. 'Did you want him to?' she yells, flinching at Ray's crow of laughter, drifting in from the balcony behind her. 'Or did he just help himself,' she demands, glancing back at him, the corners of her mouth downturned, 'like he always does?'

I swallow hard. 'I was asleep,' I say. My voice is weak and scared, and the last thing I want is for these people to know who I really am. I don't ever want them to know who I am. 'I was *asleep*,' I repeat, louder now. 'I'm waiting for Peter.'

'Asleep,' she murmurs, and sadness, or recognition, crosses her face.

I move to leave again just as Ray's words cut through the room from the balcony, where he stands in a cloud of grey smoke. 'She don't half look like our Tara, don't ya think, Maxie? You can see why I was confused.' He laughs again, a death rattle.

With an explosive scream of rage Maxine spins on her heel, and she runs at him so fast, and with such force, that he barely even sees her coming. With that single low impact he's gone, hurtling from the broken balcony, as its rusted joints give way and the front rail goes down with him. I run to the edge, instinctively catching hold of Maxine's arm to stop her toppling after him, and that's when I see him. Peter, down on the footpath below us, a grocery bag in one hand, a paper pharmacy bag in the other. He's standing beside the remains of his Great-Uncle Ray, who lies broken in Neptune's fountain, his body crumpled awkwardly in the shallow water, his head resting on the stone perimeter, a smashed and bloody pulp.

31

Maxine, Greenwich Police Station, London

Recorded interview. Present: DCI Ed Brownlee, DI Clare Painter and Maxine Gregory (suspect).

BROWNLEE: To confirm, Ms Gregory, you have declined legal representation. For the tape please.

MAXINE: Yes.

BROWNLEE: Also, to confirm, DI Clare Painter here was one of the first on the scene at your home in Neptune Court today, and she's going to read aloud her notes from that time.

PAINTER: On arrival at the premises at 12:07, I discovered the deceased, Ray Alfred Gregory, showing no signs of life, having appeared to have fallen from the third-floor balcony of the accused's flat. Standing beside the body was Peter Gregory, Ms Gregory's eighteen-year-old grandson, in a state of shock. Inside the flat were Ms Maxine Gregory, and a visitor – Eva Olsen.

MAXINE: She was waiting for my grandson, Peter.

PAINTER: Upon my entry to the flat – the door was already open – Ms Gregory immediately said, 'I've killed him. I killed Ray.' She then made a request to be arrested and brought directly to the police station.

BROWNLEE: Ms Gregory, do you agree with that version of events?

MAXINE: I do. I pushed him. I pushed Ray over the balcony.

PAINTER: The witness said the rail came away, that it was an accident—

MAXINE: Yes, but I pushed him. It was my fault. I shouldn't have pushed him.

(*pause*)

I killed my brother.

BROWNLEE: Had there been an argument? Or any form of disagreement in the lead-up to you pushing your brother?

(*pause*)

Did you have any cause for bad feeling towards your brother, Maxine? Do you remember anything at all, no matter how small?

(*pause*)

It's just that the witness, Eva Olsen, said you'd been arguing before he fell. Can you tell us a little more about that?

MAXINE: It was nothing. He was my brother – we were always bickering.

BROWNLEE: But this was more than just bickering, surely? There was a physical confrontation, and your brother ended up dead!

PAINTER: The witness said that Ray had assaulted her moments before you returned to the flat – she was certain that, had you not returned, the situation would have been far worse.

MAXINE: He did no such thing! She's lying. Ray would never do such a thing.

BROWNLEE: The witness also suggested that you were accusing Ray of molesting your own daughter – his niece – and that that was what the fight was really about.

MAXINE: No! Why would you believe her? She doesn't even know him!

BROWNLEE: (*pause*) There is also an allegation that you knew about this abuse, but failed to act on it, Maxine.

MAXINE: She said that?

(*pause*)

The girl – she said that?

BROWNLEE: (*pause*) No, not the girl.

MAXINE: Then, who? Who?

PAINTER: Your brother was still alive when they put him in the ambulance, Ms Gregory, just. He managed to say a few words before he stopped breathing.

(*pause*)

BROWNLEE: Can you guess what he said, Maxine?

(*pause*)

For the purposes of the tape, Maxine Gregory is shaking her head. DI Painter, I wonder if you can read out your notes?

PAINTER: Yes, I was with the deceased when he passed away. His last words were, 'She ain't without blame.' I asked Mr Gregory who he meant. He replied, 'My sister. Maxine. She likes to pretend like she didn't know about me and the girl. But she always knew.'

(*pause*)

I asked the victim to expand further, but he was shortly pronounced dead.

BROWNLEE: Maxine? Do you have any response?

(*pause*)

Maxine? You look upset.

(*pause*)

MAXINE: I'd like a break please.

(*pause*)

And I'd like a cup of tea. Strong, two sugars. And I think I will have that solicitor.

(*long pause*)

BROWNLEE: Interview suspended at 16:55.

32

Eva, Greenwich Police Station, London

At the police station, Peter and I are led to a family room and asked to wait for an officer to take a full statement from us, while Maxine is formally charged. The room is simply whitewashed, sparsely furnished, with just half a dozen orange chairs arranged against the walls. Posters advertise ways in which to report crimes, alongside Samaritans helplines and Legal Advice statements.

'There's nothing to worry about,' DI Painter tells us. 'Your grandmother confessed immediately, so as witnesses all you're going to need to give us is a statement to confirm what you told me at the scene. You might have to wait a while before we can do that, so is there anything you need – anyone you want to call?'

Without hesitation, I reply, 'I'll phone my friend, Rosa,' and the inspector leaves us to make the call.

As she closes the door Peter slumps back in his chair, the shock of what he's just witnessed, the death of his uncle, working its way across his face. He groans, pushing the heels of his hands hard against his eyes, as I locate Rosa in my contacts and listen anxiously to the tinny ringing on the other end of the line.

'Eva!' she yells when she picks up, and I put her on speaker-phone, so that Peter can listen in too. 'Where the hell have you been?' she demands. 'Everyone's going nuts here! Where are you?'

'Why didn't you tell me about Bern?' I ask, surprising even myself with the question. 'About me meeting up with him that night? How could you keep something like that from me?'

'We didn't keep it from you!' she replies, exasperated. 'Don't take any notice of what Lars said the other night – Bern didn't—'

I cut her off. 'Oh, just forget it, Rosa. I understand. Bern's your cousin – he's family. And I'm not.'

'*Eva*,' Rosa says now, and she sounds as though she's about to go off on a rant, but then I hear another voice in the background, and Lars faintly mentioning Bella's name. 'Listen, Eva, you stubborn cow,' Rosa says with a long sigh, 'we'll go back to the Bern thing later. But for now, you need to know, Bella is with us.'

Peter sits up, leaning closer to the handset.

'What?' I ask. 'She's with you and Lars? Why?'

'Don't worry, Mamma's here too, so it's all under control. Nettie had a fall yesterday, and her neighbour had to rush her into hospital. With your parents away we were the only people Nettie could think of to have the baby.'

'Is she alright – is Bella OK?' I'm suddenly desperate to see her, and it feels like a physical pain. 'You know she can't drop off to sleep without her velvet soother—'

'She's fine!' Rosa says. 'Mamma's all over her, as you can imagine, but I think Bella's already got the measure of her. She's got her wrapped round her little finger.'

I hear Lars again, telling Eva he needs to talk to me. *No*, I hear her say. *Let Bern do it.*

'What's going on?' I demand, at once suspicious, the knot in my stomach pulling tighter. 'What's Lars saying?'

'Nothing,' she replies firmly, and then there's the sound of a door banging, and I guess she's shut Lars out of the room. 'Where are you, Eva?' she asks, her voice softening. 'We're all worried sick. I know you hate me right now, but you have to believe me when I say we all love you. We don't want you to do anything stupid. Your parents are beside themselves.'

'They're not my parents!' I hiss. 'Don't you get it? They're *not* my parents.'

She hesitates, and I can almost hear the cogs of her mind turning. She thinks I'm unhinged; still broken. 'Don't be insane, Eva! *Of course* they're your parents. What are you even talking about? Eva?' she asks, her tone coaxing. 'Where are you right now?'

I look at Peter and make a snap decision. 'I'm in London – at Greenwich police station. You can phone my parents if you want, Rosa, I'm past caring. Tell them where I am. I'll be here for a while, if they want to come and find me.' And I hang up.

'What have you done?' Peter asks, as I clear the screen.

I blink at him, wondering if Rosa's opinion is shared by others – whether they all think I'm acting out some crazy fantasy, running away from some imagined crime. Maybe I *am* unhinged. Is Peter even who he says he is? This whole scenario *is* insane; could it be a figment of my imagination? What kind of a mother would that make me? Could they take Bella away?

'If my parents really care about me, they'll come,' I tell him. 'And where better to confront them than in a police station, in the country where the crime took place? If we let them go back to Norway, who knows whether they'll ever face justice – and we risk them taking Bella from me, especially if they claim I'm mad, like Rosa seems to think. If they can abduct a child once, what's to stop them doing it again? Here, in London, the police won't ignore it – and we'll get some real answers, Peter.'

'They won't come here,' Peter says, wretchedly, confidently. In his eyes I see my sadness mirrored, and I know he is my twin – I know that this much, at least is true. 'They've got too much to lose.'

I rest my head on his shoulder, closing my eyes and grimly wondering what kind of storm I've just set loose. I allow my mind to drift, seeking some kind of escape from thought. When my phone rings, we're both startled awake and it's Eva's number on the screen again.

'Yes?' I say, answering it immediately, but it's not Rosa who speaks, it's Bern.

'Eva – Rosa says you're in London. Are you OK?' he asks. There's urgency in his voice. 'What's going on? Why did you run off like that?'

'Bern, I know about Valentine's night,' I tell him, my voice steely.

'You know what about Valentine's night?' he asks, and he sounds genuinely confused.

'I know it was you I was meeting,' I say, desperately trying not to let my emotions get the better of me. My palms are sweating, and, before I can stop myself, all my unspoken fears come out in a mad rush of words. 'Lars told me! He said you'd asked him to set it up. I know who the driver is now, Bern

– and I know he's not responsible for Bella – and you were the one who carried out the DNA test, weren't you, so you could've fixed it to leave your own sample out, couldn't you? I don't know when or where it happened, Bern, but – but I was really starting to like you, and I don't want to believe it, but it had to be you because there's no one else—'

'Oh, for God's sake, Eva!' Bern yells down the phone at me. It's the first time I've ever heard him raise his voice. 'Stop! You're ranting! We never met that night! Understand? It didn't happen!'

Silence. In that split-second, my mind shifts, and it's as though the fog starts to lift, as memories crowd in, tumbling over each other to be known.

'Then why did Lars say it was you?' I murmur.

'He didn't! He probably said we were *meant* to meet up. Because that's the truth of it. Listen, I'd been trying to pluck up courage to ask you out for months – Rosa and Lars knew all about it. I've liked you for ages. And then these two decided to play matchmaker that night, but it never happened. I was supposed to "coincidentally" turn up to join you three at the bar, but just as I got there Rosa stormed out, telling me not to bother. I was gutted – but she was spitting feathers after your argument, and instead of coming into the bar to join you I drove them both home.'

Relief pours through me, warm and welcome. It wasn't Bern. I knew this, instinctively, in some deep, truthful place, but to hear it now, in his own words, means everything.

'So, if you're not Bella's father, Bern – then who is?'

'Well,' he says, 'that's kind of why I'm calling. We've had a breakthrough.'

I switch my handset on to speakerphone again, so Peter can listen in. 'What is it?'

'It concerns the DNA sweep we did, Eva. After that first round was unsuccessful, we went through the list again, and realised there were two or three men we'd missed, people who were out of town that week, for one reason or another.'

'And?' I feel as though my heart might burst right out through my chest.

'And we've got a match for Bella's father,' he says. 'It's a conclusive positive – and I'm not sure what you're going to make of it.'

Bern's words take my breath away. I pass the handset to Peter, and he cradles the phone between us, his ear turned towards the handset.

'Who's there with you, Bern?' I ask, suddenly wanting my friends with me. Wanting them more than anyone else in the world.

'Rosa and Lars. I'm at their house right now. I'm putting you on speakerphone, OK?'

'OK.' My head is pounding again, and the aching pain in my leg is back with a vengeance.

'Eva?' Bern says. 'Eva – I'm just going to come out with it, OK? Eva, it's Lars. Lars is Bella's father.'

For a few interminable seconds there is just silence – theirs and ours, and I find I can't reply. Instead, I hang up, the weight of fresh memories bearing down on me.

When Lars calls me, asking to meet at the boathouse, I can hear the hurt in his voice, and despite the lateness of the hour I waste no time in pulling on my snow boots and parka, to head straight down there, confident that my parents won't even notice me missing, so engrossed are they in their latest TV thriller. I smile to myself as I slip out through the front, spying them briefly, curled up together on the sofa, fire roaring, an open bottle of wine on the coffee table. I hope one day I'll have a love like theirs, I think, as I push the door shut with a soft click.

The snow has let up for a few days, and as I pass alongside the brightly shimmering lake I know Lars is already there, as the door to the boathouse stands open, and plumes of his cigarette smoke puff into the crisp air, merging with the mist from the water. Rosa is off with Olaf in town tonight, so she's not here to join as we drink whisky and smoke cigarettes, and huddle together in the shadows. In Rosa's absence, Lars can rant and swear without interruption, telling me how the lads at school had rounded on him again on the walk home that day, calling him a homo, goading him as they bragged about their sexual exploits and he wouldn't, or couldn't, join in. 'Fuckers!' he says, in his best American accent, swiping his tears away. 'Fuckers!' I agree, and when he says it again, louder this time, turning it into a howl at the moon, we find ourselves laughing uncontrollably, leaning into each other for support. Somehow, as we stand there catching our breath, shivering with cold, our faces illuminated by the light of a half-moon, our embrace of friendship turns into something else altogether. 'Do you think I'll ever meet anyone?' he asks, and I answer, simply, 'Of course . . .' – and then I kiss him.

The whole thing – an embarrassing, frantic disaster of an experience – is over before we know it, and within moments there is remorse between us, and an implicit understanding that it will never happen again, and that Rosa must never know. We're both mortified. Completely mortified. How could we have let this happen? How can things ever remain the same, after something like this?

When we arrive at Foxy Jack's a few evenings later, on Valentine's night, the three of us make a beeline for the corner

280

seat, well away from the saddos who cling to the bar, night after night. It's busy, and Foxy is in his element, handing out pink roses to all the singletons, and as usual drinking a shot of aquavit for every half-dozen drinks he serves. There's a party atmosphere as the bar fills up, and before long the three of us are well on our way to being drunk.

Gurt stops by our table, to pick up empties, and he winks at me and Rosa, looking as though he's imagining us with our clothes off.

'Hoping for a date tonight, Gurt?' Rosa asks brazenly, pointing out the rose behind his ear.

'Never know your luck,' he replies, and he lumbers off to the next table as we cringe behind our hands.

'Your round, Rosa,' Lars says, checking his watch. 'I'll have another beer.'

'Are you waiting for someone?' I ask him, my eyes following Rosa as she heads for the bar, staggering slightly. 'You must have looked at your watch a dozen times tonight.'

He smirks, and I know then that he's up to no good. 'Mind your own business,' he replies, and I lean across the table to poke him, grateful that everything is so quickly back to normal between us.

At the bar, Rosa has to wait a while to be served, and every now and then she turns in our direction to pull an impatient face, making us laugh as she sticks one of Foxy's roses in her hair and strikes a pose. Eventually, Foxy puts three fresh bottles on the counter between them, takes her money, and returns her change. Rosa gathers up the beers, making to leave, but then Foxy leans on the counter, his manner confidential, and to my surprise he points in our direction. I quickly look away, not wanting to be caught staring, only to see Lars's expression mirroring my alarm.

'What's going on?' he mutters, his eyes pointedly averted from the scene at the bar.

I shake my head, and glance back furtively, to see Rosa still there, still looking our way, her face hardening into a frown.

'Rosa looks really mad,' Lars says, chancing another look. 'What are they talking about? You don't think—'

'Shit, Lars. She looks furious.'

And then she is marching over, holding up a hand to silence Lars, cold eyes fixed on me as she tries to contain her rage. Lars stands, holding out his hand, like a gesture of peace, but Rosa bats it away.

'Are you OK?' I ask, reaching out to take my beer.

'OK?' she replies, slamming the other bottles down on the table.

Lars looks stricken. 'Rosa, what's going on. What did Foxy say?'

'You really want to talk about this here?' she replies. She bends to my level and says, 'You've let me down, Eva Olsen. You,' and now she points to Lars, 'and him.'

I'm winded by her words. How could Foxy possibly know about that? How could anyone? Lars and I had been completely alone in the woods that night. We would have heard if someone else had been there, surely?

'It was nothing,' I start to say, hoping Lars will back me up, but he appears to have been struck dumb. 'Tell her, Lars?'

He nods, but Rosa isn't even looking at him. She grabs her coat from the back of her chair and starts to pull it on. 'Let's get out of here. I don't want to stay a minute longer – we'll walk you back, Eva, and then I think we'd better stay out of each other's way for a while, don't you?'

'Let me explain—' I try to say, but she isn't having it, isn't letting me get a word in.

Over at the bar, Foxy's watching through the crowd, smirking to himself as he pours pints and gets steadily more pissed up. He's loving this.

'Are you coming?' Rosa demands when I don't budge.

I lift my bottle to my mouth and drink deeply, regret giving way to anger in the face of her pig-headedness. 'No. I'll get my parents to pick me up.'

For a few seconds, Rosa doesn't move. 'Get your coat on, Eva,' she orders me.

'Please?' Lars begs. 'We don't want you staying here on your own, Eva. We can't go without you.'

I bring the bottle to my lips again, glugging it down, hiding behind it, angry at Lars for his weakness, and at Rosa for her anger. 'I'll be fine. Pappa will fetch me. Just go, Rosa.'

And she does, with Lars trailing, shamefaced, behind her. 'Sorry,' he mouths at me as he goes.

I shake my head, dismissing him as he crosses the room, and that's when I see Bern in the doorway, looking as though he's about to walk in, until Rosa turns him around and spirits him away.

After they've gone, I stay in my corner alone, drinking first my beer and then the two that Rosa and Lars have abandoned. It occurs to me briefly that I don't actually know how I'm going to get home, and my head is spinning as I glance around, trying to stay focused, trying to come up with a plan. The clock over the bar says it's just after ten; I should ask Foxy if I can use the phone, but he's such a dick, he'll probably say no. I should let my parents know where I am.

As I pass the archway to the pool room, I see Creepy Gurt sitting on the wall bench, waiting his turn, his pool cue laid out across spread legs, his gaze locked on me. I blank him, making my way towards the bar again, holding up my bottle so that Foxy can see I want another, feigning confidence. He reaches for one, flips off the cap and thumps the full bottle on the wooden countertop, causing its contents to bubble and spill.

'Why'd they call you Foxy Jack?' I ask him, and I hear how cocky I sound. I want to get him back for whatever it was he'd said to Rosa, and the beer is making me brave. He ignores me, and I turn to look at Mad Eric, raising an eyebrow in playful challenge. 'D'you know why, Eric?' I ask.

'It's 'cause he stinks of fox shit,' Mad Eric replies, and he yowls with laughter as though it's the funniest thing he's heard all year.

Like a genie, Creepy Gurt is suddenly beside me, too close, his elbow touching mine. 'Where are your little friends?' he asks.

I turn my back on him, hooking one elbow on to the wooden counter and lifting the bottle to my lips, and a young man at the far end of the bar catches my eye. He's been watching the exchange intently, a smile forming at the corner of his mouth, as though communicating to me that he's taking my side. I smile back, seeing something familiar in the set of his face, feeling that there's something we need to say to each other. I know you, I think, as the boy breaks eye contact, and I too look away, trying to solve the puzzle as I knock back the contents of my bottle in one go.

That's when Foxy leans over the counter and whispers in my ear, 'We saw you, you little tramp. Last week. Down at the boathouse with your legs in the air, eh?'

I spin round to face him, humiliated, and slam my bottle down, watching it skid and topple across the bar, straight into Foxy's meaty hand. Desperate to escape their filthy laughter, and with the hungry burn of their eyes on my back, I stumble out into the driving snow of the night, out towards the car park and that dark and icy road.

'Why didn't Lars say something?' I ask, more to myself than to Peter. 'I mean, if Rosa already knew we'd been together, he had nothing to be afraid of. Why didn't he come forward, to say he could be Bella's father?'

Peter is sitting on the plastic seat beside me, hands clasped in his lap. 'Who knows?' he replies. 'Maybe he was scared.'

I feel the need to phone Lars straight away, to reassure him that it's all going to be OK – but I don't get that far, because the duty officer walks through the door to the family room.

And she's got my parents with her.

33

Maxine

Transcript of Recorded interview. Present: DCI Ed Brownlee, DI Clare Painter, Maxine Gregory (suspect) and John Marco, appointed solicitor for the suspect.

BROWNLEE: You claim your brother Ray abused you as a child, Maxine.

MAXINE: (*no response*)

BROWNLEE: Maxine?

MARCO: Maxine, we talked about this. You don't have to answer anything you're not happy with.

MAXINE: (*no response*)

BROWNLEE: For the purposes of the tape, Ms Gregory is nodding. And at what age did this begin?

MAXINE: The first time was the night of my father's funeral, so I must have been seven. He was nineteen.

BROWNLEE: (*pause*)

And how long, would you say, did the abuse last?

MAXINE: It never stopped.

BROWNLEE: What I mean is, when was the last time your brother sexually molested you?

MAXINE: Two days ago.

BROWNLEE: (*pause*) And where did this take place, Maxine?

MAXINE: In our bed.

BROWNLEE: (*clears throat*) You just said 'our' bed, Maxine.

MAXINE: We share a bed. We shared a bed. It was Ray's idea, not mine, though.

PAINTER: There did seem to be signs of a man sharing Ms Gregory's bedroom, sir.

BROWNLEE: And how are we to be sure that you and your brother's recent relationship wasn't consensual, Maxine – that this isn't a case of incest, rather than abuse? I mean, it's not as though we can ask for Ray's version, can we?

MAXINE: Well, you can't be sure, I suppose.

BROWNLEE: So, really, we just have to take your word for it?

MARCO: My client has answered your question, Inspector. She's made her situation clear. The abuse started when she was a child and has continued until the present day.

BROWNLEE: But you're not a child any more, Maxine. Why didn't you stop this, this 'situation' a long time ago? Why didn't you come to the police? You own your flat, don't you – it's in your name, not your brother's. Why didn't you just kick him out? Or tell someone?

MAXINE: (*no response*)

BROWNLEE: You see my problem, don't you, Maxine? Without any proof, it's just your word against his – and any decent prosecution will suggest that this is a fabricated story designed to provide you with mitigating circumstances for your crime. A reason for you to have killed him. Do you have *any* proof that abuse occurred, at any stage, Maxine?

287

MAXINE: What kind of proof would you be after?

BROWNLEE: Credible witnesses. Photographs. Letters or correspondence. That kind of thing. DNA.

MAXINE: Oh, I've got some of that. I've got my daughter's letter, and her diaries. She talks about it in there.

BROWNLEE: Why would your daughter have details of your abuse, Mrs Gregory?

MAXINE: I don't mean my abuse.

BROWNLEE: (*pause*) Ms Gregory – Maxine – what exactly are you telling me?

MAXINE: Ray was telling you the truth, what he said in the ambulance. He did it to her, too, didn't he? She wrote it all down. The papers are all together in the hat box on top of my wardrobe.

BROWNLEE: (*pause*) And, you've never reported this before?

MARCO: Maxine, I suggest—

MAXINE: How could I report it, Inspector? The shame of it would've killed him. He was a decent man for the most part, and where was the point, when she was already long gone? How could I have done that to Ray, after everything he's done for me?

BROWNLEE: Everything he's *done* for you?

PAINTER: You knew he was abusing your daughter and did nothing?

MAXINE: *No!* I didn't know for sure. I never knew for sure, not until I found that box in her wardrobe a few years back. And even then, I didn't really believe it, 'cause she was always making stuff up when she was younger. I just thought it was more of her lies. She was never right in the head, our Tara.

BROWNLEE: And what kind of things did Tara make up, when she was younger?

MAXINE: Things – things about Ray. Things about—

MARCO: (*whispers inaudibly to Maxine Gregory*)

(*long pause*)

BROWNLEE: DI Painter, could you make a note to retrieve that box following this interview? I think we need to see these documents for ourselves.

PAINTER: Noted.

BROWNLEE: Your daughter's name is Tara, you say? Do you know where we might find her, Maxine – to corroborate your claims?

MAXINE: Beaport cemetery, Inspector. Eighteen years dead. Tara Jean Gregory.

BROWNLEE: (*pause*) Is that—

MAXINE: That's right, Inspector.

BROWNLEE: Tara Gregory, as in mother of the missing child, Lorna Gregory?

MAXINE: The same.

BROWNLEE: Jesus.

(*long pause*)

Maxine, is there anything else you want to tell us before we finish this interview today?

MAXINE: (*no response*)

BROWNLEE: OK. OK.

MARCO: If that's everything, Inspector?

BROWNLEE: Yes, thank you, Mr Marco, we'll close for now. But we will want to speak with Maxine again once we've conducted our house search and taken a look at that letter and the diaries.

(*pause*)

Well, then, Maxine, in a short while, one of the desk sergeants will come and move you to an overnight cell. As we've charged you formally, you'll need to be processed – fingerprints taken, etc. – and we'll probably want to speak with you again in the morning.

MAXINE: (*no response*)

BROWNLEE: Now, is there anything else you think we ought to know about, before we stop for the day?

MAXINE: (*crying*) I never put his name on the birth certificate, but it was him. Promise me you'll keep it from Peter, Inspector Brownlee? Spare him that, at least?

BROWNLEE: What exactly are you telling me, Maxine?

MAXINE: My brother Ray – he was Tara's father.

34

Eva

'I'll leave you to it,' the duty officer says as she closes the door, and I get to my feet, knocking the chair against the wall with a crash. Peter stands beside me, tense and silent.

It's just the four of us in this tiny windowless room, Mamma, Pappa, Peter and me, and I have almost no sense of time, of where I am in the world. I think of Bella, back in Norway, missing me, and of the Bruns taking care of her, and the strange sense of calm that came over me when Bern told me that Lars was her father. I miss Bella so much; I want to hold her more than anything, to feel her soft skin against my neck, her breath in my hair.

'Who – ?' Pappa asks, gesturing towards Peter, but I won't let him speak first. I won't let these impostors control my life for another second.

'You stole me,' I whisper, looking from one to the other, knowing them, not knowing them; desperately trying to hold my rage at bay. 'You took me from some poor woman and passed me off as your own!'

'Ingrid?' Pappa says. 'This lad – isn't he—?'

But Mamma is focused on me. 'Just calm down a minute, Eva,' she says cautiously, raising her palms. 'Let us talk, will you? Hear us out.'

'Why should I listen to you?' I hiss. 'You've done nothing but lie to me since the moment I woke up in that attic room – since the moment I was born! Both of you. *Everything* that comes out of your mouths is a lie!'

Mamma doesn't deny this, but instead shakes her head wretchedly, looking to Pappa for some help.

'Eva, who is this young man?' he demands. 'Ingrid, he looks like that lad we chased off back home – that journalist.' Pappa frowns as he glances at our hands, which have at some point become intertwined.

'Journalist?' Peter says bitterly. 'I *am* that guy you chased off with your hillbilly shotgun, but I ain't no journalist.'

Mamma gasps. 'Is this who brought you here? You're the one who's been stalking Eva all these months? What do you want with her?' She makes a grab for my hand, and I recoil. 'He's using you, Eva! Can't you see? He just wants to get a story out of you – he's after a quick buck!'

Beyond the door, we hear movement in the hallway, and we all fall silent, my mother's outburst hanging in the air. My pulse races.

'This, *Mamma* and *Pappa*,' I say, pausing momentarily to gather my breath, 'is Peter Gregory. This is the twin brother you snatched me away from eighteen years ago.'

Pappa looks as though someone has slapped him, and his face slackens. Beneath his beard, his cheeks appear hollow, and I realise he's lost a lot of weight. He looks old, and yet so very young and helpless. 'Eva, sweetheart,' he says, reaching out at the same time as I take another step backwards. '*That* is not Peter.' Somewhere between this sentence and the next, Pappa loses conviction in what he's saying, because his voice falters. 'It *can't* be Peter.'

For a moment, there is nothing but silence, and the distant rumble of traffic, and all eyes fall on my brother.

He turns to look at me, and back to them, his jaw set hard. 'I *am* Peter Gregory,' he says, and there is ice in his voice.

'He is Peter,' I say, slowly and clearly. 'I *know* he's Peter.' Of this one fact, I have no doubt at all. 'All the lies!' I yell, raking my fingers through my hair. 'I – honestly – it's no wonder I thought I was losing my mind back there. Is there no end to it? When are you going to tell me the truth? You're not my parents – you're my *abductors*! You took me all those years ago, and the moment someone comes along and threatens to expose you for the fakes you are, you lock me in an attic and hope the problem goes away!'

'Eva,' Mamma says, when Pappa doesn't respond. 'The only reason we kept you in the attic for so long was because that person there – whoever he claims to be – was pursuing you! It was terrible enough that he nearly killed you in that stolen truck, but then he just wouldn't leave us be! Eva, he is *not* your brother!'

The door to the family room opens, and, just as the desk sergeant is about to speak to us, another officer passes behind, escorting Maxine Gregory. In that short moment, Maxine's head turns this way, and the look of shock and recognition on her face is startling.

'You!' she cries out, pulling back from her escort to stop in the doorway, thrusting a finger in our direction.

I feel Peter's hand tighten around mine. He hasn't seen her for months, and here she is baying at him like a harpy.

The sergeant stands aside, instinctively holding out his arms as though to keep two invisible forces apart. 'Can we move this prisoner along?' he demands, indicating towards Maxine.

'You!' Maxine repeats, resisting the hands of her officer. She flinches, her fingers now hooked on the doorframe to anchor her in place, and I realise with shock that it's not Peter she's addressing. 'Karl Gunn?' she says through a long gasp. 'As I live and breathe, it really is you, isn't it? Take away that beard, and it's Karl bloody Gunn!'

35

Eva

In a combined effort, the two officers finally extract Maxine
from our doorway, and that's the last we see of her. We're
alone again.

'Maxine,' Pappa whispers, as he stares at the back of the
closed door where she had just stood.

I watch Mamma as she brings her hands to her mouth, the
power of her earlier confidence dissolving.

Peter turns to Pappa. 'You're Karl?' he asks. 'But you killed
yourself—'

'The body was never recovered,' I murmur, realisation
dawning on me.

'You're my father?' Peter's hurt gives way to anger as he
points towards the empty doorway. 'And you left me? You
left me – with *her*?'

Pappa sinks to a chair, dropping his face into his hands.
'You can't be Peter,' he says, his voice trembling. 'I can't
believe—' When he lifts his head he gazes intently at Peter,

as though trying to decode his features. 'I thought I'd never see you again.'

'You left me?' Peter repeats, and all I want is to take away his pain, to pull him to me and shut this all out. But there's so much we both need to hear. 'If – if it wasn't for you, my mother might still be alive today.'

'Is that what Maxine told you?' Pappa asks, stricken-faced.

Something passes between Mamma and Pappa, as she too takes a seat. On the other side of the room, Peter and I do the same, facing them across what now feels like a chasm. Is this how it will be now? Them against us?

'It wasn't meant to be this way.' Pappa wipes a wrist across his face, pushing back tears. 'Tara knew I'd taken Lorna – it was her idea. We'd planned it together.'

Peter and I stare, mute with disbelief.

'Before the twins – before *you* were even born,' he continues, speaking carefully, 'your mother made it clear she wanted me to have full custody of you both. At first I tried to talk her out of it, but the more I saw of the way she was, the more I knew it was the right thing to do.'

'What do you mean, "the way she was"?' Peter asks.

Pappa hesitates, choosing his words carefully. 'She was fragile, Peter. Maxine was controlling, and it was clear Tara relied on her mother entirely. She was somehow incapable of breaking away – and she feared if you stayed with them you'd both end up in care. But when Maxine got wind of our plans she threatened to fight for custody herself, announcing that Ray was moving back in to help her.'

'Uncle Ray,' I say, feeling Peter shift beside me.

Pappa continues. 'Tara was frantic. She told me how Ray had Maxine at her beck and call – how he'd taken over their lives when she was a child. She wouldn't go into detail, but it was clear she was frightened of him. Either way, Tara wasn't up to the job of bringing up children, and her concerns about her mother and uncle just helped to convince me that I should bring you up myself.'

'What went wrong?' I ask.

'The ruling should have been straightforward, until I made the biggest mistake of my life, and got into a fight with Ray. With that one foolish act, I jeopardised everything. As far as the courts would be concerned, I was a single man in a rented flat, on a charge of assault. And there was Maxine, with a clean record, offering the twins a so-called stable family environment.'

He looks to Peter and me for a response, and I nod for him to continue.

'Tara said we just couldn't leave it to chance, and with Peter not yet ready to leave hospital she begged me to get Lorna away – just as a short fix, until custody was sorted. She was so terrified, almost out of control, and when she said she'd rather you both died than went home with Ray I got swept up in the panic of the situation, and before I knew it I'd organised your abduction. Peter was safe, in the treatment room – but I was truly worried for Lorna's safety, sleeping beside Tara when she was in that state. I honestly thought she might—'

I glance at Peter, silent beside me, his eyes never leaving Pappa's face, and at Mamma, whose hand moves in soothing circles over my father's back, urging him on.

'I worked at the hospital,' Pappa goes on. 'I was a doctor in those days, so I knew my way around the building and worked out how to avoid the security cameras.'

He pauses, taking in my disbelief.

'You were a doctor? A *doctor* – like Mamma?'

'We'd met at medical school ten years earlier,' he replies, and he bows his head, as though weighed down by his sadness. When he looks up again, he takes a deep breath. 'I had to give it all up when I returned to Norway. When I—'

'When you became Tobias Olsen,' Mamma says, filling in the words he can't say.

'With help,' he says, 'we got Eva – *Lorna* – out of the country on another child's passport, and for the next few days, while the world press went crazy over the disappearance, Tara held her nerve. A few weeks earlier I'd helped her to write to Social Services, and we were praying that by the time Peter was ready to go home we'd be able to do it all officially – legally.'

'If Tara was so worried about Maxine and Ray, why didn't she just move out, get her own place?' I ask.

'Tara confided in me that she had a history of mental illness and medication, and she believed Maxine, who'd brought her up believing she'd never be able to cope on her own.'

'But she could've put her foot down about Ray, though? Surely her mother would have understood Tara not wanting her uncle living with them?'

Pappa shakes his head. 'Tara knew Maxine would always choose Ray over her – over the babies.'

I glance at Peter. 'But no mother would do that . . .'

'You don't know Maxine,' Peter replies, his voice deadpan.

Mamma – Ingrid – gazes at me, and I see the strength returning to her as the truth slowly emerges. *She* would fight to the death for *me*, I'm certain. This thought comes to me with such clarity, I feel unbalanced by the truth of it.

The door opens, and DI Painter enters. 'Peter, we're ready to take your statement now,' she says.

I leap to my feet, blocking her view of him. There's no way I'm letting Pappa stop talking now; there's too much left unexplained. 'Could you give us ten more minutes?' I ask, indicating towards Peter. 'It was his great-uncle, you know? He's really upset.'

DI Painter gives an understanding nod and closes the door.

'The day Tara discharged herself,' Pappa goes on, 'I was there. We'd got as far as the hospital entrance, where the press was gathered, and we were preparing to make a dash for the taxi rank along the way, when Maxine pointed out Ray waiting for them in his car on the other side of the road. Tara became hysterical.' Pappa swallows hard. 'She handed Peter to me,' he says, his eyes glazing over, 'and she just ran. Straight out into the path of an oncoming press vehicle. She was killed instantly.'

Peter is listening silently, his face a blank canvas. 'And you?' he says. 'How does a person just vanish like that?'

'It was a split-second decision,' Pappa replies. 'The moment that van hit your mother, Maxine snatched you from me and took off with Ray. She left her own daughter just lying there, in the road. With Tara dead, I knew I would have no chance against Maxine, and when the police phoned me that night, saying they were on their way over to pick me up – wanting to question me further about Lorna's disappearance – I knew I was about to be arrested. I had to find another way, or risk never seeing either of you again. I dashed out a suicide note, and headed for the beach, where I left my shoes, coat and hospital ID on the shingle, praying that the police would follow my suicide note there, and conclude I really was dead.'

'And they did,' I say, visualising the newspaper cutting in Maxine's bragging book, with its tiny image of a young, clean-shaven Karl Gunn.

'The very last thing I did, Peter, was to phone Social Services, to tell them that you weren't safe. And then, to my eternal shame,' Pappa says, his face caving in again, 'I walked away.'

'You got through airport security?' I ask, remembering how tight the checks had been when I'd flown in.

'Your pappa thought that if anyone *was* still looking for him they'd be searching the flights,' Mamma says, 'so he got as far as Southampton, and made a last-minute booking on a cruise ship back to Norway.'

'Where he started a new life,' Peter says, bitterly.

Pappa nods. His expression is soft, wearied, and I can see that all he wants to do is reach out for his son.

'And Tara's letter – the one to the Social Services?' I ask.

'I never found out. She said she'd sent it, and I thought once it landed, they would have to act, to remove Peter from the Gregorys. And then I would return to England, to clear it all up – and take Peter back. But it never happened. Back in Norway, we followed the case from afar, and it soon became clear I'd been tried and found guilty by the British press, and that I could never go back without facing certain imprisonment – without jeopardising Eva's safety.'

Peter is staring intently at Pappa, his expression constantly shifting, as he finds himself faced with the father he believed to be dead all these years.

'I'm sorry, Peter,' Pappa says, tears streaking into his beard. 'I had to make a choice. It was either one of you or neither of you. I'm so sorry.'

'And you?' I ask Mamma. 'When did you come on the scene?'

'I was always on the scene,' she replies. 'We were already married when he went to England – and we continued to be married when he returned to Norway, with you.'

'You took him back, after all that?'

'I loved him,' Mamma says.

'But he'd been with – he'd had children with another woman,' I reply, trying to understand.

300

She nods slowly, sadly. 'We'd had problems the year before, and he'd taken that job in England to give us some space. But neither of us could stand to be apart. We had been trying for, and losing, babies for several years by this point, Eva, and the strain of it had pushed us apart. When your father asked this of me – to take his children in – how could I say no? Tara begged him to keep the children safe, and away from that family, and he did the best he could.'

Peter is pale, the skin beneath his eyes puffy. He's taking this all in, and barely saying a word. Peter, who remained with 'that family' for all these years.

'I loved you instantly, Eva,' Mamma says. 'From the very first moment I held you. You were always my daughter.' Now, she looks at my brother, who appears suddenly so small, and so alone. 'And Peter,' she says, 'if I'd had the chance, I would have loved you just the same.'

She stands, holding her arms wide, and stiffly, reluctantly, Peter rises from his seat and allows himself to be wrapped in her embrace, as I, exhausted, allow myself to be wrapped in my father's.

'You said you had help, Pappa,' I say, pushing back so I can look into his face. 'Who helped you to get me out of the country?'

'It was Nettie, sweetheart,' he replies, with no hesitation at all. 'Eva, Nettie's your real grandmother.'

36

Maxine

Transcript of recorded interview. Present: DCI Ed Brownlee, DI Clare Painter, Maxine Gregory (suspect) and John Marco, appointed solicitor for the suspect.

BROWNLEE: We've had a chance to search your property now, Maxine, and, before we hand you over to the justice system on the manslaughter charge, I'd like to go over a few details relating to the historic case of your granddaughter Lorna Gregory's abduction.

MAXINE: OK.

BROWNLEE: I'm showing you a letter, pre-dating your grandchildren's birth. It's handwritten, from your daughter Tara, addressed and stamped to Social Services in Dorset, with instructions to start legal proceedings giving full parental custody of her as-yet unborn children – twins – to their father, Karl Gunn. It looks as though this letter was never sent.

MAXINE: That's right. Tara gave it to me to send on my way to work, and I never posted it.

BROWNLEE: Why's that?

MAXINE: Well, I'd opened it, hadn't I? Ray said Tara might try something like that, so I opened it, and when I saw he was right I just stuffed the letter in the back of a drawer.

BROWNLEE: Did she try to contact Social Services again, at any point?

MAXINE: I couldn't say. What's the date on it? Oh, no, she had the babies less than a fortnight later, so I doubt it. And anyway, she thought they'd got this letter, didn't she? She probably thought it was all under way.

BROWNLEE: Did Karl Gunn ever pursue the matter?

MAXINE: He threatened to. But you know, he 'died' soon after Tara, didn't he? Ha! A bit hard to fight for custody when you're dead! Have you questioned him yet? Have you asked him what he's doing here, in Greenwich, when he's meant to be dead at the bottom of the sea? He's the one you want to bang up, for what did you say, John – evading arrest, is it? False something or other?

MARCO: Maxine— (*whispers inaudibly to client*)

BROWNLEE: You can leave Karl Gunn to the police to deal with, Maxine. At the moment, we're most concerned with revisiting some of the details around the time Lorna went missing. As you know, you're being charged with manslaughter for Ray's death, so, if Ray's abuse of you is a mitigating factor, getting these facts straight will be important to you. Do you agree with that summary, Mr Marco?

MARCO: Agreed.

MAXINE: But Karl Gunn—

BROWNLEE: Maxine, please rest assured that Mr Gunn – if that

303

is indeed who that man is – will be assisting us with further enquiries into Lorna's disappearance.

(*pause*)

Right, as well as this letter to Social Services, we've recovered Tara's diaries, which do indeed indicate a sustained period of abuse between the ages of eleven and fifteen. Maxine, can anyone else corroborate your claims that you – and/or Tara – had been abused by Ray? Would Tara have confided in anyone else?

MAXINE: (*inaudible*)

BROWNLEE: Again, for the tape, please.

MAXINE: She wouldn't have told anyone else.

(*pause*)

BROWNLEE: Except you?

MAXINE: (*no response*)

BROWNLEE: Maxine, at any point did *you* think that Peter would be better off away from your brother?

MAXINE: Of course not! I knew the boy would be alright. Ray had never shown any interest in boys, ever. I didn't really want to keep the boy, truth be known, but Ray said he'd be an—

(*pause*)

BROWNLEE: Ray said he'd be a what? Maxine, you need to be straight with us here. I understand that, up to a point, you were a victim in all of this too – but if you're not completely honest with us, there's nothing we can do for you.

MAXINE: (*pause*) An asset.

MARCO: Maxine, don't you think—

MAXINE: Ray said the boy would be an asset. He said he'd be paying for himself by the time he was five or six, if the press kept bugging us for interviews.

BROWNLEE: And was Ray right?

304

MAXINE: Well, Peter's appearance fees alone paid for my flat down the road, and plenty more besides. So, I suppose he was.

MARCO: (*whispers to client*)

BROWNLEE: (*pause*) You seem very cold about all this, Maxine. Doesn't it worry you that you could have come forward about the abuse sooner, to protect Tara?

MAXINE: (*pause*) A bit, I suppose.

(*pause*)

But no one ever worried about me, did they? I mean, look at my own mother – she more or less handed me over to Ray after my dad died. There were always rumours about me and Ray, you know? My brother David tried to talk to her about it – and one of the lads at the dairy got in a fight with Ray when he offered him a touch of me. But no one never did anything about that, did they?

PAINTER: Didn't that make you want to protect your own daughter even more? I've got children myself, and I know I'd do anything I could to safeguard them. Anything.

(*pause*)

BROWNLEE: You're shrugging, Maxine. Why?

MAXINE: Life's shit, Inspector. My mum told me that, very early on in my life, and she wasn't wrong, was she? Life is shit, and you take what you can.

BROWNLEE: (*pause*) You know what my mother used to say?

MAXINE: Go on.

BROWNLEE: What goes around comes around.

(*pause*)

Eventually, Maxine, life catches up with you – and you get what you deserve.

37

Eva, Bergen, Norway

It's almost two weeks before we're finally allowed to return to Norway, and we leave England under strict conditions agreed between the British and Norwegian police, which will have Pappa reporting to our local police station on a weekly basis. Nothing is clear yet, but, while the cloud of uncertainty still hangs over us, it is good to be going home.

When we land in Bergen airport, Bern is waiting for us at arrivals, conspicuous in his full police uniform amongst the tourists and business suits. He hugs us each in turn, welcoming Peter to the country with such warmth that I embrace him a second time out of sheer gratitude. Peter has grown quiet since we landed. I know he's apprehensive and hopeful in equal measures, and I want him to like it here – to like his new family.

Even before we reach the car, Bern is updating us on all the news from home, and I'm thankful to hear that Nettie's stay in hospital was only a short one, and that she's now back home with her wrist in a cast. All these years when I longed for a grandparent, when I envied Rosa and Lars theirs, and she was here all along, hidden in plain sight. As much as I'd love to announce this to the world, I know I must wait until we're certain there's no chance of Nettie getting swept up in all this. Pappa told me she'd stayed away from us for a full year after we'd arrived in Valden, during which time the police interviewed her at length, trying to work out if she was involved in my disappearance in any way. But eventually the police moved on, and so did Nettie, under a different surname, so as not to be linked to her son. If her true identity is made public too soon, her role in all this might come to light too. And that must never happen. All in good time, Pappa says, and for now I must be content that Nettie and I can know, if nobody else.

'I hope you'll enjoy Norway, Peter,' Bern says as he pulls out on to the highway. 'There are a lot of people back home, waiting to meet you.'

I'm in the front seat, with Mamma, Pappa and Peter in the back, and even without looking at him I can sense my brother's relief at being back in this breathtaking countryside, still coated in snow as spring attempts to make itself known in the little yellow flowers which have appeared along the roadside.

We pass an old stave church, strikingly white against the aqua-blue backdrop of lake and waterfall. I turn to look at Peter, and he returns a small smile, a silent communication.

Mamma has her head on Pappa's shoulder, their hands linked, his eyes on the passing landscape. I try to imagine what he's been through over these years, living with that terrible choice he had to make, and I wonder too if Mamma will ever go back to calling him Karl. How must it have felt, to leave their old life behind so completely, knowing they

307

could never return to it, never undo what they'd done? What anguish must they have suffered? They covered it well, that's for sure. At least now I know they really *did* do it all for me.

For a while no one speaks, and the open vista of sunlit water spreads out before us as we pass into Nordfjord, and I feel my heart bloom. This is where I belong.

'Can we stop, Bern?' I say suddenly, 'Peter hasn't seen much of this area – can we just get out a minute, so he can see the view to the glacier?'

Bern pulls up on the stony boundary to the lake, and we all get out to stretch our legs, to gaze over the softly undulating water, off towards the distant mountains and glacier ahead. Peter has walked away some distance, and I watch as he leans against a smooth boulder at the water's edge, an expression of stillness on his face.

'Remember all those reports Margrete made, Tobias, of seeing torchlight in your woods?' Bern says.

Pappa nods. 'Of course, we know it was Peter now.'

'Not necessarily,' Bern replies. 'Peter was back in England for some of the time when that activity was reported.'

'Then who was it?'

'Foxy and Gurt. Mac took them in last week, after we found a large stash of Class A drugs hidden in a sealed trunk beneath the floorboards of your old boathouse. You know, down by the pontoon?'

Foxy and Gurt at the boathouse. Of course, that's what they'd been up to the night they spied me and Lars together there. No wonder Foxy was so spiteful that night, stirring it up with Rosa; we'd probably screwed up their plans, got in the way of a drugs pickup. That explained why neither Foxy nor Gurt told the police about seeing me with Lars – they wouldn't have wanted to draw attention to themselves.

'You're kidding?' Pappa scratches his chin thoughtfully. 'How long has that been going on?'

'Well over a year, we think. They've always dabbled – but never enough to bother prosecuting, or to suggest they're dealing. But it seems Foxy got ambitious, and dragged his feckless lodger along in the plan.'

'Poor old Gurt,' I say, still marvelling at the fact that he managed to stay quiet about taking me to the airport right up until Nettie tracked him down the next morning, her neighbour having spotted me getting in his truck when I left hers.

Bern agrees. 'Gurt's no drugs lord. He's just a bit gullible, and with any luck he'll get off with a fine. But as for Foxy, we're expecting a prison sentence. There was a lot of gear there, and he'd been dealing it from the bar for a long time.'

I glance over at Peter, beside the lake, where he appears to be gathering pebbles, placing them in a small pile on the edge of his boulder. 'Go and talk to him,' I tell my parents, who are still cautious with him, uncertain when they don't know what he's thinking. The shock of finding out about Ray's abuse of his mother all those years ago is still something he hasn't, won't, talk about yet, but I'm hopeful it's me he'll turn to when he's ready. There have been too many secrets in this family already, too many things left unsaid.

He looks back towards me and waves, before handing Pappa a stone to skim.

Bern and I stand at the roadside, watching Peter as he skims pebbles out across the lake's rippling surface, and I breathe in the warm air, thankful to be back on Norwegian soil. As Mamma and Pappa stand beside Peter, Bern says, 'You know, Mac's British contact said it's likely your parents will receive a suspended sentence for your abduction.'

I turn to look at him, and I'm struck by the kindness in his eyes.

'It's an unprecedented case, I know, but he says there's solid written evidence of Tara's intentions that Karl should have the children. When you add to that the threat presented by her uncle, as supported by your grandmother – well, it makes for very compelling mitigating circumstances. Your father was acting to protect you from certain danger, and I'm sure any judge will rule in his favour. I don't think you've got anything to worry about, Eva.'

'I hope you're right, Bern,' I reply, my gaze following my parents as they start back towards us with Peter. I couldn't bear to lose them again.

'I'm sure I am,' Bern says. 'Mac wants to call in on you later, so you can ask him yourself.' He nudges me lightly and jerks his head towards the passenger door. 'I expect you're desperate to see your Bella, aren't you?'

My breath catches at the thought of seeing my girl again. *Bella*. My daughter.

Lars and I have spoken on the phone several times since we heard the news that he is Bella's father, and the strangeness of it melts away as we drive on to the dirt track towards home and I see him standing on that sun-drenched patch of land outside his little cottage, holding our child with ease, her colouring so like his.

'I honestly didn't think there was any way it could be mine,' he'd told me, when I'd phoned him from the station in London, demanding to know why he hadn't come forward the minute he heard about the baby. His embarrassment had flooded down the line, and I'd imagined him at the other end, colour rising in his pale cheeks. 'We were so drunk,

Eva,' he'd whispered, and it sounded all echoey, as though his hand was cupped around the mouthpiece. 'I mean, we hardly even managed—' He hadn't needed to finish his sentence, because I knew what he was getting at. The whole thing had been mortifying, finished before it even really began. 'By the time we heard you were pregnant, everyone was talking about the man who took you that night, saying the dates proved it had to be his. There was the tiniest doubt in the back of my mind – but when they started talking about rape, *jeez*, I just couldn't bring myself to come forward. You couldn't back me up, could you, stuck in a bloody coma, and I couldn't bear it if people started saying that I'd forced you. I'm an idiot, aren't I?' He'd cried then, big, rasping sobs which hurt me like physical pain, and I'd wept too. All I'd wanted was to reach down the phone line and take his shame away, to wrap him in my arms as though none of this had ever happened. 'I'm *glad* it was you,' I'd finally whispered in reply, before ending the call.

Now, I'm running towards them before Bern's even pulled on the handbrake, my trainers kicking up dried earth and leaves in my haste to see my beautiful girl, to see my friends. Bella's face tells me all I need to know: she hasn't forgotten me, she knows I'm her mother. Through the faded green door, Rosa appears, with Ann at her side, holding up a big almond cake, and all at once it's a celebration and we're heading down to the lake's edge, to the place where the early spring sunlight has thawed out the snow, and we sprawl out on picnic blankets and pass Bella between us.

Peter can't help but be swept up in all this good feeling, and I see him beside Rosa, laughing at her attempts to impress him with her flawless English, as Lars talks over her, offering Peter plates of herring bites and bread spread with jam made last autumn from the wild cloudberries that grow close to the stream. Mamma and Ann are doe-eyed with adoration of their granddaughter, and I wonder how I ever doubted Ingrid's love for me, now that I understand the lengths that she and Pappa went to, just to keep me safe. Looking at Bella, feeling the way I do about that little girl, I know there is nothing I wouldn't do for her. Would I lie to her, to keep her safe? Without a doubt. Would I lock her away? Perhaps. Would I kill?

'Are you OK?' Bern asks as he sits beside me on the fallen log, a little way apart from the others, who are now all settled on the giant picnic blanket Lars has spread out at the lakeside.

I look over to where Pappa is lying stretched out, close to Nettie, his mother, face turned towards the sun, eyes closed in a moment of quiet contentment. He shaved his beard off this week, so his whole face is visible to me for the first time ever, and the resemblance between him and Peter is startling. Even so, Mamma and I have persuaded him that he should grow it back; he doesn't look like big, strong Tobias without his grizzly beard, and I've already had enough change to last me a lifetime. I think back to our taxi drive this morning, as we left London, when Pappa told Peter about a trust fund he set up for him eighteen years ago, now containing money which is his to do with as he wishes. 'It's yours,' he told Peter. 'No strings. I'm just grateful I've been given the opportunity to pass it on to you in person.' Peter fell silent for long minutes then, before telling Pappa it was the first time anyone had ever given him anything and not wanted something in return. I hope he can learn to forgive Pappa, to love him as I do; I hope he decides to stay with us. I've dropped lots of hints about the art school in Bergen, so he might yet.

Bern nudges me, repeating a question I've missed. 'Are you happy to be home?'

'I really am, Bern,' I say. 'I'm tired, but I'm happy.'

We sit like that for some time, listening to the rise and fall of voices and laughter, watching the shifting colours as the sun slowly lowers in the sky. The silence between us is comfortable, somehow synchronised. A late-summer vision surfaces in my memory, of Mamma sitting in a deckchair at the front of the house, a bucket of windblown apples at her feet, knife in hand as she works off their skins in one smooth, continuous action.

'Did you ever work out who that hiker was?' I ask Bern. 'You know, the remains discovered over by the waterfall?'

He shakes his head. 'No. His details will just go down on record now, until perhaps one day someone comes forward looking for him.'

I gaze across at my mother, where she too sits on the blanket with Ann and Nettie, their heads close in conversation as they fuss over Bella, three generations of good women – four, when you include me. I think of the way my mother threatened Peter when she feared I was at risk, the way she guarded me against my best friends when she believed they had let me down. And I imagine her faced with a stranger on her doorstep, an investigator perhaps, set on exposing her closely guarded secret, on blowing her happy family apart – on taking me away. What would she have done in such a situation? I wonder.

Across the lawn, she looks up, perhaps sensing my gaze, and her eyes meet mine. No matter what biology says, she will always be my mother.

'She's fierce as a lioness,' I say.

Bern turns to me, his eyebrows raised in question.

'Mamma,' I explain. 'When it comes to family, she's fearless. I hope I can do as good a job with Bella.'

She's still watching me, watching Bern, reading me in that way that she's always been able to. Now, her face breaks into a relaxed smile, and there is meaning there as she winks: a single flutter of fair lashes over a pale blue eye.

I turn to Bern and kiss him on the lips, leaving him startled as I call to the others, beckoning them to follow me as I jog to the edge of the lake. Further out, the water's surface is still frozen and white, but here, where the sun hits, it is clear and sparkling, as a light mist rises, otherworldly against the dark backdrop of mountain and forest. In a single action I peel off my top layers, not even caring about the scars beneath, and to my joy I see Rosa and Lars doing the same, casting their clothes aside as they run towards me, until we're all three down to our underwear and plunging from the jetty into the heart-piercing ice water of the inky lake.

'Come on in!' Lars shouts breathlessly, waving to the others, who are all now on their feet, not knowing whether to laugh or chastise. 'Peter! Bern!'

Bern, sensible as ever, gestures to his uniform as he joins the group at the lakeside, taking Bella from Ann, holding her high so she can see us bobbing, our arms linked in a triangle. And then, in a blur of movement, I see Peter, stripping down to his boxers and racing along the jetty, bombing into the water to break up our unit, before sealing it again as his arms link with ours. He gasps with the shock of it, his eyes wide and laughing.

'Shall we show him how to play *Nøkken*?' Rosa says, mischief in her voice.

I gaze back across the water to my gathered family: to Pappa roaring with laughter as Mamma covers her eyes; to Nettie watching and waving, shoulder to shoulder with Ann; and to Bern, cradling my Bella, gently holding her chubby wrist and teaching her how to wave.

This is everything, I tell myself as I allow my body to rise to the surface, starfish-like. And when arms encircle me, pulling me down, I know they are arms that will keep me safe.

Falun Publishing International

Ms Maxine Gregory
7 Neptune Court
Greenwich
LONDON

Dear Ms Gregory

Contract between us concerning a work of non-fiction entitled: A LIFE OF LOSS (No: F3246)

Due to the unforeseen circumstances of your recent arrest, we write to confirm cancellation of the above mentioned contract for your memoir A Life of Loss, finding the manuscript to be in breach of the 'Acceptable Typescript' clause (3.a.iv). It has come to light that certain information provided by you to ghost writer Alexa Evans may be untrue, and/or violate certain confidentiality requirements set out by the Crown Prosecution Service in relation to your case.

Pursuant to clause 9 of the contract you have already received signature advance payment, which we have agreed you may retain. No further advance payments will be paid to you.

All rights in your original story will revert to you. However, we are informed that you have already attempted to offer the existing material to another publisher, and, while we cannot prevent you from doing so, we urge you to seek professional advice or risk legal sanctions relating to the ongoing police investigation under applicable British state law.

Please give this communication your utmost attention.

Yours sincerely

Monica Hart
Corporate Lawyer
FALUN PUBLISHING INTERNATIONAL

Acknowledgements

I'm often asked, 'Does writing get easier with each book?' and my answer is always the same, a resounding 'NO!' Despite being my seventh novel, *Lake Child* has been perhaps one of the hardest to write. I was in love with the story, the characters, the landscape, the tone – yet the plot was one which slithered and shifted and slipped through my fingers throughout the writing process. However, thanks to the ceaseless belief of my fiction editor Sam Eades and my agent Kate Shaw, two incredibly talented and intuitive women, *Lake Child* became the book it was meant to be. Huge thanks to *everyone* involved in the making of this novel, but particular thanks go to Kate, Sam, Karen Ball and Linda McQueen, who all had a hand in the crafting of this novel. I couldn't have done it without you x

Isabel Ashdown / 2019

Read on for an extract of *Beautiful Liars*, another gripping psychological thriller from Isabel Ashdown

A Death

It *wasn't* my fault.

I can see that now, through adult eyes and with the hindsight of rational thinking. Of course, for many years I wondered if I'd misremembered the details of that day, the true events having changed shape beneath the various and consoling accounts of my parents, of the emergency officers, of the witnesses on the rocky path below. I recall certain snatches so sharply – like the way the mountain rescue man's beard grew more ginger towards the middle of his face, and his soft tone when he said, 'Hello, mate,' offering me a solid hand to shake. *Hello, mate.* I never forgot that. But there are other things I can't remember at all, such as what we'd been doing in the week leading up to the accident, or where we'd been staying, or where we went directly afterwards. How interesting it is, the way the mind works, the way it recalibrates difficult experiences, bestowing upon them a storybook quality so that we might shut the pages when it suits us and place them safely on the highest shelf. I was just seven, and so naturally I followed the lead of my mother and father, torn as they were between despair for their lost child and protection of the one who still remained: the one left standing on the misty mountain ledge of Kinder Scout, looking down.

I can see the scene now, if I allow my thoughts to return to that remote place in my memory. I watch myself as though from a great distance: small and plump, black hair slicked against my forehead by the damp drizzle of the high mountain air. And there are my parents, dressed head-to-toe in their identical hiking gear: Mum, thin and earnest, startle-eyed; and Dad, confused, his finger pushing his spectacles up his florid nose as he interprets my gesture and breaks into a heavy-footed run. Their alarmed expressions are frozen in time. There is horror as they register that I now stand alone, no younger child to be seen; that I'm pointing towards the precipitous edge, my eyes squinting hard as I try to shed tears. There are no other walkers on this stretch of path, no one to say what really happened when my brother departed the cliff edge, but the sharp cries of distress from the winding path far below suggest that there are witnesses to his arrival further down.

It wasn't your fault, it wasn't your fault, it wasn't your fault. This was the refrain of my slow-eyed mother in the weeks that followed, while she tried her best to absolve me, to put one foot in front of the other, to grasp at some semblance of normality. 'It wasn't your fault,' she'd tell me at night-time as she tucked the duvet snugly around my shoulders, our eyes never straying to the now-empty bed inhabiting the nook on the opposite side of my tiny childhood room. 'It was just a terrible accident.' But, as I look back now, I think perhaps I can hear the grain of uncertainty in her tone, the little tremor betraying the questions she will never voice. *Did you do it, sweetheart? Did you push my baby from the path? Was it just an accident? Was it?*

And, if I could speak with my mother now, what would I say in return? If I track further back into that same memory, to just a few seconds earlier, the truth is there for me alone to see. Now at the cliff edge I see two children. They're not identical in size and stature, but they're both dressed in bright blue anoraks to match their parents, the smaller with his hood tightly fastened beneath a chubby chin, the bigger one, hood down, oblivious to the sting of the icy rain. 'Mine!' the smaller one says, unsuccessfully snatching at a sherbet lemon held loosely between the older child's dripping fingers. This goes on for a while, and on reflection I think that perhaps the sweet *did* belong to the younger child, because eventually it is snatched away and I recall the sense that it wasn't mine to covet in the first place. But that is not the point, because it wasn't the taking of the sweet that was so wrong but the boastful, taunting manner of it. '*No!*' is the cry I hear, and I know it comes from me because even now I feel the rage rear up inside me as that hooded child makes a great pouting show of shedding the wrapper and popping the yellow lozenge into its selfish hole of a mouth, its bragging form swaying in a small victory dance at the slippery cliff edge. The tremor of my cry is still vibrating in my ears as I bring the weight of my balled fist into the soft dough of that child's cheek and see the sherbet lemon shoot from between rosy lips like a bullet. '*No!*' I shout again, and this time the sound seems to come from far, far away. Seconds later, he's gone, and I know he's plummeting, falling past the heather-cloaked rocks and snaggly outcrops that make up this great mountainous piece of land. I know it is a death drop; I know it is a long way down. I can't say I remember pushing him – but neither can I remember *not* pushing him.

So, you see, I'm not to blame at all. From what I recall of

that other child – my brother – he was a snatcher, a tittle-tattle, a cry-baby, a provoker. Even if I did do it, there's not a person on earth who would think I was culpable.

I was *seven*, for God's sake.